Tyler Anne Snell genuinely loves all genres of the written word. However, she's realised that she loves books filled with sexual tension and mysteries a little more than the rest. Her stories have a good dose of both. Tyler lives in Alabama with her same-named husband and their mini 'lions.' When she isn't reading or writing, she's playing video games and working on her blog, *Almost There*. To follow her shenanigans, visit tylerannesnell.com

USA TODAY bestselling author **Barb Han** lives in north Texas with her very own hero-worthy husband, three beautiful children, a spunky golden retriever/standard poodle mix and too many books in her to-read pile. In her downtime, she plays video games and spends much of her time on or around a basketball court. She loves interacting with readers and is grateful for their support. You can reach her at barbhan.com

D0755474

Also by Tyler Anne Snell

Also by Barb Han

Discover more at millsandboon.co.uk

TOXIN ALERT

TYLER ANNE SNELL

TEXAS LAW

BARB HAN

MILLS & BOON

First Published in Great Britain 2020
by Mills & Boon, an imprint of HarperCollins*Publishers*
1 London Bridge Street, London, SE1 9GF

Toxin Alert © 2020 Harlequin Books S.A.
Texas Law © 2020 Barb Han

Special thanks and acknowledgement are given to Tyler Anne Snell for her contribution to the *Tactical Crime Division: Traverse City* series.

ISBN: 978-0-263-28057-9

1220

MIX
Paper from
responsible sources
FSC® C007454

This book is produced from independently certified FSC™ paper to ensure responsible forest management.

For more information visit: www.harpercollins.co.uk/green

Printed and bound in Spain
by CPI, Barcelona

TOXIN ALERT

TYLER ANNE SNELL

This book is for Julie Anne.
I love our powers of being awkward.

May we always use them for good.

Prologue

Noah Miller slipped his hands into his pockets, squared his shoulders against the cold and counted the bodies in silence. On a normal day he'd be the first to tell you that he didn't think Potter's Creek had a spot of ugly in it, but today? Today wasn't normal.

Today wasn't right.

And he'd guessed as much before he had come out to Amish country at the invitation of his father. A rare occurrence on its own, but nothing compared to what they were looking at on the Yoder farm.

"Twenty-four." Samuel Miller's voice was a shock against the cold quiet. Samuel nodded in the direction they were already facing. "Twenty-four cows dead," he repeated. "Make sure you don't touch anything."

Noah hadn't been planning on it but didn't say as much. He and his father hadn't been on good terms since he'd left home when he was sixteen. Now, twelve years later, they lived in the constant strain of their differences. Noah was just whom his family and their community called with an emergency, and that was still a hard pill for some to swallow. He might live only a mile from where they were now standing but that mile was the difference between the Amish world and the English world. And that difference was enough.

"What do you think it is?" Noah asked. "Poison? A virus? I've had a few cows pass on my farm before from sickness but I've never seen anything on this scale."

Out in the pasture was a sea of death. Not at all what he'd expected when he'd seen the number for the community phone pop up on his caller ID that morning.

His father hesitated. Not a great sign for an already dark situation.

"I don't know but it gets worse." Noah's brow rose at that. His father let out a long, low breath then nodded to the barn next to the pasture. "Isaiah is inside the barn. There are black sores on his arms."

"Black sores?"

His father nodded, solemn. Noah's confusion at being called out to meet him was swiftly hardening into a deep, terrible sense of foreboding. Isaiah Yoder, a loving father of five and a good guy, owned and worked the farm. Black sores on his arms and dead cows in his pasture?

This was bad.

This was very bad.

"The Haas farm lost ten cows a few days ago," his father continued, surprising Noah. "David and his sons who worked the fields became sick but then recovered. They believed it was a virus they picked up from the cows or something in the soil. Now I'm afraid that with these black sores it's something else. Something that could endanger the entire community."

Noah might have been estranged from his family but he still knew when his father was afraid. He could read it in the set of his shoulders and jaw, and hear it beneath a tone he was trying to keep even.

And he didn't blame him one bit for it.

"Whatever it is, it's bad," Noah spelled out. "We need to take Isaiah to the hospital."

His father shook his head. Fear was no match for being set in his ways.

"The Englisher doctor is in the barn examining him now."

Noah had every intention of continuing to insist but movement from the same barn pulled at their attention.

A balding man with large-framed glasses and a crease of worry along his brow stepped outside. When he saw them, he waved them over, shutting the door behind him, a palpable nervousness in his gestures.

"It's never good when the doc is nervous," Noah muttered.

His father didn't say a word as they walked over to greet the man. He introduced himself to Noah as Carson and then apologized for not shaking his hand.

That was a giant red flag to Noah even before the man got right to his point.

"It looks like Mr. Yoder is suffering from anthrax poisoning," he started, not pausing for any reactions. "In itself that's not necessarily a scary thing—anthrax poisoning can occur naturally in soil and infect cows and people—but, well, come look at this."

Noah and his father followed the doctor to an outside corner of the barn. He stopped by a pair of worn, brown work boots.

"These are Isaiah's boots. He was wearing them when I got here." Carson bent down and, without touching them, pointed between the heels. A dusting of white powder could be seen on each. "And this is what I believe to be anthrax."

Noah and his father were far from being in sync since he'd left the homestead but, in that moment, both Millers took a horrified step backward.

"As a bacterial infection, anthrax isn't contagious," the

doctor continued. "But inhaling the powder? That can be lethal."

"But where did it come from?" his father asked. "Somewhere in the field?"

The doctor shrugged.

"That would be my best guess. Though, that's maybe not what worries me most."

Noah could see his father trying to work out what the doctor was referring to, but Noah already knew.

"Does this mean that someone put the anthrax in the field intentionally?" Noah asked. "And, if so, why?"

"Good questions, son," the doctor said.

They let those thoughts mingle in with the cold around them for a moment. No one had to say out loud that their morning had gone from one of worry to something much more.

Why would anyone put anthrax in the cow pastures on purpose?

Why would anyone target the Amish community like that?

Another flash of movement pulled Noah's attention away from his current thoughts, back toward the dirt road that led from the Yoder farm to the main one.

Someone was running toward them. A teenager.

And he was terrified.

Noah's adrenaline spiked at the sight. He started to run toward the boy, his father and the doctor behind him. When they met him next to the pasture's fence, he glanced at the dead cows without an ounce of surprise and then put his hands on his knees to try to catch his breath.

"What's wrong?" Noah hurried. "Are you hurt?"

The teen shook his head and then pointed wildly behind him.

"No, but my—my father and brother need—need help,"

he panted out. "They—they collapsed in the pasture at our farm."

Noah shared a quick look with the doctor.

"We need to get there now."

While his father had never liked riding in anything but horse-drawn vehicles, he didn't push back as Noah herded everyone into his truck. Instead, he got into the front seat and directed him to the farm of the boy's family while the doctor asked the teen questions in the back seat. However, when Noah cut the engine next to the cow pasture fence, his father became quiet.

"Doc, let's go," Noah said, another surge of adrenaline going through him. "Dad, you two stay in here."

Noah didn't have time to be surprised that his father listened. He and Carson hurried out into the field with purpose and caution.

Neither did them any good.

The father and son weren't unconscious on the grass.

They were dead. Black sores on their bodies.

Noah kept his back to his truck after Carson confirmed there was nothing he could do. The two were gone.

But there were still people they could help.

"Isaiah needs to go to the hospital," Noah reiterated, voice low. "I think Mrs. Yoder will agree to that now."

Carson nodded.

"And I need to call the CDC."

He shared a look with Noah and said what Noah had circled back to thinking.

"I don't understand why anyone would do this. Especially here."

Noah gritted his teeth.

"Neither do I," he said. "But I sure as hell intend to find out."

Chapter One

Dr. Carly Welsh was in her chair less than thirty seconds before Director Alana Suzuki was in the briefing room, coffee in hand and disgust written across her face. She had been the big boss of the FBI's Tactical Crime Division since Carly had started working there three years before and, because of the team's closeness, Carly was able to register her expression now as a warning. Her news wasn't good.

Not one bit.

Then again, the cases that came to their team were never sunshine and daisies.

"There's been an attack on several farms in the small Amish settlement at Potter's Creek," she said in greeting. She motioned to the TCD tech guru, Opaline Lopez, in the corner of the room.

Opaline adjusted her neon green flower hair clip with one hand and activated the viewing screen with the other. The familiar mechanical whirl preceded the digital screen lowering at the front of the room. All five agents around the long table sat at attention, Carly included. The TCD's liaison, Rihanna Clark, and Alana's administrative assistant, Amanda Orton, came into the room and sat before the screen finished extending. Both had tablets in their hands but both turned their full focus on the first slide.

What came on screen wasn't exactly what Carly had expected to see when she'd been called in that morning.

"Are those dead cows?" Selena Lopez, Opaline's younger sister and Carly's closest friend, asked from the seat next to her.

Everyone on the team had a specialty. Selena's was surveillance, tracking and suspect apprehension, but it was her love for her partner that colored her tone concerned at the moment. Blanca was a beautiful white German shepherd who helped on just as many cases as the rest of the team. She was the reason Selena was an avid animal lover. Right now Blanca was no doubt lounging in her dog bed in Selena's office a few hundred feet away from them.

Alana nodded and gave them a second to pass over the picture once more. It was a beautiful landscape of white and green and a picturesque barn in the distance. Definitely not like any place Carly had seen in Traverse City, Michigan. Sure, they had the bay, but the simple picture captured the beauty *of* the simple. It reminded her of the many trips she'd taken with her adoptive parents to St. Joseph County.

Except for the alarming number of dead cows.

"Twenty-four to be exact," Alana continued. "At first it was thought to be something in the soil affecting this one farm but—"

She motioned to Opaline, who clicked to the next slide. She scrunched her face and pushed her pink-tipped hair over her shoulder. As if the movement would distance her from the death they were seeing on the screen.

Another picture of an otherwise beautiful scene showed more dead cattle. That picture turned into several more.

"—two other farms in the community were affected." Alana wasn't a person for dramatic pauses. In fact, she was straight to the point in every facet of her job. Yet, when

Alana's gaze swept the group, Carly thought she stuck to her a moment longer than the rest. "And then there's this."

When Opaline switched to a new slide, Carly realized why.

It was a close-up of an arm. The black sores on it stood out in absolute contrast to the tan.

Carly had seen it before.

"Anthrax," Carly said.

Max McRay, their resident explosives expert and Army veteran, shook his head. Not because he didn't believe her but because any form of warfare triggered an automatic reaction. Carly had noticed that, sometimes when he was reminded of his service, he would shift his left leg and the prosthetic attached beneath the knee.

Carly hadn't been to war but poison? Well, when it came to personal hells, that was her trigger.

And Alana was the only one in the room who knew why.

"The doctor on scene noted white powder on this man's work boots—" Alana said, motioning to the picture "—and then was called away to a neighboring farm, where they found the bodies of a father and his son. They'd been feeling ill for days, but thought it was flu and still tended their farm."

Opaline switched slides.

Aria Calletti, the former rookie of their team, shook her head along with Max. Both were parents. Aria had met the love of her life on another case the team had closed, which she'd helped solve with her expertise in drug-running.

"This is when the doctor called in the CDC. They confirmed, as Carly said, anthrax was spread across each farm's pastures. Animals in the area are now being vaccinated, and mitigation efforts are underway."

"It was deliberate," Carly made sure to emphasize.

Alana nodded.

"It was deliberate."

The slide changed to the quick facts about the town with an aerial shot. Potter's Creek was small, mostly Amish, and was under the jurisdiction of an even smaller police department and a sheriff's department that supported three other towns. Basically, no one in town had the means or know-how to deal with such a malicious attack.

Which is usually when the TCD were called in.

The last of their team finally spoke. Axel Morrow had been promoted to Supervisory Special Agent when Alana had been promoted to Director five years prior. Although he was quick to remind them that he wanted to be viewed as part of the team and *not* the leader, there were moments when authority shone through his words.

"Which means we need to find out who's behind the attacks sooner rather than later."

"Agreed." Alana found her gaze again. Carly was hyperaware of her own stillness. Everyone on the team had a set of skills, an expertise. One such person was Axel. He was a top-notch profiler and a damn near impossible man to beat at poker. If anyone was going to pick up on her slight change in behavior it was him.

Then again, considering Carly had a PhD in biological warfare and defense, it stood to reason her discomfort had everything to do with the case.

And not a past she'd tried to keep secret since she was eleven.

"Since Carly's specialty is in biochemical terrorism, she will be lead agent on this," Alana added.

Then she opened the floor up to questions.

"There's no way it was something they contracted from the soil?" Selena asked. "I mean I've heard that anthrax can occur naturally, right?"

"This wasn't natural," Carly answered. She put her hand

around her coffee mug but made sure not to stare into the drink. "Powdered anthrax spores don't just appear coating pastures. Someone put it there."

"Who would bother the Amish?" Max shifted in his seat again. "It's not like they're out there living fast and hard with questionable acts of indecency."

Aria thumbed at her engagement ring and tilted her head, thoughtful.

"Maybe it was an inside job," she said. "Someone from the community with an ax to grind. We all know vengeance can be a powerful motivator."

Opaline shook her head.

"One of the basic tenants of their religion is pacifism to the extreme," she pointed out. "They're strictly conscientious objectors to all things aggression, violence and war. They even go as far as avoiding any and all involvement with the military. They're famously not in the murder or vengeance game."

"But they are into shunning," Axel jumped in. "Those who leave or break their faith get the big boot out of the community to fend for themselves. We could be looking for someone who left trying to retaliate for being forced out."

"And they're human, after all. They could have a sociopath in their midst," added Selena.

That quieted the room as they all mulled the possibility.

Carly looked at her cell phone on top of the table. She had often admired the Amish's self-control when it came to living a more simple life. She could no more leave her phone behind than she could say goodbye to her high-tech apartment downtown. Yet the Amish made every decision with their virtues of simplicity and humility in mind.

And now someone had poisoned them?

If it wasn't an outsider, then the community of Potter's Creek was about to be rocked tenfold.

"We can talk more about religion and possible motives in transpo. We leave in two hours," Axel said, standing. He and Alana shared a look. They'd no doubt already had their own briefing before this one had started. He gave them all a sweeping smile. Like him, it was filled with boyish charm. It lightened the mood. "And I suggest no one wear their good shoes."

Opaline lightly laughed from behind her laptop.

"You heard the man, Selena," she said, looking at her sister. "That means you might want to holster any heels over three inches. I don't think Lous pair well with mud."

While it was common knowledge, and conversation, that Selena had a penchant for heels, the lighthearted tease clearly didn't land the way it was intended. Selena stiffened at Carly's side. She rallied a smirk.

"If you were in the field with us you'd know that my heels kick just as much ass as I do."

Her snark pulled a sigh right out of Carly before Opaline could pivot a comment back.

"You know, I bet Amish siblings don't snip at each other," she said. "That's part of their tenets you two might learn from."

"The Amish don't have a sister like Opaline," Selena muttered.

Everyone heard it. Opaline grinned.

"You're right. I'm one of a kind and don't any of you forget that."

The slight tension broke in the room. Carly felt the warmth of the coffee against her palm. She wanted to take a drink but stopped herself, readjusting in her seat to try to hide the redirect. One look at Alana, whose eyebrow was arched in question, and Carly knew the first moment the two were alone she'd go maternal on Carly.

But now wasn't the time.

Alana addressed the team one last time before calling the meeting to a close.

"Since the community is off the public power grid, there's only one building in town that has non-gas lighting and a phone. It's their community barn and where you'll set up for the duration of the case. And since the Amish typically aren't fans of outsiders, especially law enforcement, the area doctor who originally diagnosed the anthrax has recommended you rely on local Noah Miller as a liaison. He's a former Amish farmer who lives on the outskirts of Potter's Creek, close to town."

Former Amish?

Carly's eyebrow rose at that.

Opaline clicked to the last slide.

Intense.

That was the first descriptor that came to mind at the man staring back at her.

Tall, broad-shouldered, he was a man who worked manual labor and it showed. He wore a cowboy hat, a durable jacket, dark jeans and boots. If his dark hair couldn't be seen waving down to his chin, messy beneath the black hat, he would have looked like the poster boy for farmers of America. Someone who you, on reflex, pictured in your head when you thought of cowboys, too. Yet Carly had always imagined cowboys to be charming, outwardly hospitable people, and that wasn't the vibe she was getting from their Mr. Miller.

He wasn't looking directly at the camera, instead staring just off to the side. His green eyes had a cut to them that said he was angry, or maybe, more aptly, annoyed. Carly could almost hear the sigh that had probably escaped his lips just after the picture was taken.

Or maybe she was wrong.

Maybe Noah Miller, former Amish, was trying for smoldering and overshot the mark.

Because, regardless of his intention with the standoffish pose, there was no denying he was a good-looking man.

And their first suspect.

Rihanna stood and collected her iPad. She was a strait-laced professional from tip to tail, but she'd spent enough time with the rest of them to be less formal when it was just the team. She nodded toward the picture.

"I already let him know that we might need his help and, let me tell you, he sounded as stubborn as he looks right there," she said. "He might be as forthcoming as a rock, but he agreed to at least meet us at the barn when we arrive."

They sat with that a moment, then the meeting was over.

The team filtered out, already making calls and preparations. Carly, who could have been among them, decided to stay seated. It was better to get what came next over with now rather than later. Alana must have agreed. She was quick. The moment the last of the team was out the door, she was hovering next to Carly, a look of pure concern on her face.

"A tough case," Alana opened with. "How do you feel about it?"

Carly felt the urge to sigh, right alongside the pain that never went away. But, as she'd thought before, Alana Suzuki had thirty years under her belt with the FBI. During those thirty years she'd seen things that most never would. Not even the TCD team.

Discounting her concern was almost akin to discounting the trauma, pain and sorrow she had undoubtedly lived through.

So, Carly didn't.

Instead she finally looked down at her coffee and told the truth.

"To be honest, I don't know."

Alana put her hand on Carly's shoulder. A small moment that reminded Carly that she wasn't a kid anymore. She wasn't in that house. She wasn't in that kitchen.

No.

She was an agent with the FBI, an expert.

With a team who always had her back.

The same went doubly for their boss.

Carly felt the old fear inside of her harden into resolve.

Alana let go, realizing the change was happening.

When she met Alana's gaze, Carly was nothing but determined.

Justice wasn't just a word to her.

It was a promise.

One she was making to a stranger, someone who just didn't know it yet.

"What I *do* know is that whoever is behind this is in for a world of hurt," she said. "Because I'm coming for them and there's not a place on this green Earth where they can hide."

Chapter Two

Noah didn't know what he had expected next, but this wasn't it. He was standing outside of the community barn, hands deep in his jacket pockets and boots wet from the dusting of snow still on the ground, when the dark SUV appeared in the distance. It was followed by another SUV and a sleek black car.

Noah had spent the first sixteen years of his life seeing mostly horse-and-buggies along the main road in Potter's Creek. Even with buggy lights, it was a simpler existence. A way to stay closer to the world. Seeing the posh caravan go between open fields and modest buildings was a contrast Noah wasn't sure how to feel about now.

The group of Amish standing around the barn's doors weren't helping.

They were honest, humble men.

And they honestly and humbly did not like the idea of the Englishers invading their community with badges, guns and their own agenda.

Noah tried not to listen to his long-standing resentment as it reared its ugly head, reminding him that he was included in that group. At least as far as the outsider aspect went. His father might have called him to the Yoder farm originally, but Noah was as welcome as the group of strangers from the federal government driving up now.

Nope. Not one bit.

The Amish of Potter's Creek didn't want him at all.

Which made the fact that he'd been asked to the meeting by the Tactical Crime Division's liaison even more awkward.

Noah hadn't been rude to her, but he also hadn't been kind at the request. He was all for helping in an emergency, but any other time he'd rather be on his farm, soaking up the scenery and tending to his cattle. Not an outcast, whose father and brother, no more than five steps away, wouldn't even look him in the eyes.

That is, unless it was to glare.

Though the glaring was left mostly to Isaiah Yoder's oldest son, Isaac. The Amish might not be a violent bunch, but Noah was sure if looks could kill, he'd already be a goner from Isaac's piercing gaze. And that was saying something considering Noah's younger brother, Thomas, was present. Thomas had been three when Noah left the community. Noah was sure his younger brother had heard over the intervening twelve years just how disappointing and sinful his older sibling was.

At least you're not dead in a field.

Noah shifted against the barn's worn wall as his inner voice reminded him that his personal issues rated low to nil at the moment.

Someone had targeted the community and that had ended in the death of a father and son, plus the loss of countless heads of cattle. Lives and livelihoods had been destroyed.

Just because Noah's own father could barely stand him didn't mean he couldn't feel the loss around them weighing on his chest.

Elmer and Stephen Graber hadn't deserved to die like that. No one did.

"I don't like this," Noah's father said as the first SUV came to a stop just behind his truck. The barn behind them was almost exactly in the center of their community, equidistant from most of the farms. Yet all of the men had walked from their respective homes to meet, leaving their horse-and-buggies at home. Noah expected this was so their families had a means to get to them and their neighbors fast if something else happened.

"They are here to help, Samuel."

Their religious leader, Levi Raber, spoke the truth but there was a stiffness to his words. Noah didn't know the man well, but appreciated he was trying to keep the men around him in less hostile spirits.

Judging by the wave of tension that rolled over their group as the SUV unloaded its passengers in front of them, the bishop failed in his attempt.

It probably didn't help matters that the first person to approach was a woman wearing a tailored dark peacoat, high-heeled boots and lipstick that shone in contrast to her dark skin. She was tall and gave the immediate impression of being a professional. There was no hesitation as she strode over to the men.

"You must be Bishop Raber." She greeted Levi. Her confidence at whom she was speaking to was impressive. Noah recognized her voice as the woman whom he'd spoken to on the phone. "My name is Rihanna Clark," she continued, giving no room for a response. "I work as the liaison between the TCD team and local police, press and the public. Basically, I work at keeping everyone on the same page." She smiled and motioned to the barn behind them. "Thank you for allowing us to use your community barn for our headquarters. It will be extremely helpful to the team and the case."

Levi nodded, a curt movement.

"We were told you would need phone service. The man from the Center for Disease Control is inside using it now."

Rihanna swept her gaze across him, Noah's father and brother, and Isaac, smile holding strong.

"Great. I'll need to speak to him sooner rather than later. But first—" She turned toward the rest of her companions from the SUV. Noah watched as his father took each new member in with an impassive face.

He knew he wasn't much better.

Noah didn't have a distaste for outsiders like the rest of the community, but he wasn't enthused about an FBI team setting up camp so close to his home, either. He lived a private, solitary life. The sooner they did their job and put whoever was behind the attacks behind bars, the better. Then the community could heal after their losses, all while going back to ignoring him and his quiet life just outside of it. So he let his natural default of being the original outsider become his mask as Rihanna introduced her team.

Which was hard considering the first person up was not at all what Noah had expected when he had pictured the FBI.

"Let me introduce you to the Special Agent in Charge, Dr. Carly Welsh."

Noah struggled to hold tight to his unfazed expression. A feat, considering one of the most beautiful women he'd ever seen outstretched her hand at her introduction. She was smiling, but it wasn't friendly like the woman next to her. Instead, it almost seemed strained. Impatient, even. Like it was just one tedious thing to do before she could get right into the case.

She also didn't look like any doctor he'd ever seen. Then again, that was on him and his small-town living. There weren't many in circulation for a comparison.

"Nice to meet you," she said, adjusting the hood of her

long, black coat. The blond hair that was trapped beneath it splayed out over her shoulders. It was on the shorter side, with a wave to it. Much more free than the tight smile across her lips.

Bishop Raber shook her hand and introductions were then given for the men around him. They didn't include Noah. Rihanna extended her introductions to the last passenger, but Noah didn't catch his name. Instead, Dr. Welsh turned her dark eyes directly on him.

There was no smile this time, tight or otherwise.

He stood straighter than before as she excused herself and walked over.

There was a confidence to her walk that gave Noah the distinct impression before she even said a word to him that Dr. Carly Welsh was a force to be reckoned with.

And she had her sights set on him.

PICTURES DIDN'T DO the man justice.

Not one itsy little bit.

Their link to the Amish was more than six feet of brooding masculinity and, in any other circumstance, Carly would have had to stop a moment and revel in how attracted she would have been to him.

But it wasn't as if she was with her adoptive parents, vacationing in Amish country.

She was here to catch a murderer. One with access to and the absolute nerve to use a deadly powder that had already taken several lives.

So Carly's brain put her body on lockdown the moment she saw the cowboy leaning against their headquarters.

She had a job to do, and that job included vetting their potential link to the community.

Though, judging by the berth the rest of the group

was giving Noah, maybe Rihanna had misunderstood his significance.

In less than a minute of standing outside, Carly had already seen Isaac Yoder giving the farmer looks that could curdle butter.

It was interesting and concerning at the same time.

And absolutely the reason why she was about to take tall, dark and brooding aside and flex her FBI muscles for a quick interrogation.

"You're Noah Miller."

She didn't phrase it as a question because they both knew that was exactly who he was. Since she'd already been warned that the farmer could be standoffish, she wasn't giving him an inch to wiggle. Though Carly did know that it was easier to catch flies with honey, so she at least made sure to keep her body language loose rather than ready to strike.

To his credit, he nodded.

"And you're Dr. Carly Welsh, from what I've just heard."

His voice was a low baritone. Not only did the man look intimidating, he sounded like it, too.

Thankfully, Carly had never been someone easily intimidated.

"That's me. Call me Carly."

He extended his hand, not something the men behind them had done, and gave the first smile she'd seen since they'd gotten off of the plane. It didn't last through their handshake.

"You can call me Noah."

He must have picked up on the fact that she was already in work mode so there was no point in dillydallying.

"So I hear that you don't want to work with us, Noah. I'm curious as to why you don't want help."

That did the trick. The man switched from stoic to tense.

"Like I told Ms. Clark on the phone, I don't think I'm your best option for open communication with the community. I never said I *wouldn't* help. I just pointed out I don't think I'll *be* that much to you all."

Carly crossed her arms over her chest. The cold was no doubt turning her nose a bit red, but the jacket she'd had stashed in the back of her closet for half a year was right on the money for warmth.

"You're former Amish. Does that mean you were kicked out? Is that why you don't think you can help? Because you're an outsider, too?"

Noah didn't seem to like that line of questioning. Yet, he answered without hesitation.

"I chose to leave when I was sixteen," he said. "That decision isn't one many people around here understand or like."

Carly didn't know the man, but she'd bet every dime and nickel in her bank account that he was doing his best not to side-eye the group of men.

"Which can make communication more difficult, especially in trying times. I just don't think I'm the right guy for the job."

Carly took a small moment to consider the man. He'd *chosen* to leave. As she'd gone through her knowledge of anthrax on the plane, Axel had skimmed through Amish customs and beliefs. Some of them Carly had already known, others she'd been surprised by. Among the things she'd known about was the tradition of Rumspringa. It was a period of time where teens were allowed greater personal freedom and the ability to live outside and explore the world without Amish restrictions. After that time ended, they had to make the decision if they wanted to come back to the community or not.

What she didn't know was why Noah had been one of the few who had decided not to come back.

So she asked.

"Why did you leave? Don't you have family here?"

This time his frustration was immediate and aimed solely at her.

"That's extremely personal and, no offense, I don't have to be Amish anymore to distrust strangers." He squared his shoulders even more if it was possible, physically strengthening the wall that was him. An invisible barrier between her questions and his past.

Carly knew enough about those kinds of walls to dissuade herself from any attempt to climb the one that was Noah Miller.

She had no doubt she'd have better luck at convincing Bishop Raber to take a selfie with her. So, Carly doubled down on her conviction to get to the bottom of what was happening in Potter's Creek and dove right in to her bottom line.

"Yes. I'm a stranger and honestly, although I've spent time in St. Joseph County and picked up a thing or two in the last few years, I'm not familiar with Potter's Creek. Or you for that matter. So, no disrespect right back at you, but that's why I'm asking you these questions. I'm on a case and, from where I'm standing, you're in either one of two camps." She ticked off her index and middle fingers at each point. "You know something or did something that caused the death of human and cattle alike *or* you can help us figure out who *else* knows something or did something that has resulted in the death of human and cattle in this community. Anything less than either of those would be wasting both of our time."

Carly put her hands back into her coat pockets and

noted, while it was warm within its folds, her breath misted out in front of her when she spoke again.

"Since I know already that you have been seen tending your own farm not far from here around the times the pastures would have had to be poisoned, I still have to ask— Did you perpetrate this attack, Mr. Miller, or know who did?" Noah shook his head. His jaw was hard. He was gritting his teeth. Carly kept on. "And do you have any interest in temporarily being a liaison for us with the Amish community?"

This time he spoke.

It was low. One syllable filled with a lifetime of something Carly didn't understand or have the patience to get to the bottom of while standing there in Potter's Creek, outside of their community barn.

"No."

Carly nodded, ignoring the ping of disappointment that went off in her at his answer.

"Then I'll do us both a favor and stop wasting each other's time," she said, making sure her finality rang through just as true. "Goodbye, Mr. Miller."

And then Carly walked away.

Chapter Three

The doctor was kind and straightforward. His name was Carson and he was eager to help in any way that he could.

He was also tired.

Carly could spot that before she ever made it across the barn, and knew it to be true before he finished his recounting of what had happened on the Yoder and Graber farms.

Opaline had already done a quick workup of the man before they'd even left Traverse City. He was respected and good at what he did. Smart and skilled. But Carly knew better than most that there were some situations that got their hooks into you and didn't let up. At least, not for a while. It could beat a person down, make every part of them tired and ready for the madness to stop.

Carson might have been a good area doctor for Potter's Creek, but he was ready to go home. After Carly got the information she wanted, she obliged the man and watched him leave their temporary headquarters.

Then it was time for her to step up and call some more shots.

"Aria, Max," she started, pitching her voice so it was easier to hear in the spacious barn. Both agents snapped to attention, pausing whatever conversation they'd been having with Bishop Raber. Or, maybe *trying* to have. Aria looked frustrated. Though she did have a baby at home and had shown up to work more tired than not recently. The cold that had followed them into the barn probably wasn't helping her mood, either. They'd once joked about loading up the band and heading to Hawaii for a much-needed vacation where sunshine and warmth year-round was guaranteed.

"I need you two to go out and look for any evidence that the CDC or CSI might have missed. So far no one's found anything out of the ordinary, but it wouldn't hurt to check again. Start with the Graber farm and work your way back to the Yoder farm." Carly shifted her gaze to Selena, then Axel. They'd been in their own conversation and looked as enthused about it as Aria had. Selena was absently stroking Blanca's fur just behind her head, but there almost seemed to be some tension between her and Axel. Maybe everyone needed to get some more sleep.

"Selena and Axel, I need you two to focus on how the anthrax may have been purchased," Carly continued. "Use Opaline for whatever support you need. She's stationed at Headquarters until we say otherwise. As for Blanca, I don't want to pull her in until we have a clearer picture of what's going on."

There was no sense in sending her out into "the field" when that actually encompassed hundreds of acres of real fields and hundreds of people. Not to mention the possibility of that land being laced with more anthrax.

She'd rather have timid boots than brave snoots, as Selena often called Blanca's impeccable sense of smell, doing their first pass over.

"Aye aye, boss," Selena said. Her voice was tight. Axel glanced at her before nodding that he understood. Something strange definitely was going on between them but there was no time to dig into that now.

"Mitigation efforts have been ongoing and are almost

over. But before everyone leaves, just as a precaution, I want you to have a designated pair of work shoes for when we're out in the fields," Carly continued. "Also, make sure you have at least one pair of gloves on you, keep your set of protective eyewear I brought with us in your vehicle, and if you have a cut or get one anywhere on you, then you immediately go to a first aid kit and disinfect and bandage. And, even though it should go without saying, if you come in contact with any powder, do not inhale or touch. Instead call Rihanna, who will be coordinating with the CDC, and then me. That sound good?" Her team nodded. "Rock on, everyone."

They started to leave but Selena caught Carly before she followed.

"What are you going to do?" she asked. "Perp duty?"

Carly nodded.

"They don't realize it now, but they've won themselves an all-expenses-paid vacation to Carly Island. All my time and energy is about to shift solely onto them."

"You're Carly Town and they're the only resident," Selena said. "And the mayor."

Carly gave her a friend a quick smile. They did this sometimes. Whistled in the dark. Took a moment or two to talk nonsense to lighten the mood. Smiled and laughed and said silly things to remind themselves that there was more in the world than senseless acts of violence and murder.

Whistling in the dark.

"I'm the only member in the audience of a one-man show and I'm ready to write a scathing review," Carly pitched.

"Before you were both marooned on an island, you were allowed to bring only one item each. They brought a weapon, you *are* the weapon," Selena gave back.

"They're up the creek without a paddle…because I have all the paddles."

"And you're not giving them back."

Carly snorted.

"No way, Jose. No paddles for our perp."

Selena's grin grew. She shook her head.

"We're so lame."

"But that doesn't mean we aren't professionals."

Selena conceded to that. Then her voice went low and any amusement disappeared. She leaned in a little. Blanca brushed against Carly's leg at the new closeness.

"Heads up, I don't think our Amish buddies care if we're professional or not," she said. "I overheard Aria trying to ask some questions and they went tight-lipped."

"But we're here to help them. By them not helping *us* they're only hurting themselves."

Selena shrugged.

"Just because we have badges doesn't mean they trust us. I think our best bet might really be that tall drink of water you were talking to before we came in. The farmer."

Carly felt her lips purse in response.

"And just because I don't think he had anything to do with the attacks doesn't mean I trust him to help."

"It's your call, boss." Selena gave Blanca an absent pat on the head before pulling her gloves from her pocket. "Just make sure you keep an eye out. Cell service sucks out here and if something happens we have a lot of ground to cover. Be safe."

Carly softened momentarily at that.

"You, too."

Selena and Blanca left the barn. Carly went to Rihanna to have a quick word, even as she mentally started listing the questions she'd ask the Amish men in her drive for more information.

Yet, when she turned around, the men were gone.

Carly swore beneath her breath and hurried out of the barn.

"Excuse me," she called out. The bishop was no longer with them, but the other three were in the process of talking to another man.

Noah.

Why hadn't he left already?

"Excuse me," she repeated, pushing through her curiosity and right into their group. She knew the men by their first names—Samuel, his son Thomas, and one of the victim's, Isaiah Yoder's, son Isaac—but past that they were strangers.

Just like she was an outsider.

Which, by how quickly they zipped their mouths shut because of her presence, *was* going to be a problem.

Still, Carly hoped that wouldn't be the case.

"Like my colleague said earlier, I'm the lead agent investigating what happened and need to get started immediately," she said in greeting, careful not to let her gaze stray over to the farmer. She focused instead on Yoder's son. He didn't yet have a beard, but there was a hardness to his eyes. One that settled when worry or fear refused to go away. "If you don't mind, I'll need a list of people who might want to harm the families whose farms were affected. Anyone who might want to hurt the community as a whole, too."

Where she expected an answer, Carly only got silence.

She felt her eyebrow pull up, waiting.

The men were all still, tight-lipped.

"Um, hello? Did you hear me?"

Then the Amish men did something she absolutely hadn't expected.

They turned away from her and started to walk off.

Every instinct in Carly's body was about to show those men the mistake they'd made, but Noah cleared his throat. Carly must have had heat in her eyes, because Noah held up one hand and gave a small sigh.

"Don't shoot the messenger, but they've decided all questions and concerns you have should go through me if you want answers."

Carly rolled her eyes.

"Seriously? Is it because I'm a woman?" she asked. "Because you want to know what isn't sexist? *Anthrax*."

She might have imagined it but a smile looked like it was trying to pull up the corner of his lips.

"No, it's not because you're a woman," he said. "They're not sexist, just Amish."

Carly blew out a frustrated breath.

"And *I'm* just trying to help them."

"They don't trust 'Englishers.' It's just their way."

Noah joined her in watching the group walk away. Snow melted beneath her boots and the wind picked up enough that she had to fight a small shiver.

Usually Carly dealt with bad guys being a pain, not so much the victims.

"Listen, I can get you that list, but I'm warning you now that it'll be short." Carly heard the defeat in Noah's voice before she saw it in his expression. He didn't want to help, but he would.

"I thought you said that wouldn't work? For either you or them?"

The man kept his gaze on the retreating backs of the group.

"They might not like or understand me, but they've come to respect me over the last twelve years," he answered. "They'll answer my questions. You just need to tell me what to ask."

Carly held back a new surge of emotion at his words. It was as odd as the disappointment she'd felt at his earlier refusal to help. She still didn't have time to figure out what it was or why she was feeling it. Instead, she nodded to him and flashed what she hoped was an appreciative smile.

"The list is what I'll need first. Then I'd like a tour of the community, if that's something you can swing. They might be reluctant to finger a neighbor, but I need to know if anyone showed signs of murderous rage." They might have both been outsiders, but Carly was betting on the fact that Noah still had an ear to the ground of the community within Potter's Creek. At least way more than what she could probably get from other locals.

Noah didn't outright refuse, but he did check his watch.

"I can swing it but I suggest that's something we put on tomorrow's list of things to do." He motioned to the sky. "We've got maybe three hours left of sunlight, then this place gets as dark as the inside of a paper bag. I can still take you around, but you won't see much."

Carly actually smiled at that.

"Well we don't want to be stuck inside of a paper bag, now do we?" she asked, amused. "Tomorrow will be fine."

They exchanged numbers and he agreed to pick her up from the bed-and-breakfast they were staying at just outside of Potter's Creek the next morning. Now that he'd agreed to help, the tension had somewhat lessened in his shoulders, yet Carly could tell he was still ruminating about something in the back of his head.

And she found herself wanting to get to the bottom of it.

They said a quick goodbye, but Carly called out to him before he could get into his truck.

"Hey, Noah?"

The man paused. Then two forest green eyes were on her. "Yeah?"

Carly closed the space between them and lowered her voice.

Despite her daily attempts to keep her past in the past, she knew what she said next only partially came from what was happening in the present. The rest?

A lesson she learned what felt like a lifetime ago.

"Don't let the belief that you know the people who live here cloud the fact that one of them very well could be responsible for what's happened. Knowing someone doesn't mean they aren't capable of violence, malicious intent or even murder. Sometimes the people closest to us are really only there to hide in our blind spots." She tried to give him a cheering smile to lighten what she had just said, but her heart wouldn't let her do it. The pain that hadn't left in over two decades was a constant reminder that there were some things so low that not even light could touch them. "We need to catch who did this and that starts with that list. Amish or not, someone here has to have an idea of who might be behind it, or at least a theory."

Noah took off his cowboy hat and thumped it against his chest, almost like he was saluting her.

Only a hard rumble that stirred something else within Carly.

"I'll do my best. You have my word."

ALMOST EXACTLY THREE hours later, the Tactical Crime Division team were standing at the fence line of one of the pastures on the Yoder farm. The sun was setting, promising darkness and a close to their first day on the case.

Their first day of more questions.

Their first day of no answers.

"We didn't find anything," had been Max's greeting when he and Aria had shown up. Now Max was leaning against the slightly warped wood of the fence and looking out at the trees in the distance.

Aria, who'd stepped aside to call her fiancé, joined him when she was through. Her slight frame often got her mistaken for a teenager in just the right light. It was one reason she fought so hard to be taken seriously. But everyone on TCD knew that she might have been small, but she was mighty. Now, though, she looked like they all felt—frustrated.

"If the CDC or CSI missed anything, whatever it was didn't have a shelf life long enough to still be around now," she said. "Everything has been cleaned up so well that you can't even tell anything happened."

Aria motioned to the pasture they were overlooking now. A worn red barn stood just behind them. The same red barn where Isaiah Yoder had been first examined by the doctor.

She was right, though. The light dusting of snow blanketed the ground, hiding any evidence that twenty-four cattle had died on the field less than two days before. And the beautiful scenery around the farm? It hadn't changed a lick.

It was still beautiful, breathtakingly so.

The air was cold and crisp and highlighted the contrast between the white snow and the evergreen trees. No traffic could be heard bustling by and there wasn't an ounce of light pollution. Just stars in wait, ready to shine.

It was a simple, natural beauty.

Which made the attack that much more of a slap to the senses.

"I don't understand why anyone would do this in general," Selena said, sidling up to Carly. She leaned against the fence and breathed out a sigh. "Never mind to a community whose whole spiel is about wanting to live closer to the land."

"Which makes whoever is behind this particularly malicious." Whatever tension there was between Selena and Axel was gone for the moment as he followed up to her point. He leaned against the fence, also taking in the same view. "They poisoned the land that this community cherishes," he said.

Carly shook her head, not to disagree but a small and futile attempt to distance herself from the present...and her past.

She rolled her shoulders back to try to move even farther away from the now-rising ache and tried to focus on the sunset.

A hush fell over the team around her.

TCD had become family to Carly in the last three years, but she couldn't guess at what they were individually thinking as they all stared out across the field.

It wasn't until the sun was down and darkness invaded the world around them that they packed into their vehicles and left Potter's Creek.

If they had known they were being watched, they might have gone much sooner.

Chapter Four

The Castle in the Trees Bed & Breakfast was, as one would guess, surrounded mostly by trees. Just outside of the Potter's Creek town limits, it was a shock against the evergreens with its light blue paint, bright white porch columns, faded dark roof that was partially steepled over the two-story parlor, and warm florescent lights, pouring from the windows to let everyone know that, while it was near Amish country, it wholly embraced electricity.

It also wholly embraced the Christmas spirit.

Wreaths with fake holly were pinned above every window and door while icicle lights hung about the railing along the wraparound porch. Three Christmas trees were situated around the first floor and, from the road leading up to the inn, two of those could be seen through the windows.

It was all very festive and merry.

The newcomers who had just gone inside were not.

Dressed in their winter coats and boots and badges and guns, they were not at all what Amish country warranted.

Not at all.

"I need you to keep an eye on them."

The voice belonged to a man who didn't have a badge, but he did have a gun. It was in the waistband of his pants, hidden by his coat, but the woman knew it was there. So did the young man next to her. They both had seen it the first time they'd met him and the few times he'd thought to remind them of it.

They all stood together some distance from the inn they were observing, far enough away that they could not be seen.

"While they're here and when they're in Potter's Creek," he continued, eyes like a hawk on the men and women disappearing into the inn. A woman hesitated and looked at the bicycle leaning against the front porch stairs. Then she turned her gaze out to the woods.

The man didn't flinch as she swept over their hiding spot past the tree line.

"That one," he said when the woman finally went inside. "That one might be trouble."

"They will all be trouble," the young man whispered. She reached out and touched his wrist to quiet him, but the older man already had decided he didn't like the note.

"They might be trained but they're out of their element here." He stroked his beard. Then he was smiling. He did that a lot. It never brought anything good with it.

"We stay ahead of them and we stay off their radar. And we do that by you two telling me everything you can about them and what they're doing. Got it?"

The bed-and-breakfast twinkled in the distance. The woman adjusted the strings on her bonnet. She nodded.

"Good," he said. Then that smile was back. "Because we all would really hate for you to break our deal, now wouldn't we?"

It wasn't a question for her to answer.

It was only another excuse for him to hear his own voice.

When he left them between the trees, she wanted so much to go home.

But he was right.

They had a deal.

One she would not break.

"You will search their rooms tomorrow while they are gone," she ordered the only other person in the world who knew why she wouldn't betray the other man.

He rubbed his bare chin, a habit he'd picked up in the last few years.

"And what will you do?" he asked, his voice so quiet the wind could have taken it without a fight.

"I will protect us." She stood up straight and felt darkness in her heart, as ugly hate replaced her profound guilt. "Even if it means hurting them."

NOAH MILLER WAS an early riser.

Carly should have expected as much. He owned and operated a farm with minimal staff to cover him when he was gone. He also had mostly grown up Amish, a lifestyle that required hard work. Unless he'd left the community to shirk a hard work ethic and an early rise-and-shine time, the limited information Carly had on him showed a man who had every reason to be punctual, erring on the side of early.

Yet when she looked up from her chair out on the inn's porch, one hand hovered over her notepad, the other around her coffee thermos, she still was surprised to see his truck coming up the drive.

Never mind the trickle of excitement that danced within her.

Noah was a mystery tucked inside another mystery and, for the life of her, Carly couldn't get past the urge to want to dig a little deeper. She *had* always been a curious creature. It was one reason why Alana had said she would make an excellent agent when the offer first came her way.

That and her extensive knowledge of biochemical weapons.

He put the truck in Park and exited the vehicle with a small, polite smile. Though there was nothing polite about the thoughts that joined her trickle of excitement at the sight of him.

His long dark coat was on but open, showing a red-and-black flannel button-up that was tucked into his dark jeans, cinched together by a belt with a silver buckle that shone. All items of clothing fit him and fit him *well*. It was by no means flashy compared to what Carly saw on the daily in Traverse City, but compared to the muted, no-frills clothing of the Amish, it made the man stand out.

It also didn't hurt that Noah was undeniably good-looking. Carly thought she might have overplayed his classic good looks from the day before but, as he approached the stairs of the front porch, she mentally confirmed she had, in fact, maybe underestimated their impact. Though, without his cowboy hat on, his long, tousled hair gave him the added appearance of being more rough-and-tumble than before.

It was a stimulating sight.

And 100 percent not the right time.

"Morning," Noah said. He shook the paper coffee cup in his hand a little and motioned to the thermos she was holding. "I came with a peace offering of coffee but I see you're already drinking."

Carly tucked her notepad into her jacket pocket and tried her best to continue to look normal. Most people didn't realize how often they were offered coffee, but Carly noted every time it happened to her. It was one reason she always traveled with one or two of her thermoses.

Carly Welsh always made her own coffee.

No exceptions.

"A peace offering?" she said in return. "Normally those come after you've done something that someone else won't like. What exactly have you done that I won't like?"

She gathered her phone and coffee and mentally went through her room upstairs to try to remember if she'd left behind anything she'd need or if she'd forgotten to lock the door. Her badge and gun were already secured on her belt and in the holster at her hip. When they were on a case, she rarely was caught outside of their accommodations without either.

"It's for me saying I wouldn't help yesterday," he replied, as they walked to his vehicle. "You were only trying to do your job."

He went to the passenger side of his truck and opened the door for her. If Carly wasn't holding her coffee and her phone, she might have commented on the move. As it was, she accepted the courtesy and slid into the seat.

"But you ended up agreeing to help in the end. Which I appreciate, but I am curious why you did. You seemed pretty determined the first, and second, time you said no."

Noah sighed before closing her door and seemed to keep the sigh going until he was behind the wheel again. The cab of the truck was warm. He deposited the extra coffee in the cup holder next to his own.

"The way Isaac and the others were treating you rubbed me the wrong way. Then I realized I wasn't doing much better. Plus, I might live just outside of Potter's Creek, but the town is still my home. Someone starts attacking it like this and we all should be doing our part to help."

"Not to mention three farms have been targeted so far and you, too, happen to own a farm."

He nodded.

"There is that," he admitted. "I have more reasons to help rather than decide to mind my own business. Speaking of—" the engine came to life but he pulled a piece of paper out of the center console before reversing "—I did as much digging as my brand of shovel would allow yesterday and got the list you wanted."

A different kind of excitement started to get Carly's blood pumping.

The excitement of a lead.

Only two, by the looks of it.

"You warned me that it would be a short list," she said. "This is definitely a short list."

"And honestly it's more than I expected to get." He gave her a quick look. "You *do* have some knowledge about the Amish, right? They aren't exactly known for grudges, violence and driving people to murder."

"It's the people we never suspect of maliciousness that usually are the most capable of it. That's what makes the surprise that much worse." Carly felt her mood darken. "We can't write anyone off just because they seem like a good person."

Noah whistled.

"I thought it was innocent *until* proven guilty."

Carly rolled her eyes. She'd stepped into that one.

"In my line of work we're not here to sentence the bad guy, or even to put him on trial, we're here to *find* them. To stop the bad guys."

To make sure they don't hurt anyone ever again, she wanted to add.

But Carly could feel the cynical side starting to seep through her words. She didn't want to delve into the nitty-gritty of her past cases, or her life for that matter, so she was ready to let that thread of the convo lie.

However, Noah wasn't ready to let it go.

"I wouldn't call myself a natural optimist but, even to me, that sounds like a grim outlook to have for people. Do you really think whoever did this is from the Amish community?"

That was a question Carly and the rest of the TCD had been repeating during their shared meal at the inn the night before…and a few times before everyone went to do their own tasks that morning. It was out of character for the culprit to be Amish but, then again, without more information they couldn't rule anyone out.

"I wouldn't be doing my job if I didn't pursue every potential lead," she said, careful with her words. "I can't count how many times I've heard people say they *thought* they knew someone after that same someone did something horrific."

"Like when you see friends, neighbors and coworkers during interviews about a shooter or serial killer."

Carly nodded.

"Exactly. Most people never see it coming. And only the lucky ones can wonder about it all later."

Out of her periphery she saw Noah shake his head.

"I just can't imagine someone from Potter's Creek killing. Especially with something like anthrax. They're humble and quiet as a whole."

"And Ted Bundy was a charming man," Carly hated to point out. "Monsters don't always look like monsters. Mostly they just look like normal people."

Noah let out another long sigh.

It gave Carly a few moments to readjust in her seat, trying to find a modicum of relief from the vise tightening in her chest.

Then it was time to focus on the paper in her hands. Not spout philosophy about good versus evil in modern society.

"So you have two people here that might want to do

harm to the community?" she asked. "Are their houses a part of the tour?"

He took the turn out of the inn's long drive and pointed toward Potter's Creek. Some snow stuck to the ground but it was balding in most places, showing sprouts of dark brown and green here and there. The cold was still around, but Carly figured without checking her phone for the temperature that it was a little warmer than the day before based solely on the fact that her nose was neither cold nor runny. Still, she had her black beanie tucked into her inner jacket pocket just in case her ears became too cold.

"Only one," Noah answered. "And he just so happens to be our first stop."

Chapter Five

The Zook homestead housed a family of six and, compared to the five farms that were in Potter's Creek, was small. That didn't take away from its appeal, though. The eldest Zook still living had watched his father build the simple cottage and, through time, had made additions to it to accommodate his growing family. That family now comprised Vernon and Sarah and their children Katie, Annie, Eli and Mervin.

Carly ran her thumb over the ink on the paper Noah had given her.

It was a small, subtle movement, but Noah couldn't help but appreciate the sight.

Carly was unlike any other woman he'd met so far, from her bite, her blatant skepticism and her pinpoint focus on the mystery she was trying to solve. She was keeping him on his toes less than twenty-four hours after appearing in Potter's Creek.

Which was why he was in Potter's Creek on a Tuesday morning, pulled over on the side of the road and staring at the house in the distance.

Because he sure would have been flat-footed and on his farm right now if the FBI agent wasn't currently riding shotgun with a badge on her belt and a crinkle in her brow.

"So Eli is our person of interest," she surmised after Noah had given her a quick set of facts about the family.

Among their numbers and names, he'd also noted that they were one of the few families who had made a living in a trade rather than farming in Potter's Creek. Vernon Zook was a carpenter and had gone into business with a neighboring family five years prior. He was also one of the few Amish who had a separate shed structure out back that utilized electricity strictly for power tools, an uncommon but accepted practice given his vocation.

Noah nodded. He put on the truck's flashers and shifted to Park, cutting the engine. While Noah had gotten her the list and was her tour guide, he wasn't going to be a part of the equation when it was time to ask more pointed questions.

Right now Noah's only job was to drive her through Potter's Creek and call out facts about the Amish community. He wasn't eager to offer anything more.

Potter's Creek already had mixed feelings about him. It was probably better not to align himself completely with the investigating FBI. By the glares and stiff answers he'd gotten the day before while making the list, they were tolerating him but in no way appreciative of his presence.

The feeling's mutual, Potter's Creek.

"Yep. That's where you'll find Eli and his family," he said. "He's sixteen and, word is, has a temper."

"A temper?" Carly repeated, tilting her head a little to the side. "That's not uncommon for a teenager. Or for most adults. I personally have a temper when my caffeine runs low."

Noah could agree with that.

"*True* but apparently his temper ran a little too hot last month when Isaiah Yoder's daughter, Rebecca, also sixteen, wouldn't consider Eli for a courtship. Instead she started dating one of the Haas boys after turning him down."

Carly tilted her head to the other side in question. Her blond hair shifted at the movement, its waves softening her severe look just enough to make him wonder what she liked to do in her free time. Surely it wasn't riding with strangers with a gun strapped to her side.

"And since both the Yoder and Haas farms were affected, him being angry at getting rejected makes him a suspect?"

"I'm guessing you don't know much about how Amish courtship and marriage work," Noah said with a small snort. He was worried his dismissive tone would offend her, yet all she did was shake her head.

"Actually, I don't."

"Rule number one is that, if you're planning on being baptized and staying with the faith when you're older, you have to marry someone who plans to also stay in the faith. No one else."

"Okay so your dating pool is a little more high stakes," she guessed. "When you're turned down by someone, that dating pool shrinks without the hope of adding more to it?"

"That's the long and short of it. Not to mention it also doesn't help that everyone knows he was turned down and that now he'll have to spend years watching their courtship before being a part of the marriage portion that follows it."

This time Carly looked away from the window and at him, pulling his attention to her raised eyebrow. He noted freckles along her nose and the tops of her cheeks.

It was cute, a contrast to the gun he'd spotted at her hip when her jacket had shifted as she'd gotten into the truck.

"He'll have to spend *years* watching their courtship and then *participate* in their marriage?" she repeated. "Please give me some more depth with that one."

Noah stifled a laugh at her reaction. It had been a long while since Noah had been with someone who *didn't* know all of the Amish beliefs and customs.

"Every couple has the same steps they have to take if they wish to stay in the faith. It isn't a private thing. Intentions have to be made public and then your courtship *stays* public. If you want alone time with your sweetheart, then you spend that out on the front porch in plain view together talking. You spend it at singings. If you ride to and from church services, you do so in an open buggy and usually with a chaperone. Basically, everything you do as a couple is a public affair. *Then* the dance before marriage happens, usually around the age of twenty or so."

Noah had never experienced what he was about to explain, but he'd seen enough Amish engagements and marriages in his first sixteen years of life to be familiar.

"The first part is the same as it is for most Englishers. The young man asks his lady to marry him but then veers into a different path," he continued. "They keep their intentions a secret until around July or August, then the woman tells her family about her plans. Then the proper certification is requested after Fall communion. Then all of the couples who plan to get married are 'published' at church. The deacon tells everyone the young women's names who plan to marry. *Then* the fathers announce the date and time of the wedding and invite all members of the church to attend. After they're published, the couple only have a few days before the ceremony and are allowed to go to one last singing with their old group of friends. After that the woman helps her mother prepare for the wedding while the groom-to-be extends personal invitations to all church members. Then the day of the actual ceremony, *everyone* gets involved. There's no maid of honor or best man roles.

It's a lot of activity and not at all something you can easily ignore or just skip."

Carly returned her attention to the paper in her hand and Eli's name.

"Which means Eli wouldn't be able to avoid the fact that he was rejected by the Yoder girl for the Haas boy. He'd have a front-row seat of the entire thing, along with everyone else. Salt in the proverbial wound."

"Not an easy pill to swallow, especially for a rejected sixteen-year-old with anger issues."

Carly gave the house in the distance another long look before she pulled out her cell phone. Noah gave her privacy while she texted someone.

"Let's continue with the tour and then you can drop me off at the community barn," she said when she was done.

"Then you and your team will talk to Eli?"

She touched the second name on the list.

"Unless this David Lapp is more interesting."

Abram Lapp's eldest son had already popped into Noah's thoughts before the FBI had even shown up.

"What's that face?" Carly asked before he could reply.

"What do you mean?"

She touched the spot on her forehead between her eyebrows, then motioned to him.

"You scrunched up right there and looked like you just sucked on a lemon, all at once. I'm assuming that means you know David and he *is* more interesting than Eli."

Noah didn't want to, but he nodded to both assumptions.

"This is where my time outside of the community is going to show," he warned. "I don't know the whole story but I do know that David, nineteen now, left six months ago."

"Nineteen… So he didn't leave after his Rumspringa?"

He shook his head.

"He left after getting caught breaking church rules. Which is *interesting* considering he'd already come back from his Rumspringa with every intention of being baptized when he turned twenty."

Noah put emphasis on the word *interesting*.

"When you say he left, you really mean he got kicked out."

Now Carly was the one with a knitted brow.

"Bingo. And, before you ask, everyone went tight-lipped about what exactly he did to warrant being exiled." Noah snorted but he felt no amusement. "They might have a grudging respect for me around here but when you get down to the nuts and bolts of it, I'm still the *other* guy who left."

Carly was facing him again, but her contemplative expression had changed to something else.

Thoughtful? Sympathetic? Regret that her only resource didn't elicit enough trust from people who believed in honesty?

"Where is Lapp now?" she asked instead.

This time there was a snort of amusement from Noah. He turned the engine back on and checked over his shoulder to see if anyone was driving down the road. He didn't miss her look of surprise after he answered.

"Wouldn't you know it, he's actually my neighbor."

"Your neighbor?"

Noah nodded and pulled out onto the road since the coast was clear.

"I didn't even realize it until yesterday when I started asking around," he followed up. "I'd heard before then that David was still around Potter's Creek, but between working on my farm and not exactly having many reasons to be present in the community, I don't often get too much town news. Plus, I'd only ever met David once and that was in passing during his Rumspringa a few years back." Noah gave her a quick look. "It's not like I'm running some kind of post-Amish support group in my limited free time."

At that Carly chuckled. A nice sound that was equal parts pleasant and intriguing.

Settle down there, cowboy, Noah mentally chided himself. *You're here to help and then part ways. Not admire the FBI agent because she laughed at your joke.*

It didn't take long for them to get back to business after that.

The tour continued through the heart of the community and then by all of the businesses, farms and on to a few popular recreational spots for the town, for the Amish and tourists alike. Noah tried his best to give the facts with a few tidbits from the time he'd spent living in Potter's Creek.

Carly remained mostly quiet during the tour, asking him only to repeat family names and clarify a few details while she wrote notes. It wasn't until he was done giving his spiel on the abandoned barn at the back of the old Kellogg property that she made an observation of her own.

"You know, for a town this small, I expected every available space to be done up in some kind of Christmas decoration, but the only place I've seen anything is at the bed-and-breakfast we're staying in," she said, turning toward him in her seat, thoughtful. "Now I realize that that's probably another Amish-related thing I don't know and not just a town-wide disdain of all things jolly."

"The Amish celebrate the birth of baby Jesus in a strictly religious sense," Noah explained. "No decorations, no indoor trees, no *nonsense*."

He didn't mean to, but the last word came out sounding like a child mocking his parent.

Carly picked up on the change. Her eyebrow rose and she searched his face before her lips quirked up at the corner.

"And now that you're *former* Amish, you can go all out, right? Or do decked out Christmas trees and mistletoe not work with quiet-type farmers?"

Noah stifled a laugh at that. He hadn't been called a quiet-type farmer before.

"I actually have always loved the look of a decked-out tree—you know, the ones that look like a craft store exploded on it—but I usually keep it simple. A nod to my family, I suppose. Though, I'm sure if you ask my father, he probably assumes the inside of my farmhouse is filled to the brim with *all* things jolly."

Just like before, he hadn't meant his words to sour. Yet, they had.

Noah not only had a sparse Christmas tree, when he had spent most of his life wanting a grand, to-the-nines one, but he also spent the holiday alone looking at it. Something he'd told himself he had come to accept.

Still, there was a lonely bitterness there.

He could feel it like he could the year before.

So he handled it the same way he always had and tried to ignore it.

Noah switched gears and finished their tour. When he pulled up to the community barn where some of the TCD team was waiting, he couldn't help but feel something else weasel its way to the surface.

A pang of disappointment.

It had been a long while since he'd had someone to share the beauty of town with.

And that wasn't for nothing.

"Thanks for all of this." Carly held her notepad up, eyes still tracing her notes. "I know Potter's Creek is small, but it's always easier to have a local to help fill in the blanks.

Not to mention getting a lay of the land. It's not like Google Maps can tell us that—" she searched her notes for a piece of information "—no one uses the road behind the Kellogg property because the mud gets so bad buggies have lost wheels to it."

Noah nodded.

"It was no problem," he said. "I just hope it helps you all catch whoever is behind this. The people in town may be different from us but that doesn't mean they aren't good people."

Noah pictured two bodies in a field.

A father and son.

His fist tightened around the steering wheel until his knuckles went white.

When Carly spoke her words were surprisingly just as fierce as the anger he was feeling at the Grabers' murders.

"One way or the other, we're going to catch the person or people responsible and make them pay," she promised. "You have my word on that."

While Noah didn't know FBI Agent Carly Welsh well at all, in that moment, he found he completely believed her.

Chapter Six

The property's name had been changed to the Miller farm but the worn, wooden sign that hung out by the main gate by the road still read Tuckett Family.

Noah had owned it for upwards of five years and, in those five years, he hadn't thought to replace the sign once. The Tuckett family were good, solid people, those who'd passed on and those still here. Noah had spent his time running the place to the best of his abilities as a way to pay tribute to them, while the faded sign was a smaller token of remembrance.

Of respect.

Which was why his gut tightened when the first of his workers, a young man named Mark, took his hat off looking as guilty as sin and approached Noah after he returned from the tour he'd given.

"Hey there, boss," Mark said in greeting, his words drenched in what sounded awfully close to regret. "I heard about what happened at the Amish farms, terrible business, isn't it?"

Noah was only one step outside of his truck but he knew where this was going.

"Yeah, it is."

Mark nodded. His eyes went to the ground, then the pasture behind them, then finally back to Noah. He straightened, as if trying to prepare himself until he took a deep breath and went right to it.

"You know, I wouldn't normally do this, but the wife—well, you know she's pregnant with the twins and that in itself is already pretty risky and if there's even remotely a chance I could get them sick or infected, or worse... Well, I hate to do this, boss, but I think I need to give Potter's Creek a wide berth until everything gets sorted out."

There it was.

The first ripple effect of the attacks to touch the Miller farm, despite it not being targeted. Noah had guessed it would happen, but it still didn't feel good.

It also didn't help his anger.

Not at Mark, though. While Noah shouldered a lot of work on his own around the farm, there was a group of four to five workers who helped him. Mark was young, but had been at the farm for three years now and was as good and solid a worker as the Tucketts before him.

Now that good man was afraid that his wife and unborn children could be hurt.

And Noah couldn't fault him for that fear. He'd pick up work elsewhere pretty fast, given his good reputation.

"I don't think any of us will rest easy until whoever behind this is caught," Noah said. He clapped Mark on the back. "You go take care of your family. I'll be good here."

Mark apologized again, but didn't stay long past that. His truck wasn't even on the main road when another worker called in for her and her husband.

"I'm really sorry, Noah," Marjorie said through the phone. "We aren't saying this is forever, just until those suits can get a few days of detecting under their belts. Until then maybe you should think about taking a trip? You're welcome to come stay in our guest room if you need a place."

Noah accepted their decision but declined their offer. He didn't say it, but there was no way in hell he was leaving his farm behind. It was his home.

It was his place.

And there wasn't a soul on Earth who could move him from it.

He knew that his dedication, though, was his own and when another worker, Killian, called and recounted what he'd heard on the news and then asked if he could not come in, Noah decided it wasn't fair to expect or ask his last long-time worker to make the trip.

Regina Tuckett, however, wasn't like the rest.

She didn't answer her phone because she was already at the back of the property, wearing her snow boots despite the fact the ground was now wet, not frozen, and a look that was neither guilty nor apologetic when he walked up to her.

"This fence needs mending," she said, nodding toward the rotting wood that made up a small section between the posts. "I know it's still standing but it won't be for long. I'd rather we did it when the weather is cooperating, too. You know how I hate mending in the snow."

Noah laughed. He *did* know how much Gina hated mending in the snow because he'd heard her complain about it from when he was sixteen all the way up until the last winter at the age of thirty.

The main difference between him being sixteen and thirty was that Noah owned the farm now, not her father, and he never made her mend it alone.

"We can see about it next week," he said around a small laugh. "Until then, I think it's best you go home."

Gina turned on her heel so quick that her long silver braid slapped across her shoulder. Gina might have been in her early sixties but she hadn't moved slow a day in her

life, at least not since Noah had known her. It was mostly
due to good genes—all the Tucketts lived into their upper-
nineties—but Noah wasn't about to discount Gina's sheer
stubbornness playing a role in her ability to stay so spry.

She would dedicate her life to trying to nail jelly to a
tree if someone told her she couldn't.

"Why on earth would I go home when there's work to be
done here?" she asked, voice pitching higher than normal.
"Did you suddenly hire someone else to help with maintenance and overseeing? Because, if you did, I'd like to
meet them and see how they don't know a damned thing
about—"

"—I didn't hire anyone new *or* replace you, Gee," Noah
interrupted, holding up his hand to stop her from continuing her tirade. "Everyone else isn't coming in today because of what happened at the Yoder, Haas and Graber
farms. And I think it's a good idea. We don't know who
decided to attack them and if they're targeting other farms.
I'd rather none of you take that chance if something happens here."

Gina's eyebrow rose. Then she scoffed, surprising him.

"If you think I'm like everyone else then you don't know
me, *boy*. There's work to be done here and there's no way
I'm not going to do it because someone got their sick jollies off by preying on the defenseless." Gina motioned to
her side. A shotgun Noah hadn't seen yet, but recognized
as her father's, was propped up against her. "I'm not leaving this place until the work is finished and I dare anyone
to tell me otherwise."

Noah took a moment to try to think of a persuasive argument but accepted defeat.

"I know from experience that reasoning with you is a
loser's game," he said instead. "Just make sure you keep
your eyes open and that gun down. Last thing we need is

you shooting someone who just stopped by to snoop. Or, worse. Shoot an FBI agent."

No sooner than he said it did Noah think of Carly.

Gina's grumpy expression smoothed out and then dipped into curiosity.

"Is that why you came in late this morning?" she asked. "Were you helping them?"

Noah nodded.

"They needed a tour guide who didn't mind talking."

"Did you introduce them to your father?" Her words were genuinely curious. Gina had only met his father twice. In that time, it was apparent she wasn't too fond of him.

Then again, Gina was a Tuckett and they had never been known for being friendly, open books.

"No, it was just a point-and-give-a-brief-statement kind of tour. We didn't talk to anyone outside of the bishop when we ran into him next to the market."

Gina shook her head and turned back to the post.

"You shouldn't have to help fight for them," she breathed out hotly. "They sure didn't fight for you."

Noah knew Gina didn't intend for her words to wound, but they did.

"I'm not even sure I was all that helpful, to be honest," he said, sidestepping the reopening of the old wound. "It's not like I'm the most popular guy around town."

Gina waved a hand dismissively at him.

"Whatever you gave those suits was more than they would have gotten from the community on their own. Don't undersell yourself. If you think you're cheap then you're giving everyone else permission to think you're less-than, too." She took on a power stance, mindful to hold the shotgun with one hand so it didn't fall. "And what is it that Dad used to say about confidence?"

Noah could hear Frank Tuckett, standing in his work clothes next to the barn and wiping sweat from his brow onto his forearm.

"'Only you can make it and only you can break it.'"

Gina gave a quick nod.

"He wasn't a man who was in touch with sentiment, but he wasn't wrong."

Noah had to agree to that.

"I'll go look in the work shed to see if we have any extra posts still," he finally said after a companionable silence stretched between them. That was the Tuckett way, after all. Shared silence with bouts of work requests. "If we do I'll come find you and we can go ahead and mend this after I do my rounds. The ground's still not frozen, so we can handle it. Sound good?"

"Sounds good."

Noah started back for his truck, a chill in the air sliding into his jacket. The snow was gone but there was a forecast for rain coming up. He only hoped if it did snow, it wouldn't do it for long. He wouldn't deny that the farm and its almost one-hundred acres looked downright beautiful covered in white, but he also wasn't going to deny it was a pain in the backside to do his job when everything was covered.

Living in a scenery meant for a postcard was nice, but mending fences and other such chores with numb fingers was not.

Noah spent the next little while going about his duties, mostly maintenance since Gina had already seen to their livestock, before heading to the work shed in a hunt for extra posts. Painted a nice dark blue to make the worn wood look nicer, the shed was a small structure, half the size of the barn, near the back corner of the property. When Noah was eighteen he'd told Gina's father that the color had made the shed look like a piece of the night sky had fallen and gotten stuck in the trees. After ice had taken down a few of those trees that had once surrounded it, the rest had been cut and the fence had been built to include the shed in the field that went across one side of the property. Noah had also repainted the small building twice, keeping the same blue.

So now it was still a touch of the night sky, no longer *in* the forest. Just with a nice view of it.

Noah walked up to it with a smile, nostalgia moving through him like the chill in the air. He rounded the structure, trying to remember what all was inside before unlocking the door, but slowed in his tracks at the corner.

The shed's door was open.

Not unheard of considering the entire farm had access and anyone could be inside looking for supplies during a normal work day.

But today *wasn't* a normal work day due to the investigation and, apart from Gina, no other staff was on the farm. He doubted she'd been here or she'd have already looked for the fencing posts herself.

If that wasn't enough to raise suspicion in Noah, the blood on the wet ground in front of the opened door would have.

Without moving his gaze from the opening, he reached out and grabbed the only thing he could get his hands on as a weapon. The round-point shovel had a crack along its wooden handle but there was some heft to the tool. It would do in a pinch if needed. He flipped it upside down so one hand curved against the metal and the other around the wet wood. The muscles in his arms tightened. He moved to the door, careful with his footing so it didn't make a sound.

There were bloodstains, enough to notice but not enough indicating a substantial wound, he guessed.

If Noah hadn't been an observant person he would have missed the dark red spots, but there they were.

At his storage shed, at the back of his property.

During an investigation where farms in the community had been attacked.

Noah pushed his shoulders back and hardened his jaw.

Then, in one fluid movement, he rounded the corner, shovel held high.

It was empty.

Noah lowered his makeshift weapon after a quick glance around the room. Nothing was disturbed, though he could make out footprints that weren't his as if someone had been walking around.

They didn't stray far from the middle of the space and then they backtracked and went outside again.

Like someone had been looking for something but hadn't found it.

Noah managed to follow those footprints to the fence.

He stood there, a bad feeling starting up in his gut, and stared into the woods where they disappeared.

"What the hell?"

Chapter Seven

"I'm in a happy, healthy relationship with the love of my life, and even I can admit he's good-looking."

Aria was checking the safety on her service weapon. They were outside of David Lapp's house and readying to interview the boy as one of their two suspects. Axel and Selena had already gone off to handle talking to Eli Zook.

As for Noah?

Well, he certainly wasn't in the vehicle with them.

Which was great, considering Aria's subject change from how to approach the Lapp boy to how cute their former Amish liaison was.

Carly side-eyed Aria from the passenger's seat, eyebrow raised.

Aria gave a small shrug.

"What? I'm just saying. The farmer has that whole brooding, tall and dark-haired thing going on." She adopted a hilariously deep voice. "'I've seen things, Agent Welsh. That's why I brood.'"

Carly stifled a laugh, lest she encourage Aria to bring Noah up again when Max was back in the vehicle. For now he was just outside on the phone with Axel.

"Calling other people brooders is like the kettle calling the pot black," she replied. "You've met our team, right? We all get quite broody from time to time."

"True," Aria admitted. Then she turned toward Carly and wiggled her eyebrows. "But I noticed that you didn't disagree that Noah is a looker."

Carly rolled her eyes.

No, she wasn't going to disagree.

But she wasn't going to encourage the woman, either.

Noah had been a good, well-tempered tour guide. One who had done what he could before delivering her back to her team.

Was his past mysterious?

Did she want to know more?

Was he really that good-looking?

Yes. To all three.

But again, there was a job to do, and right now that job had them parked outside of a two-story white house at the end of a pocked dirt road that had seen better days. A job that needed them to focus on the nineteen-year-old who had been exiled. Had not left of his own volition.

Max, thankfully, appeared at the driver's-side door before Carly could respond to Aria's teasing. He was frustrated.

"That was a short phone call," Carly said after the door was opened.

Max sighed.

"And, according to Axel, that was a short-lived interview. Apparently the Zook family were as forthcoming as a brick wall. A brick wall guarded by another, taller brick wall. The dad wouldn't let the boy answer any questions and that was as much as he said himself."

Carly grumbled but wasn't exactly surprised.

"I was hoping the cold shoulder we got yesterday would have warmed when they realized we're trying to help."

She got out of the car, moving her jacket back over her hip holster and the gun inside of it. Aria followed suit and soon all three were at the bottom of the porch stairs. Even though they were still talking, they each focused their individual attention on the house. There was a car parked at the side of the home but it looked like it hadn't been driven in a while. Since the house was by itself and not a part of a farm, it was the only structure in the middle of the open stretch of land around it. Trees could be seen in the distance. Carly wondered how far away Noah's property started but didn't voice her curiosity.

It would only get another teasing rise out of Aria.

Though Axel and Selena being stonewalled by the Zook family did give her a valid reason to talk about the man.

"If we don't get anywhere with David Lapp, I'm going to reach out to Noah Miller again and see if he's willing to help us. Better than us talking to ourselves and running around in circles," Carly said.

Both of the agents next to her nodded.

Without studying their body language, Carly knew they were reverting into full detective mode. Aria was noting every entrance and exit, Max was readying for the wild card option that inevitably happened during some of their cases.

Carly?

She had split her focus into two categories: on the lookout for dangerous toxins, and readying to do a verbal dance with David Lapp to see if he had been the one behind the attack using them.

"I'll lead."

Carly bounded the steps and rapped her knuckles against the front door. She had her badge up and out by the fourth knock. By the sixth one she called out Lapp's name, then her name, her affiliation and the need to ask a few questions. When that didn't cause any movement inside, she said it was time to split up.

"Check the perimeter to see if anyone is here. But be careful. Remember we don't know anything about this David kid other than he was asked to leave the community."

"Which is kind of a red flag," Aria added.

"Agreed."

Max went the length of the porch and then hung a left around the corner. Aria did the same on the right. Carly stayed on the porch but moved to the two windows next to the door. Both had curtains drawn.

She slipped her badge back into her pocket and kept going along the front to another set of windows. No curtains or blinds blocked the view of the room here. Instead, Carly could clearly make out a good-sized dining room with a table and four chairs. All five surfaces were filled with clutter.

Magazines, books, papers. Beer bottles. An ashtray with several butts on and around it. An empty vodka bottle. There were also a few paper plates with balled up paper towels. One had half of a pizza crust on it. Carly even saw a few dirty-looking socks strewn around.

Maybe David Lapp's general hygiene and cleaning habits had led to him being kicked out?

"Carly."

Max appeared next to her, his voice sharp, direct and low.

He'd found something.

"The bedroom on the back corner of the house has been trashed. Almost everything broken."

Carly pushed her jacket aside and unholstered her gun. Max already had his out, but low.

"Sounds like probable cause to take a look inside to me. Let's go."

They moved together to the back of the house, linking

up with Aria. The back door wasn't locked so they wasted no time. In sync, the three of them raised their weapons.

Then they went into the house.

If a red flag hadn't already been waving in the wind before they entered, a trove of them were planted the second they were inside.

Stale.

Dirty.

Carly shared a look with Aria.

Max nodded toward the door nearest them.

Then it was time to clear the house.

They announced their presence a few times but were met with silence. Still they moved, guns drawn, through the first floor. At the stairs, Aria walked up while Max went along the back part of the house. Carly wound up at the door to what she thought was a pantry next to the refrigerator.

But it wasn't a pantry.

It was a set of stairs to a basement.

Carly turned her head to the side, taking a quick breath.

A different smell wafted up at her.

She couldn't place it, but it didn't matter.

Something was way beyond not right.

Something was wrong.

She descended the stairs, her stomach tightening.

At first the room seemed normal enough. It opened up on either side of the stairs, making a big box. Her gaze lit on boxes covered in dust, cloths covering bulky furniture, a few knickknacks clustered together on different surfaces.

But by the time Carly walked off the last stair, everything about the basement, the house and David Lapp changed.

"What the hell?"

What was in the middle of the space to her right was so unexpected that Carly didn't see the man right away. But she felt his knife.

Chapter Eight

The blood against her hand made Carly wish she'd kept her gloves on. It was oddly cold and concerned her a great deal. It meant that skin had been broken.

It meant that she was, in part, exposed.

It meant she was vulnerable.

It was the reason the gun she had been holding in the same hand had fallen from what was supposed to be a firm grip.

Carly internally swore.

The blood wasn't her only concern.

Maybe number four out of her five.

Her top priorities had already shifted three times in the last half hour since she'd been attacked in the basement and run after her assailant into the woods, Max coming up behind her when he'd heard her cry out. Aria had stayed to call for more help.

Now her priorities shifted again.

Find him.

Stop him.

Don't get killed.

Easy, right?

Carly swore again. This time it was from pain. A throbbing was starting to run across the right side of her face, while her lip stung to let her know without looking that it was probably busted where her attacker had socked her. Then there was the cut along her forearm.

The reason for the blood.

The reason why she had to catch the man who had done it all as soon as possible.

If he could attack a federal agent with such ferocity, there was no telling what he'd do to a hapless bystander who might have the bad fortune to be in the way.

Then again, Carly didn't expect to run into any wayward residents of Potter's Creek right now. Not several minutes deep into the woods. Which she believed was why her perp had hightailed it right into the trees when he'd first taken off.

Speeding through the dense trees and foliage would have been laborious under normal circumstances. Doing it in a pursuit was a downright pain.

A pain that Carly felt as deeply as the thumping of adrenaline trying to keep pace with her objective.

Her phone buzzed in her left hand.

She kept her pace but hit Accept.

"Where are you?" One of Max's underappreciated skills, in her opinion, was his ability to still manage complete sentences that were as clear as crystal even when he was out of breath.

Carly answered but she didn't possess the same skill. Her words were choppy and few.

She had been running for almost ten minutes under the vast tree canopy, and the pain radiating in three different places across her body was becoming an obstacle.

"No idea. Before I lost visual he kept changing direction."

Movement rustled on the other side of the call. Max was somewhere in the forest with her but, what the Amish country might have lacked in modern technology, it absolutely more than made up for in expansive acreage and nature. The fact that she hadn't seen or heard Max since they entered the wooded area highlighted just how seemingly endless their current surroundings were.

"We might need to regroup," Max said as Carly continued deeper into the unknown. "At least fall back to me since you aren't armed. Aria's getting backup, but they won't know where we are."

Carly hated it, but she knew Max was right. She hadn't seen the man she was chasing in at least three minutes. Unlike Selena and Blanca, she wasn't a tracker. Her skills leaned toward toxins, biology and the mindset of someone who would use both as a weapon. She'd already started the ball rolling on an analysis of the anthrax used in the attacks. Samples were at some of the best labs in the country with trusted colleagues looking for clues.

Now she needed to use her observational talents to figure out why her attacker would have been in that basement and if he had been connected to the spread of the deadly bacteria.

But that's why you want to catch him so badly, her inner voice reminded her. *Because what you saw in that house didn't make sense.*

Carly wanted answers.

She needed them.

"Carly," Max prodded. "Running blindly into a fight is a fast way for that fight to be a quick one. We'll find him."

He was right. Carly slowed her speed until she put her hand against a tree to catch her breath.

"If I'm not completely turned around, I think if I head east from where I am then I'll be out of here," she said after a moment. "Then we can—"

A branch snapped behind her and to the left. Carly

dropped her phone, ducked and spun around just as a towering man with wide, dark eyes swung out with a closed fist.

The hit narrowly missed her but the man himself didn't.

Whether he meant to or not his momentum carried him like a linebacker right into Carly. She barely had time to put her hands up to brace herself against his chest.

Both went down to the ground.

All the air *whoosh*ed out of her as the man grunted at the impact.

Carly didn't have time to waste.

The man wasn't just bigger than her, he had the upper hand. One of those things she couldn't change, the other she absolutely had to.

In two fluid movements she brought her knees and feet up and kicked up like a jackrabbit against his gut. Then used her hands to go for his face.

Her target was his eyes.

What she got instead was a few seconds of tangled limbs, grunts of struggle on both parts, and pain.

The force of her kick shifted him off of her but not before he pushed her hands away and angered her open wound on her forearm.

If she had had any breath left in her, she would have yelled at how it stung.

Instead she used the shift in the man's body to roll out from under him.

It was a move not without its consequences.

The man reached out and grabbed her jacket. Carly heard Max yelling out through the phone but all of her focus snapped back to her assailant the moment he used his new hold to start dragging her backward. Mud wet her face and chest. Pain from their first encounter in the basement merged with new pain.

Carly needed to end the fight now or it would be ended for her.

Using the same principle that had gotten her to the ground in the first place, Carly stopped trying to get away from the man and instead created her own momentum to use against him. She rolled back into him, knocking him flat against the ground until she was on top of him.

More pain shot through her as her knuckles hit his jaw.

Knocking him unconscious was her best bet.

Too bad she'd only brought her fists to a gun fight. Her gun had slipped again from her hands when he'd come after her.

Carly threw herself to the side half a second before the man pulled a gun and shot. Her ears rang from the sharp crack cutting the air, but she'd managed to roll out of his aim.

As Carly scrambled to her feet, he pointed the gun at her again.

She didn't have time to be surprised that he didn't pull the trigger. He struggled to stand, weapon trained on her.

What had started with close combat had turned into two people six feet apart with a gun between them.

"You know, I—I didn't want to have to kill a federal agent," he said, not at all in a cruising calm tone. He sounded frantic, unsure. "But—but I'm not above it, either."

Carly raised her hands up, trying to make herself seem helpless. Which, given the lack of distance between them and the steady hand he was aiming with, wasn't too much of a stretch to believe.

"The penalty for shooting an agent is pretty steep. Don't be foolish now. Who are you?" she couldn't help but ask. "Because I'm pretty sure you aren't David Lapp."

Not only was he at least in his mid-thirties, the man

had a shaved head, dark stubble across his face and, if the last half hour had proven anything, he was no stranger to violence. Sure, David had been exiled and was no longer a part of the Amish world, but doing such a hard one-eighty from that pacifist culture didn't seem to match the, admittedly, limited information they had on him.

The man motioned with the gun to turn around.

Carly's stomach tightened as she repeated the question and ignored the unspoken command.

"Who are you?"

That feeling of dread strengthened as the man smiled. Not an ounce of it was good.

"Wouldn't you like to know?"

He readjusted his aim to her head.

"I don't know what trouble you're in, but you're making it a hell of a lot worse. You don't need to do this," she tried.

"I know but it's easier than running." He wagged the gun at her again. "Turn around and get on your knees."

Carly had been here before. Well not *exactly* here, but in a situation where her life was a breath away from no longer being her life.

Being killed in the line of duty was always a possibility in what she did. Part of that truth was learning acceptance that a dangerous job could have a violent and unfortunate end.

But in that moment Carly didn't find even the hint of acceptance in her. There was no defeat, either.

Nope.

She was going to follow directions but try to keep him talking. Long enough for Max to show up. Or whatever backup Aria managed to get—if they could find them here in the forest.

And if she thought stalling wasn't going to work, she was going to last-ditch effort her way backward into him.

Another tussle on the ground among the mud and blood.

Because Carly wasn't leaving Potter's Creek without finding justice for the livelihoods that had been destroyed. The lives that had been taken.

And for whatever had gone on in David Lapp's basement.

She had a job to do.

Dying in the woods in Amish country wasn't how she was going to meet her end.

Not if she could help it.

"Where is David Lapp?" she repeated as her knees settled into the ground. "If you're going to kill me then at least do me the courtesy of telling me that."

The man laughed, bitterness in the sound.

"I don't owe you anything, lady."

Carly didn't have time to worry that the man wasn't a talker. That he wasn't going to take her stall. That Max still wasn't there.

She also didn't have time to employ her Hail Mary attempt to disarm him or get away.

Or at least manage to take a bullet but miss a fatal hit.

The moment the last of the word *lady* left his mouth, a noise so loud and foreign that she didn't know how to react filled the morning air around her.

Carly put her hands down and whirled around.

Then, promptly, let her jaw fall open in surprise.

The man who had been about to kill her crumpled to the ground.

Next to him was another man.

Holding a shovel, blood now on the metal.

"Noah?"

Noah Miller was still holding his makeshift weapon like a baseball bat and breathing fast. His green eyes were wide and searching.

Searching her.

"Are you okay?" he asked in a rush.

Carly hurried to the fallen gun and scooped it up. She took a few steps back and trained its aim down on her attacker. When he didn't move a breath, she squatted down to check for a pulse. His body was completely slack, but it was there.

"I'm okay," she said, back to standing and still ready to shoot if needed.

"Are you sure?" Noah's tone dipped low. A quiet man until he wanted answers. "You're bleeding."

Carly was wet in places from mud, blood and sweat and she couldn't quite figure out which was which at this point. Plus, there was a pounding and stinging that accompanied several parts of her body.

But, all in all, she felt okay.

Nothing a shower, some soap and a glass of wine couldn't fix. Hell, maybe even a shot of whiskey. After her jaunt through the woods, she felt like she deserved it.

"I'm good."

Noah didn't seem to buy it. He looked so odd with his cowboy hat and weaponized shovel.

But he also looked so good. So, so good.

Whether that was because of his hardened jaw, the unsaid promise that he was willing to fight again if he had to, or the sheer fact that he'd just saved her life, Carly didn't know.

His look of focus switched gears to a gaze Carly understood.

Now that the danger was over, he wanted answers.

"Who is he?" he asked. "And why are you out here? Someone from your team called my cell, asking if I knew where you could be."

Carly was trying to get her breathing back to normal.

Her fatigue was starting to catch up with her. She motioned with her head to the direction she'd run from. Though she had no idea if that's where she'd actually started.

"We went to David Lapp's house to talk to him. He wasn't there but we found *him*." She looked to the man on the ground. "He attacked me and ran into the woods. Max and I pursued. Aria called for help." Carly stopped herself. "Wait. Why are *you* here? And with a shovel?"

Noah lowered his weapon but didn't put it down.

"I was getting something from my storage shed and saw some blood on the ground. I followed the trail to the tree line and then heard a gunshot." He nodded to his right. "My property line is about a hundred yards that way."

The way he said it, the way he looked—eyes wild with worry—touched her. He'd been concerned. About her. Carly couldn't help but give him a small smile.

"And so you ran toward the gunshot with a shovel?"

Noah shrugged.

"It's the only thing I had so I made it work."

She glanced back down at her attacker.

"You certainly did."

A rustling sound pulled their attention back toward his farm. Carly redirected her gaze. Out of her periphery, she saw Noah raise his shovel again. A few seconds later a woman with gray hair and a shotgun ran into view.

"Don't shoot!"

Noah dropped the shovel and put his hands out, taking two long strides to get between them.

"Carly, this is Gina. She works for me," he rushed to say. "Gina, this is Carly. She's one of the FBI agents."

The woman, Gina, didn't immediately lower her weapon.

"I heard a gunshot," she said, suspicion clear in her voice.

"It was him." Noah moved so she could see the man

on the ground. Then she narrowed her eyes at Carly. "I'm okay, Gina," Noah added. "Put down the gun."

This time the woman listened. She didn't let it go, but she rested it against her leg.

"Federal agent, don't move!"

Another voice entered the area.

Max emerged, gun aimed.

Now Carly had to step in.

"They're good, Max! You can lower your weapon."

Max took a beat to look around, then listened.

Which was good considering Gina seemed ready to shoot them both.

For a moment no one spoke.

Carly took a deep breath and let it out.

It hurt.

She hurt.

But pain wasn't one of her problems right now.

What they'd found at David Lapp's house was.

Carly met Noah's gaze.

"Well, this might not be the time, but before we started a foot chase with this one here I was about to come find you."

Noah's brow slid up.

It only highlighted how attractive the man was no matter the emotion he was showing.

"Why?"

"Because we need your help." Carly let out another breath. "Because *I* need your help."

Now CARLY WAS back in the basement, absently massaging the bandage over the cut along her arm while drops of water soaked into the back of her shirt. All pain had reverted to a dull throb in the time it took for the local authorities to converge at the back of Noah's property to secure their alive, but unconscious, runner. EMS had shown up in the woods just as Carly's patience had petered out, but she'd sat there while they'd washed her cut, bandaged it and suggested she go to the hospital to get herself checked out.

Apparently she hadn't been a pleasant sight to look at.

Blood, mud and bruises.

Not the best combination to be sporting when you were trying to convince your team that you were fine.

Noah ended up being the only person out there who kept his opinion on what she should and shouldn't do to himself. Yet, she'd seen how his gaze kept flitting over to her during their wait. Aside from that, he kept his conversation with his staff member, Gina Tuckett, quiet and private. The older woman still had her shotgun against her leg when Carly was okayed to leave.

She tried not to be ungrateful for the care—it wasn't their fault that the man had given her a good beating—but she had been nothing but anxious as each TCD member had gone back to the Lapp house to dig deeper.

Then it was just her, and she'd had eyes for only Noah.

The team needed his help.

She needed his help. More than the perfunctory aid he'd given so far.

However, before she'd even gotten a word off to try to persuade him, Noah had spoken first.

"What do you need me to do?"

Now he was standing next to her in the Lapp basement, clearly as shocked as the rest of them had been.

A chair was sitting up in the center of the space.

But it wasn't a normal chair.

Not at all.

This one was metal and bolted to the ground.

If that wasn't enough to be concerning, the thick blood-covered rope attached to it was.

And that was saying nothing of the dried stain on the concrete beneath the chair.

"What has David been up to?" Noah asked after taking the scene in. "Did *he* do this or was it done *to* him?"

Carly shook her head.

"Sadly, you're as up to speed as I am at the moment. When we first came in to clear the house I was barely a step off the stairs before Broad-Shoulders-and-no-Chill came at me. We're still trying to identify him." She motioned for Noah to follow her back to the first floor. "Can you tell me if you recognize or see anything that might have a connection to the community or why David was exiled? Or maybe where he might be?"

If he wasn't a victim.

"I can look but, again, I didn't know David even lived here until yesterday."

Carly passed him an extra pair of latex gloves and together they went to every room in the house. He was gentle the few times he moved or picked something up, much to Carly's appreciation, but was quiet through his entire search. It gave Carly time to build her own theory.

Something she shared when they met the rest of her team outside by the front steps.

"We are in the uncomfortable position of knowing almost nothing, but I think it's a good bet to think that David Lapp is either in trouble or up to absolutely no good. My gut says that it's the former and we need to find him ASAP." She nodded to Noah. "We're going to go talk to his family and depending on what they say, follow up with the Zook family, too. Selena, do you think you and Blanca could look around here? See if you can find something we've missed?"

"Can do." Selena thumbed back to the SUV she and Axel had been driving. "Blanca's asleep in the car right now."

"Good. Axel, stick to the house and see if you can't try to build some kind of profile we can use to give us a better idea of who's been living here and what they might have been doing in the basement. I've already talked to Rihanna and she's going to let us know when she finds out who our Sleeping Beauty is and when he's ready to be questioned, whichever comes first."

This was the part that Carly didn't like about being the agent in charge—the uncertainty of whether or not she was making the right call. Especially given her limited information. But not doing anything could be a lot worse than doing the wrong thing sometimes and, when there was a deadly toxin at play, time was everything. So she trusted her first instinct with her last two team members.

"Until we have evidence, we can't assume the David Lapp angle, as strange as it is, is connected to the anthrax attacks. So Aria and Max, I need you to stay with our original case and keep looking into where it could be purchased and how it could be transported into the community without raising suspicion. That might get easier if we get some valuable info back from the labs I sent samples to or the folks at the CDC. But that takes time, and you can pursue other channels. I've already talked to Opaline and she's deep diving on several different angles with Alana's and Amanda's help." Carly took a small breath. The movement hurt the side of her face where she'd been sucker punched by the man twice her size. She didn't know what stung more, the fact that he'd surprised her or the busted lip he'd also caused. "Everyone good?"

The team nodded in unison, each expression turning to pure focus on their tasks. There were no jokes anymore.

No teasing or levity. Carly knew half of that was because of how bad she assumed she looked, while the other half was the image of the chair in the basement.

"Good. Everyone keep their phones on and stay alert."

They disbanded without another word.

Noah seemed to also be on the same wavelength. He walked ahead to his truck and had the passenger's-side door open for her before Carly was near it. He didn't say a word until they were headed down the drive to the main road.

"I don't want you to take this the wrong way but it might be easier to get the families talking if you…clean up a little."

Carly would have absolutely taken offense had it been any other situation, but she realized he was right. Her jacket might survive with a good washing and a strategic stitching at the arm but for now it was covered in mud.

Which might not have been all that bad had her face and hair not matched it.

Still, time wasn't on their side.

"The bed-and-breakfast is on the other side of town. I don't want to waste valuable time just so I can go wash my face."

"I was actually going to suggest my place. It's just down the road. And I promise no Gina with a shotgun this go around."

Carly couldn't help but feel a little thrill of intrigue pulling at her. She ignored it for the sensible call.

"If you don't mind, that would work for me."

Noah turned left on the road.

"I wouldn't have offered if I didn't want you to accept."

It was a normal, polite sentiment, yet Carly appreciated it more than she should have.

Chapter Nine

Carly was trying not to get blood or mud on Noah's hardwood. He could tell by the way she hesitated at the door between the screened-in porch and the kitchen.

"I run a farm," he reminded her. "You're not tracking in anything these floors haven't seen already."

Carly shook her head, then looked around to see if she'd shucked off anything at the movement.

"You saved my life today, *with a shovel*. The least I can do is be respectful of your flooring."

"There's a statement I never thought I'd hear. Or, I never thought to think about not hearing." Noah laughed and waved her in. "I got lucky is all. Now come in and don't worry about it."

She looked around herself one more time before admitting defeat, following him through the kitchen, great room and right into his bedroom.

"I don't usually have much company, so the guest bathroom is a bit bare at the moment." He opened the door to the en suite, his personal bathroom, glad that he cleaned it on a weekly basis. "There are towels in the closet just inside and you can snag any soap in there you like. If you want to give me your jacket while you clean up, I can work on making it look a little less like a Jackson Pollock painting."

Carly's eyebrow rose at that. He snorted.

"Surprised that a farmer like me knows art?"

"I'm not big on judging a book by its cover. That was just an unexpected comparison—" she looked down at said jacket "—but an apt one."

She winced as she took it off and handed it over.

Noah couldn't help but note the details after it was gone.

The ripped sleeve where she'd been cut by David Lapp's friend, *or* foe, had dried blood around it. The bandage beneath an eye-catching contrast to the crimson. The red and slight bruising along the side of her face. The dried cut above her lip.

The holstered gun she wasn't making any moves to distance herself from.

Why would she?

She'd already been attacked and come close to dying on Day Two in Potter's Creek. If Noah was her, he might even sleep with the gun beneath his pillow that night.

Just one of those details was enough to put fire into Noah's veins.

The same fire that had flamed to life the moment he'd seen the man aiming a gun at Carly.

The same fire that threatened to burn through his resolve to stay quiet while the TCD team and local authorities worked the scene.

The same fire that had seared into him the absolute need to do anything and everything to help the agents.

To help Carly.

Even though it was clear the woman could handle herself.

"I'll be in the kitchen," Noah said, trying to remain impassive. "Yell if you need me."

"Will do."

Carly disappeared into his bathroom and Noah retreated

to the kitchen, all the while replaying what had happened in the woods over and over in his head.

Violence wasn't a new concept to him, but seeing it so close to the community he'd grown up in? It was different than the attack on the farms. That had been deadly, but silent.

The man in the woods had been a loud, physical assault. Not something to overlook until it was too late.

What in the world was going on in Potter's Creek?

It was a question that added to the loop of thoughts running through his head as he tried to clean up the agent's jacket. By the time Carly emerged from the bathroom, it was his turn to admit defeat. He'd gotten the mud off, but it had seen better days, that was for sure.

The same could have been said for Carly, objectively speaking. Noah hadn't known her before yesterday, but he bet it was safe to say she didn't always have cuts and bruises on her. Yet, even with her hair slicked back, her face void of makeup, highlighting the marks along her face, there was a natural beauty to her.

A beautiful simplicity.

A glow.

She smoothed down her blouse and seemed, for a moment, uncomfortable.

But then she smiled.

It was small and unexpected.

"I guess I should have listened to Selena and packed a second jacket, just in case." She looked at her long, dark jacket spread out on the countertop. "Even from here it looks a bit rough."

"It just needs some time to dry, I think, *but* I did go ahead and grab this out of the spare room if you want to borrow it." Noah held out a coat. It was long and chestnut brown. "Beckett only ever wore it twice, so it's basically brand new."

Carly took it with another eyebrow raise. Noah could smell his bodywash wafting off of her. It felt oddly intimate.

"Beckett? I didn't realize you were married."

Noah tried not to laugh at that.

"Beckett is Gina's little sister. Their family owned this farm before I did. On the rare occasion Beckett comes to visit Gina, she stays in the guest bedroom since it used to be hers."

She slid the coat on. It was a good fit.

"Wow. That's pretty generous of you," she said. "I once met the man who rented my apartment before I did and promptly changed the locks."

Noah chuckled.

"I didn't just get the farm from the Tuckett family. I started living here when I was sixteen."

That clearly surprised Carly.

She wasn't the only one.

Gina's parents agreeing to let him stay on the farm to work for room and board when he was sixteen had caused several waves of gossip. The fact that he'd remained had caused even more.

When he'd taken ownership of the farm?

He'd felt like a gameshow contestant with the locals asking him all the same questions: Why not Gina or her sister, Beckett?

Noah never answered, partly because it wasn't their business.

And partly because he wasn't sure himself.

"So Gina is like family then," Carly guessed, surprising him that she hadn't gone for any of the normal questions. Her expression was thoughtful.

Curious, yet respectful.

It was a nice change of pace from what he was used to hearing around Potter's Creek when it came to his past.

"I wouldn't say family—Gina would be the first to tell you she's not big into people—but she is a friend."

"And an employee, too?"

He nodded.

"After I took over the farm she only asked two things of me—to give her a job maintaining this place until she was ready to retire and let Beckett stay in the main house when she visited so they didn't kill each other." Noah shrugged. "Both requirements benefit me seeing as Gina is a loyal, hard worker and when those two are stuck together in the same place for too long the yelling starts." He grimaced at the memory. "And boy, those two can get loud."

Carly snorted.

"Being cooped up can do that to some people."

She pulled her phone from her pocket and frowned at its screen. Noah took the time to grab his thermos from the counter, glad for the umpteenth time that it worked its magic by keeping his coffee warm.

Carly let out a sigh, as he appreciated the warmth after taking a long pull.

"Opaline, our tech guru, is having a hard time finding anything on David Lapp." Her fingers flew across her phone's keyboard, brow creasing. "I was hoping he would have some social media accounts we could use to find him…"

Noah watched as she mouthed what she must have been typing, her frustration clear in how her shoulders tensed.

Was this how her every day looked? How her cases played out?

Their Tactical Crime Division name certainly didn't

sound like they were dispatched to normal, run-of-the-mill issues.

"All right, I'm ready," Carly said with a nod to herself. She slipped her phone in Beckett's coat pocket and looked to him with a polite, yet small, smile.

That smile went away in a flash as her eyes went to his thermos.

Noah didn't understand the change.

"Do you want me to make you some?" He motioned to the coffee maker.

Carly shook her head, but her gaze stuck to his drink. Then she brought out another small smile.

But something had changed.

"Washing my face woke me up." Her tone was flat. Noah didn't have a chance to question it. She was out of the house in a flash.

Noah realized it was about time he added Carly Welsh to his list of mysteries currently playing out in Potter's Creek.

DAVID LAPP'S FATHER said his son wasn't home with such deep disapproval that Carly believed him on the spot. There was no way he would be hiding David on his property. That much was clear, even to an outsider like her.

And that was before she had even broached the reason why they were really there to talk to him.

"The house that David is currently renting has a chair in the basement. A chair that's *bolted* to the ground and has restraints attached to it. We believe it was used to hold someone against their will."

As Carly spoke, the patriarch's face registered two things at once.

Surprise. Disgust.

She knew before she asked that this was all news to him.

Still, Carly had to do her job.

"Do you know why that chair is down there?"

Abram Lapp shook his head so firmly that his beard trembled at the movement.

"No," he said quickly. "I have never even been to that house."

It was the first time since they'd stepped onto the Lapp home's front porch that the man had addressed her directly and not Noah.

Shock usually did that to people. They forgot to guard themselves.

"There was also a man who fled from the house," she continued, pulling up the picture of her attacker on her phone. "Do you recognize him?"

Abram pushed his glasses up his nose and leaned forward slightly. He was hesitant to look at the picture but, based on what she'd just told him, there was no doubt a curiosity there, despite him not trusting her.

"I do not," he said after squinting at the image. "Who is he?"

Carly returned the phone to her pocket.

"That's what we're trying to figure out."

Abram seemed to remember whom he was talking to and reverted his attention to Noah.

"Do you think David had something to do with this chair and man?"

Noah let out a sigh.

"I don't know a thing about him, other than both the chair and the man were in his house and that you're his father." Noah paused. "And that he'd been kicked out of the community. That's why we're here. We're asking *you* if you think David had something to do with it."

Abram Lapp took a great offense to that, though Carly

couldn't tell which part had creased his brow and made his nostrils flare.

Noah's body language changed in tandem.

He'd noticed the anger before it spewed out of Abram's mouth.

"If you had asked me a year ago about David, I would have been happy to tell you that he was abiding by our teachings and well on his way to being baptized."

"But now?" Carly interjected.

It earned her a stiff look.

"Now he's living a life separate from ours. I could no more tell you if he was in the city on the streets than I could tell you if he was walking on the moon. Since he left the community, he left us."

"But he didn't *just leave*. The church decided to kick him out," Noah said. His voice had stiffened considerably. "That's not something that happens lightly around here, especially for people who want to be baptized."

Abram opened his mouth to say something but then caught himself. Carly used the opening to apply more pressure.

"If David wasn't the one keeping someone in that chair then it's very possible he himself was being kept *against his will* in that chair. You can be mad and frustrated all you want at your son, but I have to believe, whether on the city streets or the moon, you'd still care if something bad happened to him." Abram met her gaze but made no show of wanting to respond.

So Noah brought it home.

"Abram, the TCD team is here because someone brought violence and death to the community and values you have sworn to uphold and protect." He reached out and put a large hand on Carly's shoulder. Warmth radiated from his touch.

He was humanizing her to Abram with physical contact. And it felt nice. She didn't pull away.

"Agent Welsh is only here to see that whoever is doing this is caught and held accountable, so Potter's Creek can go back to normal. So that the rest of your family doesn't have to be afraid to tend their own crops and walk their own fields. So, please, answer her questions or I'll have to go talk to Dad—" he lowered his voice "—and none of us want that."

Noah squeezed Carly's shoulder. If she hadn't been so hyperaware of it already, it might have thrown her off her game.

"We need to know why David was asked to leave here," she said, getting to the bottom line.

Abram took a second.

Then caved. He ran his thumbs beneath his suspenders.

"He violated the Ordnung," he started, dropping his voice lower. "He lied to us, stole from us and was caught sneaking out several times."

Carly raised her eyebrow at that.

"Why?"

Abram shook his head.

"Abram," Noah prodded. "What did I just—"

"He wouldn't tell us," he interrupted. "Even when being exiled was threatened, he refused to explain himself."

The man took a step back, closer to the front door. A woman could be seen through the window but she made no show to come outside.

"That is all I have to say." Abram looked to Noah. "To any of you."

He retreated into the house, leaving Noah and Carly to themselves, and nowhere closer to answering any of their questions.

It made Carly's resolve not to show her frustration crack when they were back in the truck.

"We tell him his son could be in danger or be *part* of the danger, and he gives us almost nothing to work with?" She felt a growl in her chest but was still trying to seem professional. It didn't work. She turned to face the man who had gone stoic next to her. "Is that how your father talks to you?"

She hadn't meant the last question to come out, but there it was.

This case had to be hitting on some kind of nerve for Noah, right?

He turned the engine over.

"You're assuming we talk. Until this, we didn't."

Carly had no reason to feel defensive of the man next to her, but she did.

"The Amish are all about making your own choices, right? That's why you aren't baptized until you're an adult. So if you choose not to, aren't they supposed to respect that?" she asked. "Is it really that bad to be an outsider?"

They might have been good at playing off one another to get Abram to open up the little he had, but now Carly felt the off-limits part of Noah Miller activating.

"You'd have to ask them that. Not me." Invisible walls sprung into place between them. His words had a finality to them. An *I'm not going to talk about it* in fine print.

Carly pressed on, unable to stop the line of questions queuing in her mind.

"Is that why *you* left? Did you already have problems with your dad and the others and wanted to get away from them?"

Noah put the truck in Reverse. He was as tense as she'd seen him since they met. This wasn't his usual quiet or brooding nature. No charming little smile graced his lips.

He had shut down right before her eyes.

"Why I left has nothing to do with the case now, so there's no reason to talk about it."

And so he didn't.

Not a word.

Not a peep.

with a smile.

Chapter Ten

When Carly stepped into the inn kitchen late that night to
grab a quick meal, she was surprised to discover Rihanna
had beat her to it.

"I'm not used to seeing you up this late," Carly said
with a smile. Rihanna was still in her business pantsuit,
though she'd replaced her heels with worn plaid slippers.

"And I'm not used to being one of the last ones up,"
she returned with her own smile. It was tired and led right
into the heart of the matter. "What I *am* used to is feeling
like I'm being pulled every which way on a case—that's
the entire job of being a liaison after all, trying to bridge
together two sides—but *this* case…" Her brow scrunched
as she looked down at her empty plate. She was trying to
find the right words. After a moment, she sighed and shook
her head. "It just feels like there's a lot going on and I can't
track half of it, which makes bridge building a very literal
shot in the dark. And I don't like that at all."

Carly knew the feeling. She said as much, but then tried
to be comforting. Or, at least, somewhat so.

"The great thing about the TCD is it isn't a one-man
show. It's essentially a think tank with combat training,
years of individual experience and one adorable dog. At
the end of the day, it's not just us out there looking for answers. It's a team of people who want to see the bad guys

caught and get justice." Carly patted her friend on the shoulder and then moved to the freezer to get her food. "That's all to say that this case might feel like a bunch of puzzle pieces, moving all over the place but we're moving pieces, too. We'll put it together. Soon." Carly smiled again and tried to lighten the mood with a shrug. "Or we won't. But then we'll just fail together, too, and isn't there some comfort to be had in that?"

That did it.

Rihanna raised her fist in the air with a mock cry of, "Go team!" The tension within her seemed to lessen all at once. Then she just looked tired. She waited until Carly was done preparing her noodles and walked her to the stairs, bringing a yawn along with her.

"You know, during all of this there's one person whose name keeps popping up on all sides."

"Noah," Carly guessed.

Rihanna nodded.

"Do you trust him?"

Carly was caught off guard by the question but, even more, by her answer.

"I think he's trying to help when there's no gain in it for him. And I don't think that's something we're used to seeing all that much."

Rihanna agreed to that, but before she left the stairs she paused. Carly followed what she said with a question. "Do you? Trust Noah?"

Rihanna considered that a moment. What she decided on hadn't been what Carly had expected, either.

"I don't have a lot of information on him and that makes me nervous."

They both said good-night, and Carly made her way to her room, still unsettled and restless.

She took off the robe she'd thrown on to go to the

kitchen and sat cross-legged in her T-shirt and underwear on the bed, with microwaveable noodles in her hand and thoughts of a certain farmer in her head.

It was almost midnight and, as far as she could tell, she was probably the only one still awake. Or, at least, moving around. She'd heard Selena take Blanca out in the yard an hour before, but then both had gone quiet in the next room. Axel, a pacer by nature when it came to a particularly hard case, had worn the carpet out along their hallway for a half hour in thought. If he was pacing now, it was in the quiet of his room. As for Max and Aria, Carly had heard them talking next to the bathrooms, something about their kids, an hour or so before, but now both parents were behind closed doors.

Carly poked at the plastic container with a fork. She let her thoughts wander, but they were coming back to a very specific path.

A path they had been exploring since her first moment seeing Noah in Potter's Creek. A path she had no time to travel, yet there she was.

Thinking about Noah Miller and wondering if she really did trust him.

He had good intentions, but good intentions were just actions not yet taken. They weren't worth much and could change as swiftly as the weather.

They also didn't equal trust. But there was just something about Noah. He'd come to her rescue. He'd been genuinely concerned for her, even worried.

She didn't *not* trust him. That would have to be enough for now.

Her eyes unfocused as her thoughts shifted.

Despite all of their discoveries that day, no one had any new answers. Her own contacts hadn't yet traced this strain of anthrax to a particular lab or vendor, but more

testing might yield better results. Axel had spent the re-
mainder of the day in David Lapp's house, trying to piece
together a profile, but had come up short. He wanted another crack at it in the morning. Selena and Blanca hadn't
found anything new, either, and would be turning back to
transportation angles of how the anthrax came to Potter's
Creek. Aria and Max were also trying to figure out where
one might get that much anthrax and said they had a lead
to follow first thing the next day. Opaline was also still
doing her internet thing, while Alana said she was reach-
ing out to some of her contacts in Washington for more
information that might help them.

Everyone was *working*, yet there she was in her underwear at a bed-and-breakfast, with no real progress.

She hated it.

Every day, every moment counted, and she felt like
she was wasting precious time running down information that was leading nowhere faster than they were leading somewhere.

Carly didn't realize her gaze had drifted over to her
empty coffee mug across the room until a familiar ache
thumped in her chest.

Button it up, Welsh, she thought. *Let's go back to thinking about the farmer and how he'd made a shovel sexy.*

It was a self-imposed distraction, but it did the job.

Carly imagined the man sitting next to her, his deep
voice intriguing not only her mind but her body, and repeating his earlier suspicions before he'd dropped her off
at the inn.

*"Nothing ever happens here in Potter's Creek, and
now? Biological weapons, a missing boy who happens
to be a suspect in the attack and an unknown man found
hidden in his basement along with a chair that couldn't*

have been used for anything good? That can't be a coincidence. They have to be connected, right?"

It certainly felt like they were.

But who had poisoned the fields?

Who was keeping whom in that basement?

Why couldn't they find anything on the man who had attacked her yet?

And where was David Lapp?

Carly looped a noodle around her fork's prongs.

Connected or not, him being right or wrong didn't matter. Noah stayed in her thoughts as she finished eating, brushed her teeth and eventually crawled beneath the bed sheets.

Whatever the next day might bring, she found herself looking forward to seeing him again.

Invisible walls and all.

THE AGENT TURNED off the light at fifteen minutes past one. Darkness filled the room. It triggered the camera's night-vision mode. Suddenly the small bedroom was shades of gray, green and black.

He watched as Agent Welsh turned onto her side, her hair shifting over the pillow behind her. Her phone was on the nightstand, a light flashing as it charged.

She had no idea she was being watched.

Which was good, considering this was his Plan B.

"It's not right to watch a woman like that," said the boy next to him. He was dreadfully annoying. His mother, even more so.

She wasn't with them now, but he had no doubt she would have something to say tomorrow when the boy told her. Or maybe she'd just give him that judgmental look she was so good at.

She might not have approved of him or his methods to

get what he wanted, but he had enough leverage on her so that it didn't matter what she approved of or liked.

She had to follow his instructions.

Or face the consequences they both knew she wasn't willing to face.

"I wouldn't have needed you to put the camera in if you'd done your job in the first place," he reminded the boy. "This is your fault, not mine."

The boy went quiet, a pout pushing out his lip.

"You're going to sit here until she wakes up and then tell me everything she does or says relating to the case," he continued. "Any phone calls she makes or any visitors she has. If you see her writing anything down or anything else of interest, then we'll just have to send our secret weapon in there to get whatever it is. Got it?"

The boy nodded.

"Good." He stood and stretched. He wanted a beer or some whiskey. Though he'd take some vodka if it was offered. He pulled his coat off of the back of the chair and slipped it on, the keys in his pocket rattling at the movement. When he was all situated he motioned to the bank of other monitors around the room. Five more screens showed sleeping people in shades of green, gray and black.

"The same goes for the rest of the agents."

RODNEY LEE HAD a rap sheet that was as long as his anger was deep when he finally woke up in the hospital. Opaline got a hit on his identity around the same time he managed to knock out an orderly and put the deputy guarding his room into the ICU.

Carly got the first call while she was riding in silence with Noah. It was almost ten in the morning, and they'd just left the interview with Eli Zook and his father.

Eli might have been an angry, angsty teen but as far as

Carly was concerned that's where it began and ended. Unless they found evidence to the contrary, Carly took him off their list of suspects.

"He has one count of grand theft auto, a slew of misdemeanors for drug possession and a few disorderly conducts with one drunken disorderly…" Opaline's words trailed off. Carly could hear fingers clicking across the keys on a keyboard. "The last of the charges was three years ago in Detroit. After that he disappeared."

"Disappeared?" Carly repeated. "How so?"

"The trail for him goes cold a day after he was released from the police department after spending the night in the drunk tank. He was supposed to report for a hearing a month later but didn't. According to his landlord at the time, one day he was there and the next all of his stuff was gone with no forwarding information. He even left his car in the parking garage."

"And no one reported him missing?"

There was movement on the other side of the call. Carly could imagine Opaline's pink-tipped hair nodding along with her head.

"His grandmother filed a missing persons report a week after he was released, but the detective who was working the case concluded that Lee had taken off of his own volition. He didn't figure out where that was or why."

"And there's no connection or reason you can see that Lee would be here in Potter's Creek?"

"Not so far. His grandmother is his only listed relative and the people he used to pull stunts with are still local to Detroit."

Carly took in a deep breath of frustration.

The scent of trees and spice almost made her stumble in her response—was Noah wearing cologne?—but she caught herself.

"We need more information. David Lapp is our lead suspect right now, and it can't be coincidence that a man like Lee is just chilling in his basement, waiting to attack federal agents. When he wakes up, we'll have to see if we can't get more."

The second call came as Carly asked Noah to drop her off at the community barn. Since she'd pried into his past with his father the day before, he'd gone quiet on her. Only spoken when she prompted him or if the interview called for it.

Carly decided she didn't like not talking to him, even if it was just about the case.

So much so that she was about to ask if she could treat him to some lunch for all of his help when her phone started to ring.

This time it was Rihanna.

Her words were clipped.

"Carly, Rodney Lee escaped."

That changed the rest of Carly's day on the spot. Noah, who must have heard Rihanna, kept on to the community barn but sat quiet as she made call after call. When she was finally off of the phone, lined with enough tension to give a taut rubber band a run for its money, she did one thing that normally she never would.

Carly leaned her head back against the seat and closed her eyes.

Then Noah put his hand on her shoulder, like he had standing on the Lapp front porch.

Carly opened her eyes, startled, but met his gaze.

"We'll figure it out," he said, all baritone. "I promise."

Carly didn't like promises—giving or trusting them when offered—but, in that moment, she believed Noah's.

There was just something so simple and comforting about it.

So straightforward and reassuring.

It had been a long, long time since she'd gotten that feeling from someone, and it made no sense that it had come from a man she barely knew.

Yet it had.

Carly watched as his eyes dropped to his hand. He didn't take it away.

Suddenly its weight was all Carly could think about.

Its heat was all she could feel.

The world and its terrible troubles quieted.

How complicated would it be to kiss him?

To see if his lips provided the same escape that a simple hand on her arm had already made her imagine?

He *had* saved her life, right?

A kiss could show gratitude.

A kiss could show appreciation.

A kiss could—

Carly's phone rang one more time.

Noah retracted his hand.

For a moment she was tempted not to answer, but every wandering thought she'd just entertained was a reason to pick up the call.

She was on a case.

Her team was on a timeline.

There were bad people appearing in Potter's Creek with no hesitation to do bad things.

She had to stop them.

And that could only happen if she stayed focused.

Carly answered the phone. There was a touch of excitement in Opaline's voice.

"I hope you like karaoke, because this new lead I just got you is about to get musical."

Chapter Eleven

"If you had asked me what I'd be doing this holiday season, I don't think I would have guessed this."

Carly was a sight to behold.

Her lips were turned down, dark red and pouty, and her eyes were surrounded by black eyeliner and, if Noah wasn't mistaken, glitter. She had on tight dark jeans, instead of her slacks, that made the urge to let his eyes wander instead of be respectful a constant battle, and she was absolutely rocking a long-sleeved red blouse that dipped into a low *V* and made the imagination stand at attention.

It was a definite contrast to the natural beauty that was a part of her FBI look, but tonight Carly Welsh wasn't an agent.

She was just a woman on a date.

With him.

At a bar in the city, half an hour from Potter's Creek.

"Going undercover at a dive bar with a former Amish farmer to try to get information on a criminal who just escaped from the hospital?" Noah smirked. "I don't know about you, but this is how I always bring in the holiday season."

Carly had been stiff since she'd received the call about Rodney Lee's escape. That stress had stayed throughout her meeting with her team and their new plan to try to get a lead on Lee. Now she rolled her shoulders back and snorted, letting that tension go.

Or at least hiding it before they went inside.

"I knew you were mysterious, Noah Miller, but I didn't know you were *that* mysterious."

She took a deep breath and nodded. Noah started to lead the way, but Carly caught his arm. The smell of her perfume surrounded him. It was also in the distracting column.

"And, just for the record, I'm *not* singing on any stage, no matter what Opaline suggested. Ever," she added. "Not even for a cover."

Noah chuckled.

"Understood."

The bar was called the Wallflower and, despite its more hipster name, it had the look and feel of a motel bar located near the airport. This bar, however, was down the street from The Grand Casino and, given how the waitress greeted them after they sat down in a booth in the corner, it catered to patrons when they were done with their gambling.

"We don't take poker chips as payment. Only card and cash. If you can't do that then you can leave. No swiping our Christmas decorations, either, or you'll have to answer to the boss."

Carly shared a look with Noah. He could tell she was fighting a laugh. The only decorations he could see that were holiday-themed were a few plastic light-up Santa Clauses on the bar top, clusters of candy canes with rope lights in them seemingly spread at random, and balding, metallic green garland lining the space between each booth seat and the next. It was more than he'd expected to see in the bar, but he wouldn't have thought it valuable enough to be targeted for petty theft.

Yet there the waitress was, serious as serious could be.

"None of that will be a problem," Noah assured her.

"We'll be on our best behavior," Carly added.

Another couple came through the main door, earning her suspicious gaze. Still, she took their drink orders. When she was gone Carly finally let out a little laugh.

She lowered her voice and leaned in so he could hear her whisper. The tabletop between them was small which put the smell of her perfume right back in Noah's area. He made sure to keep his eyes, once again, away from her curves at the movement.

Maybe volunteering to act as her undercover date while the rest of her team kept following their own leads down wasn't the best idea.

Yet, there they were.

"Is it bad I felt the need to go for my gun during that?" she asked. "I mean, dang, but I guess I can see how she might act like that if she has to deal with people like Lee as a regular."

At her own words, Carly looked toward the front doors. The waitress had directed them to sit in a booth that had a sightline of the entrance and the hallway opening that led to the bathroom and, he assumed, the back office and doors. The Wallflower wasn't particularly a large place, but it had several tables for seating between them and both exits. Noah watched as Carly scanned each patron sitting down with their drinks already.

"Not that I expected it, but Rodney isn't here," she said through a smile meant for a couple on a date and not an FBI agent trying to solve a case. "Neither is Rob Cantos."

Noah in turn did his own look around of the other patrons. The picture he'd been shown of Rodney Lee's friend, Rob, wasn't matching any of them.

"I still can't believe your tech guru found a connection," he admitted. "But I guess that's the pitfall of social media. One way or the other you wind up on the internet because of it."

Carly snorted.

"Especially if you're running around with someone like Rob, who obsessively posts pictures and videos on his Stories." The picture Carly had shown Noah was a selfie of Rob with Rodney in the background. It was, according to Carly's friend back at their headquarters in Traverse City, one of nearly fifteen pictures spread over the course of six months where the two had shown up together. Most of them were geo-tagged at the Wallflower. That had been enough of a lead for the tech guru to sleuth out that Rob didn't just like the small dive bar, he was a regular.

A regular who was there every night.

And if they couldn't find Rodney, then maybe his friend could help them with that.

"So you think he'll show?" Noah asked, making sure the couple two booths over didn't hear. "Rob, I mean."

"If his routine holds, yes." She checked the watch on her wrist. It was placed right where the bandage from the cut on her arm met the cuff of her sleeve. Noah had no doubt it was a strategic move to keep the bandage inconspicuous. She'd already used makeup to hide any trace of bruising or the small cut on her face. He'd had to do a double take to see if he'd imagined the wounds from the day before when he'd first picked her up from the bed-and-breakfast.

Though that second look might have been because of the simple fact that she was stunning.

However, Noah, who was more of a homebody than a bar hopper, hadn't had to do anything past leaving his cowboy hat at home and changing to a solid dark button-up instead of his normal flannel. Though he doubted anyone would recognize him regardless. He'd lived all of his life in Potter's Creek and this was his first time at the Wallflower.

"So, the plan is to sit here until he comes in," he summarized.

Carly nodded. "The team hasn't come up with a connection between him and the Amish community, so this is all we've got so far," she said. "Opaline said most of the pictures and videos he uploads from here are around eight to nine." She looked at her watch. "Which gives us a half hour to scope out the place, see if we can catch Lee or something suspicious and then see if we get lucky with Rob."

"And if none of the above happens?" Noah didn't want to be down about the plan but he genuinely wanted to know what happened next if it didn't pan out.

"Then we talk to the waitress and the owner. I'd do it now but since we're at a standstill with all other leads, I think this might be a better approach. We can't afford for anyone to rabbit because we spooked them."

The waitress appeared with their drinks. Noah waited until she was gone again to give Carly a humored look.

"To rabbit?"

She wrapped her hand around her beer bottle and smirked.

"It means to run. I dated a guy during the academy who always used to say it." She made a show of rolling her eyes. "We didn't last long, but that one phrase must have left an impression. I've had the entire TCD team poke fun at me for saying it over the last few years."

Noah had no reason to feel jealousy flare up at the mention of her dating, and he definitely shouldn't be curious if she was seeing anyone now, but there it was. Front and center before he could ignore it fully.

And before he could find a smoother way of figuring out how to answer if she was now single or not.

"So does that mean it's harder for you to date people in the same profession or do you have someone back home with a badge, too?"

Carly's eyes dragged over to his with a small, sliding smile.

He'd been caught.

"And here I thought Noah Miller was a dip-your-toe-in-the-water-to-test-it kind of guy and not a-jump-right-in guy."

Noah pulled his beer up to his lips and tried to downplay his guilt.

"I was just making conversation," he lied. "You *did* ask me yesterday if I was married, so I thought I'd learn a little about that side of your life, too."

"I said I didn't know that you were married," she corrected. "I never asked if you were."

Noah realized she was right. He nodded into his swig of beer. Carly took pity on him.

"But to *answer* your question, yes and no, and then no." She ticked off her answers with her fingers as she said them. "Yes it *can* be easier to date someone who's in law enforcement and deals with some of the same things I do, but *no* it can also *not* be easier. I once dated a guy who always tried to, for whatever reason, one-up me about work. He actually bet me he could go to the shooting range and outshoot me one time."

"And did you take him up on that bet?"

She smirked.

"We broke up out on the range after I won."

Noah laughed.

"Well done." She did a little bow.

"As for the last no, *no* I don't have anyone back home. Badge *or* civilian." Her humor fizzled a little. "This job can be...demanding. That doesn't always play well with the whole champagne flutes and long walks along the beach at sunset thing. But no harm or foul. Not all of us are made for that kind of life."

Her mood shifted, but not in the way he expected.

It was subtle. She looked down at her drink, her fingers toying with the edge of the beer's label. Then she went back to watching the patrons. Like what she said wasn't a big deal.

Just another somewhat useless stretch of conversation people put between the real issues.

Noah didn't want her to downplay what she'd just said by letting the subject change without acknowledging it.

He shrugged.

"Doesn't mean those of us who do cheap beers and dive bars with Santa decorations aren't the right kind of living, either. Simple isn't always bad."

Carly met his gaze with another subtle change. This one he couldn't read, but she tipped her bottle to him.

"I guess you're right there. I never was a woman fond of strolling any beaches. Too much sand, too many tourists. Speaking of extracurricular activities—" she motioned to the bar around them "—what does a normal night out look like for you? I've got a good idea of your day-to-day work life but I haven't really pegged how Noah Miller takes his messy yet styled hair down."

Noah chuckled at that, pleasantly surprised at how often Carly seemed to be able to make him laugh. He ran his hand through his hair for show.

"I'll take the hair compliment, thank you." Carly did another little fake bow, fluttering her fingers as if before royalty. "But as for letting it down, what I do for fun is just as simple as dive bars and beers. I like spending my time outside—hiking, fishing, the occasional building something with my hands. Sometimes I come out to the city for a drink or two with my staff, or go to their place to watch a game but, mostly, it's just me beneath the sun and moon."

Noah hadn't meant his answer to sound so *solitary* yet he heard the subtext in it before Carly's expression turned thoughtful.

"That sounds nice, but a bit lonely."

The past, *his* past, surfaced as quickly as a rising wave in a choppy ocean. It took too much of his focus to keep his body from doing what his heart wanted him to do— stiffen up and then retreat into himself. Right to the blue shed on the edge of the property that used to belong to the Tucketts. Back to the memory of the yellow house that was no longer there. Back to when he'd fought to leave a place he was told he belonged only to fall into the unknown.

An unknown that he had spent years making familiar.

Making home.

His home and no one else's.

Carly outstretched her hand and caught his on the table-top next to his drink.

The feeling of fight or flight, to swim or drown, cleared in an instant. All Noah could feel was a hand smaller than his, warm and firm. Following it up to a woman who looked more serious than smiles.

"One person's lonely is another person's choice and no one can understand that choice until they've lived the reason behind it." She ran her thumb along the top of his hand, soothing him while making her point. "So I'm sorry if that came out judgmental. It was more of an observa- tion. I'm sorry."

She released his hand as quickly as she'd taken it.

"It's fine," Noah assured her after a beat. He shook the darkness off his mood and managed a grin. "It's no secret to me that I come off as a solitary creature most of the time. I think it took the Tucketts two years to convince me to go on trips with them for the farm. Even then I don't think I really talked much until I was older."

He hadn't said it for sympathy and the way Carly smiled, she wasn't dishing it out.

"Ah, the quiet kid routine was one I had down pat. It used to drive my parents crazy the first year or so I came to live with them. My dad ended up coaxing me out of my bedroom with promises of candy and old, crummy cop movies, and yet it still took a while before I said more than a few words at a time to them."

Noah's brow furrowed, wondering if he'd heard correctly, but Carly seemed to realize the confusion.

"I was adopted when I was eleven." Carly paused. Her eyes went to the label on her beer. She started to finally peel it when she returned her gaze to him. "They're really good people, and were amazing then, but my biological mother was killed when I was ten and adjusting was hard for a while."

A part of Noah that he couldn't really define softened.

"Oh, I'm sorry," he offered.

Carly did a little shrug. The label on her bottle was already half-peeled.

"A lot of people I've met in my line of work don't get there without some kind of traumatic event that changes everything. At least, that's how it went for me. One day I wanted to be an astronomer, charting stars all night, every night, and the next?" She motioned around them. "I'm Dr. Poison. A horrible nickname my last boyfriend gave me, but I guess that left an impression, too."

That's when it happened.

Like a rain cloud passing across a sunny day.

One second Noah was appreciating her, listening to her, and worrying about what *he* said and how *he* reacted to her. And Carly? She was doing what, he had no doubt, she thought was expected of her.

She had dipped into his past on accident and so she'd given a little of hers up in payment for it.

But then she'd slipped.

For whatever reason, she'd given more to Noah than she'd meant to give.

And it hadn't been okay, whatever the memory she had been sucked into.

Noah didn't know who Carly Welsh was a week ago but *tonight*, in this moment, he believed he knew her.

At least, in a way that felt more real to him than with any other woman he'd met.

So, Noah did something he hadn't planned on—though he would have been lying if he'd said the thought hadn't crossed his mind.

Just as she had done with him, he took Carly's hand in his, and locked his eyes with hers.

There was surprise and sadness and an X factor he couldn't understand yet, pulling him in to the woman who made dive bar and beers sound like the most appealing thing in the entire world.

He knew it was his imagination, but the world around them seemed to dim. When he spoke, Noah was already hoping she'd accept what he was going to do when he was done talking.

"I have no doubt that you, Carly Welsh, leave quite the impression yourself."

Then, in sight of a poorly lit Santa Claus figurine, he took Carly's chin in his hand and kissed her.

Like the bar around them, as far as he was concerned, the rest of the world fell away.

Chapter Twelve

Carly kissed him back.

The moment Noah's lips were against hers, it was like instinct took over.

Instinct mixed with a surprising amount of desire. Well, maybe not surprising, but definitely not what she meant to overtake her.

Yet, it did.

And right after a conversation she hadn't meant to have.

It hadn't taken her academy-taught profiling skills to realize that Noah had led a solitary, possibly lonely life. What's more, she'd acted on that by questioning him for a realization she was sure she had gotten right.

Then two things had happened at once.

Noah had started to shut down again, just like he had in the truck after she'd asked him why he left the Amish community. His expression of humor had wiped away and an instant tension had lined his body.

Carly hadn't liked being the cause of it.

So much so that, while he shut down, she did perhaps the most startling thing since coming to town, or, actually if she was being honest with herself, in a long time.

He'd been shutting down, so she started opening up.

Taking his hand, letting him know she truly didn't mean

to pry and then feeling the weight of her own self-imposed walls had led her to a snippet of a story.

A nickname. An awful, accidental reminder.

Dr. Poison.

For all of her intentions to help ease Noah out of whatever she'd pushed him into, Carly had instead fallen into the trap of her own past.

Then it was Noah who had saved the day.

He'd brought her back to the present and out of her darkening, heartbreaking thoughts, with a caring, human touch.

Carly might not have known the man long, but *that* had been absolutely what she'd needed.

Him.

She'd needed him.

So Carly had kissed him back and, what's more, leaned deeper into it.

It was perfect.

That is, until the sound of a new group of patrons coming into the bar filtered into their bubble.

Perfect became ice-cold water to the face.

Carly's eyes flew open just as Noah broke the kiss.

He didn't say anything and she didn't want him to; instead they synced back up to the plan.

He took her hand again, adopted a cover-perfect smile and gave her the room to slyly examine the new group without both of them gawking.

A surge of adrenaline went through her in an instant.

"Bingo," she whispered. "Rob Cantos is in the house."

Rob was nothing like his friend Rodney. At least not in looks. While Rodney was a force to reckon with and filled with violence, Rob was stocky, short and a guy who looked like he laughed all of the time. His friends that followed him to a set of stools at the bar, however, weren't throwing out any vibes that Carly could work with. They were also more of Rodney's build. Just looking at their size made Carly's bruise beneath her foundation pulse a little.

"It looks like they're going to hang out at the bar," Carly said after a moment of watching the group. She used her free hand, the one not within Noah's hold, and took a long pull on her drink.

Noah's lips twitched at the corner.

"What? Never seen a lady take a drink of beer before deploying a ruse to question a person of interest?"

Noah chuckled this time. He made a show of doing the same with his drink.

Then it was all charm.

"And what if I said I had?" he asked.

"Then your dating life definitely was a lot more eventful than my 'to rabbit' guy."

He laughed again, but that humor was replaced with focus as Carly felt her own demeanor changing into work mode. They didn't even bring up the kiss.

Carly grabbed her purse as Noah placed a tip on the table. He let her take the lead as she scooted out of the booth and stood.

"Let's see if we can't just sweet talk our Mr. Cantos into telling us all about his friend."

RIHANNA DIDN'T NOTICE the camera in her room, but she did notice that her laptop had been moved right before she went to bed.

Before that, when she'd come back from the hospital after she'd spoken to hospital staff, deputies and then the sheriff of the county himself, she'd used her work laptop to go through some of the files Alana had sent her. Most were social media accounts to look into for a possible connection between Rodney Lee and David Lapp.

She'd gone through incident reports and community

news looking for anything that stood out as suspicious or different enough to garner a closer examination.

By the time Carly and Noah had gotten their undercover idea approved—though including Noah had gotten considerable pushback at first—Rihanna had saved only three pieces of information that had struck her as odd compared to the rest.

The first was an incident report from the year before. An unidentified male, mid-twenties, light-skinned and dark-haired, had been seen spray painting a marijuana leaf on the side of an abandoned barn on land formally owned by the Kellogg family. He hadn't been caught and no more graffiti had shown up in the town.

The second was a social media post on the county's Facebook page. It was a call to arms for any tips or information on a teenager or young woman, no one seemed to be able to pinpoint her age, who had been seen as suspicious, hanging around Potter's Creek and then running before anyone could ask why.

As far as Rihanna could tell through the comments and following news story and investigation, the woman hadn't been identified, either.

The third tidbit of information that she found was the piece she really started to get excited about. It was a Facebook comment thread on a story about local business growth and tourism in which someone talked about a local real estate developer who wanted to open up a dude ranch in the middle of Amish country. Half of the people who commented had been vehemently against it—there were enough farms in town to begin with and The Grand Casino in the city was as close as they wanted to be to more tourism—while the other commenters had been supportive but realistic.

One woman had said that, while she might have liked

the idea of getting more outsiders into town to shop at her local boutique, there was no way that the Amish families would sell out to an Englisher.

Rihanna might be a liaison, but she'd been an agent first. Her knack for keeping the peace in her current job hadn't softened the edges of knowing a good lead when she heard it. Or, in this case, read it.

She'd emailed the screenshot of the conversation to her phone and hurried downstairs to the kitchen. The owner of the bed-and-breakfast, Dot, a lover of gossip but professional as far as Rihanna could tell, was getting ready to go to her house behind the inn for the night and looked elated that she'd been interrupted. Not.

Rihanna was apologetic but then got down to business.

While Carly was doing the right thing by being sly to get clues, Rihanna had long since run out of coffee and was in no mood to be coy.

Which seemed to be fine by Dot, considering how quickly she reacted to Rihanna mentioning the realtor who had tried to start a dude ranch not too far from the inn.

"Yeah, that was Caroline Ferry," Dot said with a huff. She slung her dishrag over her shoulder and took a stance that exuded grumpiness. "She's this rich lady who lives in an honest to goodness mansion. I mean that place is three times the size of this inn and she's not even married. I heard she has a staff of five. Boggles the brain to have that much space with only one person."

Rihanna mentally locked away the name Caroline Ferry and pushed past Dot's obvious annoyance.

"So why didn't she start the ranch? If she has a lot of money, couldn't she have bought what she needed to make that happen?"

Dot shook her head, but there was a smirk on her lips.

"She wanted to build along the creek which ran smack

dab across three different properties, owned by three different Amish families. Three farms. Those families turned her and her money down flat. From what I've heard through gossip at the market, she tried to appeal to each of them, but in the end she had to scuttle the project." That smile grew. "I guess she found out the hard way that sometimes principles don't have a price tag on them."

"Do you happen to know which farms those were? What families, I mean?"

Dot didn't have to think twice. She listed off the names like she was a contestant on *The Wheel of Fortune* and she was going for a solve she knew.

"The Kline family, the Weaver farm and the Graber farm." Dot hung her head a little, sympathy spreading across her expression as Rihanna had alarm bells start ringing through her head. "I guess now if she wanted to try again she might have a better shot, since Elmer and his son passed."

Rihanna nodded.

"I guess so."

She said good-night to Dot and sent Carly a text to call her when she was done with her short undercover stint. Then Rihanna went to her room to call Opaline.

That's when she noticed something was off.

When she'd left her laptop it had been tilted *just enough* to where she could look out of the window with a glance instead of turning her head while working. Now it was centered.

Such a small thing, yet Rihanna paused.

Had she done it?

She turned to look back at her bedroom door. She hadn't locked it when she went downstairs, since no one other than FBI agents were staying inside.

Surely no one had come inside the room without asking.

Or maybe you've had too little sleep because you've too many questions bouncing around in your head.

Rihanna turned back to the laptop and decided to go with what she was sure about.

She called Opaline.

"Multitasker extraordinaire, Agent Lopez here," she answered. Rihanna laughed.

"Glad you're feeling feisty about it," she responded. "Because I need you to look up the address of a Caroline Ferry and anything odd that might stand out about her. When you have that, call Carly and tell her what you've learned."

Opaline might have had fun, but she was always professional when it was called for.

"Sure thing. Want me to send it to you, too?"

"Yes, please." She looked back at her laptop. "And send it to my phone only—text me."

Opaline didn't question it.

"Will do."

The call ended and Rihanna stood still for a moment in the middle of the room before sitting down in front of her laptop again. She slid it a little to the side again for an easier view of the window.

This time she made sure she noted exactly where it was.

HE WATCHED THROUGH the feed as the boy almost destroyed their plan. As soon as the woman left the room, the boy had taken advantage and hurried to the laptop. He'd already tried the other rooms during the day, but the agents either had their laptops in their vehicles or they hadn't used them at all.

This Ms. Clark was the only one who had been seen through the feed plugging away at hers.

But before the boy could do more than open it and see

that a lock was set up, he must have heard the liaison coming back up the stairs.

Panic had registered on his face seconds before he'd done something that not even the man would have attempted.

The boy had crawled beneath the bed to hide.

He was there now, beneath the floral-patterned bed skirt, less than a foot away from a woman whose sole purpose while in town was to take down the people behind the attacks on the community.

Which was why he couldn't let the boy get caught.

He sighed into the dark and picked up his gun, but not before looking back at the monitors.

All agents were snug in their rooms.

All except Agent Welsh.

Like the boy, she was another problem he was going to have to deal with.

And soon.

Chapter Thirteen

The rain came in the middle of the night and turned half of Potter's Creek to ice. Trees were encased by it, and windshields were annoyingly coated, but that didn't stop the community from getting up and out. The main roads were salted and still drivable once the windshields were thawed, and a horse-and-buggy were seen in the distance before Carly and Axel went in the opposite direction.

They had a job to do, though the new bite of cold wasn't helping Carly's mood.

It, like their case, was in flux.

From anthrax to David Lapp's basement to Rodney Lee escaping the hospital, every few hours a new problem popped up without a solution.

Then there was the whole kiss thing.

Noah had instigated it, yet Carly? She'd reciprocated.

And she'd wanted more.

That was as troubling as it was confusing.

Why did she feel a connection with someone she barely knew? That's not how the world worked.

Yet, she'd woken up thinking about the farmer. Just as she'd fallen asleep thinking about him, too.

It hadn't helped that the night before had driven home Carly's growing suspicion—she and Noah were a good team. He'd played his part as her date when they'd gone to talk to Rob Cantos and his friends at the bar. Rob had been an outgoing guy and had looped the two of them in for a round of drinks and a lot of idle chatter.

Noah had been the one to steer that talk to the questions they had needed answered. All without arousing any suspicion.

They'd found out that one of his buddies had fallen so hard for a girl that he'd left everything behind to come to the city to be with her. Something Rob hadn't been a fan of, from the way he said it.

"Having a lady is one thing but his focus was over one hundred percent," he'd said. "When he wasn't drinking with us, he was all about her. And even when he was with us?" Rob had tapped his temple with his finger. "He was still with her."

That's when Carly had finally shown her badge. She got more pointed with her questions and Rob hadn't had too much of an issue parting with the answers. It turned out he'd been talking about Rodney and Rodney wasn't one of his favorite people, just one of his group and that group had an order to it. One where Lee was bottom rung.

Rob had had a name for the girlfriend and a place she worked, but hadn't known where Rodney had been staying.

"Do you know exactly where all of your drinking buddies live?" he'd asked when Carly had pushed.

"I can at least point you to a zip code."

At that, Rob had shrugged.

"When we hung out it was here." He'd pointed to the front doors and then to the bar. "He'd walk in through those and sit down here and then just leave when we were done. The most I got out of him was posing for a few pics." He'd then dragged his eyes to the notepad in Carly's hand. "Plus, the quickest way to find Rodney is to find Talia. No matter what he's done, he won't leave her alone for too long."

So that was the information she'd decided to act on as she waited for news from the labs analyzing the anthrax samples she and the team had sent them. Preliminary analysis hadn't turned up anything especially unique or pointed to a trail they could follow.

Find Talia to find Rodney.

Which was starting to feel like its own investigation, an issue Carly hadn't bet on when they'd left Traverse City.

Potter's Creek sure hadn't let up on its surprises and curveballs. Not even while the TCD team had been in their rooms, ready to turn in.

Which was a big reason why Axel was frowning now behind the wheel,

"I've worked cases where I've effectively been in a war zone and felt more at ease there than here in this small town." He rolled his shoulders back. "Bioterrorism, shady development deals, bad boyfriends, Amish flying the coop. What's next, plagues of locusts?"

Axel's boyish charm was absent. He needed more sleep, she guessed, judging by the bags beneath his eyes. That and the fact that, while she'd been at the Wallflower Bar schmoozing up Rob, the team had been startled awake by several gunshots outside of the bed-and-breakfast. Three to be exact.

It had been enough to send every TCD agent to their service weapons and out into the night.

By the time Noah had dropped Carly off, they had just been finishing their search.

"It could be a hunter?" Carly had offered. Selena, in her matching pajama set, had shaken her head.

"Not for this time of year and not for here."

"It could be someone trying to rile up a building full of FBI agents," Max had guessed. "It's not like there's all that much to do around here. I imagine the youth have to get creative to get their rebel jollies off." At that, Aria had raised her eyebrow. Max had laughed. "What I mean is that it could have been out of boredom, too. A few shots into the dark to feel alive."

Axel, however, hadn't been so sure.

"Check it out in the morning," Carly had told Selena. "Just to make sure it wasn't something else."

Then they'd gone back into the inn and made a new game plan for the next day thanks to the information about Talia and the gossip Rihanna had gotten from Innkeeper Dot.

Now Carly was with Axel and almost to Caroline Ferry's mini-mansion, a residence that was somewhat secluded from the city, but the drive didn't take them that far away from the inn. It still had a good amount of trees surrounding it and, judging by the ride up the private drive, it was one of a kind in the area.

Almost like an estate fit for a celebrity.

"She's a realtor, you say?" Axel asked. He leaned toward the steering wheel to make an exaggerated show of scoping out the place. "Is she also a hired hitman for the mafia? A drug kingpin? A movie star rehearsing a role?"

Carly snorted. She looked down at her notepad and the notes she'd taken from her call with Opaline.

"According to our dear Lopez sister from afar, Caroline Ferry was a self-made real estate developer...before she exponentially increased her worth by marrying a man twice her age who had a trust fund that would put some small countries to shame."

Axel whistled.

"I was about to say, if she got all of this land and square footage from real estate, then I'm definitely in the wrong business." There was an actual half circle drive that led right in front of a set of double doors, like it was a drop-off in front of a hotel lobby. Two other cars were pulled off to the side beneath a portico. Both were sporty, but neither looked particularly new. Though Carly would have been wholly surprised if they were anything less than a hundred grand each. "Does one of these belong to Mr. Ferry?" Axel had his eyes on the two-door, slick red car closest to them. There was clear appreciation in his voice.

"No. Two years after they married he passed away from natural causes associated with old age."

Axel turned the car off and shook his head, looking longingly one more time at something he'd probably never buy for himself.

"Who knew all we had to do to get a place like this and cars like that was to marry rich and old."

"A lot of people know that one, Axel," Carly mockingly chided. "Gold diggers are real." She dropped the mocking in her tone. "Though it is extremely rude, insensitive and judgmental of us to think that's the case for Ms. Ferry before we've even met her."

Axel's grin came back.

"Don't worry. I won't judge anyone until they give me a reason."

They exited the car and were met at the front door by an older woman wearing a gray uniform with an apron. She was quick to introduce herself as a member of the cleaning staff and showed them inside and back through to a study where she lingered, as if awaiting orders.

All of it was grand and, try as Carly might not to, she formed an opinion about the woman who owned it all before setting eyes on her.

Caroline Ferry was absolutely in the top 1 percent when it came to wealth.

And she was proud of that fact.

Just as much as she was unbothered by two FBI agents being led into her home office.

"I've had a lot of people in my house before, but I don't think I've had any members of a task force. What did you say it was called again?" she asked after looking at Axel's and Carly's badges.

Axel put his badge back into his pocket. Carly followed suit as she scanned the room around them. It, like the house, was done to the nines. Modern, smooth, bright surfaces, trinkets that screamed attempts at artsy sophistication and several paintings with frames so ornate Carly bet they cost more than her apartment's rent. There were built-ins that ran the length of one wall, while the exterior wall was mostly window. It showed a view of a beautifully landscaped backyard with what looked like a lap pool in the distance.

Even Ms. Ferry matched her home's opulence. Her platinum blond hair was twisted back in a flawless bun against her head while her lipstick, manicure and white dress with gold accessories were stunning in their execution.

Ms. Ferry was certainly the most well put together suspect Carly had ever interviewed before, that was for sure.

"The Tactical Crime Division, ma'am," Axel answered, all polite. While Carly was the lead agent on this case, she followed his cue on how to speak to the woman. He was the expert profiler after all. If he went polite it wasn't because he was after an *Emily Post* etiquette award.

He did it because it was easier to catch flies with honey. Not vinegar.

"Do you mind if we take a few minutes of your time for some questions?"

Ms. Ferry swept her arm back to two love seats, also equal parts elegant and immaculate.

"Oh absolutely, why don't we take a seat. Hetty?" The

woman in the apron straightened, as if at attention. "Could you get us some refreshments, please? Would you two like some coffee?"

Carly was quick to decline because she had been caught off guard by the specific offer. Too quick. Axel gave her a look while he accepted.

Then it was the three of them in the study.

"I bet I know why you're here," Ms. Ferry started. "It's because of that nasty business with the poisoning."

Carly nodded. She wasn't surprised that the woman had brought it up. There was no other reason the team would be in town.

And with such simplicity.

Ms. Ferry touched her chest. She shook her head and breathed out. The very picture of exasperation.

"I can't believe something like this would happen in our own backyard. I mean, Potter's Creek is a stone's throw away and those people are so *modest*. I can't believe someone would do that to them and for what? It's not like they have anything. Unless maybe it was a hate crime? You know, Hetty and I talked about that. Surely no one around here has a problem with the Amish that badly. Then again, what a crazy world we live in. I mean I heard about two men fighting in the casino not too long ago because of Amish values. *Values* for goodness sake! At a casino no less! Honestly, what *is* the world coming to?"

This time Carly couldn't hide her reaction that Ms. Ferry was being open and friendly. In fact, not a whiff of suspicion had come off of her yet. She wasn't nervous. She was meeting their gaze and keeping it. In fact, if anything, she seemed excited for them to be there.

Carly shared another quick look with Axel.

He cleared his throat, bringing the woman's attention back to him.

"When you say they don't have anything, that's not exactly true. They have land. Some land you were actually interested in not too long ago."

Ms. Ferry nodded so quickly that Carly was sure her hair was going to come undone.

"Yes! The Graber farm!" She got to the edge of the love seat and spoke like she was starring in a soap opera. "When I heard what happened, I couldn't believe it. First the family is hurt, and then that beautiful land? So tragic. I wanted to reach out to them but it didn't seem right, and it's not like I could just pick up the phone to call."

"You wanted to reach out to them? Why, if you don't mind my asking?" Carly followed up.

Had Ms. Ferry tried to swoop in to buy the land from the remaining Graber family? That certainly would give credence to her having motive.

Yet, Carly was having a hard time believing Ms. Ferry was their culprit.

The older woman waved her off, like asking was no problem at all.

"I wanted to express my condolences." She sobered a little. "One widow to another."

The answer seemed genuine, but they had a case to solve and too much time had already passed without any answers.

So Axel followed up with a little more pointed series of questions.

"And what about seeing if she would sell you their land now, after everything had happened?"

That seemed to perplex her.

"What do you mean?"

Axel went at it again.

"They are one of three families who refused to sell their land to you so you could build your dude ranch, right? With their cattle being killed, their land being affected and their main workers gone, you have way more leverage to convince the Graber family to change their minds."

Ms. Ferry's brow furrowed. Just as she seemed genuine in her desire to commiserate with the Graber matriarch over being a widow, she seemed to be genuine in the confusion that followed.

"The dude ranch project was tabled. The Grabers were one of three families who refused to sell. So I let it go when it was clear they weren't interested at all." For effect, she shrugged. "I've turned my attention back to some other projects outside of Potter's Creek since then. I even have a flight booked after the start of the new year to go to Tennessee and talk to a friend about turning my focus to more charitable pursuits instead."

"So you're not interested at all in the dude ranch anymore?" Carly asked. "Just like that?"

Ms. Ferry nodded. Then her demeanor changed. She lowered her voice. Not to a whisper, but not as flamboyant as she had been.

"Honestly, I came up with the project on a whim in the first place—I mean the scenery around here is like being in a movie, why would I not try to capitalize on that if I could?—but it was my son who really ran with it."

That was news.

"Your son?" Axel asked.

"Yes. Dylan." Once again, her demeanor changed. She definitely was no longer feeling whatever excitement she had been before. "He's had a…rough time of it lately, and so I told him that if he cleaned up his act and flew straight then I'd let him be in charge of the entire ranch when it was up and running. Something he could call his own and that would give him a sense of purpose."

Carly and Axel both straightened a fraction. Carly saw it out of her periphery just as she knew he had seen her.

"What do you mean by cleaned up?" she asked.

"And what do you mean by rough time?"

Shame.

Guilt.

Frustration.

All three flashed across Ms. Ferry's expression and perfectly applied makeup.

"Dylan's father, my first husband, had a drug problem when Dylan was younger. After we divorced, Dylan went through a sort of rebellious phase...one that included gambling." She deflated a little with a sigh. "He's been in and out of different rehab programs to kick his addiction to it over the last few years. It got so bad that I had to...cut him off. No more money from me. He was going to have to learn how to fend for himself. I thought that it would help him value the things he earned himself, instead of seeing them as just more ways to fuel his addiction."

"Did he follow through?" Axel asked. "Did he fend for himself?"

Ms. Ferry sprung back up like a flower in spring. She was out of her mood.

"He did! He completed a program, got himself an apartment, kept going to meetings and told me he was ready to take on more responsibility."

"But then you ran into the issue of getting the land to build," Carly added.

Ms. Ferry frowned.

"He took the news poorly, I'll admit." She sighed. "Which is why he's in a rehab facility in Austin, Texas, at the moment. He relapsed after I broke the news to him."

After that they asked a few more questions, but none with answers that led them anywhere new. They got alibis from Ms. Ferry for the time frame when the attacks were estimated to have occurred and learned enough about her personality to make the leap that she hadn't been behind the attacks.

She also didn't know David Lapp or Rodney Lee.

"What is it about this case?" Axel asked when they were back outside. "If it is just one case we're looking at right now."

"You think it could be two." It wasn't a question. In fact, it was a theory the team had already kicked around. "Our original anthrax attack case which leads us to David Lapp who is somehow mixed up in something different with Lee. Which makes David Lapp our soft connection?"

Axel gave a half shrug.

"I know we're not big on coincidences, but that doesn't mean they don't happen."

Carly didn't believe Lee wasn't somehow connected to it all, and same with the still-missing David, but she didn't have any proof one way or the other.

Like Axel said, just coincidence.

And he was right. She wasn't a fan of those. Not in their line of work. Yet, if it was…if something else was going on unrelated to the anthrax killings…

Another attack could come soon and hurt more people.

"Until something else happens, I'll keep Max and Aria on trying to find out how the anthrax was transported and purchased, and I'll check in again on my lab sources to see if they've found anything more about the strains used," she decided. "Once Opaline finds Talia, you and Rihanna head over there with local PD as backup. If Rodney is there, take him in. If it's just Talia, question her for every ounce of information she has on Rodney, David, and if she knows anything about that damn chair in his basement."

Axel nodded. His approval of the plan gave Carly an added confidence boost. She was staying objective in his eyes.

Which was good, because her last part of the plan didn't feel as professionally detached as it should have.

"Before then, I need to pick up my rental and head to the Miller farm. I need to ask for our tour guide's help one more time."

Chapter Fourteen

Gina had her shotgun on the kitchen counter. Noah had a cup of coffee. Both were staring at Carly with their full attention.

"You two have lived around here your whole lives, right?" she asked. It was a one-question follow-up to her asking if she could come inside to talk.

Noah had been hoping she'd stop by—for what he wasn't sure—but it was an easy yes from him. Gina also seemed eager to talk, something that was definitely rare from the closed-off woman.

"Yes, ma'am. In this county and the next," she answered.

Noah nodded along.

"On an Amish farm and then on this one. Why?"

Carly had something rolled up beneath her arm. She motioned to the dining room table across from them.

"May I?"

"Go ahead."

They all circled the table while Carly unrolled a good-sized map. It was laminated and looked like a Potter's Creek–wide survey. The top corner read that it had been drawn up in 2012 but, from a quick first pass, it appeared to be more or less the same as the town now.

Carly pulled out a dry-erase marker, held up her finger

as a 'hold on' sign and started to draw a line on the plastic. Noah and Gina leaned over and watched as that line started at the town limits, then went directly into backstreets through town for a bit, before moving to a network of back Amish-land roads that led to the Yoder, Graber and Haas properties. Then she was done.

"That's the route I would take if I was bringing in enough anthrax to poison three families." Carly tossed him the marker. Noah caught it with one hand and an eyebrow raised. "Now, as locals, you tell me how you would do it."

Noah shared a look with Gina. Her gaze was already on the map.

"Well, first of all, if I was coming from anywhere outside of town, I wouldn't take these." Gina pointed to the first network of backstreets. "I'd take the main road as far as I could before turning off of it."

"And why is that?" Carly leaned over again. Her hair shifted at the movement. Noah noticed that she'd gone back to her more natural look while working. While he wasn't against her undercover style, he liked the sight. Her focus and determination to get to the bottom of the case was more appealing to him than glitter.

"The main road has less traffic than the back ones do around that area, believe it or not," he explained, agreeing with Gina. "Plus there are a few one-lane neighborhoods those open up into. If you drove an unfamiliar car around there, especially at night, it would stick out more." He drew a line along the main road and paused when he got to another that split through the heart of the Amish community. Instead of following Carly's line through the backroads she'd chosen, he drew his own while Gina made sounds of approval next to him. When he was done at the Yoder farm, she took the marker and got back to the road that went through the heart of the Amish community and went to the other side of the map, leading away from the town's main road.

Carly pointed to the first change Noah had made.

"Okay, explain why you went there."

"It's not really about why I went there, it's why I didn't go *there*." He tapped her original plan. At least, one road in particular. It didn't have a name on it. "That's the road that runs behind the Kellogg property. It's abandoned now, which makes it a good, out-of-the-way spot, but—"

"That's the road you said gets so muddy it's pulled wheels off of buggies," Carly finished, remembering their earlier conversation from their tour.

Noah nodded.

"Even when it's not muddy it's pure hell on a regular vehicle. No local would use it unless it was on foot or they had no other choice. Not with an unnecessarily high possibility of breaking down or damaging your vehicle."

"And what about leaving after the deed is done?" she asked Gina. "Why would you leave Potter's Creek on this side of town and not the other?"

"Even if you came in that way, I'd leave that way, too. Cops are never on that road. Don't ask me why. It's just been that way since I was a girl."

Carly didn't say anything for a moment. Noah watched as her gaze swept the map, thoughtful. Her wheels were spinning.

"Does that mean you think it really is David Lapp behind it? Someone who grew up around here?" he finally asked.

"I honestly don't know at this point. Everyone is out there chasing down leads from what we learned last night and from what we already knew coming into the case." She tapped the map. "But spreading that much anthrax on that much land requires a lot of work, labor and at least one vehicle large enough to transport it to and from." It also required someone who knew how to spread it without risking self-contamination, something she'd already mentioned to the team. The health and safety group tasked with mitigation had suggested this to her as they'd worked in Hazmat suits, cleaning up the fields. "If you're right then, if a local did it, they would take a completely different path and, if someone who wasn't local did it, then—" she ran her finger across the plastic until she was on the road behind the Kellogg property "—maybe they made a mistake we haven't looked for yet."

The thoughtful silence that followed ended in a flash. She rolled up the map and gave them both a quick smile.

"Thanks for this," she said, already backing up to the door. He realized with a start that she was about to leave.

Without him.

And he didn't like the feeling.

For a lot of reasons.

"Do you need me to come along?" he offered, coming around the table and trying to avoid the intrusive gaze of Gina caught in the middle.

Carly hesitated.

He might have imagined it, but it sure did look like Carly had turned a darker shade of crimson.

Gina spoke instead.

"You should take him," she said. "You'll make a good team. A local and an out-of-towner, like you said. You'll probably see more with him tagging along. Plus, he already helped me mend the fence this morning and that's all I needed from him today."

Gina cracked a grin at that. Noah snorted.

"She's right. About both of those things."

Carly seemed to think about it for a little longer than Noah liked, but then she agreed.

"You can make sure I don't destroy my rental on these backroads."

"I think I can swing that."

Noah drank the last of his coffee and offered Carly a cup. She hesitated, then declined.

It was the second time she'd stopped and started with indecision just within the last minute.

Probably because you kissed her out of nowhere during a damn FBI investigation, he chided himself. *The one guy from the community tasked with helping her and you lip-locked her at a bar.*

Noah didn't regret the kiss, but he did regret how it had happened. The fact that they hadn't talked about it at all since then, not even in the car ride back to the inn, didn't help. It also didn't help that he'd spent the morning waiting for her to show up or call only to have to remind himself several times over that Carly Welsh wasn't in town for the scenery.

She certainly wasn't there to fall for the shunned farmer of Potter's Creek.

That had been a wise, rational reminder.

Though thinking about Carly falling for him? Well, that was a slippery slope right into another question: If he was wondering about her falling for him, did that mean that he was falling for her?

Was that possible?

To have such strong feelings for someone whose middle name you didn't even know?

To know something in your heart before your head got the memo?

Now Carly was standing next to her rental, peering down at her phone, brow furrowed and lips downturned.

It wasn't a special moment, in fact it was downright normal.

Yet, it happened all the same.

One moment he was looking at her and, in the next, he was thinking about the yellow house and dreams for his life.

It was the second time in his life that he'd felt exactly what he was feeling now.

And *that* to him was the most surprising thing that had happened so far in Potter's Creek.

"So Opaline found Talia's address and Axel is there now with the city PD." Carly didn't look up as she spoke. Noah didn't think he would have been able to hide the feeling unraveling in his chest if she had. "I'm hoping that means we can finally figure out this whole Rodney Lee and David Lapp thing at least. Give us some solid ground to work with."

Noah cleared his throat and went to the passenger's side of the SUV. A new excitement was emanating from Carly as they got in, and she turned the engine over and started out of the drive.

"If we can get Talia to talk, then I'm hoping we can be done with Rodney and David."

"You don't think David was responsible for the attacks now?" he asked. They hadn't talked about the case at all after he'd dropped her off at the inn the night before. The map discussion with him and Gina was the only talk about it they'd had since their night at the bar.

"At this point, I'm hoping what we do or don't find during this little trip will help point us to a local being behind this or not." She slapped her hand against the steering wheel. "Wait! I didn't even tell you about what we found out today, did I?"

Noah laughed.

"No, ma'am, you didn't."

"Well hold onto your butt and listen to this."

Carly told him all about Caroline Ferry and her son, Dylan. Noah had met Caroline once at the market but hadn't known much past the fact that she hadn't been able to convince the families to sell. He'd never met her son or her late husband.

"So what would Dylan's motive be?" Noah asked when she was done. "Trying to get back at the community as a whole for messing up the deal? Or maybe scaring those who hadn't sold to try to sell now?"

"Neither option makes that much sense. Again, getting and spreading that much anthrax, and not even against all of the families who stopped the development before it could even begin, is a lot of work. Especially for an uncertain outcome. Then again, I've seen people who are startlingly good at the follow-through and nothing else." She sighed. "But, while Dylan would be my lead suspect now, he couldn't have done it. He's been at one of those fancy rehabs in Florida for two months. At least that's what his mother said. Opaline is chasing that down, too, just to cover all of our bases."

Carly ran a hand through her hair. He thought she was going to sigh again, yet she caught herself with a light laugh.

"You know, with all of this going on, I keep forgetting Christmas is days away," she continued. "I actually think I would have forgotten completely had Dot, the innkeeper, not reminded me before I left this morning by filling up the kitchen with platters of Christmas tree–shaped cookies." Her laugh this time dipped a little. "I always think one year I'll nail the whole holiday spirit and have this big party with all my loved ones and Secret Santa and all the Hollywood stuff you see in sitcoms. Like I'd really put the effort in and feel it. Yet, here I am having to be reminded by cookies that this year it's not happening."

"Well, this Christmas you're also working an attack that was first flagged as bioterrorism, right? That would take the holiday cheer right from anyone's sails, I'd think."

Carly moved her head back and forth, like she agreed and didn't all at the same time.

"One thing I've been learning, and I think the rest of my team has been trying to learn, is the whole light and darkness balance of what we do."

"See the good in everything so the bad doesn't crush you," he guessed.

She nodded.

"So, sure, I'm in Potter's Creek investigating a biological attack with a lot of unknown variables and seemingly unlimited questions because of those variables, *but*—" Noah caught her gaze as it swept to him. Just as quickly, she looked back out the windshield. "It sure is pretty here."

Noah couldn't help but laugh.

"That's one thing Potter's Creek will always have going for it, thick or thin—it's hard not to see its beauty through it all."

"You've got that right. I mean, I love my apartment and my job, but if I woke up to this, even just on the weekends?" She motioned to the forest in the distance, blue sky framing the expansive field in front of the trees like a painting. "I think finding the good in life might be easier."

Carly had no idea how much she'd just affected Noah with her words. They reached through his attraction to her, his respect and awe at her dedication and wit, and landed next to a younger version of him, trying to explain to an entire town why he didn't leave Potter's Creek.

It made him smile.

Really smile.

Because Carly had no idea she'd just given him something he'd been wanting almost his entire life.

Understanding.

"Maybe I can cook you dinner tonight." Noah heard himself say it before he realized how out of the blue it sounded. He hurried to expand. "I mean to try to bring some stress-free dining to a stressful case. And, well, to thank you for everything you've been doing because you might not ever get that from anyone else here."

Carly tensed. Noah was worried he'd overstepped *again*. He went back to looking out of the windshield to give her privacy to come up with a way to say no.

"Maybe if I play my cards right Dot will let me bring over some Christmas cookies."

There was a smile in her voice.

Noah chuckled.

"I wouldn't say no to that."

Their personal conversation switched gears as Noah directed them to the road that ran behind the Kellogg property. Carly pulled over onto the grass.

There was no more talk about Christmas cookies or finding the light in the darkness.

She got out of the vehicle and went right up to the dirt road, eyes down and focused.

Noah went farther down from her, eyes also on the road.

He didn't have to be a trained agent to see what she was seeing.

"It looks like someone wrecked out recently," he said when Carly showed up at his side.

"You said this road gets awful when it snows or rains,

right? It's done both since I've been here, but if someone carrying a heavy load spun out in the mud? Then it might still be here for us now."

Noah agreed. It looked like someone had gone too fast and lost control enough to use up the entire road before going into the grass, kicking up chunks of both along the way.

"So if this was the person who was carrying the an- thrax—" he started.

"Then I'd bet my badge that they weren't local," Carly finished.

Chapter Fifteen

Answers.

What Carly had been looking for since before their plane touched down.

She wasn't even picky in the beginning about how many she could get.

Just *one* would be nice.

Instead the questions came. The ones that were standard: Who was behind the attack? How did they do it? Why?

But then they split into more, complicated questions: Where was David Lapp? How was Rodney Lee involved? Were they connected to the anthrax attacks?

Never mind Carly falling prey to her own personal questions: Why was Noah Miller so attractive? Why couldn't she stop thinking about him? Had his offer to make her dinner been meant as a date?

As many questions as she had piling up, Carly nearly jumped for joy when a few answers found their way to her while inside David Lapp's bedroom an hour later.

Axel walked around the room, looking for something, clearly excited as he spoke.

"Talia's apartment was empty," he said after she walked inside. "But not *empty*. It was like someone had ransacked the place, looking for something. Just like in here." Ran-

sacked was an understatement. Max seeing David's bedroom through the window had been the reason why they'd
first come inside the house in the first place. The room
looked like a tornado had torn through it. The team had
done a search after their first encounter with Rodney at
the property, but now Axel and Carly were taking a second look.

"So, wait." Nothing was making sense to Carly. "Who
do you think was looking for something?"

Axel kept moving things around, latex gloves a flash of
blue as they crossed over the mass of clutter.

"At first I thought that maybe David somehow connected with Rodney and his girlfriend and took something
from them. Then they came back here to try to find it. Or
vice versa. Talia has no priors but since Rodney has a drug
history, I was thinking maybe David might have gotten
tied up in something like that with him."

"At first," Carly repeated. "What do you think now?"

Axel's spine zipped up, standing straight as an arrow.
There was something in his hand. It was a picture, but he
didn't show her right away.

He was grinning.

That *I got something* grin.

"This room and Talia's apartment were both basically
trashed in the same way. There was anger and aggression.
Things were destroyed even though there was no real reason to do it."

"Whoever was looking for something was pissed, is
what you mean."

Axel handed over the picture.

"I think it was Rodney, but I don't think he was looking for *something*. I think he was looking for *someone*."

It had been folded several times, making creases across
the face of a young woman. She was sitting on the floor,

back leaning against a small bed. Just by looking at the picture, Carly was left with the impression that the woman was shy. Reserved. Holding back but still smiling.

She reminded Carly of herself.

"Who is this?"

Axel's grin of knowledge only spread.

"That's Talia Clark." He stepped aside and motioned to the bed, flipped over on the floor, the wooden posts broken with unnecessary force.

"And that's the same bed from the picture," she realized.

Axel nodded.

"You said Rob Cantos used the word 'obsessed' when describing how Lee talked about Talia. He even seemed put off about the relationship, maybe subconsciously so."

"Yeah. None of them seemed to be fans."

"I think that's because it wasn't a two-sided kind of love. On a hunch, I had Opaline look into Talia's medical history and in the last two years alone she was admitted three times into the emergency room with a concussion, a broken rib and a fractured cheekbone."

"Rodney was abusing her."

Carly could still feel the occasional throb of the cut on her arm that the man had given her. Her body was still sore in places from him using his sheer power against her.

Believing he was an abuser wasn't at all a stretch of the imagination.

"But all three times she was quoted saying it was because she was clumsy and nothing more."

"So she didn't report him."

He nodded.

"She doesn't have a support system, which couldn't have helped. Her father passed away when she was in middle school and she aged out of foster care." His excitement dulled. Carly understood the feeling. Having a lead was great, but a lot of the times the lead itself was heartbreaking.

Axel pointed at the picture then thumbed back at the bed.

"Now what if, at some point, some way, David Lapp meets Talia?" he continued. "What if they become friends or fell in love?"

"His father said he was kicked out of the community for lying, stealing and sneaking out," Carly realized with a start.

"Going against the tenants of your religion and jeopardizing your entire life and connection to your family? That's not something you usually do unless there's a really good reason."

Carly looked down at the smiling Talia.

"Unless it's for love."

Her thoughts split two ways at once.

She imagined David Lapp giving up everything to be with a girl.

Then, almost in sync, she thought about Noah.

Is that why he had left the community?

For a girl?

For young love?

"I could be wrong but I think David Lapp was helping Talia hide from Rodney, and I think Rodney knew it," Axel said. "That's why this place is trashed. He was looking for something, but was pissed about it. He probably did the same at her apartment trying to figure out where she went."

Carly shook her head a little. Not because she didn't think his assessment was right—in fact, she believed it was the truth as soon as he said it—but because there was still one piece of the David Lapp puzzle that didn't make a lick of sense.

"But what about the chair in the basement?" she asked.

"That took time and forethought. Two things I'm not so sure Rodney Lee would have had if he came looking for David and Talia. I'd think, based on this mess, that he's more of a punch first, ask questions never kind of guy."

At that, Axel sighed. He looked around the room then shrugged.

"If David was here, and the dried blood is any indication, Rodney could have tortured him for information on Talia. But you're right. The setting up for the chair doesn't match up with the profile I've made of Rodney."

"Unless he had a partner." Carly didn't want to say it because it only made everything more complicated. Yet, since the first moment she'd seen the chair, she'd felt something about it didn't fit.

"If that's true then where are they and where are David Lapp and Talia now?"

Another round of questions.

Carly added to it.

"And are they connected to the anthrax attacks or did we accidentally step into another case altogether?"

"I don't know, but it sure feels like somewhere in the world a clock started ticking a lot faster."

Which was Axel-speak for they were running out of time.

For finding David Lapp and Talia? Carly wasn't sure yet.

But at least they had a profile and good guess on the David Lapp situation and Carly was going to count that as an answer.

They shared a small silence, both processing their own questions, when a bark sounded outside. Selena and Blanca were on the lawn. Selena had another answer to another question when they came outside to meet her on the porch.

"I found bullet casings in the woods outside of the inn,"

she jumped in. "From a .22. CSI came in to grab them but while I waited, Blanca and I took a look around the area." Selena's nostrils flared. "There are a lot of footsteps leading to the tree line that has an unobstructed view to the front of the inn."

"And when you say a lot…" Carly started.

"I mean at the very least three distinctive prints, despite the rain and snow we've gotten since being here," she finished.

Axel's brow pulled in together.

"Which means whoever was out there, they were out there recently," he said. "Someone's been watching us."

"It could be out of curiosity, and the shots could just be boredom or rebellion like Max guessed," Carly said, playing the devil's advocate.

Selena shook her head. Something was eating at her. Something she didn't care for.

"There was another trail that branched off from the original cluster that were fresh. I followed them right up to the back porch of the inn."

That got the hair on the back of Carly's neck to rise a little.

"You think one of our peeping Toms came in for a closer look?"

Selena's lips thinned.

"Who's to say they just stopped at the porch?"

Carly didn't like that thought. Not one bit.

THE THIRD AND fourth answers Carly was given felt more solid. She had relocated to the community barn and had been jumping between calls when Max's number showed up on the caller ID.

"We found the van, the one the perp used."

Carly actually squealed.

"You did? How? And where?"

"Since you told us about that road being harsh on a vehicle, we threw a Hail Mary and called around to see if any of the mechanics had a work order on a van or truck."

"That would be incredibly stupid not to just destroy the vehicle and move on," Carly had to point out.

"Exactly, *unless* you borrowed or rented the vehicle because you needed something bigger than you had."

"So they loaded their vehicle with anthrax and then took it to a mechanic to fix because it got busted up a little during delivery?" Carly could hear skepticism coming out clearly in her own words.

"Oh, there were no vans or trucks brought in to be fixed," Max corrected. "But there *was* a work order that the boss flagged because it was a little on the unusual side."

"Oh?"

Max waited a beat for dramatic effect.

It worked, because Carly scooted to the edge of the chair she'd been on.

"Someone called in asking for the name of the best car detailer they knew and offered big bucks to have them come do it on site *and* as quickly as possible."

Carly could feel an adrenaline surge coming. One that came with leads actually leading to something tangible. Something they could use.

"And do we know who made that call?"

Max's voice fell a little.

"Not yet, but we did trace where the call came from and where the detailing job took place. In fact, I'm standing in front of the *van* right now. Can you guess where we are?"

Max didn't give her the time. Which was fine by her. She was all about getting answers sooner rather than later.

"We're in an underground parking garage beneath The Grand Casino. And, Carly? It belongs *to* the casino. As far as we've been able to see, it has been checked out for maintenance for over a month."

"Can they prove where it was during maintenance?"

"We're running that down now but, based on how quickly they're calling up the food chain to the big boss, I'm going to take a stab in the dark and say they actually had no clue where it was until they found it down here all clean and shiny like brand new."

Carly chewed on her lip in thought. If anyone had been in the barn with her, she bet she would have looked more than a little disoriented as she ran all the questions and theories through her head before she finally landed on what she wanted to happen next.

"We need to find out who took the van in the first place, who had access to it, any security cameras that clocked it coming in and out of the parking garage, and a list of employees if it wasn't stolen." She stood, adrenaline now in full surge. "I'm coming your way now. I'll let you know when I'm there."

They ended the call and Carly went around collecting her jacket, keys and credentials, so focused on the new information that she almost didn't see the woman until she was right in front of her.

"Sorry," she said. "I knocked but I don't think you heard me."

Carly scanned the woman in a flash. Her dress was long and beige and a bonnet was wrapped on top of light brown hair in a tight bun. Her face was devoid of makeup but filled with worry. It showed on her as she wrung her hands in front of her. Carly thought the woman looked to be in her late-forties.

"It's okay," Carly assured her. "How can I help you?"

The woman looked like she wanted to say a lot but,

instead, seemed to choose her words carefully. Her eyes skirted from Carly's gaze to the ground as she spoke.

"I know you are looking for who was behind the attacks and I think I found something today that you should see."

"What is it?" That definitely wasn't what Carly had been expecting. Not only was someone from the community talking to her, the outsider, but she was trying to help.

"I wasn't supposed to tell you so we need to hurry," the woman urged.

A look of fear swept across her expression.

It propelled Carly forward in an act of comfort through close proximity.

The woman looked like a scared animal about to bolt. And Carly wasn't about to scare her off.

"What did you find?" she asked, making sure to keep her voice low and soothing.

"I'm—I'm not sure, but let me take you there and you can see for yourself." She paused. "Only you. I only trust you. Please."

Carly looked at the woman, *really* looked at her.

She'd seen something, all right.

That much was clear just by her body language.

Never mind the worry and fear written across her face.

Carly had to go.

Maybe she would get her fifth answer for the day.

"All right, show me."

Chapter Sixteen

Noah started cooking early.

Gina eyed the progress from the kitchen bar with an eyebrow raised but her opinions off. That was, until she caught Noah checking his phone.

Again.

"She's got a case to work," she finally said. "The sun hasn't even set yet. Stop counting the minutes or the hours are going to feel worse."

"I'm not counting the minutes," Noah defended.

Gina didn't buy it.

"You're not the laid-back, relaxed Noah I'm used to seeing, either. Is this dinner you invited Agent Welsh to a friendly one or romantic?" She made a point to look at the countertop. He'd pulled out all the good dishes, which meant real plates were out on the dining table. Something he planned to set up when he was waiting for stew to finish later.

Not exactly normal behavior for him.

"Friendly," he said, all gruff.

Gina snorted.

"You may say that word but I think you're hoping for the other one." Gina, who had never been one to nag him about the romance department, took a surprising stand. "I like her."

His surprise must have shown. She rolled her eyes.

"I can like people, thank you very much," she added. "It just doesn't happen often."

"I think the word *you* mean is 'ever.'"

He smiled as he said it because there was no version of him that would ever talk down to or about the Tucketts. They'd given him a safe place to learn who he was and what he wanted out of life, only ever asking for hard work and respect in return. Both of which he'd been glad to give as he made a place in the world for himself.

Gina tossed a pen from the counter at him. It was a playful move that he laughed at as he dodged the projectile. It hit the floor and skidded into a box sitting on the floor of the open pantry. Gina leaned over to get a better view of it.

"Is that our old Christmas box?"

Noah had never been one to blush, but he did feel some heat move up his neck. He'd forgotten to hide it before Gina had come in for a break.

"Yeah. I was moving some things around in the attic and found it."

He went to the box, gently pushed it into the pantry, and shut the door. Out of sight, out of mind.

But not for Gina Tuckett.

She was the hare after the carrot.

"But why is it in the kitchen and not the attic?"

Noah could have lied, maybe should have, but there was no use hiding from the truth. Not with the woman who was basically his older sister.

"Carly was down about missing out again this year on the holiday spirit, and it doesn't help she landed a case in the middle of an almost-entire town that doesn't celebrate. So I thought I'd look to see if I couldn't put up some more decorations. It's the least I can do."

Gina's eyes narrowed. Not necessarily in a bad way, just

an analytical one. She opened her mouth to, no doubt, dive into the reason behind his actions when a knock sounded against the front door.

All curiosity went from questioning the good to worrying about the bad. They shared a look, then Gina was off of her stool and scooping up her shotgun. Noah grabbed the iron skillet he'd been about to prepare, then led the way to the front. After all that had happened so far, neither of them were taking any chances.

On either side of the oak door were two narrow floor-to-ceiling windows. Through one of them, Noah saw who their unexpected guest was.

"I can count on one hand how many times he's been to this house in the last decade or so." Gina's voice had gone sour. Noah had a more complicated reaction within him.

Noah made her lower her weapon and handed over the skillet.

Then he opened the door, not at all knowing what to expect.

"Dad?"

Samuel Miller wasn't a large man, but he was solid. An entire life of working with his hands, a life spent avoiding help or shortcuts combined with a loyalty and dedication to his beliefs, made him a presence stronger than any Noah had ever encountered. Then again, maybe Noah's perspective was skewed considering he'd grown up around the man.

And then disappointed him by leaving the faith and life he'd cherished above all.

Now his father stroked his beard and looked as uncomfortable as Noah was confused. He gave Gina an equally uncomfortable nod of hello.

Then he was back to his son.

"I need to talk to you. It could be important."

He glanced back at Gina.

"I'll go make sure the kitchen doesn't burn down," she said, catching the hint. "Yell if you need me."

When she was gone, Noah motioned inside.

"Do you want to come in? We can go to the office."

His father shook his head and instead took a step back.

"Out here is fine."

Noah wanted to ask if being so close to where his son lived, and Noah himself, offended his father that much but decided now wasn't the time. Even if it had been, it wouldn't have mattered.

Like Gina said, his father had only ever been to the Tuckett farm a handful of times since Noah had moved in. Nothing had changed when Noah had taken the farm over, either.

"What's going on?" he asked, moving so they were in front of two rocking chairs that Mr. and Mrs. Tuckett used to sit in on Sunday nights after dinner.

His father stroked his beard again.

He didn't like what he was about to say. That much was clear.

"Your brother, Thomas, came to me earlier today and said he hadn't seen Aaron in two days."

Noah's brow furrowed. The name sounded familiar, but with everything going on it was harder to place than normal. His father helped him out.

"Aaron is Abram's youngest son."

Noah cocked his head to the side a bit.

"Abram *Lapp*'s son? As in David Lapp's brother?"

His father nodded.

"Your mother heard about the investigation into David and your talk with Abram, so I wanted to make sure everything was okay with them myself," he continued. "So I went to talk to Abram. He was still out working, but I found his wife, Willa." He let out a long breath and looked like he'd rather be any place but right there, telling an outsider his problems. "I've known her as long as I've known your mother and I can tell you something was wrong."

"As in she didn't know where Aaron was, either?"

"As in she told me to leave and not come back after I expressed concern."

"Did she ever say where Aaron was?"

His father shook his head.

"No. Given everything that's been happening, I thought to come to you with this." He started to say something but must have changed his mind. "Aaron is a good boy, Noah. We need to make sure he's okay."

"Agreed. Come inside so I can call Carly."

His father didn't fight the offer, but Gina met them in the hallway before they could make it to the kitchen. She already had his phone.

"An unknown number is calling."

Noah took the phone. He didn't have time to wonder whom it could be before a man's voice came through with such acute concern, Noah's gut hardened into worry.

"Is this Noah Miller?" the man asked by way of hello.

"Yes, and this is?"

"It's Axel. Agent Morrow." Noah was about to ask what he could do for the man, but Axel barreled into the reason for the call. Then the worry made sense. "Is Carly with you?"

"No. She's not."

There was no hesitation.

"Do you know where she is? When's the last time you talked to her?"

Noah didn't like these questions.

Gina and his father both watched his expression with concern.

"The last time I saw her was when I dropped her off at David Lapp's house to talk to you."

"So you don't know where she is."

"No. You don't?"

Axel let out a string of expletives that would have tested the faith. Noah was close to it himself when the agent answered.

"No, we don't. She was at the barn the last we talked. Then she was supposed to meet us here at The Grand Casino an hour ago. Now no one can get a hold of her."

"Let me guess, she doesn't normally do this on a case."

"No. She never does this."

Noah went back to the kitchen and grabbed his keys. Gina and his father followed. Both of their eyes widened when he grabbed the shotgun.

"Then it's time we find her."

CARLY HAD MADE a mistake in letting the beautiful scenery lull her into a false sense of security. She wasn't in a post-card. She wasn't vacationing with her adopted parents or spending the weekend buying beautiful handmade furniture at an Amish market.

No. She was investigating a biological attack on a community.

And it had been naive to think them all innocent.

That had been another mistake she'd managed to make. She'd forsaken years of caution, skepticism and the perspective to see the big picture beyond the details.

Now the years of personal and professional experience were flooding back in, like a river reclaiming the land past the dam it had just broken through.

Carly had made a mistake.

And she was about to find out how much it was going to cost her.

The breeze picked up and pushed a sheet of her hair along her cheek as she followed the Amish woman through a field to a barn after Carly had driven her to this spot.

She didn't move it out of the way. Her focus had become a net, one she threw around the barn and now was pulling back to her. She was listening for a snag. Something out of place. A clue. A reason why her gut had gone from calm to alert in a second flat.

And why the woman who had led her there hadn't yet given her name.

Carly unholstered her gun, but kept it low at her side.

The moment she pulled it out was the moment she realized it wasn't loaded.

How was it not loaded?

How had she not noticed?

You put the holster on with it still in there this morning. But did you actually hold the gun?

Carly didn't have an answer for either.

But she hazarded a guess as to who the stranger was walking ahead of her, leading them to the side door of the abandoned barn. It was a half mile from the stretch of road that Carly and Noah had inspected earlier that day.

The Kellogg property.

The abandoned barn they hadn't yet checked.

"I never caught your name," Carly stalled, attention still sweeping the area as best she could.

The woman kept walking. She hadn't been a fan of looking Carly in the face.

Not a sign of being shy or reserved.

It was something more.

How did you not see it before?

"Oh, I'm Katherine."

Her words were flighty.

Adrenaline.

Fear.

Guilt.

The closer they got to the door, the more she was losing the facade of innocence that had made Carly feel safe.

That had made Carly underestimate her.

"I don't think it is."

The woman hesitated. The door was a few feet from them. She walked to it, but stopped before her hand could go for the handle. Carly lowered her voice to a whisper only they could hear.

A few of the puzzle pieces to the larger picture were falling into place.

Too bad Carly was alone for it.

"I think you're David Lapp's mother, Willa." The woman turned to look at Carly so quickly she almost flinched.

She was definitely afraid.

"I don't know what you're talking about."

Carly made a show of holstering her gun. Not that it would do much harm without the bullets. Another problem for another time.

She held up her hands to show she was harmless and took a slow few steps forward.

"I think that you're David Lapp's mother, and whatever is inside of this barn is a trap. I'm guessing from the man who's looking for him or maybe the man who already has him." She took another small step forward. This was the woman Carly had seen through the window of the Lapp house when they'd tried asking questions about David Lapp. "Because I think the only leverage that would make a woman forsake her faith, lie and be a bystander to violence is a serious threat to that woman's family."

The woman glanced at the door, then back at Carly.

"You have to go into the barn," she stated. Like she was reading a script.

Carly was just as firm.

"I'm not going into that barn."

The woman, who now Carly was positive was Willa Lapp, shook her head.

"You *are* going into that barn."

"It doesn't have to be this way, Willa." Carly reached for her phone.

No one knew where she was. Not her team.

Not her boss.

And not Noah.

"I can help you," Carly stalled. "I can help David."

Willa shook her head. Fear, guilt, anger. Carly couldn't tell what she was looking at anymore, but when Willa spoke Carly knew what she was hearing.

A mother who loved her son.

"He was missing for two days before I found a cell phone with the video of him being taken on it. You showed up three days later." She shook her head. "You are late to this game, Agent Welsh, and I'm not willing to bet his life on you being better at it than *him*."

Carly should have run.

Or fought.

She should have done something the second Willa opened up.

But those damn answers were there again, taunting her.

So, Carly rolled the dice and tried to get some.

"Him? Him who? Rodney Lee?"

Willa was good. She looked like she was thinking about answering when really she was just stalling. When her eyes skirted over Carly's shoulder, it was already too late.

Carly had made mistakes.

And her life was now the cost.

Chapter Seventeen

Waking up in pain was a shock to the system.

Waking up in pain and seeing someone you didn't expect to see, staring at you, was another one.

Waking up in pain and finding yourself hanging from a complicated pulley system where your wrists were bound around a giant metal hook?

Well, that was a nightmare within a nightmare.

Carly's head was throbbing as the details lined up with the pain she was feeling. On reflex, she wrapped her fingers around the hook so that the weight was off of her wrists alone. That alleviated some of the pain.

But definitely not all of it.

Carly sucked in a breath as she looked down.

Three details filtered in late.

All of them were terrifying.

She was hanging a few feet off the ground, above what looked like snow but she knew instantly was none other than the poison that had brought her to Potter's Creek in the first place.

Anthrax.

It coated the barn floor beneath her in a messy circle.

That alone would have made her blood run cold.

But then there was the detail that her jacket was no longer on her.

Neither were her shirt, jeans, socks or shoes.

She was hanging there in her black set of underwear, cold air against her skin.

Another not-so-great development.

Yet, the third detail that combined with her pounding headache changed everything.

She'd been cut along the tops of her thighs and, what felt like, her back. Not too deep, not a lot of blood, but definitely three lines of open wounds.

Which meant that Carly was absolutely exposed to a biological agent that killed through exposure.

And the person who had set up the theatrical trap?

They knew the fastest way to kill someone with the poison.

For the briefest of moments, Carly thought about her mother, but then a man cleared his throat from a chair near the side door.

Carly wasn't surprised that Rodney Lee was leaning back with a gun resting against his leg and a smirk on his lips.

"I got worried you were hit too hard and weren't going to wake up." His eyes scanned her body up and down. If she wasn't bouncing between pain, fear and anger, she might have added disgust to the list. "Not even the knife got you going."

Carly took her own time to look around.

Willa was nowhere to be seen.

"Don't worry, your friends won't interrupt us," Rodney continued. "It'll take your team half an hour, at least, to get back from the city. That's if they even know where to look. That's the good and bad thing about not being local. We're all just bumping around in the dark after a while."

Carly didn't like how Rodney had gone from the behemoth in the woods, all aggression, to a man who sounded like he was enjoying hearing himself speak.

She was in pain.

And extreme danger.

She didn't have the patience to listen to the bad guy banter with himself.

So she got to the point.

Or *a* point.

"Why did you attack the Amish? Was it punishment for David Lapp helping Talia escape from you?"

Rodney was a hundred or so feet away from her, from the anthrax. Even at that distance, she saw the anger in him flare to life at the mention of David's name.

"Talia didn't *escape* from me. He tricked her. Took advantage of her. *I'm* the one who's trying to save *her*."

That was surprising, a feeling that was starting to lose its edge on account of how many surprises had been springing up since arriving in Potter's Creek.

Did that mean that he still hadn't found Talia?

What did that mean for David?

"So you haven't saved her yet?"

Rodney growled—actually *growled*—at her.

"That little punk hid her like it's some kind of game. And you think I'm the dangerous one."

Carly winced as the cold air made her shiver.

If any of the powder kicked up and made it to her...

Adrenaline surged through her again. It was going to exhaust her faster than her fear.

How was she going to get out of this?

You can't do it alone.

The one resounding internal thought chilled her even more because it was right. She needed help to get out of this without being infected.

She needed her team.

She just hoped they'd raised the red flag when she hadn't turned up at the casino. Though she didn't know how long she'd been in the barn unconscious. If Rodney had already set up the trap before she'd gotten there, then hoisting her up on the pulley and spreading the powder had to have taken some time, especially if he was to remain safe from the deadly substance.

Stalling until they found her was her best bet.

"Where did you get the anthrax?" she asked. "It's not the easiest thing to get, even on the black market. Or to know how to deal with safely."

Her arms were starting to burn at trying to stabilize her weight in suspension. Rodney was acting like they were having a normal conversation instead of him sitting near a circle of poison, talking to a woman hanging above it and dripping blood.

Axel would have loved to add that to his profile of the man.

"You'd be surprised at the secrets people share when there's enough money involved. And you can look up anything on the internet, you know. Even how to handle this stuff." He nodded toward the powder.

Carly didn't doubt that.

She also didn't understand the why of it all.

"So, let me get this straight—" Carly bit back a small yip of pain as she shifted to try to get more comfortable. A losing battle, she knew. "—you're trying to find and punish David for hiding Talia. But didn't you already have him? You kidnapped him and then had him in that chair in his basement, right?"

At that, Rodney stood. She couldn't read his expression as it went from anger and indignation to something akin to being thoughtful, a look that didn't really fit him.

"His family saw that he was up to no good with Talia

and everyone shunned him for it. Having him taken to his own house was the only place we were guaranteed not to be disturbed." That anger came out again, quick and hot. "I almost had him talking when you and your friends showed up to town."

"You left," she realized. "And David escaped. Didn't he?"

There was that growl again.

He took a step forward, gun in his tightened grip and aimed at the ground.

"I underestimated him. I won't do that again."

So David was still out there.

But why hadn't he come forward?

Were he and Talia gone?

And, more importantly, why was Willa helping the man who'd taken and, she assumed, tortured her son?

Carly wanted to ask—wanted to get to the bottom of something—but it was clear that whatever Rodney had been building up to was close. He did another slow look up and down her body.

Then his gaze dropped to the floor.

He grinned.

"But *you're* not getting away from me."

This wasn't like when Carly was in the woods with the man. Where she felt no need to accept that she might not make it out alive. This was different. She was absolutely vulnerable.

Carly thought of her mother again.

An ache that never left became more pronounced as an old anguish ran through it. She didn't want to, but it made her think of her father.

What would he think when he found out his daughter was killed in a similar way to his wife?

Would he be upset?

Or would he think it poetic?

The daughter who helped send him to prison for poisoning her mother, poisoned herself.

It sent a wave of regret through Carly.

Then defiance.

She didn't want to give him the chance to feel anything when it came to her.

That defiance rolled into a building rage. It came out at the man who still didn't make sense to her.

"Why the theatrics? You could have disappeared. Why grab me in the first place? Why do *all of this* and chance being caught?"

Carly's voice rose at every question until she was all but yelling.

Rodney was unaffected. His smile stayed in place. His gun, however, didn't.

He moved it up, so it was aimed at her head.

"You were getting too close."

That wasn't an answer Carly wanted.

But the writing was on the wall.

Rodney Lee was done with talking. He was done with her.

Carly closed her eyes, refusing to let her last moment on Earth happen while staring at a vile, violent man.

If she had to go out, she'd rather go out in darkness behind closed eyes.

And, at least this way, poison wouldn't be the end of her.

Carly took a small, quick solace in that.

"Don't move."

A deep baritone cut through the cold air like the gunshot she'd been expecting.

Carly opened her eyes as a flurry of motion took place at the back of the barn.

Noah Miller had come through the side door with a

shotgun trained on Rodney. He glanced over at Carly but didn't address her. His focus squared up on the man who had frozen, gun still aimed.

"Now lower it or I'll shoot," Noah commanded. The sheer power and authority in his voice surprised her.

It made something in Carly actually flutter.

But there was no time to feel anything more.

"You won't shoot me," Rodney said. "It's against your religion."

Everything happened all at once.

Rodney pulled the trigger, just as Noah pulled his. Carly yelled, expecting to be there one second and gone the next.

Yet, no new pain came and neither did a kill shot.

Rodney's body was blown back, then crumpled to the floor.

There was no way around it.

He was dead.

"Carly?" Noah's voice was filled with panic as he turned to face her.

She was ready to say she was okay—other than the obvious—but then a peculiar sound followed an odd sensation coming far above her.

Carly craned her head back to look.

"Oh my God, he shot the rope."

Rodney's bullet hadn't been meant for her head.

It had been meant to sever the rope above the hook and have her fall to the ground.

It was a lot of trouble to go through to make a statement.

But man, was it effective.

"Noah! I can't touch the ground!"

Panic spread as quickly as the rope was unraveling.

Noah sprang into action. He threw his gun down and started over.

"You can't touch it, either," Carly warned.

Noah came to a halt right outside of the circle of powder. He looked around the barn. There wasn't much to work with and there wasn't time to figure out a way to work with what there was.

Carly could see it in his expression.

There wasn't a way to grab her without risking exposing himself.

And Carly realized with such a strong force ramming into her chest the she didn't want him to risk it.

To risk himself.

She wanted Noah to be safe. To be healthy. To decorate his Christmas tree with so many ornaments and bobbles that the branches weighed down and sagged from the weight.

She hadn't known him for long but there she was, accepting exposure instead of wanting him to risk himself.

That meant something. A lot, in fact. It also didn't stop Noah from being himself.

He stripped off his coat just as Carly dropped down half an inch.

"Don't touch it," she warned him.

He didn't listen.

The rope gave way with a small snap. Carly didn't have time to yell.

Noah, however, was fast.

He ran through the powder and caught her before she could touch the ground. Sheer power kept both of them from being causalities of momentum. Instead he held her like a bride, his jacket beneath her.

Carly didn't have time to react.

Not yet.

"Walk very carefully out of this," she ordered instead.

Noah nodded and did as he was told.

He held her against his chest, bleeding and in her underwear, until they were outside. The cold hit harder now that the barn's walls weren't there to cut through it.

Carly realized she was shivering.

It took her a few seconds longer to realize it wasn't all thanks to the cold.

"Are you okay?"

Noah's voice rumbled through his body and into hers.

Carly opened her mouth to try to convince him that she was, especially now that he was there.

Yet, what came out next was something she hadn't let out in a long time.

Tears.

They poured out of Carly like the waters behind a broken dam. Her body shook which made all the pain worse.

"It's okay," Noah soothed. "I got you."

Somehow that relief only made her tears worse.

THE BOOTS WERE GONERS.

They were burned outside of the abandoned barn as a hazmat team, CSI, and the Tactical Criminal Division and local law enforcement surrounded the area. A fire truck showed up, but it was Selena Lopez who rushed Carly to the hospital.

Noah, too.

He slid into the back seat of her rental SUV without shoes and still holding Carly, wrapped up in his coat.

She insisted she was fine, but the dried blood against her skin and swollen and red eyes would have been enough to convince anyone otherwise.

Never mind that she had been *dangling* above enough anthrax to kill her.

"They're going to make sure you're good and you're going to let them," Selena had barked at her. It was obvious she cared for Carly and Carly felt the same. She gave in and didn't argue as they sped to the city.

"How did you find me?" Carly had asked instead.

"Axel called and said they couldn't find you. Your tech guru found out the last place your phone had been active was off of the road behind the Kellogg property. I realized we hadn't checked the barn yet. Then I saw your rental."

Carly nodded against him.

He could feel her wince.

He also felt her jump as she remembered something.

"Willa Lapp got me to the barn and when I realized it was a trap she admitted that David had been taken a few days before we came to town."

Noah stiffened. He felt her look up at him to see why.

"When Axel called me, my father showed up at the house. He said that my little brother was worried about his friend Aaron, David's brother. When Dad went to go talk to Willa about it she turned him away."

"Once he told us that we sent local PD out to their place," Selena added from the driver's seat. "Right before I got here, Axel got a call that they had Levi in custody but that Willa and Aaron are still missing."

Noah, who had only been in contact with Axel before he'd gone to the barn and right after he'd gotten Carly, had apparently missed a few steps the team had gone through in that time.

"Does anyone know where David is?" That was still a resounding no. Carly sighed. "Rodney didn't, either."

"Maybe he and Talia left together," Noah offered.

Carly's voice was quiet when she spoke again.

"Maybe."

The rest of the ride, Carly recapped what had been said in the barn while Selena updated her on what she'd missed at the casino.

"They said they wouldn't have known the van had been missing at all had we not shown up. There were no security cameras in the area it was originally taken from *or* returned. Opaline, Amanda and Alana were looking into any traffic cams or footage from surrounding businesses that might have caught the driver leaving with it or coming back when we realized you'd gone missing. The man who detailed the car said he was paid in cash left in a bag next to the car. Aria called the number he was originally contracted by and it was the landline at the Wallflower Bar."

That got Noah's attention.

"Where Rodney liked to drink on occasion," he said.

Selena nodded.

Carly wasn't as enthused.

Not that he blamed her given what she'd just been through.

"So it was all about Rodney's obsession with Talia? The anthrax attack on the community and abduction of David? And then stringing me up in an abandoned barn?" Noah felt her skepticism pouring off of her and onto his chest.

"You don't like this," he stated.

"It just seems like a lot of unnecessary trouble and work for an outcome that he still wasn't close to getting," she said. "It doesn't make sense."

Selena sighed.

"Just because he was bad didn't mean he had to be smart about it."

At that, they agreed.

Still, Carly was unconvinced.

She was quiet for the last few minutes of the ride.

Noah tried to ignore how warm she was against him.

Chapter Eighteen

Carly decided that, once and for all, listing things she hadn't expected to happen while she was in Potter's Creek was a useless pursuit.

Rodney, David, Talia, anthrax, the Grand Casino and the Kelloggs' abandoned barn? All unexpected.

Meeting Noah and *feeling* for him the way she was? Definitely unexpected.

Waking up in his house smelling like his body wash to the faint glow of a bedside lamp shaped like a horse shoe?

Carly decided there was no reason to deep dive with rhetorical questions about how she'd gotten there.

The short but eventful journey from touching down at the airport, to being beneath the sheets of a bed-and-breakfast's bed with a bandage around her arm, to being beneath the sheets at the Miller farm with a few more bandages and soreness had admittedly been a wild path.

But one she didn't regret for a second traveling, unexpected or not.

So she palmed the cell phone on the small side table and sat up. It was almost two in the morning and there were no new calls or texts.

Carly hadn't meant to sleep this long, but she was glad she hadn't missed out on anything. Then again, their bad guy couldn't hurt anyone anymore. He was gone.

Wasn't he?

Carly's three new wounds stung a little as she moved. The doctor at the hospital had confirmed none of them had been deep. He'd disinfected them and bandaged them with a stern warning that if she felt off at all to come back immediately, then put her on strong antibiotics just in case. But, as far as they and their tests could tell, she hadn't been exposed.

Neither had her savior.

That had somehow meant more to her.

A sound of movement from the other side of the house pushed the haze of sleep out of her in an instant. She got up from the bed and took her phone out of the bedroom, alert.

That feeling of fight or flight ebbed as she approached the kitchen. By the time she was next to the dining table, it was all but gone.

"Oh my God," she breathed out. Noah froze in front of the middle of the kitchen, his hands full. Carly laughed. "What is all of this?"

Selena and Axel had both agreed at the hospital that they would feel better if Carly stayed with someone they could trust while she got some rest. They'd meant Noah and he had quickly agreed. Carly hadn't been able to deny she liked the idea, too, especially while she slept. She felt safe with Noah around.

When they'd gotten the okay to leave and come back to the farm, Gina had even still been up and in the kitchen, right where Noah said he'd left her. She'd made his dinner that he'd been planning to make Carly and the three of them had eaten in companionable silence. Carly had liked it.

The warmth of the kitchen, the quiet of the house.

But now?

Now the kitchen was an explosion of reds, greens, silvers and golds. Garland and tinsel and little paper trees and candy canes. Ornaments decorated the table center-piece while a crimson-and-green table runner stretched beneath it. A Santa hat sat on the counter, beneath it one of four place mats covered with embroidered snowflakes.

The cherry on top of the extremely festive look?

Noah holding a baking sheet filled with Christmas tree–shaped cookies.

"I was hoping you'd be asleep a little while longer." He put the cookies down on the countertop next to the sink and looked like a child who'd just been caught trying to sneak a peek at Santa. He motioned to the holiday deco-rations around him.

"Originally I was thinking of putting some decorations out for our dinner but, well, after everything that happened Gina offered to run out to the Walmart in the city and grab something better than what we had here."

Carly was still in awe at how festive everything was. She walked over to him, staring at the garland he'd strung along the tops of the upper cabinets.

"But why?"

Noah looked, dare she think it, bashful.

"I thought it might be nice to give you some holiday cheer." He checked the time on the microwave in the cor-ner. He turned his head to do so. It was all she needed to get in front of him. "Since it's past midnight—"

This time it was Carly's turn to give a kiss that wasn't expected, the moment he turned back to her.

Every ache or pain in her body quieted, just as the bar had around them when Noah had touched his lips to hers.

And now it was Noah who kissed her back.

Warm. Soft. Brief.

As soon as it started, it was over.

Carly stepped back and met his hooded gaze.

She didn't want to leave him, but she did want to give him an out.

Just because she wanted him, didn't mean he still wanted her.

There was still a lot she didn't know about Noah Miller, and there was still a lot that he didn't know about her.

Yet, being in the barn and thinking about her mother had changed something within Carly. Or, maybe, shifted was the better word. She loved who she had become, despite her trauma. She loved her job, her team and the ability to fight for justice for those who couldn't always get it themselves.

What she hadn't acknowledged to herself, until she was staring at the man who had refused to leave her side in the hospital, was how she'd put up barriers to love.

It was easy to fake it, to go through the motions, and she'd done a good job of that through the years. Dated off and on, but never got too far. She'd had an excuse ready for every relationship's end. Usually she blamed her job. Sometimes she blamed the men. But most of the time? It always boiled down to one fact.

Carly didn't open up.

Not fully, not ever and not even to the people closest to her.

And she wanted that to change.

Starting with Noah.

"I don't let anyone make me coffee because when I was ten my mother died of arsenic poisoning," she started, jumping right into her personal hell. "The doctors didn't know why she was sick until after she died and realized she'd been poisoned slowly for weeks. The detective on the case figured out that it was something she ate or drank every day, and anyone who knew my mother knew how much she loved coffee. What *I* knew was that my father always made it for her." She took a small breath. "I don't let anyone make me coffee because my father used it to kill her. He took something she loved and used it as a weapon to punish her for his own unhappiness. Then I helped put my father in prison for life and was placed in foster care until the most wonderful couple I've ever known adopted me. The reasons I went into law enforcement, why I became an expert in biological weapons and why I drink coffee every day are all the same." She took a deeper breath this time. She'd never admitted what she said next to anyone. Not even her adoptive parents or Alana.

Noah let her take her moment, attentive and solemn.

"I do everything I do to remember and honor my mother. I try to help people and find justice for those who couldn't, I became an expert in an awful subject to try to keep people safe from it, and I remind myself with every cup of coffee that you shouldn't stop trying to love life just because there are people out there who only want to destroy it."

There it was.

She'd given her most-guarded secret to a man she'd only known a week.

Noah's expression was impassive. She'd had no idea how he would react since she'd never told anyone about her parents before.

He must have realized that.

"Why did you tell me this?"

The truth wasn't done with Carly yet. So she gave it to him straight.

"You just feel right."

Whatever the answer he was searching for, that seemed to do the trick.

Noah took her chin in his hands and dipped low for a kiss so tantalizing that Carly nearly went weak in the knees. Warm was the best way to describe Noah, followed by solid. He was a force. A quiet strength that reached out to every part of her body. That strength moved from his hands to his tongue as it swept across her lips and deepened their kiss.

It felt absolutely right.

Carly made a noise against him, unable to hide her pleasure at the move. He reciprocated the feeling by wrapping an arm around her and pulling her flush against his body. They stayed like that for a few moments, enjoying the tight and rhythmic embrace.

Until they wanted more.

Noah took a step back, lips swollen and red. His eyes betrayed him as they listed in the direction of the bedroom.

Carly, filled with heat that went from below her waistline all the way to her cheeks, found herself grinning.

Noah seemed a little uncertain.

Had she gone too fast in an already accelerated timeline?

"I can't offer you champagne or walks along the beach right now, and I can't offer you beers and dive bars, either," Noah said. "But I *can* do my best to show you a good time, if you want it."

If Carly hadn't been ready before, she sure was now.

In answer, she took his hand.

Then she led him to the bedroom.

SUNLIGHT POURED IN through the curtains and warmed the side of Noah's face. It took him a few seconds to realize what that meant.

He'd slept past the sunrise.

Something he hadn't done in a long time.

Normally that would have started his day off with an

uneasiness. Like he'd already wasted the morning by sleeping through it.

Not today.

The reason he was still in bed was in part from an exhausting few days, but mostly because of what he'd been doing in the time between the sheets leading up to falling asleep.

He'd been afraid to touch Carly for fear of hurting her or reopening any of her wounds. Carly, however, had not shared that fear. They'd split the difference of concern for a night filled with passion, care and heat.

Now Noah awoke feeling good.

Feeling...right.

The bed dipped down a little next to him. He rolled over to find Carly looked as guilty as sin and just as delicious. Her golden hair caught the morning light while his shirt engulfed her upper body. Her legs were bare, and she'd brought a plate of cookies to bed with her. She looked apologetic.

"I was going to eat these in the kitchen but then I got nervous that Gina or your dad would walk in and see me without pants and with obvious bedhead *so* I brought these in here but then I was cold so..." She held up one of the cookies he'd made her the night before. "I'm sorry for bringing cookies into your bed."

Noah laughed. A real, genuine belly laugh. He propped himself up against the headboard and swiped one of the cookies.

"Just for future reference, cookies in bed? Something you never have to apologize for." To prove his point, he took a huge bite of his own tree-shaped cookie. Unlike the mostly from-scratch stew recipe he'd begun the night before, these were the easy fifteen-minute frozen kind of cookie. But boy, they tasted good.

Or maybe it was the company that made them taste like a piece of heaven.

Carly laughed but nodded. She took a bite of her cookie as she slipped her legs back under the sheets. On reflex, Noah moved his free hand to rest on her thigh.

It pulled a quick smile from the woman.

Then her brow creased.

"What's wrong?" he asked, instantly worried. After they'd finished their nighttime activities they'd spent some time in the shower together. Then, Noah had been careful to re-dress her cuts. "Are you feeling okay?"

Carly sighed but nodded.

"Yeah. I feel fine. I mean, I feel sore and some things still sting, but it's not bad. I think sleep really helped."

"Then what's on your mind?"

Carly took another bite of cookie. As she chewed, she looked like she was working through answering that herself.

"I guess I just keep coming back to the chair," she finally said.

"The chair?"

Carly readjusted so she was facing him. He moved her legs so there was room for them to lie across his lap. She might have been half-naked in his bed, eating a plate of Christmas cookies, but in that moment Carly Welsh looked every bit the FBI agent working a case.

"The chair in David Lapp's basement. It doesn't make sense."

"How so? Rodney Lee sure seemed like a man who wouldn't mind trying to torture someone."

"See, *that* part makes sense from what we know of him. Rodney was obsessive and abusive and seemed to be prone to impulse and aggression. But bolting a chair to the floor in someone's basement and putting restraints on it? I mean,

I get him trying to muscle information out of David and needing a way to keep him from escaping, but the chair just screams premeditation. *Thought*. Finesse." She looked down at her wrists. There was some rope burn around them. Noah had put some ointment on them before they'd gone to bed. He'd had to hide how angry it had made him to see and feel physical evidence of how close Carly had come to dying. Even now it made his blood pressure rise.

"But the setup in the barn had the same feel," she countered herself. "It was *theatrical*. Like tying someone to the train tracks, when shooting them would be so much faster *and* easier."

"But shooting someone doesn't make a statement. At least, not like what I saw in that barn."

"That's what I also don't get," she hurried to say. "Rodney Lee, as far as we know, has been all about finding Talia. What statement was he trying to make? And to whom? My team? 'Hey, I'm a guy with a seemingly endless supply of anthrax who can derail an investigation by killing a federal agent.'" She shook her head. "And *that's* one more thing that's really bothering me."

She put the cookie in her hand down, completely focused.

"One *really* good way to not have the FBI, or any law enforcement, crawling around town here in the first place is to *not* spread fields' worth of anthrax randomly. And certainly not send a tape of you kidnapping a guy to his mother to use as leverage against her *to then use* to get her to help kill the FBI agent you brought to town in the first place!"

Carly let out a frustrated breath.

"I have to admit, when you put it like that it sounds like Rodney wasn't the sharpest tool in the shed."

"When I put it like that he doesn't even sound like the

sharpest tool in the superstore. I mean, I've had cases where not every loose thread is tied up, but this? It feels like it's reverted back into a ball of yarn."

"Maybe the team found something last night. Weren't they all waiting on one thing or the other?"

"I'm waiting on an update from them." She averted her gaze to the half-eaten cookie. She wasn't done with the ball of yarn yet. "David and Talia have to still be here, right? There had to be some reason Rodney was sticking around."

Her tone turned thoughtful. It matched her gaze as it moved to his.

"Why did *you* stay?"

"Why did I stay?" It was a question he'd heard over and over again, yet one he'd never answered. For a while that had been because there was no one he *wanted* to know the answer, but now?

Hadn't Carly just shared her past with him? Hadn't she let down her guard and let him in? Could he do the same?

Did he *want* to?

Yellow house, Noah. The dream for your life. Why you walked away. The freedom and peace you wanted. You already thought it once.

Carly's brows pulled together. Her face fell a little.

She knew he was debating telling her and it hurt.

Noah opened his mouth, to say what he wasn't sure, but her phone on the bed next to them blared to life.

The moment was over.

Carly put the plate down and pulled her legs off of him. When she answered her phone, she was all business.

"What's going on, Max?"

Noah couldn't hear what the agent said but, judging by Carly's expression, it was a bombshell. She flung herself out of the bed and started moving around to find her clothes. He followed suit, trying to pick up on the conversation, but could only catch a few words here and there.

It wasn't until he was dressed that Carly ended the call and found him in the kitchen.

"Rodney Lee didn't make sense because he wasn't the one pulling the strings," she nearly sang. "He had a partner."

Chapter Nineteen

"Dylan, adult son of real estate developer Caroline Ferry, never checked into the rehab facility in Florida."

Aria was using the rental SUV to block the cold wind that had picked up since Carly and Noah had arrived at the Ferry Mansion. She had her bulletproof vest on and badge pinned to it. She looked like a woman not to be tested. Small was the package, but mighty was the strength.

"The team is inside sweeping the place, but Dylan isn't here. But we *do* have several updates for you," Aria continued. "Headquarters did a lot of the work on this one. Opaline finally got the info from the rehab facility, and Amanda and Alana were able to spot the van from the casino cameras with the same plates we were looking for leaving *and* going back to the parking garage. Opaline couldn't get a good shot of his face, but Rodney was seen both times leaving through the lobby right after. Not the smartest crayon in the box."

Noah next to them smirked.

"Not the sharpest tool in the superstore, either."

Carly snorted, then asked the most obvious question she could think of.

"How do we prove that Dylan connects with Rodney?"

Just because Dylan seemed like a perfect fit for the

crime—motive, means and missing alibi—didn't mean he was guilty of it.

Aria was ready with an answer. A nice change of pace for the case.

"Well, Axel started thinking that, if Dylan was in town, there was a good chance he'd been going to the casino and maybe that was how he met Rodney." Aria pulled her phone out and went to the photo gallery app. When she found the picture she wanted, she held it up. "Amanda starting matching posts Rodney was tagged in on social media by Rob Cantos to security footage from around the same time at the casino. She got a hit from two months ago."

The picture was of two men standing outside of the casino's front sidewalk talking and smoking.

"That's Rodney," Carly confirmed, pointing to the man on the left.

Aria pointed to the man on the right.

"And that's Dylan. When he was supposed to be in rehab." She took her phone back but kept on. "Max ran with the info and went to the floor of the casino to start asking around using the photo. Turns out not only were both men regulars, they were *regularly* seen together for the last six months. Right around the time that the deal with his mother fell through is when their friendship seemed to start."

"So they definitely know each other," Noah said. "What did Dylan's mother have to say?"

Both Carly and Aria turned to him, surprised.

"Sorry, I didn't mean to overstep. You're the agents."

Carly shook her head.

"No apology necessary." She gave him a look that perhaps wasn't smart to share in front of Aria. It felt smoldering, but Carly couldn't help it.

Noah as a detective was an interesting, and stimulating, thought.

Aria smiled wide and bounced her gaze between them. Suspicious, and then somewhat excited.

Thankfully, she didn't say what she was thinking and, instead, answered his question.

"Caroline had no idea that he wasn't in rehab and when we told her the first thing she did was call her accountant. Turns out she's missing money, much to her second surprise."

"How much are we talking?"

"According to Alana, more than enough to procure a ridiculous amount of anthrax powder on the black market if you knew the right people."

Carly raised her eyebrow at that.

"And Ms. Ferry didn't notice that much money missing?"

Aria lowered her voice even though they were out in the drive.

"You know how we thought that she was really rich before? Triple that number in your head and you're in the ballpark."

"So a large amount of money draining from one of her accounts isn't going to pop up on her radar for a while, since she already has more than that," Carly finished.

Aria made a finger gun.

"Bingo."

"But, because of the seriousness of the case, Rihanna was able to get us a warrant before we knew any of this?"

A lot had happened while Carly had been sleeping. If she didn't trust her team, that would have made her skin crawl. Missing out on helping to solve the case already had Carly fighting a feeling of anxiousness. Though even she had to admit that she'd needed to take a temporary back seat after running into Rodney Lee twice.

"Yep," Aria answered. "And since then the evidence is going from circumstantial to in the direction of damning. Wanna guess what we just found in the Ferry wine cellar?"

Carly didn't try. She was nearly vibrating in anticipation.

Answers were starting to feel as good as Noah had the night before.

Almost.

"Hit me," she said.

Aria didn't disappoint.

"A bolt gun with no bolts and fibers in a package that used to hold rope. CSI will have to compare it to the rope in David's basement and the one used on you but—"

Carly interrupted with a rush of adrenaline.

"It's too much of a coincidence not to be a match." Carly turned to Noah. "That's why it was bothering me. Dylan was the one who set up the chair and the trap in the barn, not Rodney."

He smiled, almost like he was proud.

It was oddly satisfying.

Aria continued with their expert profiler's opinion.

"Axel said based on what he's seen and read on Dylan, he's a lot craftier, a lot smarter and has a lot more anger in him than we originally thought. He thinks losing the dude ranch deal might have made Dylan snap and that we're looking at a man who wants to punish those who he thinks have wronged him. Not to intimidate or use it as an opportunity to get the deal going again."

"Poisoning the community is a slow, malicious way to do damage and savor the fallout," Carly hated to say. "It's definitely a longer-lasting punishment."

She thought of her father.

Noah's jaw clenched. So did his fist at his side next to her.

"How does Rodney fit into that plan then?" he asked after a beat.

Now that Carly knew there were two suspects and not just one, she was putting together a theory in record time.

"If Opaline had not kept digging into his rehab, we might not have looked twice at Dylan past our initial contact. Everything else that we had on Rodney was enough to close the case, even with loose threads. Rodney attacked and tried to kill me twice, the second time with anthrax, admitted he had connections to get it, and might have had an ax to grind with the Amish community thanks to his hatred of David. You said it yourself, though, Dylan was craftier and smarter than Rodney, and we all know that Rodney is obsessed with Talia to the point where I bet if he was offered a way to find her, he'd do almost anything."

"So you think Dylan used Rodney for his connections and then was planning on letting him take the fall," Noah spelled out.

Carly nodded.

"If you're determined to follow through on something you know is going to pull severe heat from the law, then you're going to want to make sure someone else gets burned. Not you."

Noah conceded to that.

"Regardless of the motive and the partnership, we still have one problem." Aria shook her head. "Dylan isn't here and we can't find him. Caroline froze all of his accounts still connected with hers so if he needs money to run then he'll need that to be cash, which won't make things easy."

Carly put her hands on her hips and bit at her bottom lip.

"Why didn't he run before?" she asked after a moment.

"He wanted to see the suffering he'd inflicted?" Noah tried.

"But he had a pretty decent alibi until Opaline took a look at it. Why not leave when things started heating up? Why— Oh my God!" Carly felt her eyes go as wide as quarters. Noah and Aria both went on the defensive, startled.

Carly didn't have time to apologize.

Another piece of the puzzle fell in place.

"At the barn, Willa seemed focused solely on doing Rodney's bidding, but it was Dylan pulling the strings," Carly continued. "Even if she knew that, it didn't matter. All that mattered was her family's safety."

Carly looked up at the massive house. Then around them at the land and trees. Noah picked up on her thoughts.

"Willa wouldn't forsake her beliefs unless she had proof that her family was in danger," he said. "And she'd need more than one video on a phone, I'd think, to serve someone up to be killed."

Carly felt the same way.

"We know that Dylan set up the chair in David's basement... What if David never escaped from that chair? What if Dylan decided to use him as a way to gain leverage over a local? A mother who would be hesitant to talk to the cops, even under normal circumstances, would make a great lackey to help him stay ahead of us and out of the spotlight."

Aria understood where they were going, too, and chimed in.

"Dylan punishes the town that he thinks ruined him. He gets Rodney's help because of his connections, to poison it. Then he makes a plan to pin it all on Rodney by using David, the one person Rodney hates the most, as a way to control him."

"All while using the one person who loves David the most to play the other side," Carly finished. They shared a look with one another.

"It's all conjecture still," Aria said, playing the devil's advocate.

Carly agreed...with caveats.

"But I can tell you with confidence that my gut is saying Dylan has to have David stashed somewhere. Have you searched *all* of the property?"

Aria opened her mouth to answer, literally forming the word across her lips, when life decided to flex its muscles.

Life was often about timing.

And now was a great example of that.

Selena hustled out of the house, catching their attention. Max was quick on her heels. Blanca was in front of both.

Aria went on full alert. Carly did, too.

Then Axel rounded the team out hurrying outside. His attention went to them and he didn't stop moving as he spoke.

"We were looking through the property's security system and saw a woman crawling in the grass by the side gate."

No more needed to be said.

Carly followed behind her team while Noah came after her as everyone converged on the area they'd seen from the footage.

Selena and Blanca got there first, but it was Max who called out for an ambulance. Aria saw the woman and pivoted to make sure one was on its way, while Axel dropped down to start working on her. Carly lowered herself next to the woman and did a quick scan of her wounds.

Her knuckles were busted and her dress was stained

with dirt and blood. She had rolled over from her side to her back, giving them an easy view to the gunshot wound at her side.

But she was alive and conscious.

She was also Willa Lapp.

When she saw Carly, relief as plain as day spread across her expression.

"You're okay."

Her voice was tired, weak. Carly looked back at the path the woman had crawled along. It led into the woods.

"Where are you coming from?" Carly asked, diving right in. "And who did this to you?"

Willa cried out as Axel put pressure on the gunshot wound. Tears sprang up at the corners of her eyes, but she answered.

And what an answer it was.

"There's an old maintenance work building that way." She pointed with a shaking hand toward the trees. "He— he tried to take him so I tried to stop him."

"Who did you try to stop? Who shot you?" Carly echoed the question that everyone was hoping they knew the answer to.

"Dylan."

When Willa said his name, excitement surged through Carly. They were closer to their goal. Justice.

Willa didn't know it, but she'd found this case's magic word for the team.

"Spread out," Carly ordered but everyone was already moving.

Aria switched places with Axel, gun out, while the rest of the Tactical Crime Division team moved into and through the trees.

Noah even tagged along but kept behind them, quiet and on alert.

It wasn't until they came up to a small building, run-down and looking like it had been forgotten by the world, that Carly asked him to stay put.

He obliged with a whisper.

"Be careful."

Carly nodded. Then it was all about the building.

Small but sturdy. They took no chances as they entered and then methodically cleared the rooms.

What they contained sickened her.

One room made the hair on the back of Carly's neck stand. Axel swore. Selena did, too.

A long table housed a bank of monitors. Each of those monitors displayed a view into the Castle in the Trees Inn. More specifically, into their individual rooms.

If that was all they had found, that would have been enough.

Yet, the next room is what got to Carly the most.

She met the young man, bloodied and bruised but alive, in the middle of the room, tied to a chair and gagged. They quickly untethered him, and he stood, swaying.

"I sure am glad to finally meet you, David," Carly said.

David Lapp collapsed against Max, understandably exhausted.

"We need to get him and his mother to hospital ASAP," Carly started. "Then we—"

She didn't get to finish.

Noah burst into the room with eyes that were crazed and his cell phone clutched in his hand.

Something was wrong.

Something was really wrong.

Ice filled her veins before he could even get the words out.

"Gina called. My dad and brother Thomas came by

the house." His nostrils flared in anger but his eyes yelled worry. "And Dylan just showed up there now."

He shook his head. It hurt him to say what he did next. "He took Thomas. He took my little brother."

Chapter Twenty

It was Christmas Eve and Noah was finally spending it with his family. Every member but one.

Noah's mother, Marta, hadn't moved an inch since she'd come out to the blockade made up of SUVs and Noah's and Gina's trucks. Local PD was also there but had been told to make a perimeter around the Yoders' property while they surveyed the barn.

The barn where it had all started.

The barn where Noah's little brother was being held hostage by a desperate man with, according to him, nothing to lose.

Noah's father was less stationary than his mother. He paced a small lane between the vehicles while the Tactical Crime Division team did their recon and made their plan.

Noah wanted to help, but trusted Carly and her team to do their job.

Something he kept having to reiterate to his father.

"She can do it. *They* can do it," he said again. "I know it doesn't mean much to you, but I trust them."

That had finally gotten his mother moving. She turned around, dark hair and green eyes an identical match to his, and walked to his side.

Noah didn't know what to do for a moment. Or, more aptly, didn't know how to feel.

While his father had made the decision to label him as an outsider after he left, Noah's mother hadn't originally been happy with the decision. She'd been vocal about them still talking to and having him come over, yet that hadn't lasted past the first month that he'd left.

Now he was caught between them and worried for a brother he barely knew.

"I don't know them," his father said, words dangerously close to sounding disgusted. "And I don't know her."

That was it.

That was enough.

It wasn't the time, certainly not the place, but an anger and hurt that Noah didn't realize was still there came to the surface with startling speed.

"You don't know *me*, and yet I'm who you call when there's trouble. Sometimes life isn't fair like that and you just have to put your faith in someone other than yourself."

He hadn't meant to say it, and not with the amount of bite he had, and yet he still wanted to say more.

So he did.

"I have known Carly for a week and she and her team have shown more compassion, caring and dedication to helping this town than most people who live here. They have risked their lives and almost paid with them to protect all of us and do you know what they get in return?" Noah pointed to himself. "A liaison, because you wouldn't even *talk* to them."

Noah shook his head. Then motioned to the group a few yards ahead of them with a different barricade they'd created themselves. Carly had her bulletproof vest on and gun at her side. Noah hated that he couldn't be next to her, that he couldn't go inside that barn to rescue his brother with her, that he couldn't guarantee her safety.

So he let his feeling of helplessness pull out the rest of his hurt at his family forsaking him.

"I just want you to remember that all of the people who you ignore with such disdain are the same people who you call in your darkest hours. So to stand here and look down at any of them, at *me*, doesn't help anyone. Not an inch."

Noah's father had stopped his pacing. His mother has gone still.

Noah could have said more, but he knew it wouldn't do any good. At the end of the day, no matter his age, when he was around his parents he felt like a little kid who'd taken a left at the fork in the road instead of their right. A boy who had felt lost for years going along his path alone.

That is, until he found a yellow house, a blue shed and a home along the way.

The Tucketts.

Gina, who had not only tried to fend off Dylan, narrowly missing getting shot herself, had also taken off in her truck to chase the man until he bailed out into the closest building he'd been near. She and her family had never been fans of people in general, but they'd given him the space to decide if he wanted to be one of the few they did consider to be good.

And it was only now, standing there next to his flesh and blood, that Noah realized Gina's father hadn't given him the farm.

Noah had inherited it like a son would from a father.

Because he *was* family.

And, even though it had taken him this long to realize he hadn't been truly alone all of these years, he found the sudden clarity deflated the same anger that had brought it on.

His parents *were* good people. People who had spent their lives dedicated to their beliefs. Just as he wanted them to not fault him for the path he'd taken away from them, Noah couldn't fault them for staying on the path they'd been walking their whole lives.

Noah let out a long breath.

Then he looked between his parents and meant what he said next.

"I'm sorry. I just miss you sometimes."

A hand, small and worn, took his. Noah's mother wasn't smiling, but she squeezed his hand.

"And we miss you always. Don't you ever think otherwise."

Noah didn't know what to say to that, so he didn't say a thing. He held his mother's hand while his father looked conflicted.

Finally he let out his own breath before gazing out at the barn in the distance.

"When this is over maybe it's time we start to fix that." He turned back to Noah. "I could always use an extra pair of hands to help mend fences."

It wasn't what Noah had expected, but he took his father's olive branch all the same.

"I've gotten really good at those over the last few years."

They all shared a silence, the first one since he'd left as a teenager that wasn't filled with confusion, disappointment and resentment.

It felt nice.

But it didn't last long.

Something was happening with the TCD team.

They were splitting up. Axel went one way, Selena the other, while the rest spread out along their barricade, guns drawn.

All except Carly.

She gave her weapon over to Aria and then held her hands up in surrender.

Then she walked out into the open field.

And right into the barn.

THOMAS MILLER LOOKED like a younger version of Noah. So much so that, had they not known whom Dylan had taken, Carly would have figured it out the moment she saw him.

Even afraid and held against a desperate man without an exit strategy, a solid strength emanated out of how he held himself. Never mind his forest green eyes.

"I'm unarmed and alone," Carly called out, hands still up for emphasis. "So let's talk about this."

Dylan had seen better days.

Unlike his mother, who had been the picture of cool elegance, it was obvious he was hanging on by a thread.

The suit he wore was torn and covered in dirt. He had angry red marks with dried blood along the side of his face, courtesy of Willa Lapp she presumed, and he was sweating despite the cold.

However, the hand that held the gun pressed into Thomas's side was steady.

So was his voice.

"Stop right there," he demanded.

They were standing against the far wall of the barn. It was smaller than the abandoned one on the Kellogg property.

Which was good, but also not so good.

Carly could see all the exits as soon as she was inside. So could Dylan and, with his back against the only wall without one, that meant no surprises.

For either of them.

The main reason why the rest of the team was hanging back.

That and their belief that Dylan had already snapped once, so every complication to his plan after was just that break splintering even more. If he felt like there was no way out, he'd shoot Thomas.

And Carly wasn't going to let that happen. He'd tried to kill her, using Rodney. It had been an easy choice for her, to be the one to step up to try to get Thomas back. She wanted to face this man.

"Let's just calm down here," Carly said, stopping a few yards from him. "Your best option for this to turn out in your favor is to let him go and come with me."

Dylan didn't waste any time.

"Did you find David and Willa?"

Carly struggled to keep her expression impassive on that one.

"We did."

He didn't seem upset, which put Carly further on edge.

"Did you find Aaron?"

This time she wasn't able to hide her reaction. He actually grinned.

"See, I've been to enough support groups to know the best motivation usually comes from wanting what's best for your family. That's why I didn't just stop with Willa."

"You got her youngest son, too."

"Yep. And right now he's in an undisclosed, yet very public place, with two bags of anthrax and a cell phone." He nodded down to his jacket. "And, unless he gets a call from me in the next—" He glanced quickly at his watch. It, like the suit, looked expensive and yet wrong with his desperation. "—seven minutes, he's going to release that powder into a ventilation system… One that feeds into a wing of, drumroll please, the hospital. Which, I don't have to tell you, our resident biological weapons expert, anthrax plus hospital patients can't be a good combination."

Carly was stunned.

Absolutely stunned.

"Aaron doesn't know we found his mother and brother," she realized. "You threatened them if he didn't do this, didn't you?"

Dylan's grin turned malicious.

"You get the mother to help by threatening the son, and you get the other son to help by threatening the mother. It's the circle of life."

Carly's gears were spinning fast.

She didn't know Aaron Lapp, but his mother had almost gotten Carly killed to keep David safe. She had no doubt that Aaron would do the same for his mother.

"This place is surrounded. You can't get away," she said, changing subjects. "But if you let Thomas go and call off Aaron I'll make sure to let everyone know that you cooperated."

It was a shot in the dark, appealing to the rational side of the man holding a gun to a teenager's side.

Dylan didn't bite.

"I cooperated? Those are just words, Agent Welsh. We both know that if I get taken in that will be the end of me."

"You didn't kill anyone," she tried again. "That counts for something."

"But I orchestrated everything."

There it was.

His own admission.

Yet, she still didn't know *why*.

So she asked.

"Why, though? Why go through all of this trouble in the first place? To punish the community?"

Dylan's expression went hard.

Angry.

"Because one day everything was fine and the next I was out of money, out of my house and being sent to another place ready to tell me I needed to stop what I loved doing." He was seething. "Meeting Rodney just opened up a world of possibilities on how to finally have a win I could keep."

That's what it was.

That was who *he* was.

Standing there Carly finally saw it, clear as day.

Dylan wasn't a punisher. He was a seeker of justice. Too bad it was the wrong kind.

"You wanted to use what the community loved against them, just like you used what Rodney and the Lapps loved most against them." She looked at Thomas. "Just like you're using Thomas against me, because of Noah."

His anger transformed into another awful, no-good grin.

"We've been watching you since you got here, Agent Welsh. It's been easy to see that the fastest way to get the team to pay attention is go for their lead agent. And since Rodney failed, *twice* at that, I realized an attack against your farmer would be the next best way." He jabbed the gun into Thomas's side. "Now, you're going to go out there and tell them all to stand down and let me leave or, not only is Thomas here going to die, but somewhere out there a hospital is about to be in a really bad way."

Carly wanted to keep talking, wanted to get to know the mind behind the senseless and selfish acts of violence and destruction, but the truth was, sometimes the bad guy was one-dimensional. Sometimes they didn't make sense. Some didn't know why they did what they did, and others refused to ever say.

No one knew exactly why Carly's father had poisoned her mother. She probably never would. It was a fact that she'd struggled with since she was ten and would most likely still struggle with until it was her time to go into the great beyond.

But there were just some things you had to learn to accept or they'd eat you up.

Dylan, for whatever reason, had taken the curveball thrown at him and, instead of hitting it, had decided to blow up the stadium.

And Carly was going to have to accept that she would never fully understand why.

So there were no more questions left to ask of the case, of the man.

They had their answers.

Now it was time for the wrap-up.

"Did you get all of that?" Carly put her hand to her ear. Axel's voice came through the earpiece in a concise answer.

"Yes. We'll stand down. But, Carly? He's not going to make that call, even if we let him go. You need to get Thomas away from him before he gets into that car."

Carly nodded to Dylan. He snorted, unaware of the Plan B the TCD team had already accounted for.

"You've been on comms the entire time. Just like in the movies. That's clever."

"More like efficient," she said. "They've agreed to all stand down. The car you came in is still outside. You're free to go to it, *after* you give us Thomas and make the call."

She knew it was a no-go, but she had to make the effort.

Dylan shook his head.

"He comes with me to the car, then I'll call when I'm far enough away." He flipped his watch back and shook his head again. "Take it or leave it, because now we're down to three minutes."

"Fine, but if you hurt him, the deal is off."

"Deal. Now go ahead of us."

Carly put her hands back up and led Dylan and Thomas

out. She had to hand it to the boy, he was quiet and calm. He definitely was a Miller.

The world outside the barn was quiet. Local PD had the perimeter, but to her left she saw her team and then she saw Noah and his parents.

Everyone was watching her.

Then all eyes were on Dylan.

Carly turned around to face him and the car that was parked at the corner of the building.

"Now let him go," she said, voice low.

Dylan's flare of confidence was starting to fray. His eyes were wide as he looked at his audience. The firm grip he'd had on the gun was wavering.

All she needed was one opening.

"Dylan. Let him go."

That's when she heard it.

Small, scared and set in his own plan.

He'd done the math.

He'd used all of the aces up his sleeve.

He wasn't going to make it far, if he made it out at all.

"No."

He readjusted the gun and that's when the world was destined to become loud and chaotic.

Thomas might have been young, but he wasn't defenseless. He threw his weight forward just as Carly lunged at him. Dylan stumbled at the shift and gave Carly her only opening.

She met Thomas in the middle, grabbed his arms and used his momentum to spin him around so his back was to his family.

Just in time for her to see Noah over his shoulder as Dylan shot her in the back.

The force of the hit sent Carly and Thomas to the ground just as the yelling started. Then the gun shots over them.

Carly couldn't breathe, but she stayed on top of the boy as a shield while her team used their firepower to cover them.

The sound of a car starting preceded the screeching of tires a few moments later.

Thomas opened his eyes.

Forest green. Just like his brother's.

"Carly!"

The edge of her vision started to go black.

Someone walked past her, calm and cool.

Max.

Their Plan B.

She heard the shot he must have taken. Then the car crash.

Then she heard Noah.

But she couldn't stay awake for him.

Chapter Twenty-One

Noah spent Christmas morning making cookies. He made reindeer-shaped ones, though they didn't look that great. Selena told him it didn't matter as long as the icing was done well.

So she took over that job, while Blanca chewed on a dog bone in front of the Christmas tree.

While the rest of the team had gone back to the inn after a busy night, she'd accepted Noah's offer for the guest bedroom.

She hadn't wanted to leave her friend and, after seeing what he had yesterday, he understood.

Carly being shot was something he absolutely never wanted to see again.

"I was going to say I don't mind how they look, I'll eat the cookies, but then I heard frosting, so I'm inclined to agree with Selena."

The woman of the hour walked slowly into the kitchen. She'd changed out of his T-shirt and into a simple red dress with boots. Noah couldn't help but stare.

She laughed, then winced.

"I brought one good holiday-worthy outfit, just in case the holiday spirit found me. But, let me tell you, this look starts and stops with the dress." She slid carefully onto a barstool across from them. "It hurts to breathe so I'm not about to do my hair or make-up."

Noah frowned, remembering the moment she'd been shot.

After Carly had used herself as a human shield for his brother, he had felt like he couldn't breathe, either. He'd started running for her before Max ever took his one shot that ended Dylan's luck.

When she'd gone slack before he could get to her?

Breathing became the least of his worries.

But then he'd seen the bulletproof vest beneath her jacket.

It was only after they'd been discharged from the hospital with a few bruised ribs on her left side that he'd started breathing normally again.

"You were shot *yesterday*," Selena reminded her. "I would still be in my PJs and asleep if I were you."

Carly laughed then winced again.

"The smell of cookies and coffee is a surprisingly strong motivator. Speaking of—" Carly turned to Noah, an expression he couldn't read moved across her face. Then softened. "Do you mind making me a cup?"

It was such a simple request, but Noah knew now what it meant to ask.

It only cemented his plans for the yellow house on the hill.

"It would be my pleasure."

He went to the coffee maker and started as Selena updated Carly on everything she'd missed while she'd been in the hospital and then sleeping in his bed.

"Aria said that Dylan is out of surgery and should make a full recovery. The doctor actually complimented Max on the precision of the shot. It was enough to get him to wreck but didn't kill him." Selena snorted. "Max said he'd never gotten complimented from a doctor before about shooting someone."

"Hey, given he did it while walking through a field while Dylan was in a car speeding away? Max deserves all the praise as far as I'm concerned."

"True dat." Selena passed Noah a finished cookie while he went for a mug in the cabinet. Carly already had one in front of her, a bite missing, in the small window of time he'd turned his back to them.

It made him happy.

"And what about Aaron?" she asked after giving him a little smile. "Did he tell us anything we didn't know?"

After Max had taken the doctor-praised shot, he'd gone ahead and grabbed Dylan's phone and dialed the most recent call in the phone's log.

Aaron had answered, but hadn't believed Max until Noah's brother, Aaron's best friend, had told him that it was over.

In fact, his mother, Willa, had just been admitted into the same hospital.

Aaron had cooperated 100 percent after that. He'd stayed with the still-sealed bags of anthrax until hazmat had arrived.

They'd been the ones to discover that the bags contained flour, not anthrax.

Apparently Dylan's seemingly endless supply had had an end.

Selena nodded.

"Well, more of 'filled in some blanks.' You know the creepy surveillance room? Apparently he was the one forced to install the cameras at the inn when we were out in the field and then his job was to watch them to see if there was anything Dylan could use to stay ahead of us. He was told if he didn't do it then it was the same as killing his mother and brother. Pretty heavy for a fifteen-year-old who's never really seen violence."

"That'd be pretty heavy to me, too," Noah commented. Both women agreed.

Then Carly was all about the threads she'd been trying to weave together since they found the chair in the basement.

"Has David woken up yet?"

Selena clapped her hands, just as Carly had done the day before in excitement at remembering something.

"I meant for this to be my first bit of news to you but I got sidetracked by the cookies! Not only did David Lapp wake up, he became one of my favorite heroes." Noah had finished making the coffee and came around the breakfast bar and took the seat next to Carly, also curious. Noah had missed out on a lot of what happened since he'd been with Carly from the moment the ambulance took her from the barn.

"Turns out he met Talia in the city when he had to go in to get supplies for his father. He said it was *lightning*. Love at first sight. When he found out she was trapped in an abusive relationship with an older man who was clearly obsessed with her, he brought her to his family's house and hid her the best he could. *But* when his father confronted him about how sketchy he'd been acting, he was afraid if he told the truth that word would spread and Rodney would find her."

"So he let himself be kicked out of the community to keep her secret," Noah said, already impressed by David's compassion.

She nodded.

"Yep. She gave him the money to help rent the house and stayed there with him. Their plan was to save more money and leave town, but then Dylan grabbed him. David said he woke up in his own basement and in front of a very angry Rodney Lee." A flash of anger burned through Selena's words. "He effectively tortured David, trying to find out where Talia had gone. But that boy refused to give her up. Then, when Rodney left, that's when Dylan came back for him and took him out to the Ferry estate where he treated him like a prisoner and motivation for Willa to help Dylan. He also said that, he wasn't sure, but he thought Dylan kept feeding Rodney fake information about seeing or hearing of David around town. That's why we think Rodney stayed after he disappeared."

Carly wrapped her hand around the coffee mug. When she took a sip, Noah couldn't help but smile a little.

"Where was Talia? Was she not at David's house?"

"Get this. David was so worried about her that they came up with a safe place for her to go if she ever felt unsafe or something happened. A place that she'd be safe until he could come get her. She went there when she saw Rodney in town and had no idea David had been taken. Once she realized something was wrong, David was already missing, so she went back to wait to see if he showed up. Guess where that safe place was?"

Selena leaned in and actually cackled.

Noah was leaning in, too.

"Where?" he asked, completely invested.

"We have *no* idea."

"What?" Carly asked around a mouthful of coffee.

Selena laughed and straightened.

"Once the news broke yesterday afternoon, Talia Jones showed up at the foot of David's hospital bed late last night and hasn't left since. Aria said that Talia was the first person David saw when he woke up. They wouldn't tell us where she'd been and since the case is closed, we didn't care to keep asking." She touched her chest and made a dramatic sigh. "I know I don't know them but, damn, what a love story. I hope they make it."

Noah's father, who had asked Gina to take him to the hospital to personally thank Carly and the team, had already given him a piece of gossip that he didn't think the other two knew yet. Apparently, during their limited interactions in his captivity, David had told his mother that he loved Talia with all of his heart and planned to marry her when it was all over. Willa had in turn told her husband who had, in turn, reached out to Noah's father.

"He asked me advice on how to deal with a child who chooses to leave," his father had said.

"And what did you say?"

His father, a devout man who was as quiet as he was stubborn, had softened. It hadn't been a lot, but enough to notice.

"I told him he should learn to accept that we all walk our own paths and that's not always a bad thing. Just different."

He'd clapped Noah on the shoulder after that and then Gina had taken him home.

It wasn't a brand-new beginning for them, but it wasn't an ending, either.

Now Carly turned to him.

"Do you think he'll try to go back since he left under extraordinary circumstances?"

Noah was quick to answer.

"No. I think he's going to stick with his lightning, his love."

At that, she smiled.

The rest of the conversation bounced back and forth between the more technical details of what happened next and, Carly cringed as she said it, paperwork. They ate cookies and welcomed Gina. She was the beginning of a long line of guests, including the entire TCD team and Noah's staff. The morning turned to afternoon and, for the first time since he owned the farm, the house was filled with talking, laughter and actual cheer.

Christmas day at his house came and went. Those who couldn't get out to their families video-chatted and made promises to see them the next day, while Alana and Opaline joined in through FaceTime.

Before dessert was ready, Noah felt it was time to finally tell Carly the truth.

And ask her a question he never thought he'd ask anyone.

After making sure she felt up for it, he drove her to a part of the property she hadn't yet seen.

"Too much holiday spirit and needed a break?" she teased him after he set her up on the tailgate of the truck.

He laughed and sat next to her.

"It was just enough to show me I wouldn't mind something like this every year."

Carly smiled.

She was beautiful.

"I have to admit, it's turning me around on the whole holiday season."

He wanted to keep bantering with her, but knew it was now or never.

Noah let every wall he had down and finally told someone the truth.

"It was a yellow house."

"A yellow house?" Her tone had gone soft. She'd caught on to the change in him. He'd known her a week and she could read him better than anyone he knew.

He nodded and pointed in the distance. There was nothing but open field and sky.

"There used to be a yellow house there, owned by the

Tucketts, until it burned down about ten years ago. It was originally for the full-time staff but had been empty for twenty years before that. The first time I saw it, I was twelve. I was crossing through the farm to go home after sneaking out to fish." He let out a breath and shook his head, still unable to understand why the feeling that had followed next had happened. "One second I was a kid without any doubts in my future and then, the moment after I saw that house, everything changed. I wanted more. I wanted different.

"Then I left on Rumspringa and never went back home," he continued. "I was lucky enough to find a place on the farm to work and sleep and try to figure out what it was that I *did* want. I even thought about leaving for good, went on a few trips to see how I felt about it, but nothing ever struck me like when I first saw that yellow house."

Noah met her gaze.

"The yellow house is why I left, and then why I stayed. I don't know if it makes sense to anyone but me but, when I'm sure about something, I think of that house and know with all of my heart it's true. For David Lapp, it was lightning, for me it was a sunflower-yellow farmhouse, and up until last week I hadn't thought about that house in a long time. That is until I saw you."

Like the epiphany he'd had when he was twelve, what he did might not have made sense to anyone else, but that wasn't going to stop him.

He'd lived a guarded, quiet life.

Now he was ready to open it up and be loud with someone.

Carly, if she'd have him.

Noah pulled a thread of silver tinsel that he'd spent a maddening amount of time fashioning into the shape of a ring from his pocket. Then he got down on his knee in front of her, the perfect height to ask for her hand.

"I didn't have time to get a ring, but I sure had enough time to know I want to be with you, Carly. Whether that's here, there or both, I'd love it if you'd marry me."

Carly, who hadn't moved a muscle since he'd started talking, surprised him.

She laughed.

"You really do go all out, don't you? I tell you how sad I get about Christmas and here you are working overtime to make it my favorite holiday yet." She extended her fingers and eyed his makeshift ring. "Slip that on and then come up here so I can kiss you." She smiled wide. "I'd bend over but my back still hurts from getting shot."

Noah laughed.

"Yes, ma'am."

CARLY WAS IN her chair less than thirty seconds before Alana was in the briefing room, champagne in hand and barely contained glee written across her face.

"The case of the anthrax in Amish country is officially closed," she stated, her voice carrying along their make-shift dining table. It was a week later and dinner was on her, as it always was after a case well-handled. She extended her drink out before taking her own seat. "The bad guy will be in prison for a *very* long time and, thanks to some Grade-A accounting, we even tracked down Rodney's connections so we can make sure they never deal again. So here's to you, here's to us and here's to the future Noah Welsh!"

Carly burst out laughing just as the rest of the team around the table joined in.

"Does that mean he's taking my name?" Carly asked.

"Hey, I'm just saying, you were a rockstar this case,"

Alana added. "I mean, after all of that, *I'm* considering taking your name."

Their laughter dissolved into eating and normal chatter. Carly thumbed her new engagement ring with a sense of awe. Not at being asked to marry Noah Miller, and not at accepting without hesitation, but because no one on the team had given her any guff about it.

"I don't know," Selena had said when she'd later asked her why Selena hadn't made more of a big deal about it. "You two just kind of feel right."

Carly agreed.

It was fast. It was maybe impulsive. But it felt *right*.

Even after they'd slowed down and talked over what they both wanted at length that night in bed.

"I love my job" had been said by both, just as "I love my home" had been. Instead of that creating a problem, it had only strengthened their conviction that they would work out.

They agreed that they would split their time between Traverse City and Potter's Creek, growing roots in a straight line between the two points.

The details past that? They'd figure them out.

Together.

"You're over there smiling like a fool," Selena whispered at her ear. Carly jumped.

"And you're creeping like you're the mayor of Creep Town," she said back, swatting at her.

Selena laughed. It drew Axel's attention from his conversation with Max. He'd been looking at Selena a lot recently. If she didn't know better, Carly thought there was some tension there. Then again, maybe that was just what Selena did to some people. Most notably her sister.

That tension was noticeable and had led to many a snarky remark since being back in the same building again.

But Carly wasn't going to pry.

Not now.

Instead she was going to call her best friend a creep, drink some more champagne and think about the certain farmer who would be lying in her bed that weekend.

Not a bad Christmas after all.

* * * * *

TEXAS LAW

BARB HAN

All my love to Brandon, Jacob and Tori,
the three great loves of my life.

To Babe, my hero, for being my best friend,
my greatest love and my place to call home.

I love you all with everything that I am.

Chapter One

Sheriff Colton O'Connor took a sip of coffee and gripped the steering wheel of his SUV. Thunder boomed and rain came down in sheets. Seeing much past the front bumper was basically impossible. He'd had three stranded vehicle calls already—one of those cars had been actually submerged—and the worst of this spring thunderstorm hadn't happened yet. The storm wreaking havoc on the small town of Katy Gulch, Texas, was just getting started.

On top of everything, Colton's babysitter had quit last night. Miss Marla's niece had been in a car crash in Austin and needed her aunt to care for her during her recovery. The spry sixty-five-year-old was the only living relative of the girl, who was a student at the University of Texas at Austin.

Colton pinched the bridge of his nose to stem the thundering headache working up behind his eyelids. His mother was pinch-hitting with his twin boys, Silas and Sebastian, but she was still reeling from the loss of her husband, as was Colton and the rest of the family.

A recent kidnapping attempt had dredged up the unsolved, decades-old mystery of his sister's abduction, and his father was murdered after deciding to take it upon himself to take up the investigation on his own again. Colton was just getting started untangling his father's murder.

Considering all that was going on at the ranch, Colton didn't want to add to his mother's stress. As much as his one-year-olds were angels, taking care of little ones with more energy than brain development was a lot for anyone to handle. His mother had enough on her plate already, but she'd convinced him the distraction would be good for her.

And now a storm threatened to turn the town upside down with tornadoes and flash floods.

So, no, Colton didn't feel right about leaving his mother to care for his children, although Margaret O'Connor was strong, one of the toughest women he'd ever met.

He took another sip of coffee and nearly spit it out. It was cold. Bitter. The convenience-store kind that he was certain had been made hours ago and left to burn. That tacky, unpleasant taste stuck to the roof of his mouth.

This might be a good time to stop by the ranch to check on his mother and the twins. He could get a decent cup of coffee there and he wanted to check on his boys. His stomach growled. A reminder that he'd been working emergencies most of the night and had skipped dinner. He always brought food with him on nights like these, but he could save it for later. It was getting late.

Colton banked a U-turn at the corner of Misty Creek and Apple Blossom Drive, and then headed toward the ranch. He hadn't made it a block when he got the next call. The distinct voice belonging to his secretary, Gert Francis, came through the radio.

"What do you have for me?" He pulled his vehicle onto the side of the road. At least there were no cars on the streets. He hoped folks listened to the emergency alerts and stayed put.

"A call just came in from Mrs. Dillon. Flood waters are rising near the river. She's evacuating. Her concern is about a vagrant who has been sleeping in her old RV. She doesn't want the person to be caught unaware if the water keeps rising, and she's scared to disturb whoever it is on her own." Mrs. Dillon, widowed last year at the age of seventy-eight, had a son in Little Rock who'd been trying to convince her to move closer to him. She had refused. Katy Gulch was home.

Colton always made a point of stopping by her place on his way home to check on one of his favorite residents. It was the happiest part of his job, the fact that he kept all the residents in his town and county safe. He took great pride in his work and had a special place in his heart for the senior residents in his community.

He was a rancher by birth and a sheriff by choice. Both jobs had ingrained in him a commitment to help others, along with a healthy respect for Mother Nature.

Colton heaved a sigh. Thinking about ranching brought him back to his family's situation. With his father, the patriarch of Katy Bull Ranch, now gone, Colton and his brothers had some hard decisions to make about keeping their legacy running.

"Let Mrs. Dillon know I'm on my way." Actually, there was no reason he couldn't call her himself. "Never mind, Gert. I've got her number right here. I've been meaning to ask her how she's been getting around after foot surgery last week."

"Will do, Sheriff." There was so much pride in her voice. She'd always been vocal about how much she appreciated the fact he looked after the town's residents. The last sheriff hadn't been so diligent. Gert had made her opinion known about him, as well.

"After I make this call, I need to check out for a little while to stop by the ranch and see about things there," he informed her.

"Sounds like a plan, sir." More of that admiration came through the line.

Colton hoped he could live up to it.

"Be safe out there," Gert warned.

"You know I will. I better ring her now." Colton ended the call. Using Bluetooth technology, he called Mrs. Dillon. She picked up on the first ring.

"I hear you have a new tenant in the RV. I'm on my way over." Colton didn't need to identify himself. He was pretty certain Mrs. Dillon had his cell number on speed dial. He didn't mind. If a quick call to him or Gert could give her peace of mind, inconvenience was a small price to pay.

"Thank you for checking it out for me. This one showed up three nights ago, I think." Concern came through in Mrs. Dillon's voice. "I know it's a woman because MaryBeth's dog kept barking and I heard her tell him to shush."

"Well, if she stays any longer you'll have to start charging rent," he teased, trying to lighten the mood.

The older woman's heart was as big as the great state they lived in.

"If I started doing that, I'd end up a rich lady. Then all the young bachelors would come to town to court me. We can't have that, can we?" Her smile came through in her voice.

"No, ma'am. We sure can't."

"I hope she's okay." She said on a sigh. "Not a peep from her. I wouldn't have heard her at all if it hadn't been for MaryBeth's dog." Mrs. Dillon clucked her tongue in disapproval. Normally, her neighbor's dog was a thorn in her side. This time, Cooper seemed to have served a purpose.

"Sounds like we have a quiet one on our hands. I'll perform a wellness check and make sure she gets out before the water rises."

"I always complained to my husband that he put the parking pad to the RV way too close to the water's edge. But do you think he listened?" Her tone was half-teasing, half-wistful. Mr. and Mrs. Dillon had been high school sweethearts and had, much like Colton's parents, beaten the odds of divorce and gone the distance. The Dillons had been schoolteachers who'd spent their summers touring the country in their RV. Anyone who knew them could see how much they loved each other. They were almost obnoxiously adorable, much like his own parents had been.

Losing Mr. Dillon had to have been the hardest thing she'd gone through. Colton's heart went out to her.

"I just didn't want her to be caught off guard. If this storm is as bad as they say it's going to be, the RV will be flooded again." She heaved a concerned-sounding sigh. "I probably should've gotten rid of that thing ten years ago after the first time it flooded. But Mr. Dillon loved his camping so he could throw out a line first thing with his morning coffee." Her voice was nothing but melancholy now at the memory.

"He was one of the best fishermen in the county." Colton swerved to miss a puddle on the road that was forming a small lake. Flash flooding was a real problem in the spring. This storm was just beginning to dish out its wrath. Mother Nature had a temper and it was becoming apparent she was gearing up to show them just how angry she could become.

"That he was," she agreed.

"Who is driving you to Little Rock?" He changed the subject, hoping to redirect her from a conversation that would bring back the pain of losing her husband. After seeing the look on his mother's face at hearing the news her husband was dead, Colton didn't want to cause that kind of hurt for anyone, certainly not for someone as kind as Mrs. Dillon. His second grade teacher deserved more brightness in her day, and especially after putting up with him and his brothers when they were young. They'd been good kids by most standards. And yet they'd also been a handful. After having twins, Colton was more aware of the responsibility and sacrifice that came with the parenting job.

"Netty. You know her from my knitting club. She's heading that way to stay with her daughter, so I'm hitching a ride with her." He could almost see the twinkle in Mrs. Dillon's eye when she said the word *hitched*.

"Tell Netty to drive safe." He could barely see in the driving rain and needed to close the call in order to concentrate on the road ahead.

"I will do it, Sheriff. Thank you for checking on my

tenant." He could envision her making air quotes when she said the last word.

"You're welcome. In fact, I'll head to your house now." After exchanging goodbyes, he ended the call.

The rain was so thick he could barely see the end of his vehicle now, let alone the road. The weather had definitely turned in the last couple of minutes since he'd started the conversation.

It was a miracle he could see at all. His headlights were almost useless. If he didn't know the area so well, he'd pull over and wait it out. These kinds of storms usually came in waves. Radar didn't look promising on this one.

As he turned right onto Mrs. Dillon's street, a flash of lightning streaked across the sky, and a dark object cut in front of him so suddenly he couldn't stop himself from tapping it with his service vehicle.

A *thunk* sounded and then a squeal. The noise was quickly drowned out by the driving rain.

Colton cursed his luck, wondering if he'd been struck by debris. He hopped out of his vehicle to check. Rain pelted his face. He pulled up his collar and shivered against the cold front, praying whatever he'd hit wasn't an animal. Deer sometimes cut through town. At least he was on his way to the ranch. He could scoop it up, put it in the back and see what he could do about nursing it back to health.

Pulling his flashlight from his belt, he shined it around the area. It was next to impossible to see. Hell, he could barely see his hand in front of his face for the rain.

Squinting, he caught sight of something moving a

few feet from his passenger-side bumper. Hell's bells.
He hadn't nicked an animal at all…it was a person.

Colton dashed to the victim. He took a knee beside
the woman, who was curled in a tight ball. Her dark
clothing covered her from nearly head to toe. She was
drenched and lying in a puddle.

"My name is Colton O'Connor. I'm the sheriff and
I'm here to help." He knew better than to touch her in
case she was injured.

"I'm okay. You can go." He didn't recognize the
voice, but then it was next to impossible to hear over
the sounds of the rain. She kept her face turned in the
opposite direction, away from him.

Considering she seemed anxious to not show her
face to him, he wondered if she had something to hide.

"I'm not going anywhere until I know you're okay.
And that means being able to stand up and walk away
from here on your own," he said, figuring she might as
well know where he stood.

"I already said that I'm okay. Go away," the woman
shouted, and he heard her loud and clear this time. Her
voice was somewhat familiar and yet he couldn't place
it.

He dashed toward his vehicle and retrieved an umbrella. It wouldn't do much good against the torrent.
Water was building up on the sidewalk and gushing
over faster than the gutter could handle it. But it was
something and might help with some of the onslaught.

And he believed that right up until he opened the
umbrella and it nearly shot out of his hands. A gust of
wind forced him to fight to hold on to it and keep it

steady over the victim. Finally, it was doing a good job offering some shelter from the rain.

"Like I said, I need to see that you can walk away from here on your own and answer a few questions. I'm the one who hit you and there's no way I'm leaving. What's your name?" He bent down lower so she could hear without him shouting at her.

She didn't answer and that sent up more warning flares. Anyone could see she was injured. She'd taken a pretty hard hit. She might be in shock or maybe suffering head trauma. From his position, it was impossible to see if she was bleeding, and because of the way she'd fallen, he couldn't rule out a broken arm or leg.

Colton stood up and walked around to where she was facing. He dropped down on his knees to get a better look. Rain was everywhere—his eyes, his ears, his face. He shook his head, trying to shake off the flood.

"I'm calling an ambulance. I'm going to get some help." He strained to see her face, still unable to reach back to his memory and find a name that matched the voice. In a small town like Katy Gulch, Colton knew most everyone, which meant she was someone who'd passed through town.

She lifted her arm to wave him away.

"No can do. Sorry." He tilted his mouth toward the radio clipped to his shoulder. With his free hand, he pressed the talk button. "Gert, can you read me?"

There was a moment of crackling. He feared he might not be able to hear her response. And yet going to his SUV wasn't an option. He didn't want to leave the woman alone in the street in the soaking rain again.

She looked like she needed a hand-up and he had no plans to leave her.

With the wind, his umbrella was doing very little, but it was something.

The woman, who had been curled up on her side, shielding her face, pushed up to sit. "See, I'm okay. I'm not hurt. I just need a minute to catch my breath and I'll be fine."

Colton wasn't convinced she was able to think clearly. Often after experiencing trauma, it took a while for the brain to catch up. That was how shock worked. She might not even realize it.

"What's your name?" he asked again, trying to assess her mental state.

She shook her head, which either meant she didn't want to disclose it or she couldn't remember. Neither was a good sign.

Since she hadn't answered his question, there was no choice but to have her cleared medically before he could let her go, even if she could walk away on her own, which he highly doubted at the moment.

"I'm just going to get somebody here to take a look at you, and if everything's okay, you'll be cleared in no time. In the meantime, you can wait inside my vehicle and get out of this weather." He'd noticed that she'd started shivering.

He slipped out of his rain jacket and placed it over her shoulders.

The woman looked up at him and their gazes locked. His heart stirred and his breath caught.

"Makena?"

WATER WAS EVERYWHERE, flooding Makena Eden's eyes and ears. Rain hit her face, stinging like fire-ant bites. She blinked up and stared into the eyes of the last man she'd expected to see again—Colton O'Connor.

Still reeling from taking a wrong turn into the road and being clipped by his sport utility, she felt around on her hip.

Ouch. That hurt. She could already feel her side bruising. Mentally, she tried to dust herself off and stand up. Her hip, however, had other plans, so she sat there, trying to ride out the pain.

"I just need a minute." There was no other option but to get up and fake being well. She had no job, no medical insurance and no money. And she couldn't afford to let her identity get out, especially not on a peace officer's radio. Then there was the other shock, the fact that Colton was kneeling down in front of her. How long had it been?

"Not so fast." Colton's eyebrow shot up and he seemed unconvinced. He was one of the most devastatingly handsome men she'd ever met, and her body picked that moment to react to him *and* remind her. This was turning out to be one red-letter day stacked on the back end of months of agony. One she'd survived by hiding and sliding under the radar.

"I don't want you to try to move. We need to get you checked out first." He snapped into action, tilting his chin toward his left shoulder to speak into his radio. She could hear him requesting an ambulance. For a split second, she wondered if she could run away and get far enough out of sight for him to forget this whole situation. *Wishful thinking.* It was so not good that he knew her personally. Granted, he knew her before she'd become Mrs. River Myers, but still…

Panic squeezed her lungs as she tried to breathe through the building anxiety. She couldn't let her name go down on record. She couldn't have anything that would identify her over the radio.

"I promise that I'm not broken. I'm shaken up." Before she could say anything else, he put a hand up to stop her.

Water was dripping everywhere, and yet looking into those cobalt blue eyes sent her flashing back to her sophomore year of college. The two of them had been randomly hooked up as partners in biology lab. Even at nineteen years old, it was easy to see Colton was going to be strong and muscled when he finally filled out.

Now, just seeing him released a dozen butterflies in her chest along with a free-falling sensation she hadn't felt since college. She could stare into his eyes for days. He had a face of hard angles and planes. Full lips covered perfectly straight, white teeth.

Looking at him was like staring at one of those billboard models. The man was tall. Six feet four inches of solid steel and ripped muscle. The only reason she noticed was the survival need at its most basic, she told herself. She was in trouble and had to assess whether or not Colton could defend her.

Icy fingers gripped her spine as she thought about the past, about *her* past. About *River.* Stand still long enough and it would catch up to her. He *would* find her.

Colton might look good. Better than good, but she wouldn't let her mind go there for long. There were two things that would keep her from the attraction she felt, other than the obvious fact they'd had one class and a flirtation that hadn't gone anywhere. A badge and a gun.

Chapter Two

Makena needed to convince Colton that she wasn't injured so she could get far away from him and Katy Gulch. Coming here had turned out to be a huge mistake—one that could get her killed.

How had she not remembered this was his hometown?

Being on the road for months on end had a way of mixing up weeks. Towns were starting to run together, too. They fell into one of two categories, big and small.

Dallas, Houston and Austin fit into the big-city category. They all had basically the same chain restaurants if a slightly differing view on life. Small towns, on the other hand, seemed to share a few characteristics. In those, she was beginning to realize, it was a little harder to go unnoticed.

Getting seen was bad for her longevity.

The other thing she'd noticed about small towns in her home state of Texas was the food. Some of the best cooking came from diners and mom-and-pop shops. Since she'd run out of money, she'd been forced to live on other people's generosity.

Makena hadn't eaten a real meal in the past three

days. She'd sustained herself on scraps. The owner of the RV where she'd been staying had been kind enough to leave a few supplies and leftovers a couple of days ago, and Makena had stretched them out to make them last. Hunger had caught up to her, forcing her to seek out food.

The fact that the owner knew Makena was staying on her property *and* Makena had remained there anyway signaled just how much she'd been slipping lately. Starvation had a way of breeding desperation. Not to mention it had been so very long since she'd slept on a real bed in a real room or in a real house that she could scarcely remember how it felt. The RV was the closest she'd come and she hadn't wanted to give it up.

Makena was drenched. She shivered despite having the sheriff's windbreaker wrapped around her. She could sit there and be stubborn and cold. Or, she could get Colton's help inside the SUV and wring herself out. And at least maybe have him turn the heat on.

"If you help me up, I can make it to your vehicle," she said to him.

Colton's eyebrow shot up. "You sure it's a good idea to move? I didn't realize how badly you were hurt when I offered before."

"I'm so cold my teeth are chattering. You look pretty miserable. There's no reason for me to sit here in a puddle when I can be warm inside your vehicle." She had to practically shout to be heard. She put her hands up in the surrender position, palms up. "All I need is a hand up and maybe a little help walking."

He opened his mouth to protest.

"Sitting out here, I may end up with the death of

cold." She realized she was going to have to give him a little bit more than that. "I'm pretty sure that I have a nasty bruise working up on my left hip. It was stupid of me to run into the street. I didn't even see you."

"You must've darted out from in between the parked vehicles right when I turned." There was so much torment in his voice now.

"Sorry. I was just trying to stay out of the rain but I'm okay. Really." It wasn't a total lie. Mostly, a half-truth. Being dishonest pained Makena. She hated that she'd become the kind of person who had to cover her tracks like a criminal.

"What are you doing out on a night like this?" he asked.

"I-um…was trying to get back to my rental over by the river." The way she stammered was giving her away based on the look on his face.

He nodded as he studied her, but she could see that he wasn't convinced.

"My name is Makena. You already know that. It's Wednesday. At least, I think it is."

"Do you know where you are right now?" The worry lines on his forehead were easing up.

"Katy Gulch, Texas," she said. "And I've been out of work for a little while. That's the reason I've lost track of the days of the week."

It was her turn to look carefully at him.

"What do you think?" she asked. "Did I pass?"

Colton surveyed her for a long moment. Lightning raced sideways across the sky and thunder boomed.

"Lean on me and let me do the heavy lifting." He put his arm out.

"Deal." She grabbed hold of his arm, ignoring the electrical impulses vibrating up her arm from contact. This wasn't the time for an inappropriate attraction and especially not with a man who had a gun and a badge on his hip. She'd been there. Done that. And had the emotional scars to prove it.

Not taking Colton's help was out of the question. She had no car. No money. No choices.

Makena held onto his arm for dear life. As soon as she was pulled up to her feet, her left leg gave out under the pain from her hip.

"Whoa there." Colton's strong arms wrapped around her, and the next thing she knew he'd picked her up. He carried her over to his SUV and managed to open the passenger door and help her inside.

She eased onto the seat and immediately felt around for the adjuster lever. Her fingers landed on the control and she adjusted her seat back, easing some of the pressure from her sitting bones. Her hip rewarded her by lightening up on some of the pain.

Colton opened the back hatch, closed it and was in the driver's seat a few seconds later.

He then leaned over and tucked a warm blanket around her. "Is that better?"

"Much." She said the word on a sigh, releasing the breath she'd been holding.

"Be honest. How badly does it hurt?" he asked, looking at her with those cobalt blues.

"On a scale of one to ten? I'd say this has to be a solid sixteen."

The engine was still humming and at least she'd stopped shivering. She could also finally hear him over the roar of the weather, even though it seemed the rain was driving down even harder than a few minutes ago.

"I couldn't hear a word Gert said earlier." He flashed his eyes at her. "Gert is my secretary in case you hadn't sorted it out for yourself. And she's a lot more than that. She's more like my right arm. I'm the sheriff."

She glanced down at the word *SHERIFF* written in bold yellow letters running down her left sleeve. Even if he hadn't told her earlier, she would've figured it out. With a small smile, she said, "I put that together for myself."

"Is your car around here somewhere? I can call a tow."

"No." Talking about herself wasn't good. The less information she gave, the better. She hoped he would just drop the subject, let her warm up and then let her get back to her temporary shelter in the RV.

Her stomach growled, and surprisingly, it could be heard over the thunder boom outside.

"There's someone I need to check on. Are you hungry?" Colton asked.

"Yes. I didn't get a chance to eat dinner yet." She followed his gaze to the clock on the dashboard. It read 8:30 p.m.

With his left hand, he tucked his chin to his left shoulder and hit some type of button. "Gert, can you read me?"

Crackling noises came through the radio. And then a voice.

"Copy that, Sheriff. Loud and clear." The woman sounded older, mid-sixties if Makena had to guess.

"I need an ambulance on the corner of Misty Creek

and Apple Blossom. Stat. A pedestrian was struck by my vehicle and needs immediate medical attention. She is alert and communicative, with a possible injury to her left hip. She's lucid, but a concussion can't be ruled out," he said.

"Roger that, Sheriff. You must not have heard me earlier. There's flooding on several roads. Both of my EMTs are on calls and even if they weren't, the streets aren't clear. No one can get to you for at least the next hour."

Relief washed over Makena. However, Colton didn't look thrilled.

"Roger that." He blew out a frustrated-sounding breath. "I'll drive the victim to the hospital myself."

"County road isn't clear. There's been a lot of flooding. I don't advise making that trip unless it's life-threatening," Gert said.

Flash floods in Texas were nothing to take lightly. They were the leading cause of weather-related deaths in the state.

"We probably need to close the road since the water's rising," she continued.

Colton smacked his flat palm against the steering wheel. "Roger that."

"As soon as I warm up, you can drop me off. I think my hip just needs a little chance to rest." Embarrassingly enough, her stomach picked that moment to gurgle and growl again.

Colton's gaze dropped to her stomach as he reached under the center console of his SUV and pulled something around. A lunchbox?

He unzipped the black box and produced what looked

like a sandwich. He opened the Ziploc bag and held it out toward her. "I knew I'd be working late tonight with the storms. So I made extra. You're welcome to this one."

When she didn't immediately reach for the offering, he locked gazes with her. "Go ahead. Take it. I have more."

"I really can't take all your food." Her mouth was practically watering.

"It's no big deal. I can always swing by my house and get more. It's on the way to my office, not far from here."

"Are you sure about that, Colton?" The last thing she wanted to do was take his food and leave him with nothing. The sandwich looked good, though. And she was pretty certain she'd started drooling.

"It's fine," he reassured her with that silky masculine voice that trailed all over her, warming her better than any blanket could.

He urged her to take it, so she did.

"Thank you." She wasted no time demolishing the sandwich. Ham. Delicious.

He barely looked away from the screen on the laptop mounted inside his vehicle as he handed her an apple next.

This time, she didn't argue. Instead, she polished off the fruit in a matter of seconds while he studied the map on the screen. Just as she wrapped the remains of the apple in the paper towel he'd given her, he pulled out a thermos and handed her a spoon.

"Soup," was all he said.

Angel was all she thought.

COLTON ENTERED THE hospital's location into his computer. The screen showed red triangles with exclamation points in the center of them on more roads than not, indicating flooding or hazardous road conditions. Gert was a lifeline, going well above and beyond typical secretary duties. She'd become Colton's right arm and he had no idea what he'd do without her.

Makena needed medical attention. That part was obvious. The tricky part was going to be getting her looked at. He was still trying to wrap his mind around the fact Makena Eden was sitting in his SUV.

Talk about a blast from the past and a missed opportunity. But he couldn't think about that right now when she was injured. At least she was eating. That had to be a good sign.

When she'd tried to stand, she'd gone down pretty fast and hard. She'd winced in pain and he'd scooped her up and brought her to his vehicle. He knew better than to move an injured person. In this case, however, there was no choice.

The victim was alert and cognizant of what was going on. A quick visual scan of her body revealed nothing obviously broken. No bones were sticking out. She complained about her hip and he figured there could be something there. At the very least, she needed an X-ray.

Since getting to the county hospital looked impossible at least in the short run and his apartment was close by, he decided taking her there might be for the best until the roads cleared. He could get her out of his uncomfortable vehicle and onto a soft couch.

Normally, he wouldn't take a stranger to his home,

but this was Makena. And even though he hadn't seen
her in forever, she'd been special to him at one time.

He still needed to check on the RV for Mrs. Dillon…
and then it dawned on him. Was Makena the 'tenant'
the widow had been talking about earlier?

"Are you staying in town?" he asked, hoping to get
her to volunteer the information. It was possible that
she'd fallen on hard times and needed a place to hang
her head for a couple of nights.

"I've been staying in a friend's RV," she said. So, she
was the 'tenant' Mrs. Dillon mentioned.

It was good seeing Makena again. At five feet five
inches, she had a body made for sinning, underneath
a thick head of black hair. He remembered how shiny
and wavy her hair used to be. Even soaked with water,
it didn't look much different now.

She had the most honest set of pale blue eyes—eyes
the color of the sky on an early summer morning. She
had the kind of eyes that he could stare into all day. It
had been like that before, too.

But that was a long time ago. And despite the lightning bolt that had struck him square in the chest when
she turned to face him, this relationship was purely
professional.

Colton wasn't in the market to replace his wife, Rebecca, anytime soon. He was still reeling from the loss
almost year later. He bit back a remark on the irony of
running into someone he'd had a crush on in college
but not enough confidence to ask out. He'd been with
Makena for all of fifteen or twenty minutes now and
the surge of attraction he'd felt before had returned with

full force, much like the out-of-control thunderstorm bearing down on them.

He refocused. His medical experience amounted to knowing how to perform CPR and that was about it.

Even soaked to the bone, Makena was still stunning—just as stunning as he remembered from twelve years ago in biology lab.

However, it was troublesome just how quickly she'd munched down on the sandwich and apple that he'd given her. She'd practically mewled with pleasure when she'd taken the first sip of soup, which she'd destroyed just as quickly.

Colton glanced at the third finger on her left hand. There was no ring and no tan line. For reasons he couldn't explain, given the fact he hadn't seen Makena in years, relief washed over him and more of that inconvenient attraction surged.

No ring, no husband.

It didn't exactly mean she was single. He told himself the reason he wanted to know was for the investigation. Here she'd shown up in town out of nowhere. She was staying in an RV and, based on the brightness in her eyes, he was certain she was sober. He hadn't expected her to be doing drugs or drinking. However, his job had trained him to look for those reasons first when dealing with uncharacteristic behavior.

Darting across the road without looking, in the middle of one of the worst thunderstorms so far this year, definitely qualified as uncharacteristic. Now that he'd determined she fell into that camp without a simple explanation, it was time to investigate what she was really doing in town and why.

Again, the questions he was about to ask were all for the sake of the investigation, he told himself, despite a little voice in the back of his head calling him out on the lie.

For now, he was able to quiet that annoyance.

Chapter Three

In the dome light, Colton could see that Makena's face was sheet-white and her lips were purple. Color was slowly beginning to return to her creamy cheeks. He took that as a good sign she was starting to warm up and was in overall good health.

"I thought you were in school to study business so you could come back and work on your family's ranch." She turned the tables.

"I realized midway through my degree that my heart was not in business. I switched to criminal justice and never looked back." Colton figured it couldn't hurt to give a little information about himself considering she looked frightened of him and everything else. As much as he didn't like the idea, she might be on the run to something or *from* something. Either way, he planned to get to the bottom of it and give her a hand up. "How about you? Did you stay an education major?"

"I stayed in my field," she said.

He would've thought that he'd just asked for her social security number and her bank passwords for the reaction he got. She crossed her ankles and then her arms. She hugged her elbows tightly against her chest.

To say she'd just closed up was a lot like saying dogs liked table scraps over dry food.

"Did I say something wrong?" Colton may as well put it out on the table. He didn't like the idea of stepping on a land mine, and the response he'd gotten from her was like a sucker punch that he didn't want to take twice.

"No. You d-didn't say anything wrong. You j-just caught me off guard." The way she stammered over every other word told him that she wasn't being completely honest. It also made him feel like she was afraid of him, which was strange. Innocent people might get nervous around law enforcement, but straight-up scared? He wasn't used to that with victims.

"Okay. We better get on the road and out of this weather. I promised one of our elderly residents that I would stop by and check on her property. The rain isn't letting up and we're not going too far from here. Her home is nearby. Mind if we—"

"It's okay. You can just let me out. I don't want to get in the way of you doing your job." Panic caused her voice to shake. Colton didn't want to read too much into her reaction.

"Makena, I hit you with my SUV and the fact is going to bother me to no end until I make absolute certain that you're okay. Check that. I want you to be better than okay. In fact, I'd like to help you out if I can, no matter what you need." He meant those words.

Makena blew out a slow breath. "I'm sorry. You've been nothing but kind. I wasn't trying to put you off. Honest. I'm just shaken up and a little thrown off balance." She turned to look at him, and those clear blue eyes pierced right through him. "Don't take any of this the wrong way. It's just been…" she seemed to be searching for the right words "…a really long time since I've had anyone help me."

Well, he sure as hell hoped she didn't plan on stopping there. If anything, he wanted to know more about her. He chalked it up to nostalgia and the feelings he'd experienced when he was nineteen, the minute he sat beside her in the bio lab, too chicken to pluck up the courage to ask her out.

He'd waited for weeks to see if she felt the same attraction. She was shy back then and he was even shyer. When he finally found his courage, a kid had beaten him to the punch. Dane Kilroy had moved in.

Colton couldn't say he'd ever had the best timing when it came to him and the opposite sex. Missed opportunity had him wanting to help her now. Or maybe it was that lost look in her eyes that appealed to a place deep inside him.

He knew what it was to be broken. His family had experienced a horrific tragedy before he was born. One that had left an echo so strong it could still be heard to this day.

A decades-old kidnapping had impacted the O'Connor family so deeply that they could never be the same again. The hole could never be filled after his six-month-old sister was abducted.

Colton figured the best place to start with Makena was the basics. "Is your last name still Eden?"

He opened up a file report on his laptop.

"What are you doing?" She seemed shocked.

"Filing a report." Colton forgot that she was a civilian. She would have no idea about the process of filling out an incident report. "I need to file an accident report."

"No. That's really not necessary. I mean, I didn't get a good look at your car but there didn't seem to be any damage to your bumper. As far as me? I'll be okay in a couple of days. There's really no need to file any type of report. Won't that get you in trouble with your job?"

She was worried about him?

"My job isn't going to be on the line over a freak accident. This is what I do. This is my job, my responsibility."

"What can I say to stop you from filing that report?"

Colton couldn't quite put his finger on what he heard in her tone when she asked the question, but it was enough to send a warning shot through his system.

"Are you in some type of trouble?" he asked.

Part of him wished he could reel those words back in when he heard her gasp. Too late. They were already out there. And consequences be damned, he wanted to know the answer. Maybe he shouldn't have asked the question so directly.

"Colton, this is a bad idea. My hip is hurting right now, but it's going to be fine. There's really no reason to make a huge ordeal out of this. Despite what you said it can't be all that good for your career for you to have a car crash on your record. I can't imagine someone who drives around as part of his job wouldn't be hurt by a report being filed. I promise you, I would tell you if this was a big deal. It's so not."

The old saying, "The lady doth protest too much,"

came to mind. Colton realized what he heard in her voice. Fear.

And there was no way he was going to walk away from that. "Makena, I can't help you if I don't know what's going on. Do you trust me?"

Colton put it out there. As it was, everything about her body language said she'd closed up. There was no way he was getting any information out of her while she sat like that, unwilling to open up. And since the person closest to a woman was the one most likely to hurt her, as angry as that made him, his first thought went to her hiding out from a relationship that had soured.

Domestic disturbances were also among the most dangerous calls for anyone working law enforcement.

"It's really nothing, Colton. We're making too big a deal out of this. I'm just passing through town." She heaved a sigh and pulled the blanket up to her neck. "You asked if I stayed with teaching as my degree and the answer is yes. I did. Until the music program was cut from the school where I worked, and I decided to see if I could make it as a musician on my own."

"Really?"

"I've been traveling across the state playing gigs as often as I can set them up. I don't have a manager and I've been living in an RV without the owner's permission, but I planned to leave a note and some money as soon as I'm able to." He noticed her fingers working the hem of the blanket. "I've fallen on hard times recently and jobs have been in short supply. Really, it's only a matter of time before I get back on my feet."

"Sounds like a hard life and one that's causing you to make tough choices. And the owner knows you've been

staying there. She asked me to make sure you're okay."
Colton nodded his head. Her explanation nearly covered
all the ground of any question he could've thought of.
She'd pretty much wrapped up her lifestyle in a bow
and the reason she would be moving around the state.
But was her story tied up a little too neatly?

He decided to play along for just a minute.

"I thought I remembered seeing you on campus a
million years ago picking at a guitar." He tried not to
be obvious about watching her response.

"You saw me?" The flush to her cheeks was sexy as
hell. She was even more beautiful when she was embarrassed. But that physical beauty was only a small part
of her draw. She was intelligent and funny and talented,
from what he remembered years ago.

He wondered how much of that had changed…how
much she'd changed.

Thunder rumbled and it felt like the sky literally
opened up and dumped buckets of rain on them.

Tornado alarms blared. He owed his former father-
in-law a call. It was impossible to know if there was
an actual tornado or if this was another severe thunderstorm drill. Colton had warned Preston Ellison that
overusing the alarm would lead people to disregard it,
creating a dangerous situation for residents.

Had the mayor listened?

Clearly not. He hadn't listened to his daughter, Rebecca, either. The single father and mayor of Katy
Gulch had overprotected his daughter to the point of
smothering her. She'd rebelled. No shock there.

Down deep, Rebecca had always been a good person.
She and Colton had been best friends since they were

kids and married for less than a year when she'd died. Damned if he didn't miss her to the core some days.

But being with Makena again reminded him why he hadn't married Rebecca straight out of high school.

"ARE YOU COMFORTABLE?" Colton's question felt out of the blue to Makena, but she'd noticed that he'd lost himself in thought for a few minutes as he slogged through the flooded street. This must be his way of rejoining the conversation.

The windshield washers were working double time and had yet to be able to keep up with the onslaught.

"I'm better now that I'm inside your vehicle and we're moving toward safety. Why?" Luckily, the height of the SUV kept the undercarriage of the vehicle above water. The engine sat high enough on the chassis not to flood.

Makena strained to see past the hood. The sirens stopped wailing. The sound would've been earsplitting if it hadn't been for the driving rain drowning out nearly every other sound outside of the SUV.

"The storm's predicted to get worse." He wheeled right and water sloshed as his tires cut a path where he made the turn. The sidewalks of the downtown area and the cobblestoned streets had to be completely flooded now.

"Really?" Makena tried to shift position in her seat so that she could get a good look at the screen he motioned toward. Movement only hurt her hip even more. She winced and bit out a curse.

Colton's laptop was angled toward the driver's side

and the only thing she could see was the reflection from the screen in his side window.

He seemed to catch on and said, "Sorry. I can't tilt it any closer to you."

"No need to apologize. Believe it or not, I'm not usually so clumsy, and I don't make a habit of running out in front of vehicles. Like I already said, give this hip a few days and she'll be good as new." Makena forced a smile.

"I hope you weren't planning on going anywhere tonight." There was an ominous quality to his voice, and he didn't pick up on her attempt to lighten the mood.

"Why is that?" Actually, she had hoped to figure out her next move and get back on the road. She'd ducked into the RV to ditch a few friends of her ex-husband, who was the real reason she'd been on the run. Her marriage to an abusive Dallas cop had ended badly. Hunger had caused her to leave the relative safety of the RV. She assumed it would be safer to travel in the rain and easier to cover herself up so she could travel incognito.

It was most likely paranoia, but she could've sworn she'd seen the pair of guys she'd caught in their garage late one night, huddled up and whispering with River. She'd surprised the trio and River had absolutely lost his cool. He'd demanded she go back inside the house and to bed, where he told her to wait for him.

River's decline had become even more apparent after that night. He was almost constantly angry with her over something. Yelling at her instead of talking. Not that he'd been great at it before. Gone was the charm of the early days in their relationship.

When River's attention was turned on, everyone

noticed him in the room and he could make the most enigmatic person come to life. River's shadow was a different story altogether. It was a cold, dark cave. His temper had become more and more aggressive to the point she'd had to get out.

"According to radar, this storm's about to get a whole helluva lot worse." Colton's voice cut through her heavy thoughts.

Leaving her husband, River, one year ago had been the best decision she'd ever made. Not a night went by that she didn't fear that he'd find her.

"How is that even possible?" she asked as a tree branch flew in front of the windshield.

"Apparently, Mother Nature isn't done with us yet. We're about to see just about how big this temper tantrum is going to get."

And just when she thought things couldn't get any worse than they already were this evening, the tornado alarms blared again. Rain pounded the front windshield, the roof. And in another moment of pure shock, she realized the winds had shifted. Gusts slammed into the vehicle, rocking it from side to side.

"Normally, I wouldn't leave the scene of an accident. However, if we want to live to see the light of day, we better get out of here." Colton placed the gearshift into Drive and turned his vehicle around. Water sloshed everywhere.

"Where to? You mentioned an elderly neighbor that you need to check on." Another gust of wind blasted the front windshield. Makena gasped.

"She asked me to check on her 'guest' who was staying in her RV. Since you're right here, a change of plans is in order. My place isn't far from here. The parking structure is sound and partially underground. We should be safe there."

Before she could respond, Colton had his secretary on the radio again, updating her on his new destination. Makena figured she could ride out the storm with Colton, giving away as little personal information as she could. Their shared history might work in her favor. Any other law enforcement officer in this situation would most certainly haul her in. Her name would get out.

Makena couldn't risk River figuring out where she was. With his jealous tendencies, it wouldn't be good for him to see her around Colton, either. The Dallas cop would pick up on her attraction faster than a bee could sting.

Colton stopped at the red light on an otherwise empty street. Everyone seemed to have enough sense to stay off the roads tonight. The only reason she'd left the RV at all was to find scraps of food while everyone hunkered down.

Makena had thrown away her phone months ago, so she'd had no idea a storm was on its way. The cloudy sky and humidity had been a dead giveaway but spring thunderstorms in Texas were notorious for popping up seemingly out of nowhere. In general, they retreated just as fast.

This one, however, was just getting started.

Chapter Four

"What do you think?" Colton asked a second time. He'd blame the rain for Makena not hearing him, but she'd been lost to him for a moment.

The prospect of her disappearing on him wasn't especially pleasing. After being in the vehicle with her for half an hour already, he barely knew any more about her or her situation than he had at the start of the conversation.

The fact that she deflected most of his questions and then overexplained told him the storm brewing outside wasn't the only one.

Since she seemed ready to jump if someone said boo, he figured some things were better left alone. Besides, they were trapped together in a storm that didn't seem to have any intention of letting up over the next twenty-four hours. That would give him enough time to dig around in her story.

Colton relaxed his shoulders. He needed to check in with his mother and see if she was okay with having the twins sleep over. Again, he really didn't like doing that to her under the circumstances no matter how many times she reassured him the twins were nothing but pure joy.

"About what?" Makena asked.

"Staying at my apartment at least until this storm blows over." Colton banked right to avoid a tree limb that was flying through the air.

"When exactly might that be?"

Colton shouldn't laugh but he did. "I'm going to try not to be offended at the fact that you seemed pretty upset about the prospect of spending a couple of hours alone with me. I promise that I'm a decent person."

"No. Don't get me wrong. You've been a godsend and I appreciate the food. I was a drowned rat out there." She blew out another breath. "I wasn't aware there was a big storm coming today. And especially not one of this magnitude. I got caught off guard without an umbrella."

He didn't feel the need to add, without a decent coat. The roads were making it increasingly unsafe to drive to Mrs. Dillon's place. It looked like there were more funnel systems on the way. A tornado watch had just been issued for this and four surrounding counties. He'd like to say the weather was a shock but it seemed folks were glued to the news more and more often every year and some supercell ended up on the radar.

"You didn't answer my question." The reminder came as she stared at the door handle.

Makena sat still, shifting her gaze to the windshield, where she stared for a long moment. She heaved another sigh and her shoulders seemed to deflate. "I appreciate your hospitality, Colton. I really do. And since it doesn't seem safe to travel in this weather, going to your place seems like the best option. I have one question, though."

"And that is?"

"It's really more of a request." She glanced at the half-full coffee sitting in the cupholder.

He knew exactly what she wanted. "I have plenty of coffee in my apartment. I basically live off the stuff."

"I haven't had a good cup of coffee in longer than I care to count."

His eyebrow must've shot up, because she seemed to feel the need to qualify her statement. "I mean like a really good cup of coffee. Not like that stuff." She motioned toward the cupholder and wrinkled her nose.

He laughed. At least some of the tension between them was breaking up. There was no relief on the chemistry pinging between them, though. But he'd take lighter tension because he was actually pretty worried about her. He couldn't imagine why she would be living even temporarily in an RV that didn't belong to her in a town she didn't know. She was from Dallas and they'd met in Austin. Again, his thoughts drifted toward her running away from something—he wasn't buying the broke musician excuse. And since he hadn't seen her in well over a decade, he couldn't be one hundred percent certain she hadn't done something wrong, no matter how much his heart protested.

Something about the fear in her eyes told him that she was on the run from someone. Who that would be was anyone's guess. She wasn't giving up any information. Keeping tight-lipped might have been the thing that kept her alive. Didn't she say that she'd been on the road for months with her music? There were more holes in that story than in a dozen doughnuts. The very obvious ones had to do with the fact that she had no instrument and no band. He figured it was probably customary to bring at least one of those things on tour.

"To my place then," he said.

The light changed to green. He proceeded through the intersection, doing his level best to keep the questions at bay.

His apartment would normally be a five-minute drive. Battling this weather system, he took a solid fifteen and that was without anyone else on the road. A call home was in order and he needed to prepare Makena for the fact he had children.

As he pulled into the garage and the rain stopped battering his windshield, he parked in his assigned parking spot, number 4, and shut off the engine.

"Before we go inside, I need to make you aware of something—"

Makena scooted up to sit straighter and winced. His gaze dropped to her hip and he figured he had no business letting it linger there.

"Now, there's no reason to panic." It was clear she'd already done just that.

"Was this a bad idea? Do you have a girlfriend or wife in there waiting? I know what you already said but—"

"Before you get too twisted up, hear me out. I have twin sons. They're with my mother because the woman who usually lives with me and takes care of them while I work got called away on a family emergency and had to quit. She hated doing it but was torn, and blood is thicker than water. Besides, I told her to go. She'd regret it if she wasn't there for her niece after the young woman was in a car crash."

"I'm sorry." Much to his surprise, Makena reached over and touched his hand. Electricity pinged. Turned out that the old crush was still alive and well.

"Don't be. It was the right thing for her to do." He debated these next words because he never spoke about his wife to anyone. "I was married. I didn't lie to you before about that. My wife died not long after the babies were born."

"Oh no. I really am sorry, Colton. I had no idea." She looked at him. The pain in her eyes and the compassion in her voice sent a ripple of warmth through him.

He had to look away or risk taking a hit to his heart.

"Why would you?" He'd gotten real good about stuffing his grief down in a place so deep that even he couldn't find it anymore.

When he glanced over at Makena, he saw a tear escape. She ducked her head, chin to chest, and turned her face away from him.

"I'm not trying to upset you…" This was harder than he wanted it to be. "I just didn't want you to walk into my place and be shocked. You've been through enough tonight—" longer if he was right about her situation "—and I didn't want to catch you off guard."

She sat perfectly still, perfectly quiet for a few more long moments. "You have twin boys?"

"Yes, I do. Silas and Sebastian. They are great boys."

When she seemed able to look at him without giving away her emotions, she turned to face him, wincing with movement and then covering. "I bet they're amazing kids, Colton."

It was his turn to smile. "They are."

"Are they at your house?"

"My mom is watching them for me at the family's ranch while I work. She'll be worried with all the weather. I need to check in with her and make sure the boys are asleep."

"How old did you say your boys were?" She seemed to be processing the fact that he was a father.

"One year old. They're great kids." He needed to contact his mother. But first, he needed to get Makena inside his apartment with the least amount of trauma to the hip she'd been favoring. "How about we head inside now?"

He half expected her to change her mind, especially with how squirrelly she'd been so far.

"It would be nice to dry off."

Colton shut off the vehicle's engine and came around to the passenger side. He opened the door. She had her seat belt off despite keeping the blanket around her. Color was returning to her creamy skin, which was an encouraging sign.

"It might be easier if I just carry you up."

"I think I got it. I definitely need some help walking but I want to try to put some weight on this hip."

Considering Makena knew her identity and didn't slur her speech—a couple of key signs she was lucid—his suspicion that she might have a concussion passed. Although, he'd keep an eye on her to be safe. He figured it wouldn't hurt to let her try to walk; he had to trust her judgment to be able to do that.

"Okay, I'm right here." He put his arm out and she grabbed onto it. More of that electricity, along with warmth, fired through him. Again, he chalked it up to nostalgia. The past. Simpler times.

Makena eased out of the passenger seat, leaning into him to walk. He positioned himself on her left side to make it easier for her. With some effort, she took the first couple of steps, stopping long enough for him to close the car door.

His parking spot was three spaces from the elevator bank, so at least she didn't have far to go.

"You're doing great," he encouraged. He couldn't ignore the awareness that this was the first time in a very long time that he'd felt this strong a draw toward someone. He hadn't been out on a date since losing Rebecca. He'd been too busy missing his wife and taking care of their boys. Twelve months since the kiddos had been born and soon after that, he'd lost his best friend and wife in one fell swoop. He never knew how much twelve months could change his life.

MAKENA LEANED HEAVILY on Colton. She couldn't help but wonder if he felt that same electrical impulse between them. If he did, he was a master at concealment.

Thankfully, the elevator bank was only a few more steps. Pain shot through her if she put any weight on her left leg. But she managed with Colton's help. Despite having told him repeatedly that she'd be fine, this was the first time she felt like it might be true.

The elevator did nothing to prepare her for the largeness of Colton's penthouse apartment. Stepping into the apartment, she realized it took up the entire top floor of the building, which was three stories on top of the parking level.

It felt like she'd been transported into a world of soft, contemporary luxury. "This place is beautiful, Colton."

She pictured him sharing the place with his wife and children. Losing the woman he loved must have been a crushing blow for a man like him. Colton was the kind of person who, once he loved you, would love you forever.

Why did that hurt so much to think about?

Was it because she'd never experienced that kind of unconditional love?

It was impossible not to compare Colton to River. She'd been so young when she and River had gotten together. Too naive to realize he was all charm and no substance. He'd swept her off her feet and asked her to marry him. She'd wanted to believe the fairy tale. She would never make that mistake again.

Colton's apartment comprised one great room and was built in the loft style, complete with a brick wall and lots of windows. The rain thrashed around outside, but the inside felt like a safe haven. In the space cordoned off as the living room, two massive brown leather sofas faced each other in front of a fireplace. In between the sofas was a very soft-looking ottoman in the place of a coffee table. It was tufted, cream-colored and stood on wooden pegs. She noticed all the furniture had soft edges. The light wood flooring was covered by cream rugs, as well.

There was a pair of toy walkers that were perfect for little kids to explore various spots in the room. A large kitchen, separated from the living room by a huge granite island, was to her right. Instead of a formal table, there were chairs tucked around the white granite island, along with a pair of highchairs.

Seeing the kid paraphernalia made it hit home that

Colton was a dad. Wow. She took a moment to let that sink in. He gave new meaning to the words *hot dad bod*.

The worry creases in his forehead made more sense now that she knew that he'd lost his wife and was navigating single parenthood alone.

Makena had once believed that she would be a mother by now. A pang of regret stabbed at the thought. She'd known better than to start a family with River once she saw the other side of him. She was by no means too old to start a family except that the pain was still too raw from dealing with a divorce. The dream she'd once had of a husband and kids was the furthest thing from her thoughts as she literally ran for her life. She still felt the bitter betrayal of discovering that the person she'd trusted had turned out to be a monster.

It had taken her years to extract herself from him. Now she'd be damned if she let that man break her. Her definition of happiness had changed sometime in the last few years. She couldn't pinpoint the exact moment her opinion had shifted. Rather than a husband and kids, all she now wanted was a small plot of land, a cozy home and maybe a couple of dogs.

"Are you okay?" His voice brought her back to the present.

"Yes. Your home is beautiful, Colton," she said again.

Now it was his turn to be embarrassed. His cheeks flamed and it was sexy on him.

"I can't take the credit for the decorating. That was my mother." Not his wife? Why did hearing those words send more of those butterflies flittering around in her chest again?

"She did an amazing job. The colors are incredible."

There were large-scale art pieces hanging on the walls in the most beautiful teal colors, cream and beige. The woman had decorating skills. The best part was how the place matched Colton's personality to a T. Strong, solid and calm. He was the calm in the storm. It was just his nature.

She took a few more steps inside with his help.

"Can I ask a personal question?" she asked.

He nodded.

"Didn't your wife want to decorate?"

"She's never been here." She felt a wall go up when it came to that subject.

"How about we get you settled on the couch and I get working on that cup of coffee?" he asked, changing the subject. His tone said, case closed.

"Are you kidding me right now? That sounds like heaven." She gripped his arm a little tighter and felt nothing but solid muscle.

He helped her to the couch before moving over to the fireplace wall and flipping a switch that turned it on. There were blue crystals that the fire danced on top of. It was mesmerizing.

She tried to keep her jaw from dropping on the carpet at the sheer beauty of the place. It was selfish, but she liked the fact that he'd only lived here as a bachelor, which was weird because it wasn't like she and Colton had ever dated, despite the signals he'd sent back in the bio lab. She had probably even misread that situation, because he'd never asked her out. The semester had ended and that was that.

Makena again wanted to express to Colton how sorry she was for the loss of his wife. Considering he had one-year-old twins, his wife couldn't have died all that long ago. The emotional scars were probably still very raw.

"If you want to get out of those wet clothes, I can probably find something dry for you to wear for the time being." He seemed to realize how that might sound, because he put his hands up in the air. "I just mean that I have a spare bathrobe of mine you can wear while I throw your clothes through the wash."

She couldn't help herself. She smiled at him. And chuckled just a little bit. "I didn't take it the wrong way and that would be fantastic. Dry clothes and coffee? I'm pretty certain at this point you've reached angel status in my book."

He caught her stare for just a moment. "I can assure you I will never be accused of being an angel."

A thrill of awareness skittered across her skin. A nervous laugh escaped because she hoped that she wasn't giving away her body's reaction to him. "I wouldn't accuse you of that, but I do remember what a good person you are. I wouldn't be here alone with you right now otherwise."

She surprised herself with the comment as he fired off a wink. He motioned toward an adjacent room before disappearing there. He returned a few moments later with a big white plush bathrobe that had some fancy hotel's name embroidered on the left-hand side.

Colton held out the robe. When she took it, their fingers grazed. Big mistake. More of that inconvenient attraction surged. She felt her cheeks flush as warmth traveled through her.

He cleared his throat and said, "I'll go make that coffee now. You can change in here. I promise not to look."

Again, those words shouldn't cause her chest to deflate. She should be grateful, and she was, on some level, that she could trust him not to look when she changed. Was it wrong that she wanted him to at least consider it?

Now she really was being punchy.

Makena took in a deep breath and then slowly exhaled. Colton made a show of turning his back to her and walking toward the kitchen. Despite pain shooting through her with every movement, she slipped out of her clothes and into the bathrobe while seated on the couch. The wreck could've been a whole lot worse, she thought as she managed to slip out of her soaked clothing and then ball it all up along with her undergarments, careful to keep the last part tucked in the center of the wad of clothing.

"Do you still take your coffee with a little bit of sugar and cream?"

"Yes. How did you remember after all this time?"

He mumbled something about having a good memory. Was it wrong to hope that it was a bit more than that? That maybe she'd been somewhat special to Colton? Special enough for him to remember the little things about her, like the fact she took her coffee with cream and sugar?

Logic said yes, but her heart went the opposite route.

Chapter Five

"I'm surprised you don't live on the ranch." Makena watched as Colton crossed the room. He walked with athletic grace. If it was at all possible, he was even hotter than he'd been in college. He'd cornered the market on that whole granite jawline, strong nose and piercing cobalt blue eyes look. Based on the ripples on his chest and arms, he was no stranger to working hard or hitting the gym. His jeans fit snug on lean hips.

"I have a place there where I spend time with the boys on my days off." He handed over a fresh cup of warm coffee. She took it with both hands and immediately took a sip.

"Mmm. This is quite possibly the best cup of coffee I've ever had."

Colton laughed and took a seat on the opposite couch. He toed off his boots and shook his head, which sent water flying everywhere. He raked his free hand through his hair. He was good-looking in that casual, effortless way. "I got this apartment so I could be closer to my office, after..."

The way his voice trailed off made her think he was going to tell her more about his wife. He shook his head again and recovered with a smile that was a little too forced. He took a sip of coffee. "You don't want to hear my sad story."

Before she could respond, he checked his phone.

"I do, actually," she said softly, but he didn't seem to hear. Strangely, she wanted to hear all about what had happened to him since college. Even then, he'd been too serious for a nineteen-year-old. He'd seemed like he carried the weight of the world on his shoulders. His eyes had always been a little too intense, but when they'd been focused on her they'd caused her body to hum with need—a need she'd been too inexperienced to understand at the time.

He picked up the remote and clicked a button, causing one of the paintings to turn into a massive TV screen. Makena had known his family was successful, but she had no idea they had the kind of money that made TVs appear out of artworks on the wall.

Color her impressed.

It was a shock for many reasons, not the least of which was the fact that Colton was one of the most down-to-earth people she'd ever met. She was vaguely aware of the O'Connor name, having grown up in Texas herself. But being a big-city girl, she had never really been part of the ranching community and had no idea until she'd seen an article about his family years ago. That had been her first hint that they might be wealthier than she'd realized.

Makena had had the opposite kind of childhood. She'd been brought up by a single mother who'd made plenty of sacrifices so that Makena could go to college without having to go into massive debt. And then a couple of years into Makena's marriage with River, long after the shine had worn off and she realized there was no other choice but to get out, her beloved mother had become sick.

Leaving her husband was no longer the number one priority. Her mother had taken precedence over everything else, despite River's protests that helping her ill mother took up too much of her time. He'd had similar complaints about her work, but her job had kept her sanity in check while she watched the woman she loved, the woman whose sacrifices were great, dwindle into nothingness.

Makena reached up and ran her finger along the rose gold flower necklace she wore—a final gift from her mother.

Despite River's protests, Makena remained firm. But with a sick mother who needed almost round-the-clock care in her final months, Makena had been in no position to disappear. And she'd known that was exactly what she had to do, when she walked away from River after his threats.

When Makena looked up, she realized that Colton had been studying her.

"What's his name?" he asked. Those three words slammed into her. They were so on point it took her back for a second.

She opened her mouth to protest the question, but Colton waved her off before she could get a word out.

"Makena, you don't have to tell me his name. I'll leave that up to you. Just don't lie to me about him existing at all."

Well, now she really felt bad. She sat there for a long

moment and contemplated her next move. Having lived alone for six months after losing her mother, barely saying a word to anyone and focusing on the basest level of survival, she now wanted to open up to someone.

She just wanted to be honest with someone and with herself for a change.

"River."

She didn't look up at Colton right then. She wouldn't be able to bear a look of pity. She didn't want him to feel sorry for her. It was her mistake. She'd made it. She'd owned it. She would've moved on a long time ago if it hadn't been for her mother's illness.

"Was he abusive? Did he lay a hand on you?" The seriousness and calmness in Colton's tone didn't convey pity at all. It sounded more like compassion and understanding. Two words that were so foreign to her when it came to her relationship with a man.

"No." She risked a glance at him. "He would've. We started off with arguments that escalated. He always took it too far. He'd say the most hurtful things meant to cut me to the quick. I didn't grow up with a father in the house. So I didn't know how abnormal that was in a relationship."

"No one should have to." There was no judgment in his voice but there was anger.

"Things escalated pretty badly, and one day when we were arguing I stomped into the bedroom. He followed and when I wouldn't stop, he grabbed my wrist like he was a vise on the tightest notch. He whirled me around so hard that the back of my head smacked against the wall. I was too prideful to let him know how much it hurt. It wasn't intentional on his part. Not that part. But he immediately balled his fist and reared it back."

Makena had to breathe slowly in order to continue. Her heart raced at hearing the words spoken aloud that she'd bottled up for so long. Panic tightened her chest.

"What did you do to stop him from hitting you?" Colton's jaw muscle clenched.

"I looked him dead in the eyes, refusing to buckle or let him know that I was afraid. And then I told him to go ahead and do it. Hit me. But I cautioned him with this. I told him that if he did throw that punch he'd better sleep with one eye open for the rest of his life because we had a fireplace with a fireplace poker and I told him that he would wake up one morning to find it buried right in between his eyes."

A small smile ghosted Colton's lips. "Good for you. I bet he thought twice about ever putting a hand on you again."

"Honestly, I don't think I could ever hurt another human being unless my life depended on it. But I needed him to believe every word of that. And he did. That was the first and last time he raised a fist to me. But his words were worse in some ways. They cut deep and he tried to keep a tight rein on who I saw and where I went."

"Can I ask you a question?"

"Go ahead." She'd shared a lot more about her situation than she'd ever thought she would with anyone. Part of her needed to talk about it with someone. She'd never told her mom because she didn't want her to worry.

"Why did you stay?"

"My mom. She was sick for a couple of years and

then she passed away." Makena paused long enough to
catch her breath. She tucked her chin to her chest so
he wouldn't see the tears welling in her eyes. "That's
when I left him. Before that, honestly, she needed me
to be stable for her. She needed someone to take care
of her and she needed to stay with the same doctors.
I couldn't relocate her." Makena decided not to share
the rest of that story. And especially not the part where
River had threatened her life if she ever left him. He
seemed to catch onto the fact that she'd at the very least
been thinking about leaving.

But Makena didn't want to think about that anymore,
and she sure as hell didn't want to talk about herself.
She'd done enough of that for one night. She picked
up her coffee and took a sip before turning the tables.

Catching Colton's gaze, she asked, "How about you?
Tell me about your wife."

"There isn't much to tell. Rebecca and I were best
friends. She lived across the street and we grew up together. Her father is the mayor. We dated in high school
and broke up to go to different colleges. Her older sister
had married her high school sweetheart and the relationship fell apart in college, so Rebecca was concerned
the same thing would happen to us."

"And what did you think?"

"That I was ready for a break. I looked at our relationship a lot like most people look at religion. When
someone grows up in a certain church, it's all they
know. Part of growing up and becoming independent is
testing different waters and making certain it's the right
thing for you and not just what's ingrained. You know?"

"Makes a lot of sense to me." She nodded.

"Before I committed the rest of my life to someone, I wanted to make damn sure I was making the right call and not acting out of habit. That's what the break meant to me."

"Since the two of you married, I'm guessing you realized she was the one." Why did that make Makena's heart hurt?

"You could say that. I guess I figured there were worse things than marrying my best friend."

Makena picked up on the fact that he hadn't described Rebecca as the love of his life or the woman he wanted to spend the rest of his life with, or said the two of them had realized they were perfect for each other.

"We got married and the twins came soon after. And then almost immediately after, she was hit by a drunk driver on the highway coming home from visiting her sister in Austin. She died instantly. I'd kept the twins home with me that day to give her a break."

"I'm so sorry, Colton."

"I rented this apartment after not really wanting to live on the ranch in our home. The place just seemed so empty without her. I go there on my days off with the twins because we still have pictures of her hanging up there and I want the twins to have some memories of growing up in a house surrounded by their mother's things."

"Being a single dad must be hard. You seem like you're doing a really great job with your boys. I bet she'd be really proud of you."

"It really means a lot to hear you say that. I'd like to think she would be proud. I want to make her proud.

She deserved that." A storm brewed behind his eyes when he spoke about his wife.

"How long were the two of you married?" Makena asked, wanting to know more about his life after college.

"We got married after she told me that she was pregnant."

Was that the reason he'd said he could've done worse than marrying his best friend? Had she gotten pregnant and they'd married? Asking him seemed too personal. If he wanted her to know, he probably would've told her by now. The questions seemed off-limits even though they'd both shared more than either of them had probably set out to at the beginning of this conversation.

Despite the boost of caffeine, Makena had never felt more tired. It was probably the rain, which had settled into a steady, driving rhythm, coupled with the fact that she hadn't really slept since almost running into the pair of men she'd seen with River, not to mention she'd been clipped by an SUV. She bit back another yawn and tried to rally.

"Losing her must've been hard for you, Colton. I couldn't be sorrier that happened. You deserve so much more. You deserved a life together."

COLTON HADN'T EXPECTED to talk so much about Rebecca. Words couldn't describe how much he missed his best friend. There was something about telling their story that eased some of the pain in his chest. He was coming up on a year without her in a few days. And even though theirs hadn't been an epic love that made his heart race every time she was near, it had been built on friendship. He could've done a lot worse.

Being with Makena had woken up his heart and stirred feelings in him that he'd thought were long since dead. In fact, he hadn't felt this way since meeting her sophomore year. He'd known something different was up the minute he'd seen Makena. Rebecca had texted him that day to see how he was doing and it was the first time he hadn't responded right away.

Rebecca had picked up on the reason. Hell, there were times when he could've sworn she knew him better than he knew himself.

Being here, with Makena, felt right on so many levels. It eased some of the ache of losing his best friend. Not that his feelings for Makena were anything like his marriage to Rebecca. He and Rebecca were about shared history, loyalty and a promise to have each other's back until the very end.

Colton felt a lot of pride in following through on his promise. He'd had Rebecca's back. He'd always have her back. And in bringing up the twins, he was given an opportunity to prove his loyalty to his best friend every day. Those boys looked like their mother and reminded him of her in so many ways. A piece of her, a very large piece, would always be with him.

He reminded himself of the fact every day.

Right now, his focus was on making certain the residents in his county were safe and that fearful look that showed up on Makena's face every once in a while for the briefest moment subsided. She'd opened up to him about living with a verbally abusive ex. Colton had a lot of experience with domestic situations. More than he cared to. He'd seen firsthand the collateral damage from relationships that became abusive and felt boiling hot anger run through his veins.

He flexed and released his fingers to try to ease out some of the tension building in him at the thought of Makena in a similar predicament. He'd also witnessed the hold an abusive spouse could have over the other person. Men tended to be the more physically aggressive, although there were times when he saw abuse the other way around. Women tended to use verbal assaults to break a partner down. He'd seen that, too. Except that the law didn't provide for abuse that couldn't be seen.

Texas law protected against bruises and bloody noses, ignoring the fact that verbal abuse could rank right up there in damage. The mental toll was enormous. Studying Makena now and knowing what she'd been like in the past, he couldn't imagine her living like that.

"How long were you married?" he asked.

"Nine years." The shock of that sat with him for a long minute as he took another sip of fresh brew.

"Was your mother the only reason you stayed?" he asked.

"Honestly?"

He nodded.

"Yes. She got sick and couldn't seem to shake it. I took her to a doctor and then a specialist, and then another specialist. By the time they figured out what was wrong with her, she had a stroke. It was too late to save her." She ran her finger along the rim of her coffee cup.

The look of loss on Makena's face when she spoke about her mother was a gut punch. She didn't have that same look when she talked about her ex. With him, there was sometimes a flash of fear and most definitely defiance. Her chin would jut out and resolve would darken her features.

"I miss her every day," she admitted.

Since the words *I'm sorry* seemed to fall short, he set his coffee down and pushed up to standing. He took the couple of steps to the other couch and sat beside her. Taking her hand in his, he hoped to convey his sympathy for the loss of her mother.

"She's the reason that I got to go to college. She, and a very determined college counselor. It was just me and my mom for so long. She sacrificed everything for me."

"Your mother sounds like an incredible person."

"She was." Makena ducked her head down, chin to chest, and he realized she was hiding the fact that a tear had rolled down her face.

"I can imagine how difficult it was for her to bring you up alone. There are days when I feel like my butt is being kicked bringing up my boys. Without my family by my side, I don't even see how it's possible to do it. I don't know what I'd do without my tribe and their help."

"Whoever said it takes a village to bring up a child was right. We just had two people in ours and it was always just kind of us against the world. It wasn't all bad. I mean, I didn't even realize how many sacrifices my mom made for me until I was grown and had my first real job out of college. Then I started realizing how expensive things were and how much she covered. I saw what it took to get by financially. She didn't have a college education and insisted that I get one. She worked long hours to make sure that it could happen without me going into a ridiculous amount of debt. I never told her when I had to take out student loans because I wanted her to feel like she was able to do it all."

"It sounds like you gave her a remarkable gift. Again, I can only compare it to my boys but I also know that I want to give them the world just like I'm sure your mom wanted to with you. The fact that she was able to do as much as she did with very little resources and no support is nothing short of a miracle. It blows me away."

He paused long enough for her to lift her gaze up to meet his, and when it did, that jolt of electricity coursed through him.

"It's easy to see where you get your strength from now." Colton was rewarded with a smile that sent warmth spiraling through him before zeroing in on his heart.

"Colton…" Whatever Makena was about to say seemed to die on her lips.

"For what it's worth, you deserve better, with what you got from your marriage and the loss of your mother so young," he said.

She squeezed his arm in a move that was probably meant to be reassuring but sent another charge jolting through him, lighting up his senses and making him even more aware of her. This close, he breathed in her unique scent, roses in spring. The mood changed from sadness and sharing to awareness—awareness of her pulse pounding at the base of her throat, awareness of the chemistry that was impossible to ignore.

He reached up and brushed the backs of his fingers against her cheek and then her jawline. She took hold of his forearm and then pulled him closer, their gazes locked the entire time.

When she tugged him so close, their lips were inches apart, and his tongue darted across his lips. He could only imagine how incredible she would taste. A moment of caution settled over him as his pulse skyrocketed. His caution had nothing to do with how badly he wanted to close the distance between them and everything to do with a stab of guilt. It was impossible not to feel like he was betraying Rebecca in some small measure, especially since his feelings for Makena were a runaway train.

He reminded himself that his wife was gone and had been for almost a year. It was a long time since he'd been with someone other than her, and that would mess with anyone's mind. Not to mention the fact he hadn't felt this strong an attraction to anyone. In fact, the last time he had was with the woman whose lips were inches from his.

Makena brought her hands up to touch his face, silently urging him to close that gap.

Colton closed his eyes and breathed in her flowery scent. He leaned forward and pressed his lips to hers. Hers were delicate and soft despite the fiery and confident woman behind them.

All logic and reason flew out the window the second their mouths fused. He drove the tip of his tongue inside her mouth. She tasted like sweet coffee. Normally, he took his black. Sweet was his new favorite flavor.

Makena moved toward him and broke into the moment with a wince. She pulled back. "Sorry."

"Don't be." He wanted to offer more reassurance than that but couldn't find the right words. Either way, this was just the shot of reality that he needed before he let things get out of hand. Doing any of this with her right now was the worst of bad ideas.

They were two broken souls connecting and that was it. So why did the sentiment feel hollow? Why did his mind try to argue the opposite? Why did it insist these feelings were very real? The attraction was different? And it was still very much alive between them?

"I'm sorry if I hurt you," he finally said.

"You couldn't have. It was my fault. I got a little carried away." Her breathing was raspy, much like his own.

He'd never experienced going from zero to one hundred miles an hour from what started as a slow burn. Don't get him wrong, he'd experienced great sex. This was somehow different. The draw toward Makena was sun to earth.

Colton was certain of one thing. Sex with Makena would be mind-blowing and a game changer. With her hip in the condition it was, there was no threat it was going to happen anytime soon. That shouldn't make his chest deflate like someone had just let the air out of a balloon. He chalked it up to the lack of sex in his life and, even more than that, the lack of companionship.

This was the first time he realized how much he missed having someone to talk to when he walked in the door at night. Having the twins was amazing but one-year-olds weren't exactly known for their conversation skills.

Colton took the interruption from the hip pain as a sign he was headed down the wrong path. Granted, it didn't feel misguided, and nothing inside him wanted to stop, but doing anything to cause her more pain was out of the question.

A voice in the back of his mind picked that time to remind him of the fact he'd struck her with his vehicle. He was the reason she was in pain in the first place.

The idea that she'd been adamant about not filing a report crept into his thoughts. As much as she'd insisted not doing so was for his benefit, he'd quickly ascertained that she didn't want her name attached to a report. Colton had already put two and two together and guessed she was hiding out from her ex. But living in a random trailer and hiding her name meant her situation was more complicated than he'd first realized. No matter what else, this was a good time to take a break and regroup.

"I'm sorry. That whole kissing thing was my fault. I don't know what came over me." Makena's cheeks flushed with embarrassment and that only poured gasoline onto the fire of attraction burning in him.

"Last I checked, I was a pretty willing participant." He winked and she smiled. He hadn't meant to make her feel bad by regrouping. In fact, the last thing he wanted to do was add to her stress. Based on what she'd shared so far, her marriage had done very little to lift her up and inspire confidence.

Was it wrong that he wanted to be the person who did that for her?

Chapter Six

Embarrassment didn't begin to cover the emotion Makena should be feeling after practically throwing herself at Colton. It was impossible to regret her actions, though. She hadn't been so thoroughly kissed by any man in her entire life. That was a sad statement considering she'd been married, but wow, Colton could kiss. He brought parts of her to life that had been dormant for so long she'd forgotten they existed.

She wanted to chalk up the thrill of the kiss to the fact that it had been more than a decade in the making, but that would sell it short. He'd barely dipped the tip of his tongue in her mouth and yet it was the most erotic kiss she'd ever experienced. She could only imagine what it would feel like to take the next step with him.

And since those thoughts were about as productive as spending all her paycheck on a pair of shoes, she shelved them. For now, at least.

Makena blew out an awkward breath. Yes, dwelling on their attraction was off the table, because not only was it futile, but there was no way she could compete with a ghost. Colton had said so himself. He'd married his best friend. His beloved wife had died shortly after giving birth to their twins and making a family.

Despite the fact that he hadn't described his relationship with his wife as anything other than a deep friendship, it would be impossible to stack up to that level of love.

Colton's gaze darted to his coffee cup. "Mine's empty. How are you on a refill?"

"I'm good. I think I've had enough." She bit back a yawn. "If it's okay, I'd like to just curl up here and rest my eyes for a few minutes."

"Make yourself at home." Colton stood. The couch felt immediately cold to her, after his warmth from a few moments ago. He scooped up his coffee mug and headed toward the kitchen. She could've sworn she heard him mumble phrases like "another time and place and things might be different," and "bad timing." She couldn't be certain. It might've just been wishful thinking on her part to believe there was something real going on between them.

An awkward laugh escaped. She'd never been the type to latch onto someone, but then this wasn't just anyone. Was she seriously that lonely?

This was Colton O'Connor and they shared history. And based on the enthusiasm in his kiss, an attraction that hadn't completely run its course.

Makena counted herself lucky that embarrassment couldn't kill a person. Actually, maybe it wasn't embarrassment she felt. Maybe it was that strong attraction that caused her cheeks to heat. When she really thought about it, she hadn't done anything to be embarrassed about.

The past six months, being alone, had done a number on her mindset. That was certain. But it hadn't knocked her out. And it wouldn't. She would get through this, rebound and pick her life up again. A life that seemed a little bit colder now that she'd been around warmth again.

Makena figured it was too much to hope that she'd find her feet rooted in the real world again. And real world started with a few basics. "Hey, Colton. Any chance you have a spare toothbrush and a washcloth I could use?"

Her clothes were in the dryer, so she might as well go all in wishing for a real shower rather than a bowl of warm soapy water by the river like she'd done the past few days at the RV.

"Like I said, make yourself at home." He tilted his head toward the hallway where he'd disappeared earlier to bring her the robe. "You'll find a full bathroom in there. Spare toothbrushes are still in the wrappers in the cabinet."

With some effort, Makena was able to stand. Colton turned around and a look of shock stamped his features.

"Hold on there. I can help you get to the bathroom."

"It still hurts, I'm not going to lie. But it's not as bad as it was an hour ago. I'd like to see if I can make it myself." She wasn't exactly fast and couldn't outrun an ant, but she was proud of the fact that she made it to the bathroom on her own. She closed the toilet seat, folded a towel and paused a moment to catch her breath. It was progress and she'd take it.

As she sat in the bathroom waiting for the pain in her hip to subside, she couldn't help but inhale a deep breath, filling her senses with Colton's scent. The bathrobe she wore smelled like him, all campfire and outdoors and spice. It was masculine and everything she'd remembered about sitting next to him in biology lab. His scent was all over the robe.

She needed to get her head on straight and refocus. Thinking much more about Colton and how amazing and masculine he smelled wasn't going to help her come up with a plan of what to do next.

It would probably be best for all concerned if she could put Colton out of her head altogether. She appreciated his help, though.

Taking another deep breath, Makena reached over and turned on the water. Using the one-step-at-a-time method, she peeled off the bathrobe and then took baby steps until she was standing in the massive shower. She had no idea what materials actually were used, but the entire shower enclosure looked like it was made of white marble. There were two showerheads. The place was obviously meant for a couple to be able to shower together. However, a half dozen people would fit inside there at the very least.

Now that really made Makena laugh. Images of single father and town sheriff Colton in a wild shower party with a half dozen people didn't really fit well together.

They tickled her anyway.

And maybe she was just that giddy. Exhaustion started wearing her thin, and her nerves, nerves that had been fried for a solid year and really longer than that if she thought back, eased with being around Colton.

The soap might smell clean and a little spicy, but

it was the warm water that got her. Amazing didn't begin to cover it. She showered as quickly as possible, though, not wanting to keep too much pressure on that hip. Her left side bit back with pain any time she put pressure on it.

After toweling off and slipping back into the robe, she brushed her teeth. She had a toothbrush at the RV, in the small bag of shower supplies she kept with her at all times while on the move. But this was a luxury. It was crazy how the simple things felt so good after being deprived. Simple things like a real shower and a real bathroom.

Speaking of which, the cup of coffee that she'd had a little while ago had been in a league of its own.

Makena reminded herself not to get too comfortable here. It was dangerous to let her guard down or stick around longer than absolutely necessary. Being in one place for too long was a hazard, made more so by the fact her identity could be so easily revealed by Colton.

She tightened the tie on the bathrobe before exiting the bathroom and making her way back into the living room. She might move slow, but this was progress. If she could rest that hip for a couple of hours and let the worst of the storm pass, she could get back to the RV and then…go where?

Thinking about her next step was her new priority. She'd been so focused on surviving one hour at a time that she'd forgotten there was a big picture—an end game that had her collecting evidence against her ex. Time had run out for her in Katy Gulch.

Inside the living room, Colton was in mission control mode. He was so deep in thought with what was going on and talking into his radio that he didn't even seem to hear her when she walked into the room.

Rather than disturb him, she moved as stealthily as possible, reclaiming her spot opposite him on the couch. He glanced up and another shot of warmth rocketed through her body, settling low in her stomach. Colton's deep, masculine voice spoke in hushed tones as she curled up on her side on the sofa. He almost immediately shifted the laptop off his lap and grabbed the blanket draped on the back of the sofa.

He walked over and placed it over her before offering her an extra throw pillow. She took it, laid her head on it and closed her eyes.

With all the stress that had been building the six months and especially in the past couple of days since she thought she'd seen River's associates, there was no way she could sleep.

Resting her eyes felt good. That was the last thought she had before she must've passed out.

Makena woke with a start. She immediately pushed up to sit and glanced around, trying to get her bearings. Her left hip screamed at her with movement, so she eased pressure from it, shifting to the right side instead.

Daylight streamed through the large windows in the loft-style apartment. She rubbed blurry eyes and yawned.

Looking around, she searched for any signs of Colton as the memory of last night became more focused. She strained to listen for him and was pretty sure she heard the shower going in the other room. The image of a naked, muscled Colton standing in the same shower she'd showered in just a few hours ago probably wasn't the best start to her morning. Or it was. Depending on how she looked at it. Makena chuckled nervously.

The events from the past twelve hours or so came back to her, bringing down her mood. She opened up the robe to examine her hip on the left side. Sure enough, a bruise the size of a bowling ball stared back at her. Pain had reminded her it was there before she'd even looked.

Movement hurt. She sucked in a breath and pushed past the soreness and pain as she closed her robe and stood. Then she remembered that Colton had some of the best coffee she'd ever tasted. Since he'd instructed her to make herself at home, she figured he wouldn't mind if she made a cup.

Her stomach growled despite the sandwich, apple and soup he'd given her. She glanced at the clock. That had been a solid ten hours ago. How had she slept so long?

Makena hadn't had that much sleep at one time in the past year. Of that she was certain. She cautioned herself against getting too comfortable around Colton. She'd already let way too much slip about her personal life, not that it hadn't felt good to finally open up to someone she trusted and talk about her mother and other parts of her life. It had. But it was also dangerous.

A part of her wanted to resurface just to see if River had let his anger toward her go by now. If he'd let *her* go by now. Being on the run, hiding out, had always made her feel like she'd done something wrong, not the other way around.

Standing up to fight a Dallas police officer who ran in a circle just like him could wreak complete havoc on her life, so she had erred on the side of caution.

But should she start over now, after she'd found

Colton again? There was something almost thrilling about seeing him, about finding a piece of herself that had been alive before she'd lost her mother...before River.

If Makena was being completely honest with herself, she could admit that part of her disappearing act had to do with wanting to shut out the world after losing her mother. She'd succumbed to grief and allowed fear to override rational thought.

But where to start over? Dallas was out. Houston was a couple hours' drive away. Maybe she could make a life there? Get back to teaching music. It was worth a shot.

Living like she had been over the past few months, although necessary, wasn't really being alive.

Makena saw a coffee machine sitting on a counter-top. It was easy to spot in the neat kitchen. There were drawers next to it and so she went ahead and made the wild assumption that she'd find coffee in one of them.

She didn't. But she did find some in the cupboard above. It was the pod kind. She helped herself to one that said Regular Coffee and placed it in the fancy-looking steel machine. She glanced to the side and saw a plastic carafe already filled with water.

There was only one button, so that was easy. The round metal button made the machine come to life. It was then that she realized she hadn't put a coffee cup underneath the spout.

"Oh no. Where are you?" She opened a couple of cupboards until she found the one that housed the mugs. She grabbed one and placed it under the spout just in time for the first droplets of brown liquid to sputter out.

"Good save." She mumbled the words out loud and, for the second time since opening her eyes, chuckled.

Her lighter mood had everything to do with being around Colton again. The kiss they'd shared had left the memory of his taste on her lips. And even though their relationship couldn't go anywhere, the attraction between them was a nice change of pace from what she usually felt around men. After being with River, she'd become uneasy interacting with the opposite sex.

Makena slowly made her way to the fridge. Quick movement hurt. Walking hurt. But she was doing it and was certain she could push through the pain.

In the fridge, she found cups of her favorite thing in the world, vanilla yogurt. She took one and managed to find a spoon. She polished it off before the coffee could stop dripping.

The carton of eggs was tempting, but she needed to take it easy on the hip. Standing in front of the stove was probably not the best idea. The yogurt would hold her over until she could rest enough to gather the energy to find something else to eat or cook.

Cup of coffee in hand, she slowly made her way to one of the chairs at the granite island. It would be too much to ask for sugar and cream at this hour, especially with the amount of pain she was in. She hadn't asked for ibuprofen last night, not wanting to mask her injury. Today, however, she realized the injury was superficial and she would ask for a couple of pain relievers once Colton returned from the shower.

Speaking of which, she was pretty certain the water spigot had been turned off for a while now.

Nothing could have quite prepared her for the sight of

Colton O'Connor when he waltzed into the room wearing nothing but a towel. The white cloth was wrapped around lean hips and tucked into one side.

"Good morning." The low timbre of his voice traveled all over her body, bringing a ripple of awareness.

"Morning to you." She diverted her gaze from the tiny droplets of water rolling down his muscled chest.

"I see you managed to find a cup of coffee. It's good to see you up and around. How's that hip today?" His smile—a show of perfectly straight, white teeth—made him devastatingly hot.

"It's better. I managed the coffee minus the cream." She decided it was best to redirect the conversation away from her injury. "This coffee is amazing straight out of the pot. Or whatever that thing is." She motioned toward the stainless-steel appliance.

Colton's eyebrow shot up and a small smile crossed his lips—lips she had no business staring at, but they were a distraction all the same.

"You want cream and sugar?"

"It's really no big deal." She'd barely finished her protest when Colton moved over to the fridge and came back with cream that he set on the counter in front of her. He located sugar next and tossed a few packets in her direction.

She thanked him.

"You seemed pretty busy last night. Is everyone okay?" she asked.

"The storm was all bark and no bite thankfully. Roads were messy, but folks respected Mother Nature and she backed off without any casualties."

"That's lucky," she said.

"There were a few close calls with stranded vehicles. Nothing I could get to, but my deputies could."

"That's a relief." She took a sip of coffee and groaned. "This is so good."

He shot her a look before shaking his head. "That's a nice sound. But not one I need in my head all day and especially not after...never mind."

The words on the tip of his tongue had to be *that kiss*. She'd thought the same thing when she saw him half-naked in the kitchen.

"I can't remember the last time I slept as well as I did last night." She stretched her arms out.

"If you slept that well on the couch, imagine what it would be like in a real bed." He seemed to hear those words as they came out and shot her a look that said he wanted to reel them back in.

The image that had popped into her thoughts was one of her in bed with him. Considering he still stood there in a towel, she needed to wipe all those thoughts from her head.

Seeing him again was making a difference in her mood and her outlook. Somewhere in the past six months after losing her mother, she'd given up a little bit on life. Looking back, she could see that so clearly now.

This morning, she felt a new lease on life and was ready to start making plans for a future. She hadn't felt like she would have one, in so long.

She took another sip of coffee. "I know that I said last night was the best cup of coffee I'd had in a long time, but this beats it."

He practically beamed with pride. "Are you hungry?"

"I already helped myself to yogurt. I hope that's okay."

"Of course it is. I make a pretty mean spinach omelet if you're game."

The man was the definition of hotness. He cared about others, hence his job as sheriff. And now he decided to tell her that he could cook?

"You're not playing fair," she teased. "I really don't want you to go to any trouble."

"If it makes you feel any better, I plan to make some for myself. No bacon, though. I'm out."

"Well, in that case, forget it. What kind of house runs out of bacon?" She laughed at her own joke and was relieved when he did, too. It was nice to be around someone who was so easy to be with. Conversation was light. This was exactly what she remembered about biology lab and why she'd been so attracted to him all those years ago. Sure, he was basically billboard material on the outside, with those features she could stare at all day. But how many people did she know who were good-looking on the outside and empty shells on the inside? A conversation with a ten on the outside and a three on substance made her want to fall asleep thinking about it.

Physical attraction was nice. It was one thing. It was important. But she'd learned a long time ago that someone's intelligence, sense of humor and wit could sway their looks one way or the other for her.

On a scale of one to ten, Colton was a thirty-five in every area.

Chapter Seven

Colton whipped up a pair of omelets and threw a couple slices of bread into the toaster while Makena finished up her cup of coffee at the granite island.

"Is there any chance I can have some pain reliever?" she asked.

"I have a bottle right here." He moved to the cabinet at the end of the counter. Medicine was kept on the top shelf even though his sons had only just taken their first steps recently. "Ibuprofen okay?"

"It's the only thing I take and that's rare."

"Same here." He grabbed a couple of tablets and then put a plate of food in front of her. "You probably want to eat that first. Ibuprofen on an empty stomach is not good."

She nodded and smiled at the plate. Tension still tightened the muscles of her face but sometime in the past twelve hours they'd been together, she'd relaxed just a bit. Given her history with men, it was wonderful that she could be this comfortable around him so quickly, and Colton let his chest fill with pride at that, although her ease was tentative, as he could tell from her eyes.

"Are you serious about these eggs?" She made a show of appreciating them after taking another bite.

Colton laughed. He realized it had been a really long time since he'd laughed this much. The roller coaster he'd been on since losing Rebecca and then his father had been awful to say the least.

To say that Colton hadn't had a whole lot to smile about recently was a lot like saying The New Texas Giant was just a roller coaster.

The exception was his twin boys. When he was with them, he did his level best to set everything else aside and just be with them. He might only have an hour or so to play with them before nighttime routine kicked in, but he treasured every moment of it. The last year had taught him that kids grew up way too fast.

"I'm glad you like the eggs."

"*Like* is too weak a word for how I feel about this omelet." Her words broke into more of that thick, heavy fog that had filled his chest for too long.

"The roads are clearing up. After you eat, I should make a few rounds."

"Can you give me a ride to the RV?" she asked.

"Happy to oblige," he teased. "I just need to get dressed."

Her cheeks flushed and he wondered if it had anything to do with the fact that he was still in a towel. A rumble of a laugh started inside his chest and rolled out. "I just realized that I'm walking about like I don't have company. Pardon me. I'll just go get dressed now."

"Well, it hasn't exactly been hard on the eyes." Now it was her turn to burst out laughing. "I can't believe I just said that out loud."

He excused himself and headed into his bedroom, where he threw on a pair of boxers, jeans and a dark, collared button-down shirt. He pulled his belt from the safe and clipped it on. It held his badge and gun.

Colton located one of his navy windbreakers that had the word *SHERIFF* written in bright, bold letters down the left sleeve. He finger-combed his hair and was ready to go. Walking out into the living room and seeing Makena still sitting there in his robe was a punch to the chest.

"I'll go and grab your clothes from the dryer." His offer was met with a smile.

"I can go with you. Or you could just point me in a direction. I think I can find my way around," she said.

"Down the hall. Open the door in the bathroom. You probably thought it was a closet, but it's actually a laundry room."

"That's really convenient." She tightened her grip on her robe and disappeared down the hallway.

He was relieved to see that her hip seemed in better condition today. She was barely walking with a limp. Even so, he wondered if he could talk her into making a trip to the ER for an X-ray.

Ten minutes later, she emerged from the hallway. She'd brushed her hair and dressed in the jeans and blouse she'd had on yesterday. "Ready?"

"Are the pain pills kicking in yet?" he asked.

"It's actually much better. I mean, I have a pretty big bruise, but overall, I'm in good shape. The ibuprofen is already helping. I won't be riding any bucking broncos in the next few days, but it'll heal up fine."

"I like the fact that you're walking more easily, but

I would feel a whole lot better if we stopped off at the county hospital to get it checked out. The roads are clear on that route." He hoped she'd listen to reason.

She opened her mouth to protest, but he put his hand up to stop her.

"Hear me out. You won't have to pay for the cost of the X-ray. It's the least I can do considering the fact that I hit you."

"Technically, I ran out in front of your car and you didn't have enough time to stop. You also couldn't see me because of the rain. So, technically, I hit you."

Well, Colton really did laugh out loud now. That was a new one and he thought he'd heard just about every line imaginable in his profession. He couldn't help himself, and chuckled again. It was a sign she was winning him over, and he didn't normally give away his tells.

"I'm glad you're laughing, because you could be writing me up right now or arresting me for striking an official vehicle. Does that count as striking an officer?" She seemed pretty pleased with that last comment.

"All right. You got me. I laughed. It was funny. But what wouldn't be funny is if there's something seriously wrong with your hip and it got worse because we didn't get it checked out." Was it him or had he just turned into his old man? He could've sworn he'd heard those same words coming out of Finn O'Connor's mouth for most of Colton's life. His dad was great at coaxing others to get checked out. He didn't seem to think he fell into the same category.

And it was only recently that Colton and his brothers had found out his father had been dealing with a health issue that he'd kept quiet about until his death.

"Don't you think we would know by now? Plus, what's the worst it could be? A hairline fracture? I had one of those in my wrist in eighth grade PE. It's an incident I don't talk about because it highlights my general inability to perform athletics of any kind. But there wasn't much they could do with it except wrap it and put it in a sling. It wasn't like I needed a cast. I'm sure my hip falls into the same category. I need to rest. I need to take it easy. Other than that, I think I'm good to go."

What she said made a whole lot of sense, and Colton knew in the back of his mind she was right on some level. The thought of dropping her off at the RV to fend for herself after witnessing the way she'd gobbled down food last night and cleaned her plate this morning wasn't something he could stomach doing.

He wanted to help her, but he didn't want to hurt her pride. He needed to be tactful. "Since you're going to be resting for a few days anyway, why not do it here?"

The question surprised even him. But it was the logical thing to do. He had plenty of room here. He could sleep on the sofa. He'd done that countless times before, unable and unwilling to face an empty bedroom.

"That's a really kind offer. Maybe under different circumstances I could take you up on it…"

"I didn't want to have to pull this card out, but since you mentioned it, you're leaving me no choice." He caught hold of her gaze and tried his level best not to give himself away by laughing. "If you don't stay here and let me help you heal, I might be forced to handcuff you."

He mustered up his most serious expression.

Makena's jaw nearly dropped to the floor, and a twinge of guilt struck him at tricking her.

"That's blackmail. You wouldn't do that to me. Would you?" Her question was uncertain and he suspected she'd figured out his prank.

"I don't know." He shrugged. "Is it working?"

She walked straight toward him with her slight limp on the left side and gave him a playful jab on the shoulder. "That wasn't funny."

"Actually, I thought it was ingenious of me." Seeing the lighter side of Makena and her quick wit reminded him of why he'd been willing to walk away from the relationship he'd known his entire life, for someone he'd met in biology lab.

Deep down, behind those sad and suspicious eyes, she was still in there. Still the playful, intelligent, perceptive woman he'd fallen for.

"I'm probably going to regret this, but I'll think about staying here until I get better. Maybe just a day or two. But…"

"Why is there always a *but*?" He rubbed the day-old scruff on his chin.

"But I sleep on the couch. You only have two bedrooms here. One is yours and the other has two cribs in it. The door was open on the way to the bathroom. I couldn't help but notice," she said in her defense.

"Yes, you can stay here. Thank you for asking. And who sleeps on the couch is up for debate. We'll figure out a fair way to decide." There was no way he was going to let her curl up on the sofa when he had a king-size bed in the other room. Most of the time, he nodded off with a laptop open next to him and a phone in his hand anyway. It was easier than facing an empty bed on his own.

"And hey, thanks for considering my proposal," he added.

Colton appreciated how difficult her situation must be for her to feel the need to hide in a random stranger's RV, and he appreciated the confidence she put in him by staying with him last night.

In the ultimate display of trust, she'd fallen deeply asleep.

She didn't speak, but he could see the impact of his words. Sometimes, silence said more than a thousand words ever could.

Colton put his hand on the small of Makena's back as he escorted her to the elevator. Emotions seemed to be getting the best of her, because she'd gotten all serious and quiet on him again. The lighter mood was gone and he wondered if it had something to do with what he'd said or the simple fact they were going back to the RV where she'd been staying.

There were so many unanswered questions bubbling up in his mind about Makena and her need to hide. Abusive exes he understood. But she'd been in hiding for months, and he wondered how much of it had to do with losing her mother. He knew firsthand what it was like to have a close bond with a parent who died. Colton and his siblings were still reeling from the loss of their father. Worsened by the fact none of them could solve the decades-old mystery about their only sister's abduction from her bedroom window.

Frustration was building with each passing day, along with the realization their father had gone to his deathbed never knowing what had happened to Caroline. Plus, there was the whole mess of Caroline's kidnapping being dredged up in the news ever since there'd been a kidnapping attempt in town a couple of months ago.

Renee Smith, now Renee O'Connor after marrying his brother Cash, had moved to Katy Gulch with her six-month-old daughter, Abby, in order to start a new life. Her past had come with her and it was a haunting reminder of what could happen when a relationship went sour.

Renee's ex had followed her to Katy Gulch unbeknownst to her and tried to take away the one thing she loved most, in order to frighten her into coming home.

Was Makena in the same boat?

At least in Makena's case, she knew what she was dealing with. Renee had been caught off guard because her ex had cheated on her and was having a child with a coworker before deciding no one else could have Renee. That was pretty much where the comparisons between the two ended.

He'd brought up a good point, though. Colton wanted to know more about Makena's ex so he could determine just how much danger she might be in.

The fact she'd left the man a year ago stuck in Colton's craw. The way he'd found her and discovered how she'd been living made him think that she'd either run out of money or couldn't get to hers.

But then, he didn't know many people who could go a year without working and survive. Colton may have come from one of the wealthiest cattle ranching families in Texas, but all the O'Connors had grown up with their feet on the ground and their heads out of the clouds. Each one was determined to make a mark on this life and not rely on the good graces of their family to earn a living despite loving the land and the family business.

Colton helped Makena into the passenger seat, where she buckled herself in. The drive to Mrs. Dillon's place was short. Colton checked in with Gert on the way and the rest of the car ride he spent mulling over what he already knew.

He hoped Makena was seriously considering his offer to let her stay at his apartment. He couldn't think of a safer place for her to heal. It dawned on him that he hadn't even asked her if she liked children. He just assumed she did.

That was one of the funny things about becoming a parent: he was guilty of thinking that everyone loved kids. Growing up in Katy Gulch didn't help, because most people were kind to children in his hometown.

Colton had to stop a couple of times to clear the road of debris. So far, it was looking like Katy Gulch had been spared the storm's fury.

Gert had reported in several times last night and first thing this morning to let him know that very few people had lost power. Neighbors were pitching in to make sure food didn't spoil and people had what they needed. It was one of the many reasons Colton couldn't imagine bringing up his boys in any other place.

The twins were fifth-generation O'Connors, but whether or not they took up ranching would be up to them. Both seemed happiest when they were outdoors. Colton prayed he could give them half the childhood he'd been fortunate to have. He and his brothers had

had the best. Of course, they'd also had their fair share of squabbles over the years.

Garrett and Cash seemed to rub each other the wrong way from just about the day Garrett was born. Make no mistake about it, though. Either one would be there for the other in a snap. Help needed? No questions asked.

Was it strange that Colton wished the same for Makena? He wished she could experience being part of a big family. It sounded like since losing her mother, she'd lost all the family she had. He couldn't even imagine what that would be like.

She'd remained quiet on the way over. They were getting close to Mrs. Dillon's and the river.

"Everything all right over there?" he asked her.

"Yeah, I'm good." The words were spoken with no conviction.

From the way she drawled out those three words, he could tell she was deep in thought. Her voice always had that sound when she was deep in concentration. He'd once accidentally interrupted her studying and heard that same sound.

He'd given her a lot to think about. To him, it was a no-brainer decision. Knowing Makena, she wouldn't want to live off him for free even for a few days.

It occurred to him that he was momentarily without a sitter. He wasn't even sure if she was up for the job, considering her left hip. She was walking better today, but she would know better than anyone else if she'd be able to keep up with the boys.

For the time being, it was a lot of bending over and letting them hold your fingers while they practiced walking. They also had swings and walkers and every other kid device his mother could think to buy for them.

He could put gates up to make it easier for her. More and more, he liked the idea. It would give her some pocket money and a legitimate place to stay. She wouldn't have to feel like she was imposing, if she took a short-term job with him just until he found someone permanent.

"How are you with children?"

"They seem to like me. I have been a music teacher in an elementary school. I don't know about little-littles. I don't have much experience with anyone younger than the age of five. But I do seem to be popular with eight-year-olds." Hearing her voice light up when she talked about her career warmed his heart. "Why?"

"It's just an idea. I already told you my babysitter had an emergency in Austin and had to quit. I also mentioned having my boys with my mom at the ranch isn't ideal for anything less than short-term. We have a lot going on in our family right now with our father passing recently. I was just wondering if you'd be interested in helping me out of a pinch. Would you consider taking care of the boys until I could find someone else full-time?"

He gripped the steering wheel until his knuckles went white, as he waited for an answer.

"When would you need me to start?"

Was she seriously considering this? Before she could change her mind, he added, "Now would be good. My mom can hang on for a couple more days if needed."

"Can you give me a few hours to think about it?"

"Take all the time you need, Makena. I don't have

any interviews set up just yet. Mom is on board with helping for a few days. I'm just trying to lighten her load."

"Okay." She nodded, giving him the impression that she liked the idea. "It's definitely something to think about. Maybe I could just meet the boys and see if they even like me."

"That's a good first step. I'm sure they will, though. They're easygoing babies. It might be good for you to see if that age scares you, without the pressure of signing on for a commitment." He liked the idea of taking some of the burden off his mother, considering everything she was going through. And the thought of Makena sticking around for a while.

"I've been so focused on my situation that I haven't considered what your family must be going through," she said. The conversation ended when Colton parked at Mrs. Dillon's house.

Makena had opened the passenger door and was out of the vehicle before Colton could get around to help her. "I just want to pick up the few things I always have with me."

As she walked toward the RV, a bad feeling gripped him.

He glanced around, unable to find the source that was causing the hairs on the back of his neck to tingle.

Why did it feel like they were walking into a trap?

Chapter Eight

The silver bullet–style RV sat on a parking pad behind the farmhouse and near the river. Makena had placed a foot on the step leading into the RV when she heard Colton's voice in the background, warning her. She craned her neck to get a good look at him.

"Stop." That one word was spoken with the kind of authority she'd never heard from him before. It was the same commanding cop voice she'd heard from River.

Colton locked gazes with her. "Take your hand off the handle slowly. Don't put any pressure on the latch. And then freeze."

Makena stood fixed to the spot as a chill raced up her spine at the forceful tone. The "cop voice" brought back a flood of bad memories.

Would it always remind her of River when she heard Colton talk like that? Even a simple friendship, let alone anything more, was out of the question if her body started trembling when she heard him give an order.

She also knew better than to argue with him. He'd obviously seen something and was warning her.

"Stay right where you are. Don't move." He was by her side in a matter of seconds.

Makena's heart hammered against her rib cage, beating out a staccato rhythm. Panic squeezed her chest, making inhaling air hurt.

"Stay steady. Don't shift your weight." Colton dropped down to all fours. In that moment, she knew exactly what he was looking for.

A bomb.

Sweat beaded on her forehead and rolled down her cheek. She focused on her breathing and willed herself not to flinch. She reminded herself to slowly breathe in and out. Her hands felt cold and clammy.

Although she couldn't exactly say she'd been living the past six months, she didn't want to die, either. And especially not here.

Her mouth tried to open but her throat was dry, and she couldn't seem to form words. Fear was replaced with anger. Anger at the fact that by hiding, she'd allowed River to run her life all these months. She'd been miserable and lonely, and had nearly starved because of him. But she'd survived. Now there'd be no going back.

Makena decided by sheer force of will that she would live. No matter what else happened, she would make it through this. It was the only choice she would allow herself to consider.

"There's a device strapped to the bottom of this step. Stay as still as you possibly can. We're going to get through this." Colton pushed up to standing and quickly scanned the area. Based on the expression on his face, which was calmer than she felt, she knew the situation was bad. He was too calm.

From the few action movies she'd seen, it seemed like if she moved, she'd be blown sky-high. She was afraid even to ask, because a slight shift in her weight, no matter how subconsciously she did it, would scatter her into a thousand tiny bits. More of that ice in her veins was replaced by fire.

River didn't get to do this. If anything happened to her, she needed Colton to know who was responsible. "My ex." She slowly exhaled, careful not to move so much as an inch.

"His name is River Myers. He works at the Dallas Police Department as an officer. He's the reason I've been on the run for the past six months. He has threatened me on numerous occasions. I walked away from a man who is armed and dangerous. He's calculating. He'll destroy me if he finds me before I locate evidence against him," she said in a voice as steady as the current in the river next to them.

"Don't you give up on me now. You're going to be fine. But the clock is ticking. I have no idea how much explosive is here and we're running out of options."

With that, he literally dove on top of her, knocking her off the step and covering her with his own body. When a blast didn't immediately occur, he said, "Let's get out of here."

With one arm hooked under her armpit, he scrambled toward a tree near the riverbank. He rounded the tree, placing it in between them and the RV. He hauled her back against his chest. He leaned back against the tree and dropped down, wrapping his arms around her.

Not two seconds later, an explosion sounded.

Her first thought was that she was thankful for Colton. If he hadn't been there, she'd be dead. Her brain couldn't process that information. It was going to take a while for that to sink in. Her second thought, as Colton's arms hugged her in a protective embrace, was that everything she'd owned in the past few months was gone.

The guitar her mother had given her had been blown to smithereens. The few clothes she had were gone along with it. It wasn't much but it was all she owned in the world.

A few tears of loss leaked out of her eyes. She sniffed them back, reminding herself this could've been a whole lot worse. It was hard to imagine, though. She had so little left from her mother.

She brought her right hand up, tracing the rose necklace with her fingers. Thankfully, she had at least one thing left from her mother.

A little voice in the back of her head pointed out that she had someone in her corner for the first time in a very long time. It wasn't the security of her mother's guitar or the few articles of clothing that meant something to her. But she had the necklace and she had Colton.

She would have to rebuild from there.

And then another thought struck. She was in danger. Real danger. Colton had a young family, and because of her, his twins had been almost orphaned. She'd never been more certain of the fact that she couldn't accept his help any longer.

Moving forward, she planned to ask him for a loan, some kind of cover identity and a ticket out of town. She'd been crazy to stay in Texas. It was only a matter of time before River and his buddies would find her there. She'd adopted the hiding-in-plain-sight strategy and it had backfired big time.

Staying in the country was no longer an option. Since Mexico bordered Texas, she could slip across the border and make a new life. Maybe she could get down to one of the resorts and work in a kitchen or someplace where she'd be hidden from view.

A ringing noise in her ear covered the sound of Colton's voice. The only reason she realized he was talking at all was because she felt his chest vibrate against her back. The blast had been deafening. And at least temporarily, she'd lost hearing. Bits of metal had blown past her and the last thing she'd heard was the bomb detonate.

Everything felt like it was moving in slow motion. It was like time had stopped and everything around her moved in those old-fashioned movie frames and some mastermind stood behind a curtain clicking slides.

When the last of the debris seemed to have flown past and everything was still, Colton scooted out from underneath her and whirled around to check the damage.

Her heart went out to the owner, the sweet woman who'd just lost a remnant from her past.

Makena balled her fists and slammed them into the unforgiving earth in frustration.

Colton had disappeared from view. She rolled around onto all fours to see for herself. The door had been blown completely off its hinges. Many of the contents had gone flying. The RV was on fire. Colton had raced to his sport utility and returned with a fire extinguisher before she was able to get to her feet.

River hadn't just sent a potent message. His intention had been to kill her. All those times he'd threatened her came racing back. And so did the memory of the pair of men she'd seen the other day.

WITHIN THE HOUR, Colton had cordoned off the crime scene. A few of his deputies arrived on-site to aid in the investigation. There was no need to call in a bomb expert. The one that had caused the kind of damage the RV had sustained was a simple job. One that anyone could've logged onto the internet and bought materials to make.

Hell, any person old enough to know how to use a phone and have access to a credit card could grab the materials used here. The bomb was crude but would've done the job of killing Makena if he hadn't been there.

A ringing noise still sounded in Colton's ears, but his hearing was coming back at least. People didn't have to shout at him anymore for him to hear what they were saying.

Deputy Fletcher walked over. He had on gloves. His palm was out, and a key chain was on top. It was a classic hotel style, with the words *Home sweet home* inscribed on the black plastic.

"What's this?" Colton asked his deputy.

Fletcher shrugged. "Found it about fifteen feet from the RV."

"Let's check with Makena to see if she recognizes it." He led Fletcher over to the spot where she was being examined by EMT Samantha Rodriguez. There were no visible signs of bleeding, so she'd been spared being impaled by debris. Colton, on the other hand, hadn't been so lucky. He'd taken a nick to his shoulder, and he was holding a T-shirt pressed to the wound to stem the bleeding.

Samantha's partner, Oliver Matthew, had tried to get Colton to stop long enough for treatment, but he had a crime scene to manage and wouldn't take any chance that evidence could end up trampled on.

"Does this look familiar to you?" he asked Makena, pointing toward the key chain on Fletcher's palm.

She gasped.

"I bought one just like that for River after moving in together. He kept losing his key, so I ordered a key chain for him. That looks exactly like the one I bought," she stated.

"Bag it and see if you can lift a print," he said to Fletcher.

"Yes, sir." Fletcher turned and walked toward his service vehicle after thanking Makena for her confirmation.

Although any Joe Schmo could make this bomb, Colton had zeroed in on one name: River Myers. And now he might have proof. Colton was a little too familiar with the law enforcement statistics. Police officers battered their spouses in shockingly high numbers. The stress of the job was partly to blame and the reason why Colton, as a law enforcement leader, went to great lengths to offer programs and resources to help combat a pervasive issue with his deputies and employees. He saw it as his responsibility to ensure the mental and physical fitness of the men and women who served under him.

However, he could only keep an eye on his employees and do his level best to ensure they had plenty of tools to manage the stress that came with a career like theirs. He couldn't force them to take advantage of a program. An old saying came to mind: "You can lead a horse to water but you can't make it drink."

One of the advantages of running a smaller department like his office came in the form of being able to be up-front and personal with each one of his employees. A large department like Dallas wouldn't have that same benefit. Running an organization that large presented challenges.

In no way, shape or form was Colton condoning or justifying what a cop under duress might do. He held his people to the highest standards. Part of the reason why he was so selective in the hiring process. In a bigger setup, it would be easier to slip through the cracks.

When the site had been secured and medical attention given, he made his way back to Makena. Samantha turned to him.

"Her hearing should return to normal in a few days. Other than that, she was very lucky."

The last word Colton would use to describe Makena was *lucky.* Bad things happened to good people sometimes. But he understood what Samantha meant. The situation could've been a whole lot worse, with neither one of them walking away from it.

They'd also been fortunate that the pressure on the step had set off a timer and not a detonator. Those critical fifteen seconds had saved both of their lives.

"I'm so sorry, Colton. I should've known something like this would happen." Makena's pale blue eyes were wide. Fear flashed across them for a moment, followed by anger and determination. Two emotions that could get her in trouble.

"You know this isn't your fault." He needed to reassure her of the fact. He thanked Samantha.

The EMT folded her arms, put her feet in an athletic stance and shot him a death glare. "You are going to let me check out that shoulder now. Right?"

Samantha knew him well enough to realize he would put up a fight. Colton always made sure everyone around him was okay first.

"I'm standing here right now, aren't I?"

"Good." She didn't bother to hide the shock in her voice. She bent down to her medical bag and ordered him to take off his shirt, which he did.

"This is the only injury I sustained other than the ears, just like Makena."

Samantha stood up and made quick work tending to the cut in his shoulder. Within minutes, she'd cleaned the wound, applied antibiotic ointment and patched it up with a butterfly bandage.

"This should help it heal up nicely. I'd try to talk you into stopping by the ER for a few stitches, but I didn't want to push my luck."

"I appreciate the recommendation. This should be good." He'd grown up working a cattle ranch, so it wasn't the first time he'd ended up with a scar on his body. Nor would it be the last. He thanked Samantha for doing a fine job, which she had.

She told him it was no trouble at all before closing up her bag and heading toward the driver's seat of her ambulance. He would've just patched himself up but didn't want to appear a hypocrite in front of Makena after urging her to seek care.

Before he could open his mouth to speak, Makena threw herself into his chest and buried her face. He stroked her long, silky hair, figuring this was a rare show of emotion for her.

He couldn't be certain how long they stood there. Being with her, it was like time had stopped, and nothing else mattered except making sure she was okay.

When she pulled back, his heart clenched as he looked at her. She wore the same expression as she had that last day of biology lab. He'd been so tempted to ask her out despite the fact that it had been made clear she was with someone else. It would've gone against everything he believed in. Honor. Decency. He'd never break the code of asking someone out who was married, in a relationship, or dating someone else.

He'd cleaned up his own relationship at home, realizing that he and Rebecca would never have the kind of spark that he'd felt with Makena. He'd decided right then and there, with his nineteen-year-old self, that he'd hold out for that feeling to come around again. Little did he know just how rare it could be.

All these years later, he'd never felt it again until recently. It was then he realized what he and Makena had had was special.

"It's not safe for me to be here anymore, Colton. I know you need a statement from me, but I'd like to keep my name as quiet as possible. He obviously found me here and he'll find me again. I'll be ready next time. I took his threats too lightly. Not anymore."

"I do need a statement from you. And I have no authority to force you to stay in Katy Gulch. Whether or not you do, a crime happened here in my jurisdiction. Someone's property was damaged and there was an attempted murder and that makes it my responsibility. So, whether you're here or not, I plan to investigate." Why did the news of her wanting to run away impale him?

She had every right to do what she felt was necessary to protect herself. Now that he knew her ex was in law enforcement, so many of her reactions made sense to him. That fact alone made a relationship between them practically impossible.

Given Colton's line of work, she would always be reminded of her ex.

Makena shook her head furiously. "I understand you have to file a report. Believe me when I say you don't want to chase this guy down. Look what he's capable of, Colton. You have a family. You have young boys who depend on you. I won't have your life taken away from them because of something I did."

"Is that what you believe? That any of this is somehow your fault?"

"I didn't mean it like that. I know what River did in the past and now is completely on him. I didn't deserve it then and I don't deserve it now. I won't take responsibility for any of his actions. That's all on him. But *I* brought that man to your doorstep. That's the responsibility I feel."

"You're right about one thing. You did nothing wrong."

Her chin quivered at hearing those words, so he repeated them. "You did nothing wrong."

She was nodding her head and looked to be fighting back tears. "I know."

"Sometimes we just need to hear it from someone else."

"Thank you, Colton. You have no idea what you've done for me in the past twenty-four hours and how much that has truly meant to me, which is why I can't burden you any more than I have."

Colton had his hands up, stopping her from going down that road again. "In case you hadn't noticed, Makena, this is my job. This is what I do. And yes, there are personal risks. Believe me when I say that I don't take them lightly. Also, know that I take safety very personally. I have every intention of walking through the door every night to my boys as I watch them grow up. There is no other option in my mind. And if this had been anyone else but you in this situation, I would still be following the same protocol. Most law enforcement officials are there for all the right reasons. It's rare for them to go completely rogue or off the chain. But when they do, they aren't just a danger to one person. They will be a threat to women, to children and to men. That's not something I can live with on my conscience. Not to mention the fact that I'm a law enforcement officer. Being on this job is in my blood."

He stopped there. He'd said enough. He gave her a few moments to let that sink in while he walked her over to his SUV.

Makena took in a deep breath. "Okay."

She blew the breath out.

Colton hoped that meant she'd heard what he said and was ready for him to continue his investigation.

"Let's do this. Let's make sure that River Myers never hurts another soul again. I'll tell you everything I know about him."

Colton helped her into the passenger seat before closing the door and claiming his spot. Pride filled his chest. It wasn't easy for anyone to go against someone they'd cared about or, worse yet, someone they were afraid of. It took incredible courage to do what she was doing, and he couldn't be prouder of her than he was right then.

After giving Colton a description of her ex, his badge number, his social security and his license plate, she dropped another bomb on him.

"Abuse is not the only thing he's guilty of. I don't know the names of the people he was talking to one night in my garage but I'd heard a noise and when I went to investigate, River flipped out. He rushed me back inside the house and threatened me. He told me that I had no idea what I'd just done. All I can figure is that I walked in on some kind of meeting between the three of them."

"Did you hear what they were talking about, by chance?"

"I wish I had. He rushed me out of there too early and I was too chicken to go back." Her hands were balled fists on her legs. "I guess they were planning something or talking about something they didn't want anyone else to know about. They sounded threatening and there was a handprint around River's throat. I thought I overheard something about getting someone to pay but I have no idea what that means."

"Were the other men in uniform?"

"No. They weren't. They were in regular street

clothes but they acted like cops." That didn't mean they weren't officers.

"Did you get a good look at them?"

"Yes. As a matter of fact, I did. And I saw them here three days ago. It's the reason I ducked into the RV and didn't leave for three days straight."

That explained why she'd practically starved to death by the time she'd walked out to find food. So many things clicked in the back of his mind. Like the fact that she'd gone out in a driving rain when there were no cars out. It must have been to forage for food. The way she'd gobbled down that sandwich and apple made more sense to him now.

He'd wondered how long it had been since she'd had a meal.

"I knew I'd stuck around too long and I was preparing to move on. Seeing them scared me to the core. River had always been clear. If I left him, he would hunt me down and kill me. He would see the divorce as the ultimate betrayal."

Another thought dawned on Colton. River may not have been trying to kill her. His cohorts, on the other hand, seemed ready to do the job.

They could be in league with River. They may or may not be cops themselves, but they definitely could be doing his dirty work.

"Describe them to me in as much detail as you can remember."

Chapter Nine

"The first one I saw was around six feet tall. He had a football-player build, with a clean-shaven face. His hair was light red...kind of strawberry blond. He had a thick neck and big hands. Other than that, I remember that he had light skin and freckles." Makena remembered the men vividly because they were so different.

Colton nodded.

"The second guy had one of those 1970s mustaches on an otherwise clean face. Black hair with big bushy eyebrows. He had these puffed-out cheeks like he had a big wad of gum or tobacco in his jaws. His hair was short and thick and a little wavy. I remember that he was several inches shorter than Red. They were so distinct-looking and oddly matched. Opposites. That's what I remember about them from that night."

"Did you have a chance to hear their voices? Would you recognize them if you heard them?"

She shook her head.

"Cops?" he asked.

"I don't know for certain. I can't be one hundred percent sure. They looked like they were law enforcement. They had that cop carriage, if you know what I mean."

Colton nodded. He seemed to know exactly what she was talking about. There was just a cop swagger. Being on the job, wearing a holster for long shifts day in and day out caused them to hold their arms out a little more than usual. They also walked with the kind of confidence that said they could handle themselves in almost any situation. They had the training to back it up.

"What shift did your ex work?" Colton asked.

"Deep nights. He requested them. Said he liked to be out and about when everyone else was asleep." She couldn't imagine anything had changed in the past few months since she'd been gone, considering the fact that River had been on deep nights for almost fifteen years.

"A couple of my brothers work in law enforcement," he said.

"Oh yeah?"

"U.S. Marshals. They would help if we brought them up to speed." Colton had scribbled down descriptions of Red and Mustache Man. He also made notes about River's shift preference. Considering it was only ten thirty in the morning, River would be home and still asleep.

"I'm not sure it's such a good idea." A lot was coming at her, fast. She needed a minute to process. "Can I think about it first?"

He nodded and then moved on. "Could he afford the residence you shared on his own?"

"I moved into his bachelor pad and fixed it up. It's likely that he's still there. He doesn't really like change."

Colton checked the clock on his dashboard. It was almost like he read her thoughts. He started the engine of his sport utility. "I have a few calls to make that might go a little easier in my office. You okay with that?"

What he was really asking was would she stay with
him? She could read between the lines. Since she had
nowhere to go, literally, and no friends in town, she
nodded. The honest truth was that she didn't feel safe
with anyone but Colton. Being with him was warmth
and campfires despite the dangers all around.

She leaned her head back and brought her hands
up to rub her temples. Her head hurt. A dull ache was
forming between her eyes. The headache distracted
her from her hip pain. Now, there was something. She
was getting punchy.

Makena appreciated the fact that the ride to Colton's
office was short. She climbed out of the sport utility,
her hip reminding her that it wasn't quite finished with
her yet.

The driver's-side door of a blue sports sedan popped
open two spots down, the driver having cut off the engine almost the minute she stepped out of the SUV.
Makena flinched.

The person held something toward Colton. As the
youngish man, early thirties if she had to guess, bum-
rushed them, Colton tensed. His gaze bounced from
being locked onto the guy he seemed to recognize and
then across the rest of the cars in the lot. The way he
watched anything that moved reminded her just how
out in the open they were in the parking lot.

The jerk with what she recognized as his phone in
his hand caught up to them. "Sheriff O'Connor."

"Mike."

"Sir, do you care to comment on your sister's kidnapping and the recent crime wave in Katy Gulch?"

Colton stopped dead in his tracks. He turned to face

the guy named Mike, who Makena assumed was a reporter. "That story has been dead for decades, Mike. What's wrong? Slow news week?"

"Sir, I—I—I…"

"I accept your apology, Mike. Now, if you don't mind, I have business to attend to in my office." Colton turned his back on the reporter and started walking toward the building. He said out the side of his mouth, "But if there are any new leads, you'll be the first to know."

Considering Colton's stiff demeanor, it was clear to Makena the story about his sister's kidnapping was off-limits.

Mike stood there, looking dumbfounded.

Makena heard what was said, and she couldn't help but think about the fact that Colton's father had just died. She wondered if the two incidents were connected in some way. That had to be unlikely, given that Colton himself had said his sister's kidnapping was decades old. Colton had also mentioned a kidnapping attempt on his newly minted sister-in-law's adopted daughter and then there was his father's death. A family like the O'Connors could be a target for any twisted individual who wanted to make a buck. A shudder raced through her. She could only imagine based on her experience of living in fear for the months on end what it must be like living on guard at all times.

Colton had mentioned that a couple of his brothers had gone on to become US marshals. He was sheriff. She had to wonder if their choices to go into law enforcement had anything to do with a need to protect each other and keep their family safe.

The minute Colton walked through the front door and into the lobby, a woman who seemed to be in her late sixties popped up from her desk, set the phone call she'd been on down, and ran over to give Colton a warm hug. The moment was sweet and the action seemed to come from a genuine place.

"Thank heavens you're okay." The woman had to be Gert, Makena guessed from the sound of her voice. It also made sense that she would be at Colton's office.

When Gert finally released him from the hug, he introduced her to Makena.

"I'm pleased as punch to meet you. I'm sorry for the day you've had. Can I get you anything? Coffee? Water?"

"Coffee sounds great. Just point me in a direction and I can get my own cup." Makena echoed Gert's sentiments. Now that she'd had a minute to process the fact that her ex had tried to blow her to smithereens, she needed a strong cup of coffee.

"Don't be silly. I'd be happy to get you a cup. I just put on a fresh pot."

"If you're offering, I'll take a cup of that coffee, too." He placed his hand on the small of Makena's back and led her through a glass door that he had to scan his badge to enter. He hooked a right in what looked to be a U-shaped building and then led her halfway down the hall. His office was on the right.

"Make yourself comfortable," Colton said. "Is there anything else you'd like besides coffee?"

"No, thank you." The shock of the day's events was starting to wear off. The annoying ringing noise was a constant companion as she moved to the leather sofa and then took a seat.

Colton moved behind his desk. "Professional courtesy dictates that I make a call to Mr. Myers's chief before questioning him."

"Won't that give River a heads-up that you want to speak to him?" The thought of being in the same room again with her ex fired more of that anger through her veins. It needed to be a courtroom, the next time. And he needed to be going to jail for a very long time. One way or another, she would find a way for justice to be served and keep him from harming other innocent people. But the River she knew wouldn't exactly lie down and take what was coming his way. Without a doubt, he'd deny any involvement.

The explosion and fire would have made certain there were no fingerprints. When she really thought about the crime, it was an easy way on his part to get away with murder. No one would know her in Katy Gulch. That meant she would most likely have ended up a Jane Doe. She'd quit her job and disappeared. No one would miss her.

She could vanish and there was no one to notice. How sad had her life become since marrying him, since her mother's drawn-out illness, that Makena could die at the hands of her ex and no one would know?

The only person she knew in Katy Gulch was Colton. He would have had no reason to suspect a blast from the past. He wouldn't have been looking for her. And if she'd been badly burned, which seemed like the plan, her face would have been unrecognizable anyway. It had been a near-perfect setup.

She flexed and released her fingers a couple of times to work out some of the tension. She rolled her shoulders back and took in a couple of deep breaths. She couldn't imagine trying to hurt someone she supposedly cared about.

Colton's voice broke through her heavy thoughts. She realized he was on a call.

"Yes, sir. My name is Sheriff Colton O'Connor and I need to speak with Chief Shelton. This is a professional courtesy call and I need to speak to him about one of his officers." Colton was silent for a few beats. And then came, "Thank you, sir."

A few more beats of silence, and then someone must've picked up on the other line. Gert walked in about that same moment with two mugs of coffee in her hands. She set the first one down on Colton's desk, which was the closest to her. The other one she brought over to Makena, who accepted the offering and thanked Colton's secretary for her kindness.

Gert produced a couple packets of sugar and a pack of creamer from her pocket and set them down on the coffee table along with a stir stick. Gert made eye contact and nodded. The sincerity, warmth and compassion in her gaze settled over Makena. It was easy to see the woman had a heart of gold. She disappeared out of the room after Makena mouthed a thank-you.

"As I said before, this is a professional courtesy call to let you know that the name of one of your police officers came up in the course of an investigation today." Colton was silent for a moment. "Yes, sir. The officer's name is River Myers. A few more seconds of silence followed. "Is that right?" A longer pause. This time the silence dragged on. Colton glanced at her, caught her eye and then nodded. She could tell there was a storm brewing behind his cobalt eyes.

After Colton explained to the Dallas police chief that he wanted to speak to River in connection with an attempted murder case, there was even more silence.

Colton ended the call by thanking the chief for his time and by promising that he would keep him abreast of his investigation.

"What did he say?" She waited for Colton to hang up before asking the question.

"He wished me luck with my investigation. He said his office was fully prepared to cooperate. And then he informed me that River Myers is on administrative leave pending an investigation."

Makena gasped as all kinds of horrible thoughts crossed her mind. "Did he say what River was being investigated for?"

Colton's earlier words that she needed to speak up so she could prevent anyone else from getting hurt slammed into her. Had River done something to another woman he was in a relationship with?

"The chief said he really can't share a lot of details for an ongoing investigation, but in the spirit of reciprocity, he said an internal affairs division investigation was underway on two counts of police brutality and one count of extortion."

Relief washed over Makena that River wasn't already being looked at for murder. He was, now. "What does being placed on administrative leave mean?"

"It's basically where he would be required to hand in his department-issued weapons along with his badge until the investigation is over and it's decided whether or not any criminal charges would be filed." Colton took a sip of coffee.

Makena brought her hand up to her mouth. If River had still been on the job, they would know exactly where to find him. "Does this mean what I think? That he's out there somewhere? Going rogue?"

"That is a distinct possibility." Colton's grip on his coffee mug caused his knuckles to go white. With his free hand, he drummed his fingers on his desk. "I need to issue a BOLO with his name and description. I don't want my deputies being caught unawares if they happen to run into him personally or on a traffic stop."

Colton mentioned a couple of other things before jumping into action. Not five minutes later, he'd had Gert issue the BOLO, he'd started the report on the explosion, and he'd nearly polished off his second cup of coffee. Once he'd taken care of those preliminary details, he looked at her. "My next call needs to be to my mother. But first, I want to know where you stand. Will you stay with me until the investigation runs its course?"

The look on his face suggested he expected an argument. She had none.

"I appreciate the offer. You already know my concerns about bringing danger to your doorstep. And then there's your boys to consider."

"Don't worry about my sons. For the time being, they'll be safe at the ranch. I know my mom will pull through and yet she's the one I worry about the most. I have two new sisters-in-law I forgot about before, who I can ask to pitch in. The ranch has a lot of security in place already, and I don't mind adding to it. In fact, it might not be a bad idea for me to take you to my home there. Times will come up when I have to leave for the investigation or for work, and I want to know that you're safe."

Makena could stay on the ranch safely with all the extra security. She could not live with bringing danger around Colton and his children. "I'll stay with you at your apartment or I'll wait here at your office if you need to investigate someone without me there. But I won't go to the ranch. It's too dangerous for the people."

Colton rubbed the scruff on his chin. He took a sip of coffee. "That's fair."

She hoped so, because it was the only offer on the table. If she had to sit in the office for an entire day, she would. There was no way in hell she was going to risk his family. Granted, River wanted her. But she couldn't be certain that he wouldn't use one of them to draw her out. It was a gamble she had no intention of taking.

Makena rolled up her sleeves and drained her cup. She set the mug down on the coffee table. She placed her flat palms on her thighs and looked at Colton.

"What's next?"

"You tell me everything you can think of about your ex. His favorite restaurant. Whether or not he's a fisherman and has a fishing lease. Is he a hunter? Does he have a hunting license? Who are his friends? And then, I go track him down."

"Hold on there. I'm the best person to help find him. I want to go to Dallas with you."

"Not a chance. The agreement we just made was that you would stay here while I investigate. It's either here or my apartment. I need to know that I can trust you to do what you say you're going to do."

"I wouldn't lie to you. I just thought it would be easier to track him down with me involved."

"If you're his target and he sees you, it could be game over."

"I'm not arguing. However, trying to blow me to pieces on a timer once I thought I was safely inside an RV doesn't exactly make me feel like he wants to be connected to my murder in any way. In fact, he seems to be taking great pains to kill me without leaving any trail back to him."

"True enough. The explosion was most likely meant to cover his tracks. We also have to broaden the scope. You saw his friends…or…acquaintances might be a better word. You said yourself they were speaking in hushed tones. We can go after them, too. They might be acting on his behalf or they might be on their own."

"Oh, I doubt anyone would do that. Not with River's temper. He never struck me as the type to step aside."

"We have to keep unbiased eyes on the case and we have to follow the evidence. Right now, you saw two people from your past in town three days ago and that spawned you to disappear into the RV."

"Allegedly saw. I mean, they were far away and I can't be one hundred percent certain it was them."

"Okay. What are the chances the two guys you saw, even at a distance, weren't the men you saw in your garage?" He was playing devil's advocate. She could see that. Looking at the case from every angle probably made him a good investigator.

It was impossible for Makena not to lead with emotions in this case. For one, the explosion was targeted at her. And for another, River's threats echoed in her mind. To her thinking, he was delivering on threats he'd made six months ago.

Chapter Ten

Colton spent the next hour getting to know River Myers. He then made a quick call to his mother, and she agreed the twins staying on with her would be for the best, at least for a couple of days.

He knew better than anyone that investigations often took far longer than that, but he hoped for a break in this one. If Makena's ex was determined to erase her and she was constantly at Colton's side, he would have to get through Colton first. Makena had made a list of River's known hangouts. Colton had handed the list over to Gert, who'd meticulously called each one to ask when the last time River had been in.

So far, no one had seen or heard from River for the past month. Of course, the couple of places that were known cop hangouts most likely wouldn't admit to seeing him if he was standing in front of their faces.

Other than that, he frequented a popular Tex-Mex restaurant and a couple of taco chains. None of the managers or employees admitted to seeing the man in the past few weeks if not a month.

The timing of River sticking to himself coincided with when he was put on leave according to the chief.

It was odd, since the guy would've had more free time on his hands. Usually, that meant being seen in his favorite haunts more often. In River's case, he seemed to be hunkering down.

A call to one of his neighbors revealed that it didn't seem like he'd been home, either. There were no lights left on in the evenings, and the neighbor hadn't seen his truck in a couple of weeks.

"What are the chances he has a new girlfriend?" Colton asked Makena.

She looked up from her notebook, where she'd been trying to recall and write down all the places he could've possibly gone to.

"Anything is possible. Right?" She tapped her pencil on the pad. "I mean, he's not really the type to be alone and he was served with divorce papers not long after I disappeared. I worked through my lawyer to finish up the paperwork."

"If River is spending all his time at a new girlfriend's house, it might be harder to track him down." His personal phone number had changed. Colton had his guess as to why that might have happened.

As word spread about the morning's incident, Colton's phone started ringing off the hook. Everyone in the community wanted to pitch in and help find the person responsible for blowing up Mrs. Dillon's RV. Colton couldn't give any more details than that and it was impossible to keep this story completely quiet considering how much neighbors watched out for each other in Katy Gulch.

After hours of receiving and making phone calls, Colton realized it was past dinnertime. Not a minute later, Gert knocked on the office door. It was a courtesy knock because Colton had a long-standing open-door policy.

"It might be time to take a break," Gert said. They both knew she would go home and continue working on the case, but it was her signal she was heading out.

"Let me know if you get any leads or figure out anything that I've missed," Colton said. He stretched out his arms and yawned, realizing he'd been sitting in the same position for hours. It was no wonder his back was stiff. His ears were still ringing from the explosion this morning but there was improvement there, too.

"You know I will, sir." Gert waved to Makena before exiting the room. Before she got more than a few steps down the hall she shouted back at them. "I'll lock the front door."

Colton turned to Makena. "What do you think about taking this back to my apartment? We should probably get up and get our blood moving. And then there's dinner. You must be starved by now."

"That's probably a good idea. I'm not starving, but I could eat. The bags of nuts and trail mix that Gert has been bringing me have tided me over."

"I'll just close up a couple of files and log out and then we can go." Colton tried not to notice when Makena stood up and stretched just how long her legs were. She had just the right amount of soft curves, and all he could think about was running his hand along those gorgeous lines…

He forced his gaze away from her hips—a place he had no business thinking about. He straightened up his desk and then closed out of the files on his desktop. His laptop had access to the same system, and he could get just as much done at home. He figured Makena would be more comfortable there anyway.

It also occurred to him that she'd lost everything she owned except the clothes on her back. He stood up and pushed his chair in. He gripped the back of his chair with both hands. "We can stop off anywhere you need on the way to my house. I'm sure you want a change of clothes and something to sleep in."

"I appreciate the offer, but pretty much everything I own was blown up. I don't have any ID or credit cards with me." He realized that she wouldn't want to carry ID in case she got picked up. Now that he knew her ex was a cop, he understood why she'd gone to the lengths she had to keep her identity a secret.

"How about I take care of it for you? It really wouldn't be any trouble—"

"You're already doing so much for me, Colton. It's too much to ask. I'll be fine with what I have."

"I promise it isn't. We don't have to do anything fancy. We can stop off at one of those big-box stores. There's one on the way home. We can let you pick up a few supplies. It would be a loan. Just until you get back on your feet. I have a feeling once we lock this jerk away for good, you'll get back on your feet in no time. For old times' sake, I'd like to be the one to give you a temporary hand up."

Colton hoped he'd put that in a way that didn't offend her. He wasn't trying to give her a handout. All he wanted was to give her a few comfort supplies while they located the bastard who'd tried to kill her.

She raked her top teeth over her bottom lip, a sure

sign she was considering his offer. Then again, with her back against the wall, she might not feel like she had any options.

"I promise it's no trouble, and if you don't want to take the stuff with you, you could always leave it at my place. One of my new sisters-in-law will probably fit the same clothes. Renee looks to be about your size, if leaving them would make you feel better. It would certainly make me feel better to be able to help you out. Besides, you're probably the only reason I passed biology lab."

That really made her laugh. "I was terrible at biology lab. If you hadn't helped me, I would've failed and I'm pretty certain I dragged your grade down."

"I might have been better at the actual work than you were, but you were the only reason I kept going to class."

Her smile practically lit up the room. It was nice to make her smile for a change after all she'd been through. She deserved so much better.

"I tell you what. I'll let you buy me some new clothes. But once this is over, maybe I can stick around a few days and watch the boys for you as a way to pay you back. I'm not sure I'm any good with kids that age and they might not even like me, but I'm willing to try. And who knows, we might actually have some fun. It would make me feel so much better if I can do something nice for you."

"Deal." He wouldn't look a gift horse in the mouth. This was something nice, and she made a good point. He was halting his nanny search so he could throw himself completely into this investigation. As much as the process would take time, he was also keenly aware that the colder the trail, the colder the leads. His best bet at nailing the bastard would come in a window of opportunity he had in the next seventy-two hours. If the investigation dragged on longer than that, the apprehension rate would drop drastically.

Unless there was another attempt. Colton didn't even want to consider that option.

"Do you want to take a minute to order a few things on the laptop? We can put a rush on the order, and they'll have it ready by the time we swing through. I just need to turn off a few lights and double-check the break room." He handed his laptop over.

"Sure." She sat down in one of the leather club chairs across from his desk and studied the screen as he headed down the hallway.

Turning off the lights had been an excuse to give her a few minutes alone to order. In reality, he didn't like the idea of her going out in public where she'd be exposed. A skilled rifleman could take her out from the top of a building or beside a vehicle.

And then there was the gossip mill to consider. Most of the time, he didn't mind it. For the most part, people were trying to be helpful by sharing information. Being seen with him would be news. Like it or not, the O'Connors were in the public eye and people seemed to enjoy discussing the details of his family's private lives.

He took his time checking rooms before returning. The laptop was closed. She stood up the minute she heard him come in the room. "Ready?"

"All set," she said, handing over the device. He tucked it under one arm before placing his hand on the small of her back and leading her out the rear of the building. He guided her down the hall and outside, deciding it would be safer to take his personal vehicle home.

His pickup truck was parked out back.

"I don't want to run into Mike or anyone else sniffing around for a story." It was true. But he also didn't want to risk going out the same way he'd come in, just in case River or one of his cohorts was watching. That part Colton decided to keep to himself.

Colton finally exhaled the breath he'd been holding when they were safely inside his truck and on the road. It was past seven o'clock, and it wouldn't be dark for another hour and a half this time of year.

Being out in the daylight made him feel exposed. He kept his guard up, searching the face of every driver as he passed them. He stopped off at the box store and pulled into the pickup lane. A quick text later, an employee came running out to the designated curbside area.

Colton thanked the guy and handed him a five-dollar bill. The rest of the ride to his apartment took all of ten minutes. He pulled up to the garage and punched in the security code before zipping through the opened gate.

From a security standpoint, the place wouldn't be that difficult to breech on foot. But the gate kept other drivers from coming in and closed quickly enough after he pulled through that it would be impossible to back-draft him.

Colton had spent part of the drive thinking through something that had been bugging him since he'd gotten off the phone with the DPD chief. If River was being investigated for serious charges like police brutality and extortion, there had to be a reasonable complainant involved. Considering there were several charges against him, he wondered what kind of huddle Makena could've walked into that night, when she'd interrupted River and the other two men.

It was obviously a meeting of some kind. The fact that River had ushered her away so fast meant that he was trying to protect his group, or her. Possibly both. In his twisted mind, he probably believed that he loved his wife.

Abusers usually thought they cared for their partners. Forget that their version of caring was tied up with control and abuse, sometimes physical. When they realized that, they seemed to have some sense of remorse. For others, it was just a way of life.

Thinking back, Colton wondered if Makena's life would've turned out differently if he'd somehow plucked up the courage to ask her out.

But then, his own life might've turned out differently, too. Having the twins was one of the best things that had ever happened to him. He wouldn't trade his boys for the world. And even though his wife had died, he wouldn't trade the years of friendship they'd had, either.

Since regret was about as productive as stalking an ant to find cheese, he didn't go there often. Life happened. He'd lost Rebecca. He'd gained two boys out of their relationship.

Makena's life might not have turned out differently even if they had dated. There was no way to go back and find out. And even if they could…change one thing and the ripple effect could be far-reaching.

Returning his focus to the case, he thought about Red and Mustache Man. The what-if questions started popping into his mind.

What if Red and Mustache had been working to shake someone down? Considering one of the charges against River was extortion, it was a definite possibility.

If Mustache and Red had come to Katy Gulch, were they sticking around? Were they acting alone? Were they after her because they thought she'd heard something in her garage that night?

Alarm bells sounded at the thought. He felt like he was onto something there.

This could've been an attempt to…what?

Hold on. Colton had it. If River had gone into hiding and the guys blew up Makena, would that be enough to bring him out?

COLTON THREW A PIZZA in the oven while Makena mixed together a salad from contents she'd found in the fridge. Working in the kitchen with her was a nice change to a frozen dinner in front of his laptop after the boys were in bed.

They'd just sat down at the island to eat when his cell phone buzzed. He glanced at the screen and saw Gert's name. Makena was sitting next to him, so he tilted the screen in her direction before taking the call. He held the phone to his ear.

"This is Colton. I'm going to put you on speaker. Is that okay?" There was some information that was sensitive enough that Makena shouldn't hear.

"Fine by me, sir."

Colton put the call on speaker and set it in between

him and Makena on the island. "Okay. Makena and I are listening."

"Sir, Deputy Fletcher was canvassing in Birchwood and stopped off at a motel along the highway. He got a hit." Her voice practically vibrated with excitement. Gert loved the investigation process. "The clerk told Deputy Fletcher a man matching River Myers's description had been staying at her motel for the past four days. The clerk's name is Gloria Beecham and this place is a rent-by-the-hour type, if you know what I mean. She said he was a cash customer. Given the amount of time he'd been there and the fact that he kept the Do Not Disturb sign on the door the whole time, housekeeping was freaked out by the guy."

Colton wasn't surprised. Hotels and motels had tightened up their processes to ensure every room was checked.

"Housekeeping alerted the clerk to the fact. She made a call to let him know that housekeeping had to check his room every twenty-four hours by law. She said that when they came to clean, he would stand in the corner of the room with the door open and his arms crossed over his chest."

"Odd behavior," Colton noted.

"It sure is." She made a tsk noise. "They never did find anything suspicious, and honestly, admitted to getting in and out of there just as fast as they could."

"And this mystery man matched River's description?" he asked.

"Yes, sir."

"He was staying in the room alone?" This could be

a solid lead. Colton looked at Makena, who was on the edge of her seat.

"Yes, sir."

"Did they say whether anyone else ever came in or out of the room?"

"No. No one to her knowledge. She started keeping an eye on the room by the camera mounted outside. This place has no interior spaces. It's the kind of place where you park right in front of your door and use a key to go straight inside. So there are cameras along the exterior overhangs. She said it was something the owner had insisted on installing over a year ago. The funny thing is, he struck her as odd because his face was always pointed the opposite direction of the nearest camera."

"He was smart enough to realize that cameras might be in use."

"So much so, in fact, he wore a ball cap most of the time. He kept his chin tucked to his chest as he walked in and out of the building."

"Did they, by chance, get a make and model on his vehicle?" Colton asked.

"No, sir. They did not. He never parked close enough to the door for the cameras to pick up his vehicle."

Colton wished there were parking lot cameras. Even a grainy picture would give him some idea of the kind of vehicle River was driving, if that was in fact him. The coincidence was almost too uncanny.

The possibility the clerk could've picked up on any details of the bombing case from the media was nil. He'd kept a very tight rein on the details of the morning's event on purpose. He'd released a statement that said there had been an incident involving an RV and a homemade explosive device, and there'd been no casualties or injuries. Technically, that part was true. The scratch on his arm would be fine and his hearing would return to normal in a few days. The ringing was already easing.

Evidence was mounting against River.

"And this witness was certain, without a shadow of a doubt, that the man at the motel matched the BOLO?"

"Not one hundred percent," Gert admitted. "She said she wouldn't exactly bet her life on it, but it was probably him."

Colton cursed under his breath. He needed a witness who would testify they were certain it was River, not someone who *thought* it might be him.

"This is something. At least we have someone who can most likely place him in town or at least near town. Birchwood is a half-hour drive from here."

"That's right, sir."

"Is he still there, by chance?" He probably should've asked this already, except that Gert would've known to lead with it.

"That's a negative sir." Gert's frustration came through the line in her sigh. "You're going to love this one. He checked out first thing this morning, at around six thirty."

Colton had figured as much, even though he'd hoped for a miracle. River, or anyone in law enforcement, would be smart enough to stay on the move. "You mentioned the place was basically a cash-and-carry operation. Is that right?"

"Yes, sir. And I confirmed that the person who'd stayed in room 11 paid with cash."

"Good work, Gert." Colton pressed his lips together to keep from swearing.

Makena issued a sharp sigh. "So close."

"Thanks for the information, Gert. It gives us confirmation that we're on the right track."

"My pleasure, sir. And you know me. Once I'm on a trail, I stick with it."

"I've never been sure who was the better investigator between the two of us. I appreciate all your efforts." He knew it made Gert's chest swell with pride to hear those words. He meant them, too. She was a formidable investigator and she'd proven to be invaluable in many cases.

Colton thanked her again before ending the call.

"I knew it was only a matter of time before he caught up to me." Makena's voice was a study in calm as she stabbed her fork into her salad. Almost too calm. And yet, Colton figured she was much like the surface of the river. Calm on top with a storm raging below the surface.

If River checked out at six o'clock this morning, he could've set the bomb at the RV. He'd had a specific detonation in mind. It made sense to Colton that he'd wanted Makena to be stepping on the platform as she headed inside the RV to blow her up. Otherwise, if she stepped on the platform to go outside, then the bomb could've been a warning. It was possible, maybe unlikely, the ordeal was meant to be a scare tactic.

Without knowing much about River, it was difficult to ascertain which. But what would he have to gain by scaring her months later?

River had had some time on his hands recently to stew on his situation. It was clear the guy had a temper.

He'd used that on Makena during their marriage. And yet a hothead didn't tend to be as calculating. That type was usually more spontaneous.

In Colton's years of investigating domestic violence cases, of which there'd been sadly too many, it was generally a crime of passion that led to murder. A spouse walked in on another spouse having an affair. The unsuspecting spouse got caught up in the moment, grabbed a weapon and committed murder.

Makena had not had an affair in this case. She'd left. That was a betrayal someone like River wouldn't take lightly.

Chapter Eleven

Makena pushed around a piece of lettuce on her plate. The fact that River had been in town at the very least on the morning someone had attempted to take her life sat heavy on her chest. It wouldn't do any good to look back and question how on earth she'd ever trusted him in the first place.

It was time to move forward. And then something dawned on her. "Did I hear right? Did Gert say River checked into that hotel four nights ago?"

"That's the same thing I heard. Gert will write it all up in a report, but yeah, that's what I heard." Colton rocked his head. He pushed the phone away from their plates.

"So River shows up four days ago. It's now been four days since I saw Red and Mustache Man." A picture was taking shape, but it was still too fuzzy to make out all the details.

"So these three have met in your garage and now they are in town at the same time without staying in the same room. We don't know if they rented a room next door." Colton got up, found a notepad and pen and then reclaimed his seat. He scratched out a note for them to check with the early-morning-shift clerk to see if anyone matching the description of Red or Mustache had checked in or been seen coming into or out of River's room.

"Gert said River had no visitors," she corrected, distinctly remembering Gert's words.

"True." He scratched out the last part. "Which didn't mean they didn't meet up somewhere."

She was already thinking the same thing.

"Maybe they thought I overhead them and that's why I left my husband. Maybe in their twisted-up minds they think I know something, which meant the meeting in the garage could've been some kind of planning meeting."

Colton was already nodding his head. "It makes sense. When we look at murder or an attempted murder case, we're always looking for the motive. In your case, one could make the argument that River was still jealous months after you left and that it took him that long to hunt you down. That would make sense. It's a story that, unfortunately, has been told before. The twist in this case is Mustache and Red. If River was here because of a jealousy that he couldn't let go of or because he didn't want you to ever be with anyone else, which is another motive in domestic cases, there wouldn't have been anyone else with him."

"That's exactly my thinking. So if I did walk in on a meeting that day and they think I know something, which I assure you I don't no matter how much I wish I did, they're willing to kill me to make sure I'm silenced. River has already gotten in trouble with his department for extortion. At least, he's under investigation for it." They were finally on a path that made some sense to her. Granted, it was still twisted and unfair, and she didn't like anything about it, period, but it made sense. "Okay, what do we do next?"

"Tonight? We eat. We try to set the case aside at least for a little while. Overly focusing on something and overthinking it only creates more questions. Tomorrow, six a.m., we pay a visit to Gloria Beecham and see if she remembers seeing Red or Mustache anywhere in the area. If we can link those three up, it's a story that makes sense."

Colton was holding something back.

"What is it?"

"There's another story that says all three of them are in town and in a race to see who gets to you first."

Makena shuddered at the thought. It was a theory that couldn't be ignored. It would still take a while to wrap her thoughts around the fact that anyone would want her dead, let alone three people. But it was possible each person was acting on his own, trying to be the one to get to her first to see what she knew and if she had evidence against any one of them.

"Think you can eat something?" Colton motioned toward her plate. "It's important to keep up your strength."

"I can try." She surprised herself by finishing the plate a few minutes later. Colton was right about one thing—overthinking the case would most likely drive her insane.

When the plates were empty, she picked up hers and headed toward the sink. She stopped midway. "I can clean yours while I'm up." At least the ringing noise in her ears was substantially better if not her left hip. The bruise was screaming at her, making its presence known. Colton was right. All she wanted was to stand under a warm shower and to curl up on the couch and watch TV to take her mind off the situation.

Colton was on his feet in the next second, plate in hand. He was such a contrast to River, who, in all the years she spent with him, basically set a plate down wherever he was and got up and walked away without a thought about how it got cleaned and ended up back in the cabinet the next day. He'd blamed his disinclination to do the house chores on being tired after working the deep night shift. The truth was that he thrived on that schedule. And the other truth was that he was lazy.

"It's not that hard for me to rinse off a second dish and put it in the dishwasher."

Colton set his dish down next to the sink. "For the last year, I've done everything for myself. Well, for myself and two little ones. I'm not trying to be annoying by doing everything myself, but I can see how that might get on someone's nerves. Especially someone who is strong and independent, and also used to doing things for herself. The truth is, being in the kitchen together making dinner tonight, even though it was literally nothing but pizza and salad, was probably my favorite time in this kitchen since I moved in."

Well, damn. Colton sure had a way with words. His had just touched her heart in the best possible way and sent warmth rocketing through her. She stopped what she was doing, turned off the spigot and leaned into him.

"It's been a pretty crazy twenty-four hours since we literally ran into each other, but it's really good to see you again, Colton."

It was so easy in that moment to turn slightly until her body was flush with his and tilt her face toward him. She pushed up on her tiptoes and pressed a kiss to his soft, thick lips. Being around Colton again was the easiest thing despite the electricity constantly pinging between them. Instead of fighting it…she was so very tired of fighting…she leaned into it.

Colton took a deep breath. And then he brought his hands up to cup her face. He ran his thumb along her jawline and then her chin as he trailed his lips in a line down her neck. He feathered a trail of hot kisses down her neck and across her shoulder. She placed the flat of her palms against his solid-walled chest, letting her fingers roam.

She smoothed her hands toward his shoulders and then up his neck, letting her fingers get lost in that thick mane of his as he deepened the kiss.

There was so much fire and energy and passion in the kiss. Her breath quickened and her pulse raced. Kissing Colton was better than she'd imagined it could be. No man had ever kissed her so thoroughly or made her need from a place so deep inside her.

He splayed one of his hands across the small of her back and pressed her body against his. Then his hands dropped, and she lifted her legs up and with help wrapped them around his midsection. He dropped his head to the crook of her neck.

Colton held onto her for a long minute in that position before he released a slow, guttural groan and found her lips again.

He fit perfectly and all she wanted to do was get lost with him.

THE ATTRACTION THAT had been simmering between Colton and Makena ignited into a full-blown blaze. He wanted nothing more than to strip down and bury himself deep inside her.

Her fingernails dug into the flesh of his shoulders. Considering her injury, this was about as far as he could let things go between them. There was another reason. A more obvious one. He knew without a doubt that taking their relationship to the next level would be a game changer for him, and he hoped it would be for her, too.

But she had trust issues and he still hadn't gotten over the loss of his best friend. Besides, as much as Makena fit him in every possible way, he had zero time to commit to a new relationship. He had the boys to think about and the fact that they might not be comfortable with him moving a stranger into the house. Somewhere in the back of his mind, his brain tried to convince him these were excuses. Maybe they were.

But if he was ready, he doubted his mind would try to come up with reasons they shouldn't be together. The biggest of which was the fact that she hadn't gotten over the experience with her ex.

Colton had seen that fear in her eyes one too many times. Granted, her anxiety had never been aimed at him and he would never do anything knowingly to hurt her. He wouldn't have to. His badge and gun might prove to be a problem for her.

Plus, she'd changed her life in every sense of the word. She needed to reemerge and find a footing in her new life.

Makena moaned against his lips, and it was about the sexiest damn thing he'd ever heard. Let this go on too much longer and no cold shower in the world would be able to tame the blaze. Because he was just getting started.

He dropped his hands from her face, running his finger down to the base of her neck. He lowered his hand to her full breast and then ran his thumb along her nipple. It beaded under his touch and sent rockets of awareness through his body. Every single one of his muscles cried out for the sweet release only she could give. His need for Makena caused a physical ache.

Sleeping together at this point would only complicate the relationship. She was beginning to open up to him more and more. He sensed she was beginning to lean on him, and he liked the fact her trust in him was growing.

She needed to be sure how he felt about her before taking this to the next level. And since he was just now trying to figure that out himself, he pulled back and touched his forehead to hers. Their breathing was raspy. A smile formed on his lips.

Having twin sons had sure made one helluva grown-up out of him. Not that he'd taken sex lightly in the past. He preferred serial dating before he married Rebecca, and always made certain that his partners knew one hundred percent that the relationship would be based on mutual physical attraction. The likelihood anything emotional or permanent would come out of it was off the table.

"What is it, Colton? What's wrong? Did I do something?"

"You? Not a chance. It's me. And before you think I'm giving you the whole 'it's not you, it's me' speech, it really is me. I think whatever we have brewing between us could turn out to be something special. But the timing is off. I think we both realize that." He almost couldn't believe those words had just come out of his mouth. They were true. They needed to be said. But, damn.

He felt the need to explain further, because he didn't want her to be embarrassed or have any regrets. "For the record, I think that was probably up there with the best kisses of my life."

He could feel her smiling.

"Okay, I lied. That was the best kiss of my life. And it gets me in trouble because I don't want to stop there. I want more. And when I say more, I don't just mean physical." He could almost hear the wheels spinning in her brain and could sense she was about to do some major backpedaling.

"I hear what you're saying, Colton. I feel whatever this is happening between us, too. I don't exactly have anything to give right now." Ouch. Those words hurt more than he was expecting them to.

"You don't have to explain any of that to me. I feel the same."

"I'm sorry. This is the second time I've put you in this position. I promise not to do it again." She pulled back and put her hands up in the surrender position, palms out.

"Well, that's disappointing to hear." Colton laughed, a rumble from deep in his chest rolling up and out.

She looked at him with those clear blue eyes, so honest and still glittering with desire. The way his heart reacted, he thought he might've made a huge mistake in pulling back. Logic said that he had done the right thing in preparing her. His life didn't have room for anyone else, and she was just about to figure out what her new life was going to be. She didn't need him inserting himself right in the middle and possibly confusing her.

A sneaky little voice in the back of his mind said his defense mechanisms were kicking into high gear. He hushed that because it was time to think about something else.

"We could watch a movie to take our minds off things. We could talk." Normally, that last option would've felt like pulling teeth with no Novocain. But he actually liked talking to Makena. Go figure.

"I think what I would like more than anything is to curl up on the sofa with you and turn the fireplace on low. And maybe have something warm to drink. Maybe something without caffeine."

"Sounds like a plan. As far as the hot beverage without caffeine, I'm kind of at a loss on that one."

It was her turn to laugh. She reached up and grabbed a fistful of his shirt and tugged him toward her. She stopped him just before their lips met. "Thank you, Colton. You've brought alive parts of me that I honestly didn't know existed anymore. You've shown me what a strong, independent man can be."

This time she didn't push forward and press a kiss to his lips, and disappointment nearly swallowed him.

He smiled at her compliment and squeezed her hand, needing to refocus before he headed down that emotional path again.

"Good luck if you want something warm in this house that doesn't have caffeine."

"If you have water, a stove and maybe a lemon or honey, I can get by just fine."

"I definitely have honey. It's in the cupboard. Gert makes a point of bringing some back for everyone in the office when she visits honeybee farms. She's made a goal to visit every one in the state before the end of the year. I should have a few bottles in there to choose from. As far as lemons go, I actually might have a few of those in the bin inside the fridge. I'll just make a call and check on my boys. I really want to hear their voices before they go to sleep. So if you'll excuse me, I'll take the call in the other room while you make up your warm batch of honey-lemon water."

His smile was genuine, and when she beamed back at him his heart squeezed. His traitorous heart would have to get on board with the whole "he needed to slow the train down" plan. It was on a track of its own, running full steam ahead.

Makena pushed him back a little bit in a playful motion. He hesitated for just a second, holding her gaze just a little too long, and his heart detonated when he turned to walk away. He exhaled a sigh and grabbed his phone off the granite island before heading into the bedroom.

He gave himself a few moments to shake off the haze in his mind from kissing Makena. He was still in a little bit of shock that one kiss could ignite that level of passion in him. He chalked it up to going too long without sex. That had to be the reason. He hadn't felt a flame burning like that in far too long.

After a few more deep breaths, he was at a ready point to hear his sons' little babbling voices. He pulled up his mother's contact and let his thumb hover over her number.

He dropped his thumb onto the screen and put the phone to his ear. It took a couple of rings for his mother to pick up. When she did, he could hear the sounds of his little angels in the background, laughing. He'd recognize those voices anywhere.

"Hi, son. I was just drying off the boys after their baths. How are you doing?" she asked. He listened for any signs of distress in her voice that meant taking care of the boys was too much for her right now.

"All is well here. We're moving forward with the investigation and I'll be up and out early tomorrow morning to go interview a potential witness. Making progress." Hearing his sons' laughter in the background warmed his heart.

"Colton, what's really wrong?" His mom could read him and his brothers better than a psychic.

"The case. I know the intended target from college. We go way back and she's a good person. She definitely doesn't deserve what's being handed to her." It would do no good to lie to his mother. She'd be able to hear it in his tone and he wouldn't feel good about it anyway. He'd been honest with her since seventh grade, after he'd hidden his phone in his room so he could call Rebecca when they were supposed to be asleep.

A young Colton hadn't slept a wink that night. He'd come clean about the deception in the morning and his mother said he'd punished himself enough. She expected him to leave his phone downstairs before he went up to bed just like the others did. Garrett had always sneaked back down to get his, but that was Garrett and beside the point.

Lying had taught Colton that he was an honest person.

Plus, his mother had been around him and his brothers who worked in law enforcement long enough to realize they wouldn't be allowed to divulge details about an ongoing investigation. She wouldn't dig around.

And she wouldn't ask. There were lines families in law enforcement never crossed.

"I'm sorry to hear such a nice-sounding person is having a rough go of it." He could hear more of that innocent laughter come across the line and he figured his mother knew exactly the distraction he needed. "The boys have had a wonderful day. They've been angels with just enough spunk in them for me to know they're O'Connor boys through and through."

"That's good to hear."

"Do you want me to put them on the line? I can put the phone in between them. They're here on the bed. Well, mostly here on the bed. Renee is here helping me and they keep trying to move to get away from the lotion." His mom laughed. It sounded genuine, and there'd been too much of that missing in her life over the past few months. It made him feel a lot less guilty about having the boys stay over with her for a few days. They might be just the distraction she needed.

"I would love it. Put them on." He could hear shuffling noises, which he assumed was her putting the phone down.

Her mouth was away from the receiver when she said, "Hey, boys. Guess who is calling you? It's your Dada."

It warmed his heart the way his family had accepted Silas and Sebastian despite the circumstances of their birth.

"Hey, buddies. I hope you are behaving for your Mimi and Aunt Renee." In truth, there wasn't a whole lot to say to one-year-olds. All he really wanted to hear was the sound of their giggles. Knowing how well they were being cared for and how much his mother loved them. It was kind of Renee to help.

One of the twins shrieked, "Dada!"

The other one got excited and started chanting the same word. Colton didn't care how or why his boys had come into his life. He was a better man for having them. He kept the phone to his ear and just listened.

A few minutes later, his mother came back on the line.

"Well, these two are ready for a little snack before bedtime," she said.

"Sounds good, Mom." He wanted to ask how she was really doing but figured this wasn't the time. Instead, he settled on, "They really love you."

"Well, that's a good thing because I love them more. And I love you." There was a genuine happiness to her tone that made Colton feel good.

They said their goodbyes and ended the call. Colton glanced at the clock. It was after eight. He needed to grab a shower and get some shut eye soon. Four o'clock in the morning would come early and he wanted to be at the motel the minute the clerk started work.

Colton took a quick shower, toweled off and then threw on some sweatpants and a T-shirt. By the time he joined Makena in the other room, she was curled up on the couch. She'd figured out how to flip the switch to turn on the fireplace. He didn't want to dwell on how right it felt to see her sitting there in his home, on his sofa, looking comfortable and relaxed.

If it was just the two of them and she was in a different mental space, letting this relationship play out would be a no-brainer. But he had his children to think about and how the loss of their mother at such a young age would affect their lives. He also had to consider how bringing someone into their lives who could leave again might impact them. He couldn't see himself getting into a temporary relationship or introducing them to someone who might not stick around for the long haul.

"Shower's free. I left a fresh towel out for you and a washcloth. It's folded on the sink," he said, trying to ignore his body's reaction to her. His heart—traitor that it was—started beating faster against his rib cage.

Sitting there, smiling up at him, Makena was pure temptation. A temptation he had to ignore—for his own sanity.

Chapter Twelve

The shower was amazing and quick. Makena couldn't help but think about the case, despite trying to force it from her thoughts. It was impossible for questions not to pop into her mind after the update they'd received from Gert.

It was probably odd to appreciate the fact that she knew River. He had a physical description and a job. She couldn't imagine being targeted by someone without any idea who it could be or why.

Granted, in her case, the why was still a question mark. It could be his jealous nature. Or it could be that he believed she'd overheard something.

At least she wouldn't walk down the street next to the person targeting her without realizing it. Even Red and Mustache were on her radar.

And then there was Colton. She couldn't imagine having a better investigator or a better human being on her side. He'd grown into quite an incredible person, not that she was surprised. His cobalt blue eyes had always been just a little too serious and a little too intense even in college. He saw things most people would never notice. After hearing more about his family, she was starting to get a better understanding of him and what made him tick.

To say her feelings for him were complicated barely scratched the surface. She got dressed and brushed her teeth before venturing into the living room.

Colton sat in front of the fire, studying his laptop. Her heart free-fell at the sight of him looking relaxed and at ease. Butterflies flew in her stomach and she was suddenly transported back to biology lab at the time they had first met. Those feelings were very much alive today and sent rockets of need firing through her.

"Hey, I thought we agreed. No more working on the case tonight." She moved to the kitchen and heated more water. The lemon and honey water had done the trick earlier.

"I was just mapping out our route to the motel tomorrow morning. I wanted to be ready to go so that we're there the moment Gloria Beecham checks in for work."

"That sounds like a plan." The buzzer on the microwave dinged and she poured the warm water into the mug she'd used earlier.

"It's about a half hour's drive, so we should probably get on the road at five thirty at the latest."

"In the morning?" She gripped the mug and added a slice of lemon along with another teaspoon of honey. After stirring the mixture, she made her way back to the sofa, noticing how badly her attempt at humor had missed the mark.

Colton continued to study the screen without looking up. She hoped she hadn't offended him earlier before the showers but the air in the room had definitely shifted. A wall had come up.

Makena pulled her legs up and tucked her feet underneath her bottom. She sat a couple of feet from Colton and angled herself toward him. From this distance, she'd be less likely to reach out and touch him. The feel of his silk-over-steel muscles was too much temptation. It would be so easy to get lost with him.

But then what?

There was no way she wanted to do anything that might drive a wedge between her and Colton. He was her best and only friend right then. She had no plans to cut off her lifeline. An annoying voice in the back of her head called her out on the excuses.

"So, the way I understand it, there's a story behind why everyone in law enforcement got there. What's yours?" She wanted to know why he'd chosen this profession versus taking up ranching.

He chuckled, a low rumble in his chest. "Do you mean more than the fact that I grew up with five brothers, all of whom were close in age?"

"That would challenge anyone's sense of justice," she laughed.

"I think it was always just inside me." He closed the laptop and shifted it off his lap and onto the sofa. Then he turned to face her. "We all used to play Cops and Robbers. Growing up on a ranch, we had plenty of room to roam and enough time to use our imagination. I was always drawn to the cop. For a while, I tried to tell myself that I was a rancher. Don't get me wrong, ranching is in my blood and it's something I think I've always known I'd do at some point. We all pitch in, especially me before the boys came. I think I always knew it was just a matter of time. I want to take my place at the ranch. Later. I'm just not ready. So in college, when my parents tried to get me to go to the best agricultural school in the state, I rebelled. Our university had a pretty decent business school, and that's how I convinced my parents it was right for me. They weren't really trying to force me into anything so much as trying to guide me based on what they thought I wanted."

"They sound like amazing parents."

"They were…my mom still is," he said.

"I'm guessing by that answer there's no news about who is responsible for your father's death. I'm really sorry about that, Colton. About *all* of it."

"Before I checked the map, I was digging around in the case file. I couldn't find anything else to go on."

"Maybe no one was supposed to find him," she offered.

"It's possible. There are just so many unanswered questions. When I really focus on it, it just about drives me insane."

She could only imagine someone in his shoes, someone who was used to giving answers to others in their darkest moments, would be extremely frustrated not to be able to give those answers to his own family. She figured that between him and his brothers who worked for the US Marshal Service, they wouldn't stop until they found out why their father was killed. Their sister's kidnapping must have influenced their decisions to go into law enforcement in the first place. "How long has it been?"

"A couple of months now. He was digging around in my sister's case."

"You mentioned that she was kidnapped as a baby.

Thirty-plus years is a long time. Wouldn't any leads be cold?"

"Yes. The trail was almost instantly cold and has remained so to this day. We're missing something. That's what keeps me up at night. It's the thing that I don't know yet but know is out there, which gives me nightmares. It's the one piece that, when you find it, will make the whole puzzle click together. That's been missing in my sister's case for decades."

This was the first time she'd ever heard a hint of hopelessness in Colton's voice. Despite knowing just how dangerous this path could be, she reached over and took his hand in hers. He'd done so much for her and she wanted to offer whatever reassurance she could. The electricity vibrating up her arm from their touch was something she could ignore. She needed to ignore it. Because it wasn't going to lead her down a productive path.

She couldn't agree more with Colton about timing.

"I wish there was something I could say or do to help."

"Believe it or not, just being able to talk about it for a change is nice. We never talk about Caroline's case at home. Our mother has a little gathering every year on Caroline's birthday and we have cake. She talks about what little she remembers about her daughter. It isn't much and it feels like Caroline is frozen in time. Always six months old. I've already had more time with my sons than my mother did with my sister. And I can't imagine anything happening to either one of my boys."

"It hardly seems fair," she agreed.

Colton rocked his head and twined their fingers together.

"We better get some sleep if we intend to be out the door by five thirty." He squeezed her fingers in a move that she figured was meant to be reassuring. He got up and turned off the fireplace. From the other room, he grabbed a pillow and some blankets. "For tonight, I'll take the couch."

"I thought we already talked about this." The last thing she wanted to do was steal the man's bed. It was actually a bad idea for her to think about Colton and a bed because a sensual shiver skittered across her skin.

"We did. I said I'd take the couch tonight and you'll take the bed. If I have to, I'll walk over there, pick you up and carry you to bed." At least there was a hint of lightness and playfulness in his tone now that had been missing earlier. There was also something else…something raspy in his voice when he'd mentioned his bed. And since she knew better than to tempt fate twice in one night, she pushed up to standing, walked over and gave him a peck on the cheek…and then went to bed.

COLTON SLEPT IN fifteen-minute intervals. By the time the alarm on his watch went off he'd maybe patched together an hour of sleep in seven. It was fine. He rolled off the couch and fired off a dozen pushups to get the blood pumping. He hopped to his feet and did a quick set of fifty jumping jacks. He'd been sitting way more than usual in the past thirty-six hours and his body was reminding him that it liked to be on the move.

He followed jumping jacks with sit-ups and rounded out his morning wake-up routine with squats. As quietly as he could manage, he slipped down the hall past his master bedroom, past the boys' room, where he lingered for just a second in the doorway of the open door. And then he made his way to the master bath where he washed his face, shaved and brushed his teeth.

Makena didn't need to be up for another hour. There was something right about her being curled up in his bed. He didn't need the visual, not this early in the morning. So he didn't stop off at the master bedroom on his way to the coffee machine.

The supplies were all near the machine, so he had a cup in hand and a piece of dry toast in less than three minutes. It didn't take long for the caffeine to kick in or for questions to swirl in the back of his mind.

At first, he thought about his father's case. Colton had a dedicated deputy to untangle Mrs. Hubert's financials and the contact information that had been found in her computer. Her files were all coded and his deputy was presently on full-time duty trying to crack the code. The older woman who was murdered a few months ago had ties to a kidnapping ring. Had she been involved in Caroline's case?

As a professional courtesy, and also considering the fact they were brothers, he was sharing information with Cash and Dawson. Those two were working the case in their spare time, as well. Even with a crack team of investigators, it would take time to unravel Mrs. Hubert's dealings. Time to get justice for Finn O'Connor was running out. A cold trail often led to a cold case. It occurred to Colton that his mother could be in danger, too.

There could be something hidden around the house, a file or piece of evidence their father had been hiding that could lead a perp to her door.

Colton tapped his fingers on his mug. He thought about time. And how short it could be. How unfair it could be and how quickly it could be robbed from loved ones.

It was too early in the morning to go down a path of frustration that his boys would never know their mother. Besides, as long as he had air in his lungs, he would do his best to ensure they knew what a wonderful a person she was.

Colton booted up his laptop and checked his email. Several needed attention, so he went ahead and answered those. Others could wait. A couple he forwarded on to Gert. She'd been awfully quiet since the phone call last night, which didn't mean she wasn't working. It just meant she hadn't found anything worth sharing.

He pinched the bridge of his nose to stem the headache threatening. Then he picked up the pencil from on top of his notepad. He squeezed the pencil so tight while thinking about the past that it cracked in half. Frustration that he wasn't getting anywhere in the two most important cases of his life got the best of him and he chucked the pencil pieces against the wall.

Colton cursed. He looked up in time to see a feminine figure emerge from his bedroom. Makena had on pajama bottoms and a T-shirt. The bottoms were pink plaid. Pink was his new favorite color.

"Morning." She walked into the room and right past the broken pieces of pencil.

"Back atcha." He liked that she knew where everything was and went straight to the cabinet for the coffee. She had a fresh cup in her hands and a package of vanilla yogurt by the time he moved to the spot to clean up the broken pencil.

"How'd you sleep?" he asked her as he tossed the bits into the trash.

"Like a baby." She stretched her arms out and yawned before digging into the yogurt. The movement pressed her ample breasts against the cotton of her T-shirt.

Colton forced his gaze away from her soft curves. "How's your hip today?" He'd noticed that she was walking better and barely limped.

"So far, so good," she said. "I don't think I'm ready to run a marathon anytime soon, but I can make it across the room without too much pain. The bruise is already starting to heal." She motioned toward her hip, a place his eyes didn't need to follow.

Colton made a second cup of coffee, which he polished off by the time she finished her first.

"I can be dressed and ready in five minutes. Is that okay?" she asked.

"Works for me." He gathered up a few supplies like his notebook and laptop and tucked them into a bag.

Makena emerged from the bedroom as quickly as she'd promised, looking a little too good. He liked the fact that she could sleep when she was around him, because she'd confessed that she hadn't done a whole lot of that in recent months.

He smiled as he passed by her, taking his turn in the

bedroom. He dressed in his usual jeans, dark button-down shirt and windbreaker. He retrieved his belt from the safe and then clipped it on his hip.

He returned to the kitchen where Makena stood, ready to go.

The drive to the motel took exactly twenty-nine minutes with no traffic. The place was just as Gert had described. A nondescript motel off the highway that fit the information Gert had passed along—that it rented rooms by the hour. There was an orange neon sign that had M-O-T-E-L written out along with a massive arrow pointing toward the building. Colton had always driven by those places and wondered why people needed the arrow to find it. He could chew on that another day.

"It's best if you stick to my side in case anything unexpected goes down. I'm not expecting anything, but should River still be in the area or pop in to rent another room, I want you to get behind me as a first option or anything that could put the most mass between you and him. Okay?"

She nodded and he could see that she was clear on his request. She'd been silent on the ride over, staring out the window, alone in her thoughts. Colton hadn't felt the need to fill the space between them with words. It had been a comfortable silence. One that erased the years they'd been apart.

The office of the motel was a small brick building that had a screen door in front of a white wooden one. The second door was cracked open enough to see dim lighting. He opened the screen door as he tucked Makena behind him.

With his hand on her arm, he could feel her trembling. River's connection to this place seemed to be taking a toll on her. A renewed anger filled Colton as he bit back the frustration. Of course, she'd be nervous and scared. She'd been running from this guy for literally months and here she was walking inside a building where he'd recently stayed.

Inside, they were greeted by a clerk whose head could barely be seen above the four-and-a-half-foot counter. The walls were made of dark wood paneling. The worn carpet was hunter green, and the yellow laminate countertop gave the place a leftover-from-another-era look.

"How can I help you, Sheriff?" The woman didn't seem at all surprised to see him, and he figured his deputy might've let her know someone would most likely swing by to speak to her.

"Are you Gloria?" he asked. Aside from the long bar-height counter that the little old lady could barely see over, there were a pair of chairs with a small table nestled in the right-hand side of the room. To his left, in the other corner, a flat-screen TV had been mounted.

"In the flesh." She smiled.

"I understand you spoke to one of my deputies yesterday. My name is Sheriff Colton O'Connor." He walked to the counter and extended his right hand. "Pleased to meet you."

The little old lady took his hand. Her fingers might be bony and frail but she had a solid handshake and a formidable attitude.

"Pleased to make your acquaintance, Sheriff. You're in here to talk to me about one of my clients." She had the greenest eyes he'd ever seen. He didn't get the impression she'd had an easy life. The sparkle in her eyes said she'd given it hell, though.

"Yes, ma'am. This is a friend of mine and she's familiar with the case." He purposely left out Makena's name.

Gloria nodded and smiled toward Makena. "My name might be Gloria but everyone around here calls me Peach on account of the fact I was born in Georgia. I've lived in Texas for nearly sixty years but picked up the name in second grade and it stuck."

Peach's gaze shifted back to Colton. She nodded and smiled after shaking hands with Makena.

"Can you tell me everything you remember about the visitor in room 11?" Colton asked, directing the conversation.

"The name he used to check in was Ryan Reynolds. I can get the ledger for you if you'd like to see it."

"I would." Ryan Reynolds was a famous actor, so it was obviously a fake name. Colton figured that Makena could confirm whether or not the handwriting belonged to River.

Peach opened a drawer and then produced a black book before finding a page with the date from five days ago.

"I get folks' information on the computer usually, but my cash customers like to sign in by hand the old-fashioned way." He bet they did.

She hoisted the book onto the counter and, using two fingers on each hand, nudged it toward Colton. He looked at the name she pointed at. Ryan Reynolds. The movie star. Somehow, Colton seriously doubted the real Ryan Reynolds would have come all the way to this small town to rent a motel room. Last he'd checked, there were no movies being made in the area. But this wasn't the kind of place where a person would use his or her real name, and Peach clearly hadn't asked for ID.

Colton leaned into Makena and said in a low voice, "Does that handwriting look like his?"

"Yes. He always makes that weird loop on his Rs. I mean, wrong name, obviously. But that's his hand-writing."

"Do you mind if I take a picture of this?" Colton glanced up at Peach, who nodded.

Colton pulled out his phone and snapped a shot.

"I'd also like to keep this book as evidence. Did Mr. Reynolds touch the book or use a pen that you gave him?"

"Now that I really think about it, I don't think he did touch the book. I can't be sure. But the pen he used would be right there." She reached for a decorated soup can that had a bunch of pens in it.

"If you don't mind, I'd like to admit that as evidence." Colton's words stopped her mid-reach.

"Yes, sir. I'm happy to cooperate in any way that I can."

"Thank you, ma'am." Colton tipped his chin. "Has anyone else who looked suspicious been here over the last week or two?"

"You'll have to clarify what suspicious means, sher-iff. I get all kinds coming through here," she quipped with a twinkle in her eye.

Chapter Thirteen

Okay, bad question on Colton's part. "Let me ask another way. Did you have anyone new show up?"

"I have a couple of regulars who come in once a month or every other week. This is a good stop for my truckers who are on the road."

"Anyone here you haven't seen before other than Mr. Reynolds?" he clarified.

"I've had a couple of people come through. I'd say in the last week or so there've been four or five, but we've been slower than usual."

"Has anyone say around six feet tall with light red hair, maybe could be described as strawberry blond, been in?"

She was already shaking her head before he could finish his sentence. "No. I would remember someone like that."

"How about anyone with black hair and a mustache?" he asked.

"No, sir." Her gaze shifted up and to the left, signaling she was trying to recall information. So far, she'd passed his honesty meters.

"I can't really recall anyone who looked like that coming through recently."

"Is it possible for me to view the footage from the occupant of room 11 as he came and went?" Colton asked.

"I can pull it up on the screen behind you now that I have here one of those digital files." She smiled and her eyes lit up as she waited for his response.

"That would be a big help." Colton turned his head and shifted slightly to the left. He put his right elbow on the counter, careful not to disturb the cash ledger.

The next few sounds were the click-click-clicks of fingers on a keyboard.

"Here we go," she said with an even bigger smile. "It should come up in just a second."

Colton's left hand was at his side. He felt Makena reach for him and figured she must need reassurance considering she was about to see a video of the man she'd been in a traumatic relationship with. He twined their fingers together and squeezed her hand in a show of support.

She closed what little distance was between them, her warm body against his. He ignored the frissons of heat from the contact. He'd never get used to them, but he had come to expect the reaction that always came and the warmth that flooded him while she was this close.

The TV set came to life and the sound of static filled the room. The next thing he knew, the volume was being turned down on the set. There was a large picture window just to the left of the TV screen and Colton surveyed the parking lot of the small diner across the street. There were five vehicles: two pickup trucks, a small

SUV and a sedan. He figured at least one of those had to belong to an employee, possibly two.

"Here it is. Here's the day he checked in." Peach practically beamed with her accomplishment of finding his file.

Just as Gert had explained, the video was grainy as all get-out. The man in the video wore a Rangers baseball cap and kept his chin tucked to his chest. Out of the side of his mouth, Colton asked, "Is that about his height and weight?"

"Yes." There was a lot of emotion packed in that one word and a helluva lot of fight on the ready. He couldn't help being anything but proud of her. When some would cower, she dug deep and found strength.

"I don't have a whole lot of video of him, just his coming and going." Peach fast-forwarded, pausing each time his image came into view. The time stamps revealed dates from five days ago, four days ago and three days ago. Then it was down to two days and the same thing happened every time. He'd walk in or out of the room with his chin-to-chest posture. He didn't receive any visitors during that time except for daily visits from housekeeping. He didn't come and go often, mostly staying inside. He didn't have food delivered, which meant he either packed some or went out for food once a day. His eating habits would definitely classify as strange.

And then on the last day, the morning he checked out, he did something out of character and strange. He took off his hat as he left the room and glanced up at the camera, giving the recording device a full view of his face.

Makena's body tensed and she gripped Colton's hand even tighter.

River, she'd said, was a solid six-foot-tall man with a build that made it seem like he spent serious time at the gym. He had black hair and brown eyes. And was every bit the person who'd looked straight at the camera.

From the corner of Colton's eye, he now saw a man matching the description of River exit the diner and come running at full speed toward the motel office. He put his hands in the air, palms up, in the surrender position to show that he had no gun in his hands and he was surveying the area like he expected someone to jump out at him.

MAKENA HAD NOTICED the moment she and Colton had exited the vehicle earlier that he'd rested his right hand on the butt of his gun. Having been married to someone in law enforcement, she knew exactly the reason why. It was to have instant access to his weapon. The seconds it took for his hand to reach for his gun, pull it out of the holster and shoot could mean life or death for an officer. It also reminded her of the risks they were taking by visiting the place River had been in twenty-four hours ago.

As she followed Colton's gaze, she saw her ex-husband, to the shock of her life. Her body tensed. River was running straight toward them, hands high in the air, no doubt to show that he wasn't carrying a weapon.

Colton drew his, like anyone in law enforcement would.

"Get down and stay below the counter, Ms. Peach," he directed the clerk.

He tucked Makena behind him and repositioned him-self so they were behind the counter. She wanted to face River and ask him why in hell he'd tried to blow her up yesterday morning, but she wasn't stupid. She wanted to make sure she did it safely. Colton had told her to either hide behind him or put some serious mass between her and River.

She dropped Colton's hand as it went up to cup the butt of the weapon she recognized as a Glock. She glanced around, looking for some kind of weapon. There was a letter opener. She grabbed it and tight-ened her fist around it.

If River somehow made it past Colton to get to her, she'd be ready.

Her left hand was fisted so tightly that her knuckles went white. Anger and resentment for the way she'd had to live in the past six months bubbled up again, burning her throat.

Colton crouched so only a small portion of his head and his weapon were visible as River opened the door.

Her ex was out of breath, and the expression on his face would probably haunt her for months to come. She expected to find hurt and anger and jealousy, emotions that had been all too common during their marriage. Instead, she found panic. His eyes were wide, and he kept blinking. He was nervous.

"I swear I'm not here to hurt anyone. You have to believe me," he said. He still had that authoritative cop voice but there was a hint of fear present that was com-pletely foreign coming from him.

"Give me one good reason we should listen to you."

Colton didn't budge. "And keep your hands up where I can see them.

Colton had that same authoritative law enforcement voice that demanded attention. Hearing it from River had always caused icy fingers to grip her spine, but her body's reaction was so different when she heard it come from Colton.

All the angry words that Makena wanted to spew at River died on her tongue. It was easy to see the man was in a panic. Whatever he'd done was catching up to him. That was her first thought.

"I swear on my mother's life that I'm not here to hurt anyone." His face was still frozen on the TV that was positioned behind him. He'd taken a couple of steps inside the room and then stopped in his tracks.

"How'd you know I was here?" Makena asked.

"I saw you come in, and they will, too," came the chilling response.

"Who are *they*?" Colton asked.

"I can't tell you and you don't want to know. Believe me. The only thing you need to be aware of is that your life is in danger." River's voice shook with dread and probably a shot of adrenaline.

A half-mirthful, half-frustrated sigh shot from Makena's throat. He wasn't telling her anything she didn't already know.

Makena locked eyes with the terrified older woman at the other end of the counter. Peach kept eye contact with Makena when she pointed at something inside a shelf. It was hidden from view and Makena had a feeling it was some kind of weapon, like a bat or a shotgun.

Makena shook her head. Peach nodded and tilted her head toward it.

"Talk to me, River. Tell me why they would be after me. Is it because of you?" As much as Makena didn't believe that anymore, she had to ask. She needed to hear from him that wasn't the case, and she needed to get him talking so she could understand why it seemed like the world was crumbling around her.

"It's not important *what* you know. It's what they *think* you know. Even more important right now is that you get the hell out of here. Stay low. Stick with this guy." He motioned toward Colton. "He can probably protect you if you stay out of sight. Just give me time. I need time to straighten everything out."

"Time? To what? Plant another bomb?" she said.

She'd never seen River look this rattled before. And also…something else…helpless? His eyes darted around the room and he looked like he'd jump out of his skin if a cat hopped up on the counter.

This close, she could see his bloodshot eyes and the dark circles underneath. They always got that way when he went days without sleep. He was almost in a manic state and part of her wondered if deep down he actually did care about her well-being or if this was all some type of self-preservation act. To make it seem like he was a victim. But to what end?

"I knew they were planning something, but I had no idea…" River brought his hands on top of his head. His face distorted. "Everything's a mess now. I made everything a mess. I never meant for you to get caught up in this. Bad timing. But just do what I say and lie low. Trust me, you don't want to get anywhere near these guys."

His words sent another cold chill racing down her spine.

"You're not getting off that easy, River," Colton said. "Start talking now. I can work with the DA. I can talk with your chief if you give me something to take to him."

River's emotions were escalating, based on the increasing intensity of his expression.

This was not good. This was so not good.

"Are you kidding me right now? It's too late for me. It's too late to go back and fix what's wrong. I messed up big-time. There's not going to be any coming back from this for me but there's still time for me to fix it for you."

"Hold on. Just do me a favor and slow down." Colton's deep voice was a study in calm. "This doesn't have to end badly. Whatever you've done... I can't promise any miracles, but I can say that I'll do everything in my power if you talk. You need to tell us what's going on. You need to tell us who those men are and exactly why they're after Makena. It's the only way that I can help you."

River seemed more agitated. "You just don't understand. You don't get this and you don't realize what I'm going through or what I've done. It's too late. It's too late for me. I can accept that. But not her. She didn't do anything wrong."

The fact that River was concerned about her when it appeared his own life was on the line told her that she hadn't married a 100 percent jerk all those years ago.

There had been something good inside him then and maybe she could work with that now.

Makena stood up taller so that she could look River in the eye, hoping that would make a difference. "I don't know what happened, River. But I do know there was a decent person in there at one time. The person I first met—"

"Is gone. That guy is long gone. Forget about the past and forget that you ever knew me. Just lie low and give me some time to get this straightened out."

"I've been in hiding for half a year, River. How much more of my life do I need to give up for whatever you did?" she asked.

Instead of calming him, that seemed to rile him up even more. She'd been truthful and her words seemed to have the effect of punching him.

"I know, Makena. I realize that none of this makes sense to you, and it's best for everyone else if it doesn't. If I could go back and change things, I would. Time doesn't work like that and our past mistakes do come back to haunt us."

Makena remembered that he was on leave for some pretty hefty charges. Maybe if she pretended like she already knew, he would come clean. "The men who are after me, who tried to blow me up…are they related to your administrative leave?"

River issued a sharp sigh and then started lowering his hands.

"Keep 'em up, high and where I can see them." Colton's voice left no room for doubt that he was not playing around. He could place River under arrest, she knew, but he seemed to be holding off long enough to get answers. She took it as a sign he believed River might give them useful information.

River's hands shot up in the air. Being in law enforcement, he would be very aware just how serious Colton was about those words. Colton's department-issued Glock was still aimed directly at River. All it would take was one squeeze of the trigger to end River's life.

Considering the man was standing not ten feet away, Colton wouldn't need a crackerjack shot to take him out.

"What did you do, River?" Makena asked again, hoping to wear him down and get answers. "You can help me the most if you tell Colton what you're involved in."

Hands in the air, River started pacing. He appeared more agitated with every forward step. His mood was dangerous and volatile. Deadly?

She scanned his body for signs of a weapon, knowing full well there had to be one there somewhere. On duty, he'd worn an ankle holster. It wasn't uncommon for him to hide his Glock in another holster tucked in the waistband of his jeans.

He mumbled and she couldn't make out what he was saying. And then he spun around to face them. "Did you say his name is Colton?"

"Yes, but I don't see how that has any bearing on anything."

"Really? Isn't that your ex-boyfriend from college? I used to read your journals, Makena."

Her face burned with a mix of embarrassment and outrage. She hadn't kept a journal since their early years of marriage. And yes, she had probably written something in it about Colton. But it had been so long ago she couldn't remember what she'd written.

"Colton was never my boyfriend. He wasn't then and he isn't now. But even if he was, that's none of your business anymore. In case you forgot, we're divorced. And this is my life, a life that I want back." She'd allowed him to take so much time of hers. No more.

Makena took in a deep breath because the current assertiveness, although she deserved to stand up for herself, wasn't exactly having a calming effect on River.

In fact, she feared she might be making it worse. She willed her nerves to calm down and her stress levels to relax.

"I won't pretend to know what you're going through right now." Colton's voice was a welcome calm in the eye of the storm. "I know you're facing some charges at work but if you help in this case it'll be noted in your jacket. It won't hurt and might convince a jury to go easier on you."

River looked at Colton. His gaze bounced back to Makena.

"Man, it's too late for me now."

And then the sound of a bullet split the air, followed by glass breaking on the front door.

The next few minutes happened in slow motion. Out of the corner of her eye, Makena saw Peach reach into the shelf. The older woman came up with a shotgun in a movement that was swift and efficient. It became pretty obvious this wasn't the woman's first rodeo.

She aimed the barrel of the gun right at River. But it was River who caught and held Makena's attention.

As she ducked for cover, the look on his face would be etched in her brain forever.

At first his eyes bulged, and he took a step forward. She could've sworn she heard something whiz past her ear and was certain it was a second bullet. Before she realized, Colton positioned his body in between her and River.

River's arms dropped straight out. His chest flew toward her as he puffed it out. It was then she saw the red dot flowering in the center of his white cotton T-shirt. His mouth flew open, forming a word that never came out.

Shock stamped his features. He looked down at the center of his chest and said, "I've been shot."

He looked up at Makena and then Colton before repeating the words.

Colton was already on the radio clipped to his shoulder, saying words that would stick in her mind for a long time. She heard phrases like "officer down" and "ambulance required." This was all a little too real as she saw a pair of men, side by side and weapons at the ready, making their way across the street and toward the motel.

"I have to get you out of here," Colton said to Makena. The truck was parked behind the motel and she saw the brilliance of his plan now.

"Okay." It was pretty much the only word she could form or manage to get out under the circumstances. And then more came. "What about River?"

"There's nothing we can do to help him right now. The best thing we can do is lead those men away from the motel." Colton turned to Peach. "Is the back door locked?"

"Yes, sir." She ran a hand along the shelf and produced a set of keys. She tossed them to Colton, who snatched them with one hand. "You need to come with us. It's not safe here."

Peach lowered her face to the eyepiece of the shotgun. "I'll hold 'em off. You two get out of here while you can. I'll hold down the fort."

"I'm not kidding, Peach. You need to come with us now."

The woman shook her head and that was as much as she said.

"Help is on the way," Colton shouted to River, who'd taken a few steps back and dropped against the door, closing it. He sat with a dumbfounded look on his face.

"Reach up and lock that," Peach shouted to him.

Surprisingly, he obliged.

"We have to go." Colton, with keys in one hand and a Glock in the other, offered an arm, which Makena took as they ran toward the back.

He unlocked a key-only dead bolt and then tossed the keys into the hallway before fishing his own keys out of his pocket. The two of them ran toward the truck, which was thankfully only a few spaces from the door.

Once inside, he cranked on the ignition and backed out of the parking spot. "Stay low. Keep your head down. It's best if you get down on the floorboard."

Makena did as he requested. She noticed he'd scooted down, making himself as small as possible and less visible, therefore less of a target. He put the vehicle into Drive and floored the gas pedal.

In a ball on the floorboard as directed, Makena took in a sharp breath as Colton jerked the truck forward.

It was a big vehicle and not exactly nimble. Size was its best asset.

"They have no idea who they're dealing with," Colton commented, and she realized it was because they were in his personal vehicle and not one marked as law enforcement.

A crack of a bullet split the air. It was then that Makena heard the third shot being fired.

Chapter Fourteen

Colton tilted his chin toward his left shoulder where his radio was clipped on his jacket. His weapon was in the hand that he also used to steer the wheel after they'd bolted from around the back of the motel.

Peach would be safe as he drew the perps away from the building and onto the highway. River had been shot and it looked bad for him, but he was still talking and alert, and that was a good sign.

Getting Makena out of the building and Birchwood had been his first priority. River was right about one thing. She'd be safer if she kept a low profile.

Colton also realized the reason the perps were shooting was probably because they didn't realize they were shooting at a sheriff. Even so, it had been one of his better ideas to slip out the back of his office yesterday and take his personal vehicle, because it seemed as though the perps had zeroed in on Makena's location at the RV.

They also seemed ready and able to shoot River though he was an officer of the law. With River's professional reputation tarnished, plus the charges being lobbed against him, they must think they could get away with shooting him.

"Gert, can you read me?" He hoped like hell she could, because she was his best link to getting help for River and for him and Makena.

Birchwood was in Colton's jurisdiction. One of his deputies passed by this motel on his daily drive to work, and Colton hoped that he was nearby, possibly on his way into work.

Gert's voice came through the radio. "I read you loud and clear."

"I have two perps who have opened fire on my personal vehicle. And an officer is down at the motel. Makena is in my custody and we're heading toward the station, coming in hot."

"Do you have a vehicle or a license plate or can you give me anything on who might be behind you?"

"The shooter was on foot." Colton took a moment to glance into his rearview mirror in time to see the pair of perps running toward a Jeep.

With the weight of his truck, he didn't have a great chance of outrunning them. "It's looking like a Jeep Wrangler. White. Rubicon written in black letters on the hood. I don't have a license plate but I imagine it won't take them long to catch up to me. If they have one on the front of their vehicle, I can relay it."

He heard Makena suck in a breath. She scrambled into the seat and practically glued her face to the back window. "What can I do?"

"Stay low. Stay hidden. I don't have a way to identify myself in the truck. My vehicle is slow. But I'm going to do my level best to outrun them."

Makena didn't respond, so he wasn't certain she bought into his request. He was kicking up gravel on the service road to the four-lane highway. He took the first entrance ramp, and despite it being past seven o'clock in the morning on a Friday, there were more cars than he liked.

"Where are they now?" Makena asked.

"They're making their way toward us on the service road." Colton swerved in and out of the light traffic, pressing his dual cab truck to its limits. What it lacked in get-up-and-go, it made up for in size. If nothing else, he'd use its heft to block the Jeep from pulling alongside them.

Of course, the passenger could easily get off a shot from behind.

Colton leaned his mouth to his shoulder. "Where's the nearest marked vehicle?"

"Not close enough. I'm checking on DPS now to see if I can get a trooper in your direction. How are you doing? Can you hold them off until I can get backup to you?"

"I don't have a choice." Colton meant those words.

The Jeep had taken the on-ramp onto the highway and it wouldn't be long before it was on his bumper. He glanced around at the traffic and figured he'd better take this fight off the highway rather than endanger innocent citizens.

River was in trouble at work. Colton knew that for certain. What he wasn't sure of was his partners.

Colton relayed the description of the perps to Gert. "Call Chief Shelton at Dallas PD and see if any of his officers matching those descriptions have been connected in any way to River Myers. I want to know who River's friends were. Who he hung out with in the department and if any of them had visited the shooting range lately."

Most beat cops couldn't pull off the shot Red had at that distance and through a glass door. Whoever made the shot would get high scores in marksmanship at the range. Other officers would take note. Someone would know.

Between that and the physical descriptions, maybe River's supervising officer could narrow the search.

"Hold on, I'm going to swerve off the highway," he said, noting his chance.

At the last minute, he cranked the steering wheel right and made the exit ramp. It was probably too much to hope the perps lost him in traffic. There were plenty of black trucks on these roads.

He cursed when the Jeep took the exit.

"Gert, talk to me. Do you have someone at the motel?" Colton's only sense of relief so far was that he'd drawn the perps away from Peach and River. He also had a sneaky suspicion that Peach could take care of herself and could keep River there at gunpoint. Colton had no doubt the woman could hold her own until River received medical attention.

He could only hope that River would come clean with names.

Again, all they needed was a puzzle piece. At least now they knew that River had some connection to Red and Mustache. There was something the three of them had concocted or were doing they believed would land them in jail if someone found out. That someone, unfortunately, ended up being Makena. And again, he was reminded of how timing was everything.

If Makena had gone out to that garage five minutes before, maybe the men wouldn't have been there yet. Maybe River could've convinced her to go back to bed and she could be living out a peaceful life by now after the divorce.

His mind stretched way back to college. He'd wanted to ask her out but hadn't. Again, the ripple effect of that decision caused him to wonder about his timing. Now was not the time to dredge up the past. Besides, the Jeep was gaining on him. At this pace, it would catch him.

There were fields everywhere. One was a pasture for grazing. The other was corn stalks. The truck could handle either one and so could the Jeep. Colton couldn't get any advantage by veering off road. Except that in the corn, considering it was already tall, maybe he could lose them.

The meadow on the other side of the street was useless. The last thing he needed was more flat land. And while he didn't like the idea of damaging someone's crop and potential livelihood, he knew that he could circle back and make restitution. What was the point of having a trust fund he'd never touched if not for a circumstance like this one?

"Hang on tight, okay?" he said to Makena.

When she confirmed, he nailed a hard right. The truck bounded so hard he thought he might've cracked the chassis but stabilized once he got onto the field. The last thing he saw was the Jeep following.

Colton's best chance to confuse them was to maybe do a couple of figure eights and then zigzag through the cornfield. It would at the very least keep the perps from getting off a good shot. He was running out of options.

So far, the Jeep hadn't gotten close enough to them for him to be able to read a license plate if there was one on the front. Law required it to be there. However, many folks ignored it.

Considering these guys had good reason to hide any identifying marks, they most certainly wouldn't have a plate up front.

Gert's voice cut through his thoughts. "I got you pulled up on GPS using your cell phone. I have a location on you, sir. Can you hold tight in the area until I can get someone to you?"

"That's affirmative. I can stick around as long as I keep moving." He tried to come off as flippant so Gert wouldn't worry about him any more than she already was.

Makena was getting bounced around in the floorboard. At this point, it would be safer for her to climb into the seat and strap in. So that was exactly what he told her to do.

She managed, without being thrown around too much.

The crops had the truck bouncing and slowed his speed considerably. He cut a few sharp turns, left and then right…right and then left. A couple of figure eights.

There was a time in his life when a ride like this might've felt exciting. His adrenaline was pumping and he'd be all in for the thrill. Even having a couple of idiots with guns behind him would've seemed like a good challenge. A lot had changed in him after he'd become a dad last year.

He took life more seriously and especially his own. Because he knew without a shadow of a doubt those boys needed their father to come home every night. And he would, today, too.

He checked his mirrors and was feeling pretty good about where he stood with regard to the perps. Until he almost slammed into the Jeep that had cut an angle right in front of him.

Slamming the brake and narrowly avoiding a collision, Colton bit out a few choice words.

Gert's voice came across the radio again. "Sir, I have names. Officer Randol Bic and Officer Jimmy Stitch were known associates of River Myers and fit the descriptions you gave. Bic is a sharpshooter. They're partners in East Dallas and both of their records are clean."

A picture was emerging. Was River taking the fall for Bic and Stitch?

Had they threatened him? Were they holding something over his head?

"I've heard those names before," Makena said.

Gert's voice came across the radio. "Sir, I think the GPS is messing up. It looks like you're driving back and forth on the highway."

Colton couldn't help himself; he laughed. "Well, that's because I'm presently driving in a cornfield near the highway. GPS probably can't register that location."

"I feel like I should have known it would be something like that." Now Gert laughed. It was good to break up some of the tension. A sense of humor helped with keeping a calm head, which could be the difference between making a mistake or a good decision.

The Jeep circled back, and Colton could hear its engine gunning toward him. He cut left, trying to outrun the perps.

"Gert, how are you doing over there?" Colton needed an update. Actually, what he needed was a miracle. But he'd stopped believing in those after losing Rebecca, and he figured it was best to keep his feet firmly planted on the ground and his head out of the clouds.

"Sir, I have good news for you. Do you hear anything?"

Colton strained to listen. He didn't hear anything other than the sound of his front bumper hacking through the cornfield. He hated to think what he was doing to this farmer's crops. But again, he would pay restitution.

"I don't hear much more than the noise I'm making and the sound of an engine barreling toward me." He was barely cutting around.

The Jeep was close, he could hear and feel it, if not see it.

"Well, sir, the cavalry is arriving. If you roll your window down, I think you'll be happy with what you hear. DPS got back to me and a trooper should be on top of you right now."

Well, maybe Colton had been too quick to write off the likelihood of miracles happening.

"That's the best news I've heard all day." When he really listened and got past the sounds of corn husks slapping against his front bumper, he heard the familiar wails of sirens in the distance.

Makena was practically glued to her seat, with her hands gripping the strap of her seat belt.

"If you like that news, I've got more. An ambulance is en route to the motel. Help is on the way, sir."

"Gert, remind me the next time I see you that you deserve a raise."

"Sir, I'm going to hold you to that when it's time for my review." Again, lightening the tension with teasing kept his mind at ease and his brain able to focus. The minute he thought a situation was the end of the world was the minute it would be true.

Colton circled around a few more times, ensuring that he was on the move and as far away from the Jeep as possible. He figured the perps had probably given up once they'd heard sirens.

Since they were cops with clean records, they would want to keep them that way. When he really thought about it, they'd concocted the perfect scenario. The puzzle pieces clicked together in one moment.

They had some type of hold over River. That was obvious and a given. They believed that Makena could possibly link them to River and so they would get rid of her. All the while implicating River, who was already known to have a temper and a bad relationship with his wife.

When the different parts of their plan made sense like that, he realized the genius of their plot. However, he had seen them. He knew who they were. That was where they'd messed up. Now they'd gone and left a trail.

"Are they gone?" Makena looked around as Colton slowed down.

"I believe so."

Makena sank back in the chair. "I hear the sirens."

Colton nodded as he tried to navigate back toward the highway.

"I can patch you through to Officer Staten," Gert said.

"Ten-four. Great work, Gert." But before Colton could speak to the highway patrolman through the radio, he saw the cruiser. Colton flashed his headlights and cut off his engine.

Hands up, he exited his truck and told Makena to do the same.

After greeting Officer Staten, Colton said, "It's a shame I didn't get a plate. A white Jeep Rubicon in Texas doesn't exactly stand out."

"The two of you are safe. That's the most important thing to me right now," Officer Staten said.

There was no arguing with that point.

"Do you need assistance getting back to your office?" Staten was tall and darker-skinned, with black hair, brown eyes and a deceptively lean frame. Every state trooper could pull his own weight and more in a fight. These officers traveled long distances with no backup in sight. To say they were tough was a lot like saying Dwayne Johnson had a few muscles.

Colton looked to Makena. "Any chance I can convince you to take a ride back to my office with the officer?"

Makena was already vigorously shaking her head before he could finish his sentence. He figured as much. It was worth a try. He wanted her to be safely tucked away while he circled back and checked on River and Peach.

She seemed to read his mind when she said, "I'm going with you."

There was so much determination in her voice he knew better than to argue. No use wasting precious time.

Colton turned to Officer Staten and said, "Can I get

an assist to the motel where an officer was fired on? I'd like to go back and investigate the scene. And considering I have a witness with me, I think it might be best if I have backup."

Staten seemed to catch on, because he was already nodding. "I'm happy to help in any way I can."

Professional courtesy went a long way and Colton had gone to great lengths to build a cooperative relationship with other law enforcement agencies.

Once their destination was agreed upon, Colton retreated to his truck with Makena by his side.

The drive back to the motel surprisingly took half an hour. Colton didn't realize they'd gotten so far from the motel, but then he was driving back at normal speed limits, whereas he'd flown to get away from there.

There was a BOLO out on the Jeep. If they were as smart as they appeared to be, they would ditch the vehicle. The new problem was that they'd been made and now they had nothing to lose. Dangerous.

They couldn't possibly realize that Colton had figured out who they were. So Colton had that on his side.

By the time they reached the motel, it looked like a proper crime scene. An ambulance was there. The back had been closed up and it looked as though they were about to pull away.

"Hold on a sec," Colton said to Makena.

He hopped out of his pickup, knowing that Makena would want to know River's status.

He jogged up to the driver's side of the ambulance and the driver rolled down the window. Fortunately for him, he still had on his windbreaker that had the word SHERIFF in big bold letters running down his left sleeve, so it was easy to identify that he was in law enforcement.

"How is your patient in the back?" Colton asked. "I was here at the time of the shooting. I had to get a witness out of the building. What is the status of your patient?"

"GSW to the back, exit wounds in his chest. We need to rock and roll, sir. No guarantees on this one. Still breathing, but a lot of blood loss by the time we got here."

Colton took a step back and waved them on. "Go."

It wasn't good news, but River was still alive and Colton had learned that even a tiny bit of hope was better than none. As done as Makena was with the relationship, and he had no doubt in his mind the marriage had been over for a very long time, she was the type of person to be concerned for someone she'd once cared about.

He wished he could give her better news.

Glancing toward the truck, he expected to see her waiting there. A moment of shock jolted him when he saw that she was gone. Then, he knew immediately where she would go. He raced inside to see her standing next to Peach, who was sitting in one of the chairs on the right-hand side.

Makena was offering reassurances to the older woman while rubbing her shoulders. Peach had blood all over her flowery dress.

"I did everything I could to help him, but there was so much blood. He was already pale by the time we got help. His lips were turning blue." The anguish in the older woman's voice was palpable.

"Peach, what you did was admirable. If he has any chance at all, it's because of you," Colton said.

Peach glanced up at him, those emerald green eyes sparkling with gratitude for his comments.

"I mean it. You very well could've saved his life here and I know you saved ours. I would work beside you in law enforcement any day." He meant every word.

Her chin lifted with his praise.

"I appreciate your saying so, Sheriff. It means a lot."

Colton crouched down to eye level with her before taking her statement. And then Makena took Peach into a back room where she washed up.

Makena stayed by the elderly woman's side long after the blood had been rinsed off and Peach had changed clothes.

The highway patrolman stayed outside, guarding the front door in case the perps returned. The front door was cordoned off with crime scene tape.

"My deputy here is going to process the scene. Can one of us give you a ride home?" Colton asked Peach.

"I'll be all right in a few minutes," Peach said. Her hands had steadied. "I have my car out back and I don't want to leave it here overnight."

"What's the owner's name? I'll give 'em a call and ask for someone to cover your shift."

Whatever he said seemed to tickle Peach.

"You're looking at the owner. I owned this place with my husband, God rest his soul."

"Can I call someone? It's not a good idea for you to be alone right now." The shock of what had happened would wear off and her emotions could sneak up on her.

Colton didn't want her to suffer. She'd shown incredible bravery today.

"I have a daughter in town," she said. "I'll see if she'll make up the guest bedroom for me tonight."

"Any chance you could get her on the phone now?" Colton asked.

"My purse is underneath the counter where Rapture was hiding." She motioned toward her shotgun that was sitting on top of the counter. It had been opened and the shells looked to have been removed.

As he waited for Peach to call her daughter, Colton took stock of the situation. He now had names. He had motive. All he needed was opportunity to seal Bic and Stitch's fate.

Chapter Fifteen

Makena heard Colton's voice as she sat with Peach. He was talking about shock and the need to keep an eye on her. The concern in his voice brought out all kinds of emotions in Makena. She could tell that he genuinely cared about Peach and it was just about the kindest thing Makena thought she'd ever witnessed. But that was just Colton. He was genuine, kind and considerate wrapped in a devastatingly handsome and masculine package. There was nothing self-centered about him. In fact, there was a sad quality in his eyes that made him so real.

"Bernard and I spent our whole lives here at this motel. He never would take a vacation. I used to tease him about what he'd turn into with all work and no play." A wistful and loving look overtook Peach's face when she spoke about her husband.

"He sounds like an honest, hard-working man," Makena said.

"That he was. He was good to me and I was good to him. We had two daughters. One who succumbed to illness as a child, and the other who your boyfriend is on the phone with now. She looks after me. She's been on me to sell the business for years." Peach exhaled. "It's difficult to let go. Here is where I feel Bernard's presence the most. I always thought I'd start a little restaurant. Even had a name picked out, but I never did find the time. I always would rather be feeding people. The motel was Bernard's baby."

The fact that Peach had referred to Colton as Makena's boyfriend didn't get past her. She didn't see this as the time to correct the elderly woman.

She glanced up, and it was then that the flat-screen TV caught her attention. She remembered the date stamp and the time stamp on the screen when River had looked up. He'd looked up at exactly 6:12 a.m., which meant he was at the motel and not anywhere near Katy Gulch and he must have known something was going to happen even if he didn't know what because he'd given himself an alibi. Birchwood was a solid half hour from town. He'd been inside his room the entire night, based on the camera footage. The only window was in front, next to the door. If he'd tried to climb out, the camera would've picked it up.

As far as she knew there were no other exits in the room, which pretty much ensured that he was innocent.

A flood of relief washed over her that he hadn't been involved in the bombing attempt. Bic and Stitch's whereabouts had yet to be known, and she had plenty of questions for the pair.

Makena sat with her hands folded in her lap. She refocused on the story Peach was telling her about how her beloved Bernard had singlehandedly patched up a roof after a tornado. Peach was rambling and Makena didn't mind. The woman's smooth, steady voice had a calming effect, and she figured Peach needed to keep her mind busy by talking.

Colton stepped back into the room and then handed the phone to Peach, who took it and spoke to her daughter.

While Peach was occupied, Makena motioned for Colton to come closer. He bent down and took a knee beside her. She liked that he immediately reached for her hand. She leaned toward his ear and relayed her discovery.

He rocked his head. "That's a really good point. If he was here all night, he couldn't have been the one to set the bomb. We have two names, and their department will want to be involved. I promise you here and now justice will be served."

Makena hoped he could deliver on that promise before they could get to her. Bic and Stitch had proven they'd go to any length to quiet her.

"I already figured out they were setting River up. It's a pretty perfect setup and that's the reason we found the black key chain at the scene." After everything she'd been through with River, she probably shouldn't care one way or the other about it. She just wasn't built that way. She did care. Not just about him but about anyone who'd taken a wrong turn.

"Any chance we can stop by the hospital when we leave here?" Makena asked.

"I think that can be arranged."

She really hoped so, because she wanted to see with her own eyes that River was okay.

"Since we know he's a target, will there be security? How will that work?" she asked.

"I just called in a report that he's a material witness in an attempted murder case. One of my deputies is with him and we'll make sure he's not left unattended in the hospital while he fights for his life." Colton's words were reassuring.

"Excuse me, sir." Trooper Staten stepped inside the room.

"How can I help you?"

"Since you have a deputy here, I'd like to offer backup to one of my buddies who has a trucker pulled over not far from here. If you think you'll be good without me, I'd like to assist."

"We're good. Thank you for everything. Your help is much appreciated." Colton stood up, crossed the room and shook the state trooper's hand.

Deputy Fletcher worked to process the scene while Colton and Makena waited for Peach's daughter to show. She did, about twenty minutes later. The young woman, who looked to be in her late twenties, had a baby on her hip and a distressed look on her face as she approached the motel.

Rather than let her step into the bloody scene before it could be cleaned up, Colton met her at the door. He turned back in time to say, "Makena, do you want to bring Peach outside?"

"Sure. No problem." She helped Peach to her feet.

The older woman gripped Makena's arm tightly and it gave her the impression Peach was holding on for dear life. It was good that her daughter was picking her up. She needed someone to take care of her.

Seeing the look on her daughter's face as soon as they stepped outside sent warmth spreading through

Makena. The mother-daughter bond hit her square in the chest, and for the first time, Makena thought she was missing out on something by not having a child of her own.

When Peach was settled in her daughter's small SUV and the baby had been strapped in the back seat, the older woman looked up with weary eyes.

"Maybe it is a good idea for me to sell. My handyman, Ralph, can keep things running until the sale. He can see to it if anyone needs a rental. You were right to have me call my daughter," she said to Colton. "Good luck with everything. Take care of yourselves." Peach glanced from Makena to Colton and back. "And take care of each other. If you don't mind my saying, the two of you have something special. That's probably the most important thing you can have in life."

"Thank you, ma'am," Colton said.

Again, Makena didn't see the need to correct Peach despite the thrill of hope she felt at hearing those words. Peach had been through a traumatic experience and Makena wasn't going to ruin her romantic notions by clarifying her relationship with Colton. He had become her lifeline and that was most likely the reason the thought of being separated from him at some point gave her heart palpitations, not that she'd reactivated real feelings for him. The kind of feelings that could go the distance.

COLTON CHECKED HIS WATCH. He surveyed the area, well aware that it had only been a short while ago that two perps had been walking across that same street.

A second deputy pulled up. Colton motioned for him

to go on inside. He didn't want anyone working alone on this scene or this case.

He turned to Makena. "River is probably still in surgery. Do you think you could eat something?"

Peach wasn't the only one in shock. Makena was handling hers well, but she'd had months of being on the run and hiding to practice dealing with extreme emotions.

Makena closed the distance between them and leaned against him.

Colton looped his arms around her waist and pulled her body flush with his. This time, he was the one who dipped his head and pressed a kiss to her lips. He told himself he did it to root them both in reality again, but there was so much more to it, to being with her.

The thought of how close he'd come to losing her sent a shiver rocketing down his back. He'd lost enough with Rebecca and he didn't want to lose another friend.

Makena took in a deep breath. "How do you think he knew?"

Colton knew exactly what she was talking about. She was picking up their conversational thread from a few minutes ago.

"It's possible he didn't. It's likely he assumed that something could happen. He might have followed them here. Maybe they disappeared for a couple of days, and he realized they were searching for you and had found you. So he must've decided following them was his best chance at finding you. You were the wild card. They had no idea when you were going to show up and what evidence you might bring with you. They've probably been looking for you this entire time, and the fact that you disappeared when you did made it look that much more like you had something to hide or fear."

"Timing," she said on another sigh. It was a loaded word.

She blinked up at him and those crystal clear blue eyes brought out feelings he hadn't felt since college. He had no idea what to do with them. Complicated didn't begin to describe their lives. But he liked her standing right where she was, her warm body pressed against his and his arms circling her waist.

Colton glanced around, surveying the area. Even with two deputies on-site he couldn't let his guard down.

"What do you say we eat at the cafeteria in the hospital?" Makena asked.

"I need to let these guys know where we're headed and communicate with Gert so she can keep someone close to us." Traveling this way was cumbersome and frustrating. An idea sparked. He twined his and Makena's fingers before walking back inside the building. "How about one of you gentlemen lend me your service vehicle? I can leave my truck here. I don't want either one of you driving it. I'll have it towed back to my office. And then the two of you can buddy up on the way back to the office, where you can pick up another vehicle."

Both of his deputies were already nodding their agreement.

Deputy Fletcher pitched a set of keys to Colton, which he caught with one hand. He figured that he and Makena would be a helluva lot safer in a marked vehicle than his truck. Not to mention Bic and Stitch knew exactly what he drove. They may have even pulled some strings and run the plates by now, which would work in Colton's favor. He highly doubted they would've shot at a sheriff if they'd known.

Colton led Makena out to the county-issued SUV.

The drive to the hospital was forty minutes long. Colton located a parking spot as close to the ER doors as he could find. He linked his and Makena's fingers before walking into the ER bay. He was ever aware that a sharpshooter could be anywhere, waiting to strike. But what he hoped was that Bic and Stitch had gone back to Dallas to regroup.

Now that their chief was aware, they would be brought in for questioning. It would have to be handled delicately. Their plan to set up River had blown up in their faces, as had their plans to erase Makena.

The strangest part about the whole thing was that they were targeting her based on what they thought she knew, while she really knew nothing. But now Dallas P.D and the sheriff's office knew what the men were capable of.

On the annual summer barbecue night, Colton and his staff would sit around a campfire way too late and swap stories. Conversation always seemed to drift toward what everyone would do if it went down, meaning they had to disappear.

The first thing people said was obvious. Get rid of their cell phone. The next was that they'd stay the heck away from their personal vehicle. Another thing was not to go home again. That seemed obvious. Most of the deputies said they'd go to the ATM and withdraw as much money as they could before heading to Mexico. At least one said she would head toward Canada because she thought it was the opposite way anyone would look for her.

Bic and Stitch had to have a backup plan. It was just a cop's instinct to talk through worst-case scenarios. And if they thought like typical cops, like he was certain they did considering they had twenty-six years of police experience between them, he figured they had an escape plan, too.

So the thought of them going back to their homes or to Dallas was scratched. Their cover was blown.

But did they realize it?

One thing was certain: they didn't have anything to gain sticking around town. In fact, it would do them both good to hide out until this blew over. And then take off for the border.

What would their escape plan be? He wondered where they'd been hiding while River booked the motel room.

It was a lot to think about. Colton needed a jolt of caffeine and he probably needed something in his stomach besides acid from coffee. The piece of toast he'd had for breakfast wasn't holding up anymore.

He stopped off at the nurses' station in the ER.

"Can you point me to the cafeteria?" It wouldn't do any good to ask about River yet and these women most likely wouldn't know. He would go to the information desk, which would be in the front lobby.

"Straight down this hallway, make a right and then a left. You'll find a lobby, which you'll need to cross. You'll get to a hallway on the exact opposite side and you'll want to take that. You can't miss it from there."

Colton thanked the intake nurse and then followed

her directions to a T. A minute later, they were standing in front of a row of vending machines that had everything from hot chocolate to hot dogs.

"Does any of this look appetizing?" he asked Makena.

She walked slowly, skimming the contents of each vending machine. She stopped at the third one and then pointed. "I think this ham sandwich could work."

Colton bought two of them, then grabbed a couple bags of chips. She wanted a soft drink while he stuck with black coffee.

There was a small room with a few bright orange plastic tables and chairs scattered around the room. Each table had from three to six chairs surrounding it. There were two individuals sitting at different tables, each staring at their phone.

Makena took the lead and chose a table farthest away from the others. The sun was shining, and hours had passed since breakfast.

"So I noticed you didn't ask about River." Makena took a bite and chewed on her ham sandwich.

"No, the intake nurses either wouldn't have information or wouldn't share it. There's an information desk we can stop at after we eat. I know most of the people who work there and figured that would be the best place to check his status" He checked his smartwatch. "Gert would let me know if the worst had happened, if River had died."

"Have you given much thought to what your life might look like once this is all behind you?" Colton asked Makena after they'd finished eating.

"Every day for the past six months I've thought about

what I would do once this was all over. To be honest, I never really had an answer that stuck. I went through phases. One of those phases was to just buy a little farmhouse somewhere away from people and live on my own and maybe get a golden retriever for company."

"There are worse ways to spend your life."

She smiled and continued. "Then, I had a phase where I wanted to move far away from Texas and live in a major metropolitan area where there would be people everywhere, but no one would bother me unless I wanted them to. If I wanted to be left alone, people would respect that. But I would be around life again. I'd be around people doing things and being busy. I wouldn't have to hide my face." She looked out the window thoughtfully. "None of those things stuck for more than a month."

"And how about now?"

"I have a few ideas." She turned to face him and looked him in the eyes. "Now I feel like I know what I want, but that maybe it's out of reach."

Before he could respond, a text came in from Gert that River was out of surgery. Gert had connections in most places and the hospital was no different. Glancing at his watch, he realized an hour had passed since they'd arrived at the hospital.

Colton made a mental note to finish this conversation later, because a very large part of him wanted to know if she saw any chance of the two of them spending time together. It was pretty much impossible for him to think about starting a new relationship while he had one-year-old twins at home, especially with what was going on with his family.

His mind came up with a dozen reasons straight out of the chute as to why it was impossible and wouldn't happen and could never go anywhere. Why he couldn't risk it.

But the heart didn't listen to logic. It wanted to get to know Makena again. To see if the fire in the kisses they'd shared—kisses he was having one helluva time trying to erase from his memory—could ignite something that might last longer than a few months.

Logic flew out the window when it came to the heart.

"River is out of surgery and I can probably get us up to his floor if not his room."

Makena looked like she wanted to say something and then thought better of it.

"Let's do it." She took in a sharp breath, like she was steadying herself for what she knew would come.

Colton cursed the timing of the text, but it was good news. He led them to the information desk where he could get details about which floor River was housed in. Trudy, a middle-aged single mother who lived on the outskirts of Katy Gulch, sat at the counter.

As sheriff, Colton liked to get to know his residents and look out for those who seemed to need it. Trudy had been widowed while her husband had been serving in the military overseas. She'd been left with four kids and not a lot of money. Colton's office led a back-to-school backpack drive every year in part to make sure her children never went without. Gert always beamed with pride when delivering those items.

Gert organized a toy drive every year for Christmas, a book drive twice a year and coats for kids before the first cold snap.

"Hey, Trudy. You have a patient who just got out of surgery, and we'd like to go up to his floor and talk to his nurse and possibly his doctor," Colton said after introducing Trudy to Makena.

"Just a second, Sheriff. I'll look that up right now," Trudy said with a smile. Her fingers danced across the keyboard.

Makena's gaze locked onto someone. Colton followed her gaze to the man in scrubs. The doctor came from the same hallway they'd entered the lobby from, and then headed straight toward a bank of elevators.

The hair on Colton's neck prickled. Trudy's fingers worked double time. Click-click-click.

As the elevators closed on the opposite side of the lobby, something in the back of Colton's mind snapped.

"The patient you're looking for is on the seventh floor. He's in critical condition. No visitors are allowed." She flashed eyes at Colton. "No normal visitors. That doesn't mean you. He's in room 717."

Colton thanked her for the courtesy and realized what had been sticking in the back of his mind. The doctor who'd crossed the lobby wore a surgical mask and regular boots. Every doctor Colton had seen had foot coverings on their shoes. They usually wore tennis shoes with coverings over them for sanitation purposes.

This guy had on a surgical mask and no boot covers?

One look at Makena said she realized something was up. Colton looked at Trudy before jumping into action the minute he made eye contact with Makena and realized she was thinking along the same lines.

"Trudy, call security. Send backup to the seventh floor and help to room 717." Colton linked his fingers with Makena and started toward the elevator. Of course, he had a deputy on-site and the hospital had its own security. So imagine his shock when the elevator doors opened and his deputy walked out.

"Lawson, what are you doing?"

His deputy seemed dumbfounded as Colton rushed into the elevator.

"What do you mean? I'm going to get a cup of coffee. Hospital security relieved me and said you authorized a break."

"And you didn't think to check with me first?" Colton asked.

Lawson's mistake seemed to dawn on him. He muttered a few choice words as he pushed the button for the seventh floor, apologizing the whole time.

It seemed to take forever for the elevator to ding and the doors to open. At least, they knew where one of the men was; the other had to be close by. The two seemed to travel as a pair.

As soon as the doors opened, Colton shot out. He shouted back to Lawson, "Make sure no one comes down this hallway."

There were two hallways and several sets of stairs, but Lawson could make sure no one followed Colton.

Unwilling to let Makena out of his sight, Colton held on to her hand as he banked right toward room 717. As suspected, there was no security guard at the door.

Colton cursed as he bolted toward the open door.

Inside, he interrupted a man in a security outfit standing near River's bedside. The man in uniform had a black mustache, neatly trimmed.

"Sheriff, I saw him. Someone was in here. He ran out the door."

"Put your hands where I can see them," Colton demanded.

Chapter Sixteen

From behind the curtain dividing the room, a window leading to the outside opened.

"Hands where I can see them," Colton repeated, weapon drawn, leading the way. River lay unconscious with a breathing tube in his mouth as multiple machines beeped.

The security guard dropped down on the opposite side of the bed. And then, suddenly, an alarm began to sound on one of the machines. Was it unplugged?

Another wailing noise pierced the air.

Colton kept Makena tucked behind him as he took a couple of steps inside the room. He planted his side against the wall, inching forward.

A nurse came bolting in and froze when she saw Colton with his gun drawn. The divider curtain blew toward him with a gust of wind. Colton saw a glint of Mustache as he climbed out the window.

Red must've been on the other side of the divider all along. He must've made it inside the room. Colton assumed he'd be the one wearing the surgical gear.

"Freeze." Colton took a few more tentative steps before squatting down so he could see underneath the curtain. He saw no sign of shoes and assumed both men had climbed out the window and onto the fire escape they'd seen earlier. And since assumptions in his life of work could kill, he proceeded with extra caution. Someone could be standing on the bed or nightstand. Hell, he'd caught a perp climbing into the ceiling tiles at the bank before.

There was no more sound coming from that side of the room. He took a few more steps until he was able to reach the curtain and pull it open. He scanned the room before checking on the other side of the bed.

"Clear. Nurse, you're okay." It was all Colton could get out as he heard the sounds of feet shuffling and her scurrying to plug in the machines that were most likely the reason River was still breathing.

Colton rushed to the window and looked out in time to see someone wearing scrubs along with Security Dude climbing down the fire escape and around the side of the building.

He glanced back at Makena.

"Stay here. Someone will come back for you. Stay in this room. Nurse, lock this room and stay with her. As soon as I'm out of this window, I want you to lock it."

A moment of hesitation crossed Makena's features. She opened her mouth like she was about to protest and then clamped it shut.

Colton climbed out the window and followed the path of the perps. He climbed down to the corner, stopping before risking a glance.

The second he so much as peeked his head a shot rang out, taking a small chunk of white brick before whizzing past his face.

Colton quickly jerked back around the side of the building and pulled himself back up. His body was flat against the building, his weapon holstered.

There was no way these guys were escaping him twice.

He scaled the wall a couple more floors, refusing to look down. He wouldn't exactly say he was afraid of heights, but he wouldn't call them his friend, either.

When Colton made it to the third story, gripping the windows for dear life, he risked another glance around the side of the building, hoping they would still be looking for him on the seventh floor. This time, thankfully, Red and Mustache were too busy climbing down to realize he'd looked. They probably still thought he was up on the seventh.

Colton continued his climb down with his stomach twisted in knots, but he made it to the ground. Without a doubt, they'd made it to the ground first. There were also two of them and only one of him. Not the best odds. One was a sharpshooter. That would be the person who would most likely wield the weapon.

And then there was the fact that they were both cops. Maybe he could find a way to use that to his advantage.

With his back against the wall and his weapon extended, Colton leaned around the building. The pair of men were making a beeline for the parking lot. He scanned the area for the Jeep but didn't see it.

They could have another vehicle stashed by now. Since it was early evening, there was a little activity. He wouldn't risk a shot. He, like every law enforcement officer on the job, was responsible for every bullet he fired. Meaning that if he accidentally struck a citizen, he was answerable, not to mention it would be horrific.

When Red and Mustache made it to the lot, one turned around.

They took cover behind a massive black SUV. One turned back, Red, and Colton figured that of the two, he was the marksman. He had his weapon aimed at the seventh floor, where he must expect Colton to be.

He figured Mustache was looking for a vehicle to hotwire, since they didn't immediately go to a car.

Colton figured his best line of defense was to get to his county-issued vehicle and try to circle around the back and come at them from a different direction. He got on his radio to Lawson and Gert as he bolted toward his SUV.

He slid into the driver's seat and blazed around the opposite side of the lot as he informed Gert of the situation. Lawson chimed in, stating that he was on his way down and heading to the spot Colton had just left.

Colton slowed his SUV down to a crawl as he made his way around the back of the parking lot. He located a spot in the back of the lot and parked. He slipped out of his windbreaker, needing to shed anything that drew attention to him. He toed off his boots as he exited the vehicle.

As the shooter's attention was directed at the building, Colton swung wide to sneak up on him. He was ever aware that Mustache was creeping around the lot, likely looking for a vehicle.

Lawson peeked his head around the building and Red fired a shot. While Red's attention was on Lawson, Colton eased through cars and trucks.

With Red distracted by Lawson, Colton came in stealth. He rounded the back of the SUV and dove at Red, tackling him at the knees. His gun went flying as Colton wrestled him around until his knee jabbed in the center of Red's back. As tall and strong as Red was, he was no match for a man of Colton's size.

Face down, Red spit out gravel as he opened his mouth to shout for help. Colton delivered a knockout punch. The man's jaw snapped.

From there, Colton was able to easily haul Red's hands behind his back and throw on zip cuffs.

It was then that Colton heard the click of a gun's hammer being cocked.

"Make one move without me telling you to, and you're dead."

Out of the corner of his eyes, Colton could see Mustache. He cursed under his breath.

"Hands in the air where I can them." Mustache was in authoritative cop mode.

Colton slowly started lifting his hands, his weapon already holstered. And at this rate, he was as good as dead. His thoughts jumped to Lawson. Where was he?

"Uncuff my friend. You're going to help me get him into my vehicle."

The retort on Colton's lips was, *like hell*. However, he knew better than to agitate a cop on the edge.

"You won't get away with this. Your superiors know what you've done and they know you're connected to Myers. But you can get a lighter sentence. You haven't dug a hole that you can't climb out of yet. No one's dead. A murder rap is not something you can ever come back from."

"Shut up. I don't need to hear any more of your crap. The system pays criminals better than it pays us. When Bic's kid needed medical care and his insurance ran out, who do you think covered his mortgage?" Stitch grunted. "It sure as hell wasn't the department."

Psychological profiles were performed on every officer candidate to ensure a cop could handle the pressures that came with the job. The tests could give a snapshot of where a candidate's head was at the time of his or her hiring. What it couldn't do 100 percent accurately was predict how someone would handle the constraints of the job over time.

The stress could compound and end up looking something like this.

"I never said it was easy being on the job. But you and I both know you didn't get into it for the money."

Mustache laughed. "Yeah, I was a kid. What did I know about having real bills and a father-in-law with dementia who lost his business and I had to support?"

"This isn't the answer. You can still make this right. You can still go back and untangle this. Make restitution."

A half laugh escaped Mustache.

"You know what? I think I'm just going to kill you instead. Not because I have to but because I can."

Colton had no doubt Mustache was trigger-happy. A man with nothing to lose was not the kind of person Colton needed to have pointing a gun at him.

"You're going to help me put my friend in my vehicle and then I'm going to give you ten seconds to run."

Colton knew without a doubt that the minute he put Red into a vehicle, his life was going to be over. He needed to think fast. Stall for time. He glanced over to see if Lawson was on his way.

Mustache laughed again.

"Your friend isn't coming. I don't know if you noticed but he's bleeding out over there. Guess it's too late for me after all."

Colton slowly stood with his hands in the air.

"Keep high and where I can see them. I'm going to relieve you of your weapon."

The crack of a bullet split the air.

Colton flinched and dropped to his knees. When he spun around, it was Mustache taking a couple of steps back. With his finger on the trigger, all it would take was one twitch for Colton to be shot at in point-blank range.

He dove behind the sport utility and came up with his weapon. It would take Mustache's brain a few minutes to catch up with the fact that he'd been shot. Right now, he was just as dangerous as he had been, if not more so.

Using the massive sport utility for cover, Colton drew down on Mustache.

"Hands up, Stitch." All Colton could think of was securing the area and getting to Lawson.

Another shot sounded.

Colton glanced around and saw Lawson's body. As he rounded the back of the vehicle, he heard a familiar voice.

"Drop your weapon *now*." From behind a vehicle, Makena had her arms extended out with a Glock in her hands. Red's weapon? The barrel was aimed at Mustache.

Colton was proud of the fact she'd listened to his earlier advice and used the vehicle to protect her body.

Mustache seemed dumbfounded as he took a couple of steps and locked onto her position. "You."

He brought up his weapon to shoot her and she fired again. This time, the bullet pinged his arm and his shoulder drew back. His weapon discharged, firing a wild shot, and his shoulder flew back. His Glock went skittering across the black tar.

Colton dove toward it and came up with it after making eye contact with Makena. He tucked and rolled on his shoulder and then popped up in front of the vehicle Makena used as cover.

There was no way to know if Mustache had a backup weapon, which many officers carried in an ankle holster.

"You just saved my life," Colton said to Makena. He moved beside her and realized that her body was trembling.

Her eyes were wide.

"You're okay," he said to soothe her before turning to Mustache, who was slumped against the back tire of a vehicle. "Get those hands up."

Much to his surprise, Mustache did.

It was probably the shock of realizing he'd been shot multiple times. Colton immediately fished out his cell and called Gert, telling her the perps had been subdued and that Lawson was down. She reassured Colton a team of doctors was waiting at the ER bay for word.

Before Colton could end the call, he saw the doctors racing to save Lawson's life.

Mustache's once light blue shirt was now soaked in red. Colton ran over and cuffed Mustache's hands. After a pat-down, he located a backup weapon.

"If either one of these men moves, don't hesitate to shoot," he said to Makena.

Lawson was flat on his back as he was being placed on a gurney.

"I'm sorry. I let you down," Lawson said.

"No, you didn't. I'm alive. You're alive. Those bastards are going to spend the rest of their lives behind bars. You did good."

In less than a minute, Lawson was on his way to surgery. The bullet had nicked his neck.

Colton bolted back to Makena.

"It's over," Makena said. She repeated herself a couple more times as Colton took her weapon before he pulled her into an embrace, keeping a watchful eye on the perps.

"You did good," he whispered into her ear as she melted against him.

"I found the gun on the ground," she said quietly.

Red popped his head up and shook it, like he was shaking off a fog.

"What the hell happened?" His gaze locked onto his partner, who had lost a lot of blood.

"You and your partner are going away for a very long time," Colton said. He held Makena, trying to calm her tremors.

An emergency team raced toward Mustache. In another few minutes, he was strapped and cuffed to a gurney with security in tow and another deputy on the way.

Colton pulled Red to standing after patting him down. He walked the man over to his service vehicle. "You're taking a trip in the back seat for once."

Makena climbed into the passenger side and kept silent for the drive back to Katy Gulch.

Deputy Schooner met them in the parking lot and took custody of the perp.

"You would do what you had to if your kid was sick," Bic practically spat the words. "Look as sanctimonious as you want, but I had bills stacking up and a mortgage to cover. I did what was necessary to take care of my family."

"There are other ways to accomplish the same thing and stay within the law," Colton said.

"That's what you say. Don't you get tired of watching them get away with crimes every day? Don't you get sick of seeing criminals drive better cars and wear better clothes than us?"

"Fancy clothes were never my style," Colton said. "But why River?"

"He was on to us, so we turned the tables on him. His nose wasn't clean, either. He liked to play it rough," Bic said. "She was the problem. She threatened everything we were doing. It took months to track her down but she made mistakes and River led us right to her."

Colton was done talking. He turned to Makena. "Are you ready to go home?"

She stood there, looking a little bit lost.

"I don't have a home to go to, Colton."

"Then come home with me while you figure out your next move." He brushed the backs of his fingers against the soft skin of her face. He'd missed his opportunity with her once and did not intend to do so again. "Come home with me and stay."

"And then what?" She blinked up at him, confused.

"Stay. Meet my boys. See what you think about making a life together. I know what I want and it's you. I love you, Makena. And I think I have since college. I was too young and too dumb to realize what was happening to us in college. I had no idea how rare or special it was. But I do now. I'm a grown man and I won't make that same mistake twice."

He looked into her eyes but was having trouble reading her. Maybe it was too much. Maybe he shouldn't have thrown this all at her at once.

"But if you don't think this is right, if you don't feel what I'm feeling, then just stay with me until you get your bearings. I don't care how long. You'll always have a place to stay with me."

"Did you say that you love me?"

Colton nodded. "Yes, Makena. I love you."

"I love you, too, Colton. I think I always have. Seeing you again brought me back to life. But then what? You have boys. You have a life."

"I'd like to build a life with *you*."

"Are you sure about that, Colton? Because I have no doubts."

"I've never been more certain of anything in my life other than adopting my boys," he admitted.

She blinked up at him, confused.

It dawned on him why. He'd never told her about his twins.

"Rebecca and I had been high school sweethearts. We didn't know anything but each other. We decided to take a break in college and see if this was the real deal. I loved her and she was my best friend. But then I met you and it was different. I felt things that I had never felt with Rebecca. There was a spark inside me that said you were special and then I wanted more than a best friend as a partner. I went home and told Rebecca that I didn't think I was coming back to her."

"But you ended up together?"

"Yes, but not for years. We went our separate ways as a couple but stayed close as friends. Years later, long after she and I broke up, she ended up in a bad relationship with a man who didn't treat her right. When he found out she was pregnant he accused her of cheating on him. He questioned whether or not the boys were his and that crushed her. She said she couldn't come home pregnant to her father's house without a husband or a father for her kids. We'd always promised to have each other's back, so that's what I did. Her father, who's the mayor of Katy Gulch, got over the fact she was pregnant and still not married as soon as he found out she was marrying an O'Connor. I felt like I could've done a lot worse than marry my best friend. I figured that what you and I had was a one-and-done situation. So I asked Rebecca to marry me. I loved her, but there was no spark in our marriage, not like what I'd experienced with you. But then, no one else made me feel that way. And make no mistake about it, those boys are my sons. They are O'Connors through and through, and always will be. Can you live with that?"

"Colton, you are the most selfless man I've ever met. I think I just fell in love with you even more."

"Just so you're clear, we can take a little time for you to get to know the boys, and we can make certain this is the life you want. But I'm in this for the long haul, and I have every intention of asking you to be my bride," he said.

"If your sons are half the person you are, I already know that I'll love them. And just so you know, when you ask me to marry you, I'll be ready to say yes. I never felt like I was home around anyone until I met you and then I lost it. I've definitely been in the wrong relationship and that taught me exactly what I wanted in a person. And it's you. It's always been you."

Colton pulled Makena into his arms and kissed his future bride, his place to call home.

"I have one condition," she warned.

"Anything." He didn't hesitate. He wanted to give her the world.

"You asked me before if I had any idea what I wanted to do once I had my freedom back."

He nodded.

"I want to volunteer at the motel to help out Peach. She told me about her and her husband building that place together and that the motel made her feel closer to him. She's considering selling, but I could tell nothing in her heart wanted that to happen. It would cut her off from the man she built a life with and she deserves so much more than that. She deserves to have her memories of him surrounding her until she takes her final breath."

"It sounds like the perfect plan to me." Colton kissed his future, his soon-to-be bride, his home.

Epilogue

"I have news."

Makena sat on the kitchen floor, playing with her favorite boys in the world. She'd taken them into her heart the minute she'd looked at those round, angelic faces. Someday, she wanted to expand their family, but after living with twins 24/7 for the past month, she realized her hands were full.

"What is it?" she asked Colton as he walked into the kitchen wearing only jeans hung low on his hips. He was fresh from the shower, hair still wet. Droplets rolled down his neck and onto his muscled chest.

She practically had to fan herself.

"Myers has agreed to testify against Bic, who will be put away a very long time for attempted murder and police corruption, among other charges."

Stitch hadn't made it, but Bic was the brains of the operation.

"Good for him," she said. "I'm so ready to close that chapter of my life. I'm done with running scared and I'm done hiding. He put me through hell and I'm just ready to move on and never look back."

Colton walked over to her and sat down behind her,

wrapping his arms around her. He feathered kisses along the nape of her neck, causing her arms to break out in goose bumps and a thrill of awareness to skitter across her skin.

"I can't wait to be alone after we put the boys to bed tonight," he whispered in her ear.

She smiled as she turned her head enough for him to find her lips. The kiss sent more of that awareness swirling through her. Tonight felt like a lifetime away.

One of the boys giggled, which always made the other one follow suit. Their laughs broke into the moment happening between Makena and Colton.

"What's this?" she asked as she witnessed one pick up a block and bite it before setting it down only for the other to copy him.

Laughter filled the room and her heart.

This was her family. These were her boys. This was her home.

* * * * *

COMING SOON!

We really hope you enjoyed reading this book.
If you're looking for more romance, be sure to
head to the shops when new books are
available on

Thursday 10th December

To see which titles are coming soon, please visit
millsandboon.co.uk/nextmonth

JOIN US ON SOCIAL MEDIA!

Stay up to date with our latest releases, author news and gossip, special offers and discounts, and all the behind-the-scenes action from Mills & Boon...

 millsandboon

 millsandboonuk

 millsandboon

It might just be true love...

MILLS & BOON

HISTORICAL

Awaken the romance of the past

Escape with historical heroes from time gone by. Whether your passion is for wicked Regency Rakes, muscled Viking warriors or rugged Highlanders, indulge your fantasies and awaken the romance of the past.

MILLS & BOON

MODERN

Power and Passion

Prepare to be swept off your feet by sophisticated, sexy and seductive heroes, in some of the world's most glamourous and romantic locations, where power and passion collide.

MILLS & BOON
MEDICAL
Pulse-Racing Passion

Set your pulse racing with dedicated, delectable doctors in the high-pressure world of medicine, where emotions run high and passion, comfort and love are the best medicine.

Eight Medical stories published every month, find them all at:

millsandboon.co.uk